RUNAWAY GROOM

WEDDING FEVER
BOOK 3

FIONA LOWE

RUNAWAY GROOM

Dear Reader,

I'm thrilled to bring you this updated edition of **Runaway Groom,** the final book in the **Wedding Fever** trilogy.

Amy Sagar's life is in ruins. Fired from her fast-track job and dumped by her double-crossing boyfriend, she retreats to Whitetail, Wisconsin, to lick her wounds and regroup. Meeting an impossible, sexy Australian isn't part of her strategy for getting back on track.

Ben Armytage is running away. After being left at the altar and publicly humiliated, he's taking his vintage motorcycle on an extended road trip from Argentina to Alaska. Having his journey interrupted by a breakdown and sharing a house with a curvy, redheaded lawyer in a town obsessed with weddings was never on his itinerary.

Though being stuck in a luxury log cabin isn't really a hardship, living *together* with their broken hearts isn't easy. When the attraction between Amy and Ben proves unstoppable, they'll both begin rethinking their plans...

Although I'm not writing straight romance fiction these days, the same humor and romantic elements are found in my recent women's fiction novels, despite the more serious undertones. I like to think my wedding books are more of a romp!

As a side bar, since I researched and wrote these books, I have enjoyed the hands-on experience of being a huge part of my eldest son's garden wedding. We had to deal with a gum tree flattening the marquee two days before the wedding! But that's another story for another book.

Happy Reading!

Fiona x

For more weddings in Whitetail, check out **Saved by the Bride** and **Picture Perfect Wedding**, available now!

PRAISE FOR FIONA LOWE

"With the perfect mixture of romance, sadness and Australian/American wise-cracking, **Boomerang Bride** is one of the best romance novels this reviewer has read in a long time. Top Pick" RT Book Reviews

"With **Boomerang Bride** I got a Kristan Higgins and Nora Roberts feel. You get the fun sharp wit with very likable characters like Kristan Higgins and then the hot and steamy scenes like Nora Roberts. There are no negative words to say when it comes to this book. I mean, come on, if you read a book and you wish you were the characters best friend then you know it's good." 5 . *Chick Lit = The New Black*

"Oh guys! How much did I love this book? The answer? A lot. A lot. So much!" *Kate Cuthbert*

WEDDING FEVER SERIES

Saved by the Bride, Picture Perfect Wedding
& Runaway Groom

"***Saved By The Bride***, the first in the Wedding Fever series, is a fun, romantic romp in a quirky small town. Anni and Finn are well matched in both wits and stubbornness. Their journey from enemies to friends to lovers is one that will keep readers turning pages." 4* RT Review

"***Saved by the Bride*** has such a wonderful humor and sense of fun about it. Fiona Lowe, you have created a couple, and a town, that you just can't help but cheer for." 5/5 My Written Romance

"If you like small-town contemporary romances with heat, humor, and heart-winning characters, I think you will enjoy it as much as I did. I recommend ***Picture Perfect Wedding***." Just Janga

"Oh my. Ms. Lowe writes a charming, entertaining, and sometimes wrenching story in ***Picture Perfect Wedding***." Fedora Chen Goodreads Reviewer.

"Fiona Lowe has a way of mixing comedy with a sweet, hot, romance, ***Runaway Groom*** was no exception." Kristen Johnson Goodreads Reviewer

"If you're a fan of well-written contemporary romance, I would suggest ***Runaway Groom***. You get THREE HEA's in one novel!" Harlequin Junkies.

ALSO BY FIONA LOWE

The Wedding Fever Series

(Romance Fiction)

Saved by the Bride

Picture Perfect Wedding

Runaway Groom

Women's Fiction Novels

Daughter of Mine

Birthright

Home Fires

A Home Like Ours

A Family of Strangers

Coming in 2023

The Money Club

Did you know BookBub has a new release alert? www.bookbub.com/
authors/fiona-lowe

Romance Novels

Fiona has an extensive backlist of Australian-set romances. For a full list head
to http://www.fionalowe.com

RUNAWAY GROOM

First Published by Carina Press in 2014
This revised edition published in 2022 by Fiona Lowe
Copyright © 2014 by Fiona Lowe.
All rights reserved.
www.fionalowe.com

RUNAWAY GROOM
ISBN 978-0-6456187-7-8

Cover Design By Barton Lowe

Published by Fiona Lowe

Special thanks for this updated 2022 edition go to Barton Lowe for the perfect cover, Vicki Nelson for a final read and to Norm who runs the business side of things.

I couldn't do it all without you!

CHAPTER ONE

Had Amy Sagar known that sabotage wore Giorgio Armani, she would have paid a lot more attention. If she'd had even a hint at what was to come, she'd have broken her open-door policy the day Jonathon Wiseman walked into her office and slammed the oak door shut in his face. She most definitely would not have slept with him.

As it happened, she'd been oblivious to his calculating deceit and utter betrayal, which was why she was stood on the front porch of a neat and tidy home in Whitetail, Wisconsin. It was 420 miles from Chicago and the Fortune 500 company she'd called home for the past five years. It may as well have been another planet.

She rang the bell, listening to the high-pitched peep of the frogs while she waited for the door to be answered.

An older woman with short, pink hair opened the door, her face friendly and inquisitive. "May I help you?"

I hope so. "Mrs. Norell?"

"Yes."

"I'm Amy Sagar. It's been a long time but my family used to rent a cottage from you and—"

"*You're* little Amy Sagar?" Delight spun through the words.

Amy shrugged. "I am. Only now I'm all grown up." *And it totally sucks.*

"What a lovely surprise," Mrs. Norell said. "Why, the last time I saw you and your sisters, you must have been, what?"

"Fourteen."

"Oh, my! It can't have been eighteen years, can it?"

Amy didn't quite know what to say, except the obvious *yes*, which was an easier reply than *and it makes me thirty-two*.

Mrs. Norell stepped out onto the porch, opened her arms and enveloped Amy in a hug before stepping back. "Now, just look at you."

Amy wished she wouldn't. The last shower time she'd showered was the previous morning when her life was as it should be—organized, scheduled and career totally on track. Now she stood in a crushed business suit, pantyhose with spectacular runs and ballet flats, along with a ketchup stain on her blouse courtesy of the burger she'd eaten when she'd taken a break on the long eight-hour drive.

"It's good to see you again, Mrs. Norell."

"Call me Ella." Concern hovered in the older woman's eyes. "Is everything all right, dear?"

Remembering how good Mrs. Norell's hug had just felt, Amy had to work really hard at ignoring the caring expression on her face. It beckoned strongly, tempting her to tell all.

Stay strong. No one must know. Ever!

Amy refused to give in to a momentary needy weakness and admit that her life was in the toilet. And it wasn't just because she didn't want to look tragic in anyone's eyes, although who ever enjoyed being pitied? No, it was more that her own stupidity was the cause of her current situation.

Smiling against aching muscles, she said, "Everything's great. I just had a hankering to see the lake and I thought, why not today. There's no time like the present, right?"

Ella frowned. "It's hard to see the lake in the dark, dear."

Amy ignored the implication that perhaps she hadn't thought this trip through. "Do you still rent out the cottage, Mrs.—Ella?"

She shook her head slowly. "No, dear. I sold it a long time ago."

"Oh." Amy wrung her hands. The idea that the cottage wouldn't be available hadn't even occurred to when she'd fled Chicago nine hours earlier.

At ten this morning, when she'd walked into her apartment clutching the box of personal effects from her desk, she could barely breathe, let alone think. What had started off as a normal, everyday Friday had ended ten minutes into the working day. Her stellar career in corporate law was demolished faster than a house of cards, and she hadn't even seen it coming.

Shocked and numb, she wasn't certain how she'd even got home on the El. She had no clue how long she'd curled up on her sofa clutching her knees and rocking back and forth, but she did remember the moment she'd raised her head and had seen the photo of her at the lake all those years ago. She'd adored that vacation. She'd been happy. Purposeful. Filled with hope for her future.

The memory had penetrated the monotone in her head that had been running continuously since security had escorted her from the M.M. Enterprises building. The one that said, *You allowed a rat bastard to kill your career. You can't trust anyone.*

Returning to the lake had seemed so logical that she'd jumped off the couch, grabbed two suitcases, frantically dumped in whatever clean clothes had been on hand, put her house plant in a sink of water then jumped into her car. On the long drive north, it had been the memory of that cottage on the lake that had kept her from driving headfirst into a tree.

"If you're just here for the night, dear, you're welcome to stay with me," Ella said kindly.

Amy bit her knuckle. "Thank you, but I really want to stay longer. It's been forever since I had a vacation."

Ironically, the fact she hadn't taken any vacation time in the past five years, other than the prescribed holidays, meant her severance pay included many weeks of vacation time. If having her job stolen out from under her had a silver lining, she supposed this might be it.

Ella tapped the doorjamb as if it helped her think then she smiled. "The Rasmussens' vacation house is empty."

Hope soared. "Would they mind if I used it?"

"I think they'd be happy someone was living there in the off-season. Sometimes we get break-ins, especially when it's obvious the house is empty. The only thing is, it's not quite in the same league as my cottage."

The old cottage had been pretty basic, which was the only reason her family had been able to afford the rental. Amy hadn't done basic in years unless she counted four-star accommodations. "It's not *too* rustic, is it?" she asked with some trepidation.

Ella laughed. "Put it this way. It gives a whole new definition to the word. I'll just go get the keys, a flashlight and I'll draw you a map."

Amy slumped. A new definition of rustic? Could this day possibly get any worse? Apparently yes, it could. With exhaustion clawing at her, she just wanted to curl up on a bed and put an end to this horrendous day.

Why? Tomorrow won't be any different. You still won't have a job and your career will still be dead.

Sadly, that truth was inarguable.

CHAPTER TWO

SWEAT POURED off Ben Armytage as he pushed his extremely heavy, red, vintage Harley-Davidson up the road. The sign he passed read, Two Miles to Whitetail, the Home of Weddings That Wow. The irony of the situation hadn't escaped him. His beloved bike, which had carried him without mishap over the thousands of miles between Argentina and Alaska, had chosen to break down four hundred miles away from Milwaukee. The home of Harley-Davidson and the place Red had been made.

The fact it had happened outside a town that celebrated weddings was just an added extra on the irony scale and a lot like rubbing salt into a wound. After all, this entire two-continent trip was the result of a wedding. Or, to be more precise, the lack of a wedding. His. He unzipped his leather jacket, needing the breeze. Had the bike not weighed so much, and if there'd been another town that was closer, *nothing* would have enticed him to step foot in Whitetail.

Over the past two hundred and eighty days, he'd come to think of his bike in terms of the ideal woman. She didn't talk back, she sat between his legs and more often than not she was a little bit dirty.

"Red, you could have planned this better."

She dripped oil on his boots.

If his lungs weren't cramping so much from exertion, he probably would have enjoyed the fresh scent of pine on the early evening air. As it was, he could barely appreciate the vivid autumnal colors—the red of the maple, the yellow of the poplar and the orange of the beech—all glowing incandescently, backlit by the setting sun. It was very different from his native Australia and the evergreen gum trees.

He heard the hum of an engine behind him and moved Red to the edge of the narrow road.

The truck slowed and an older man with a shock of white hair stuck his head out the window. "You outta gas, son?"

"No. She's fueled up but she started running rough. Now she won't start."

The driver leaned over and opened the door. "Get in and I'll take you into town."

"I appreciate the offer but I'm not keen to leave Red on her own."

The man nodded in perfect understanding. "Oh, yeah, she's a sweet ride. Hydra-Glide, eh? What year?"

Ben was used to answering questions about Red, but getting one from someone who recognized her straight off the bat was unusual. "Nineteen fifty-seven."

"I've got a '41 chopper myself." He got a faraway look in his eyes. "Back in the day I ruled these roads on that baby."

Ben laughed, thinking of the motorcycle club his father belonged to whose motto was Grow Old Disgracefully. "You probably still can and should."

"Mebbe you're right. Just lately I got too much work to ride her much." He tugged on his beard. "Your baby's gonna be fine here. It'll only take ten minutes to get back with the tow truck and we'll have her tucked up safe by nightfall. Meanwhile, you look like you could use a beer, eh?"

Ben grinned. He'd only been in Wisconsin one day but the locals' love affair with beer almost matched Australia's. He pulled his wallet, phone and passport out of a saddle bag and got into the truck. "Thanks, mate. I'm Ben."

"Al Swenson, Whitetail's mechanic." He shook Ben's hand before putting the truck in gear and moving off. "Is that an accent I hear?"

Ben tried not to laugh because Al sounded like a character off *A Prairie Home Companion*. "Yeah. I'm Australian."

"An Aussie on a Harley in Wisconsin, eh?" Al slapped the top of the steering wheel with his palm. "Damn. Now, that's not something we see every day. Welcome to Whitetail, son. It's a nice little town. Why not stay awhile, eh?"

Ben saw an advertising flyer on the dash for Feel Like a Star Car and Carriage Service. It featured a photo of a bride in a horse-drawn carriage. He shuddered.

"I'll think about it," he said. But it was sheer politeness.

Nothing short of the apocalypse could keep him in a town that celebrated weddings.

Half an hour later, Ben stood in an auto repair workshop not quite able to believe his luck that not only had Al driven past when he needed him but he was a mechanic with a passion for bikes. Not that Ben didn't know his way around Red's engine; he did. He tinkered with it constantly and, truth be told, he probably took better care of it than he took of himself. But Al would be great backup if he couldn't fix Red himself and a good contact if he needed parts.

He glanced around, noticing the set up. It appeared that Al was also a lover of all things that provided transport. The vehicles in the front section of the building looked relatively modern, but the back was filled with old engines, worn buggies that had once been pulled by elegant horses and something that looked like it might be a rusted-out Mustang. It reminded him of his dad's shed.

"Interesting collection," Ben said.

"Some people say I collect junk but I know different. Did up an old landau a while back and now it's a wedding carriage." Al rose from a squat after taking a quick look at Red. "Going on what you told me,

Ben, the problem could be anything from valves to the manifold. I'll take a look at her first thing in the morning." He threw a tarp over Red.

"It might just be dirty fuel. We could work on her now." Ben was eager to find the problem, fix it and get out of town.

"Son, you just finished telling me you've been on the road for over two hundred days. Red needs rest and, looking at you, you need a home-cooked meal. What's your hurry, eh? We'll deal with it tomorrow." He opened the door and flicked off the lights as if the topic was now closed for discussion. "My daughter's putting supper on the table right about now."

Ben was used to the beat of his own drum. "I don't want to hold you up but if you're happy for me to work here alone, I'm sure I can solve the problem. I've kept her going this long."

"And risk her breaking down on you again and this time in the dark?" Al gave him a look that said Ben was clueless. "It's over a hundred miles to Eau Claire and there's no town bigger than Whitetail in between. It's not like you need to be anywhere in particular tonight, eh?"

Al had him there. The whole point of life on the road was to take it as it comes. He was an expert at doing that but he didn't want to do it in this town. Without transport, though, he was stuck and he could hardly break into the workshop and fix her.

Recognizing a fait accompli, he reluctantly followed Al back to the truck. "Can you suggest somewhere cheap I can stay?"

Al scratched his chin. "Oh, hell. I just remembered there's a wedding tomorrow and everywhere's booked solid."

Ben's gut tightened. A town filled with happy and excited wedding guests was the last place he wanted to be. He turned back toward the garage door. "Let me take a look. It's probably just the spark plugs."

Al's beefy hand shot out and clamped on his shoulder. "You're not going anywhere except to my house for supper."

Ben wasn't used to such insistent hospitality and he got the strong impression it would be easier to give in, but that wasn't something he was very good at.

"I'd invite you to stay with me," Al continued, "but my family's visiting from Saint Paul for the wedding." He sighed. "The house is full of excited women."

Ben thought he'd just dodged a bullet. "No worries. I'll pitch my tent."

Al shook his head again. "The mornings are mighty chilly this far north."

Ben had camped in a lot worse places. "I'll cope. I saw a sign about a campground near the lake."

"It closed last week." The mechanic's pale blue eyes suddenly lit up. "But I know just the place and it's right on the lake. How about I lend you my chopper and you head out there straight after supper, eh?"

The thought of a sweet ride on a chopper silenced every concern about spending time in the wedding town. He shot out his hand. "It's a deal."

CHAPTER THREE

AMY EASED the car down the long, overgrown driveway, with her heart sinking fast. If the cabin was in the same state as the driveway, she knew it would be a dump. God, she hoped there weren't spiders. Or mice. She shivered at the thought and gripped the steering wheel harder. Ella had said there were clean sheets and towels and at this point of her day, and her life, that was all she cared about. She needed a shower to wash away the filth of the day—well, physically anyway. Nothing could wash away the poison of Jonathon's words.

You know more about the law, Amy, than you do about sex.

How had she been so stupid? How had she managed to lose everything she'd worked so hard for so quickly? She didn't know who she hated more right now—Jonathon or herself for being so blind.

She peered into the darkness and a small building came into view so she pulled off and parked behind some trees. Grabbing her flashlight, she got out of the car and looked for a path. There wasn't one. As she approached the log cabin she thought it odd that there were no windows on the back wall, especially as there wasn't a chimney either. She walked around the rectangular building, looking for the door. She stopped short as the yellow beam of her flashlight bounced off a padlock.

Oh, God, it was worse than she thought. This wasn't even a cabin. It was some sort of shed. It probably reeked of fishing bait or Jet Ski oil. She pressed her forehead against the metal doors and tried not to cry. She didn't have the heart to open it and face the contents.

Go back to town.

The thought tempted her so much she felt herself giving in. Ella had a lovely house with a hot shower and she could stay the night and rethink her plan tomorrow.

Ella will ask questions.

Suddenly the idea of sleeping with the scent of engine oil and fish didn't seem quite so bad. She fingered the bunch of keys in her hand and wondered what they were all for. She couldn't imagine what could possibly be inside a one-room shed that would need so many keys.

As she tramped back to the car to grab her bag, she noticed what looked like a path off to her left. It probably led to the lake. Despite the fact there was only a half-moon and she wouldn't be able to see much, she had an overwhelming need to see the water. Moving her flashlight back and forth in a wide arc, she walked slowly with her gaze on her feet so she didn't trip over. At the end of a grove of pine trees, the path suddenly opened up into a large clearing.

Bright lights came on and she stared, blinking, as she heard her stunned gasp echoing back to her on the night air. There was no lake. Instead, towering above her was the biggest house she'd ever seen. Scarcely able to believe its existence, she quickly crossed the driveway and walked straight to a wide wooden door that was housed under a portico.

She frantically tried almost every key in the bunch until the sixth one yielded entry. She quickly passed through a vestibule and then she was standing inside a massive room that had to be more than thirty feet high. She supposed that, as there were exposed log beam walls, this was technically a log cabin. Everything else about it screamed *mansion.*

On one side of the great room was a floor-to-ceiling river-rock fireplace, the size of which put a Tudor castle's to shame. On the other side was an enormous glass prow wall, the height of the house, and she'd stake her life it gave uncompromising views over the lake. She tried not to meet the glass eyes of the deer head that had pride of place on another wall along with other trophies of large fish. After all, this was the Northwoods and people took their hunting and fishing very seriously.

As she moved through the house, the lights came on automatically. She ran up the wide staircase to a catwalk and still the huge ceiling beams were far above her. Deliberating for a moment whether to go left or right, she chose left. She discovered bedroom after bedroom until she got to the end of a wing and found herself in the master bedroom. The king-size bed barely made a dent in the enormous room and she leaped on it.

Oh, my God. Sheer comfort enveloped her as she sank into pillow softness and let out a squeal of pure delight. A moment later, excitement lurched her back to her feet and she found a control panel for the lights in all parts of the house. The question, *Honey, did you turn off the kitchen lights before coming upstairs?* never needed to be asked in the Rasmussens' house. She bypassed the walk-in closet and went directly to the master bathroom. Like the rest of the house it was decorated in elegant and expensive rustic chic complete with a jetted tub and fluffy towels. She might never leave.

Praying that the hot water hadn't been turned off, she turned on the tub's faucets. Cold water ran for thirty seconds and she was about to concede defeat and then the hot kicked in. *Yes.* Finally, after living the crappiest day of her life, something was going right. She rifled through a vanity drawer and found a bottle of mango body gel and squirted it in. The tropical scent rose on the steam and she stripped off her soiled clothes and stepped in.

As the water covered her body she leaned back, closed her eyes and sighed. She'd just found the perfect haven to stay while she worked out exactly what she was going to do with the rest of her life.

Amy didn't realize her eyes had fluttered closed until they jerked open in fright. The loud and throaty sound of an engine reverberated around her, sending fear skimming along her veins. She sat up fast, her hands gripping the edge of the bath so hard it hurt. The house was well set back from the main road so traffic noise wouldn't penetrate, which meant this engine noise was coming from just outside.

It died away and a moment later she relaxed. It must have been a boat belonged to an enthusiastic fishermen or maybe a local. She remembered there were some people who lived on the lake and used boats to travel to and from the town in summer months as it was quicker than the road. Who knew, maybe they used their boats until the lake froze?

While she'd dozed, the water in the bath had cooled and the lights in the bathroom had automatically switched off. She stood and the lights came on. She stepped carefully out of the deep-sided tub and picked up the gloriously soft and enormous bath sheet. As she rubbed herself dry, she heard a squeaking sound. She immediately paused, listening for it again but when she didn't hear it, she figured it must have been the floorboards creaking under her feet.

It's just new house jitters. You'll get used to the sounds. She returned to drying herself and was just about to pop the edge of the towel between her toes when the bang of a door made her jump.

Her heart leaped in her chest. Someone was in the house!

Sometimes in the off-season, we get break-ins.

Ella's words amplified her fears and she realized the throaty engine noise she'd heard hadn't been a boat at all. It was a motorcycle.

A gang?

Don't be ridiculous. It was one engine.

Every stereotype ever created about bikers filled her with panic.

It might be a woman.

And pigs might fly.

With an engine that loud and thundering, it had to be ridden by a man who had a serious ego and put himself above the law. That would be the only reason why he hadn't ridden away the moment the outside security lighting had come on. Why the sight of her car hadn't deterred him.

Amy shoved her fist into her mouth to stifle a scream. He wouldn't have seen her car. She'd parked it well off the driveway and it was hidden behind trees. The biker wouldn't know she was in the house. Oh, God! The news was full of the unpredictable things thieves did when they were unexpectedly confronted.

Her breaths now came in short, choppy rifts. She was alone in a huge house with a probable violent intruder and no neighbors close enough to hear her scream. Why had she been so against the idea of carrying a small gun in her purse?

Think, Amy, think.

Tying the large bath sheet firmly under her arms, she reentered the bedroom. The low glow of the bedside lamps came on instantly and she threw herself at the switch, turning them off. There was no way she could move in this house without activating the lights and drawing attention to her presence. Her body took another jolt of fear-induced adrenaline but instead of paralyzing her, it activated her brain.

The control panel.

She turned on the long-handled flashlight Mrs. Norell had given her and pointed it at the panel, praying there'd be an obvious master switch to turn off the lights and keep them off. She didn't want to press random buttons and risk turning on every light in the house. Sending up a prayer, she pressed the switch that read, Good-night. Then she tried to get the lamps to turn on. Nothing happened.

Yes!

Her relief was short-lived. A lack of light didn't change the fact that a dangerous man was downstairs and she had to find him first, not the other way around. She eased her way out of the room and carefully and quietly made her way along the hallway until she stood in the shadows of the catwalk.

Heavy footsteps—loud and ominous—echoed around the house followed by the scrape of wood against wood. Next came a dull thud.

"Shit!"

The male voice confirmed her suspicions but the way he'd said the curse was odd. It sounded sort of flat and elongated.

She crept forward and saw a small spill of light. He was holding a phone. The light silhouetted him as he bent over rubbing his shin. He straightened up.

Her mouth dried. She was five feet ten inches tall in flat feet but this guy was taller. Exactly how much more was hard to tell because he was wearing a motorcycle helmet, but she guessed he was well over six feet. But it wasn't his height that was intimidating, it was his breadth. The square tilt of his shoulders and the way they filled his leather jacket said he could squish her like a bug if he chose.

Not if I get to you first, buddy.

Her hand tightened on the flashlight. If she could somehow get downstairs without him realizing she was here then maybe she could sneak up on him and...

What? What? Years of arguing for a living and reading dry contracts had hardly prepared her for a stakeout and a raid.

The guy turned and started walking slowly back across the great room. Amy thought she heard him mumble, "Bloody lights" but perhaps she'd been watching too much British television on late-night cable. Why would he want to turn on the lights if he was going to burglarize? He was either not very bright or very certain the house was isolated enough for no one to notice. The fact he didn't have a flashlight indicated the former.

He disappeared through a doorway that Amy hadn't explored and she took her chance. Holding her towel tightly against her chest, she pressed her body against the banister and walked down the stairs.

Don't come back, don't come back, don't come back, she chanted silently to herself as she touched each step. She finally reached the bottom and left the safety of the banister, walking toward the doorway he'd exited through. If or when he returned, she'd be there ready to hit him with her flashlight.

She was halfway across the great room when the enormous antler chandelier above her head lit up.

Terror froze her to the spot. He must have found another control panel. Any minute he'd reappear and find her. She glanced around frantically, taking in the entire open space and running through her very limited options. Hiding behind one of the four-seater leather sofas put her at risk of being discovered crouching and vulnerable. Unless she could jump up and surprise him.

Wearing a towel?

Okay, bad idea.

Why the hell hadn't she thought to put her clothes on?

Just move! Like a sprinter hearing the starter's gun, she raced to the doorway and flattened herself up against the wall. Sucking in her breath as if that would make her even less noticeable, she raised the flashlight high above her head.

Come on, come on.

Seconds ticked by, followed by a full minute and then another. The muscles of her upper arms burned. Why had she spent so much time in the office instead of lifting weights and working out at the gym?

Because your job was your life.

And hadn't all of that worked out just peachy. Now she was out of her job, she had jelly arms and a widening butt, and she was trying to stave off an attacker. The burn moved, spreading across her shoulders and down along her arms. Pins and needles tingled in her fingers and the bath sheet felt loose over her breasts.

Come on. Where the hell was he?

The faint sound of boots against the polished maple floorboards increased in volume. She tried tightening her grip on the flashlight but the numbness in her hands made it impossible to feel anything.

The door opened.

Now!

He moved past her into the room and she swung the flashlight toward the back of his now-uncovered head, planning to knock him out cold. But with screaming arm muscles and numb hands, she misjudged the distance and clipped him hard on the shoulder.

"Jesus." He spun around fast, his left arm reaching for his right shoulder. "What the hell?"

He was so close she could see the shock in the depths of his wide, emerald-green eyes. She saw the exact moment his survival instincts kicked in.

He lunged. His left arm shot out, grabbing for her. She dodged, avoiding his grasp but his hand caught the edge of the towel. As it tumbled down her body, she brought her knee up hard into his groin.

With a sucking gasp, he staggered backward before slumping over. Taking advantage of his exposed position, she threw herself at his right shoulder, knocking him to the floor. The momentum took her flying over his head and she heard him grunt in pain. *Good.* Half a second later, her hip hit the floorboards with a bone-chipping thud.

"Argh." Agony ripped through her and silver stars danced in her head. She was sprawled, chest-down with no air in her lungs, gasping for breath.

His hand locked around her ankle, his fingers digging into the small triangular space. "Are...you...done?" he asked, panting.

No way. She kicked out and connected with something hard that she hoped was his head.

"Fuck." The word held every level of pain but his grip tightened.

If she had any time to think, she'd swear he had an accent.

"Listen, lady, I don't know who you are or what your problem is, but you need to stop. Right now."

He sounded utterly pissed but she didn't care. If she could have moved, she'd have scrambled around and pummeled him with her fists. "Why, so you can hurt me instead?"

"No." This time he sounded insulted.

"I don't believe you." God, she wished she could reach her towel. Right now he had a perfect view of her naked butt.

He breathed out a long, pained sigh. "Don't you think that if I wanted to hurt you, I would have done it by now instead of lying here on the floor?"

His logic managed to sink into her fear. He had a point.

"So why haven't you?"

"A, I don't beat up women. B, I've seen you naked and you're not my type."

"Thank God for that." She hated that this stranger's words, which should be reassuring to her, only made Jonathon's vicious parting words from this morning boom loud in her head. *I lowered my standards dating you.*

The intruder grunted. "And C, you dislocated my shoulder."

She dug deep to banish the insecure little girl with red hair and freckles and tried to find her inner toughness. "If that were true, you'd be writhing in pain."

"Believe me," he ground out, "if I thought it was safe to let go of you, I would. But given your actions so far, you'd just kick me in the ribs."

Was it possible that she'd really injured him? Trying to move so she could see him and yet at the same time not expose her breasts, she craned her neck.

Sweat beaded on his forehead and he looked extremely pale.

Jonathon suckered you. This guy will too. She pulled hard against his manacle grip but it only tightened. She could feel his nails pinching her skin and imagined the half-moon marks.

"We can stay here all night if you want," he said, jerkily. "I'm not the one who's going to get cold."

With the towering ceiling, there was scant heat on the floor of the great room and just thinking about it made her shiver. "If you were a gentleman, you'd let me get my towel to cover myself."

He made a strangled sound. "If you were a lady instead of an armed assassin, I'd consider it."

Armed assassin? "My only weapon is the flashlight and as you can see I don't have it anymore. I'm hardly dressed to hide a weapon."

He was silent for a moment except for jerkily expelled breaths that indicated all movement was excruciating. "If I'd known you were in the house..." he dragged in a breath, "...I would have knocked."

Her teeth started chattering. "And what, then gone on to rob another house?"

He released her ankle. "Bloody hell, woman! I have a key."

Taking her chance, she pushed to her feet. Keeping low, she scampered behind the furniture until she reached her towel, all the time listening for sounds that told her he'd risen to his feet to chase her.

The only sounds she heard were muffled groans.

She quickly wrapped the bath sheet around her and picked up the flashlight for protection before rechecking his position. He hadn't moved off the floor and his right shoulder was definitely sagging, but he held up his left arm. Dangling from his ring finger was a set of keys complete with a moose key ring. An identical key ring to hers.

The contents of her stomach turned to stone. Oh, God, he'd been telling the truth.

"You're not a burglar," she said softly.

He grimaced and his square jaw tensed with pain. "And she finally gets it."

No longer fearing for her life, Amy took a moment to really look at him. He was dressed top to toe in black bike leathers but he didn't look scary or terrifying. Sure, his tousled, sandy-brown, sun-kissed hair needed a cut and his jaw sported a three-day growth but instead of making him look like a thug, it gave him a rakish look. In fact, the lines around his mouth indicated that when he wasn't rendered incapacitated, he probably smiled widely and often.

She bit her lip at the horrible thought she may have attacked a member of the Rasmussen family and her minutes in this lovely house were numbered. "Who are you and where are you from?"

His jaw tightened, giving him an intransigent look. "Do you think we could do the pleasantries *after* you've put my shoulder back into its socket?"

She stared at him, not having anticipated the request and feeling completely out of her depth. What if she did him even more damage? "Shouldn't you go to the emergency room?"

"Probably, but this will end the pain faster. You *can* follow instructions, right?"

She pursed her lips at the implication she was dim-witted. "Yes."

"Good. I'll tell you what to do."

Her stomach rolled. "Won't it hurt?"

The left side of his mouth drew down. "Don't worry. It's only going to hurt me."

A surge of resentment pierced her guilt. "I didn't mean—"

"You're going to have to come closer to me to do it. I'd appreciate it if you put down the lethal weapon first."

"Right, of course." She placed the flashlight on the coffee table, tugged the towel super tight across her breasts and walked over.

His cheeks were pale under his tan but the pain seemed to have made his vivid green eyes even brighter. There was something about his direct and uncompromising gaze that made her feel— What, exactly? Intimidated? No, that wasn't it. She was no longer scared of him, but whatever it was, it definitely made her feel uneasy.

"Hold my right hand and lift up my arm," he said.

His hand was wide, warm and calloused. The slight roughness of it surprised her and she realized she'd become used to the soft touch of men whose jobs meant their hands only worked with phones and computers. Men who paid for other men to do the chores that coarsened hands. For some reason she remembered her father's hands. Just like her dad's, this guy's hands dwarfed hers.

The moment she raised his arm the skin around his lips blanched. She hated that she was causing him more pain. "You should take something first..." she thought about the Westerns she'd watched as a kid, "...a slug of whiskey?"

"No." His eyes glazed over and he closed them for a second. Surprisingly long, chocolate-brown lashes brushed his cheeks. "Just put your foot in my armpit."

"Excuse me?"

"Your foot. My armpit. Now." He ground out the instructions, each word hitting her with the velocity of a bullet. "Listen," he continued after her foot was in place, "no matter how loud I yell, keep pushing down with your foot and pulling my arm toward you. Use your entire body weight." His voice dropped to a mumble. "At least I lucked out there."

His jibe at her weight bit hard, lessening her sympathy. It was only her guilt that she'd injured him that kept her from dropping his arm and telling him where to go.

"Push. Pull. I got it," she said. "Ready?"

"Not really. I know what's coming." His eyes fluttered closed again. "Just do it."

She breathed in. "One, two, three." She hauled as hard as she could while at the same time pressing her foot deep into his armpit.

His roar of visceral pain exploded around her, gaining volume and echoing back off the high ceiling before spiraling through her, carrying both culpability and blame. As much as he'd ticked her off, it felt so wrong to be hurting him so much. She had to work hard against the overwhelming desire to stop.

Just when she thought she couldn't bear his pain a moment longer, she heard a pop and the tension suddenly changed.

"You can stop now," he said, panting hard.

"Really? Are you sure?"

"Yeah. It's back in place."

Relief swept through her. "Thank goodness."

He stared up at her silently, his face impassive and his intriguing chocolate-fringed eyes devoid of any readable emotion.

A prickle of sensation started at her spine and spread outward until it raced all over her, leaving her hot, bothered and confused. If the circumstances had been totally different she might have said she was aroused, but given everything that had happened to her today, including the past ten minutes, that was utterly impossible.

Feeling rattled, she broke the silence. "What?" she said more curtly than she intended.

His nostrils flared. "You might want to go and put some clothes on."

His quietly spoken words rocked through her and she wanted to die on the spot. Burning with embarrassment, she realized that how she was standing gave him a completely unobstructed view of everything nestled between her legs. Everything she rarely showed anyone, let alone a complete stranger. She'd never felt so exposed in her life.

She jerked her foot away fast, desperate to leave. "I...um...I'll be back in a minute."

"Take your time," he said, his voice raspy. "I'm not going anywhere."

And that's what worried her.

CHAPTER FOUR

BEN HEARD the woman's retreating footsteps and blew out a breath. Screaming pain combined with an uninterrupted view of a curvaceous naked woman with curly red hair both on her head and on her map of Tasmania, had his body so confused he couldn't see straight, let alone think.

How was it possible to be in absolute agony and aroused at the same time? It must be some sort of nervous system overload-meltdown thing, because getting hard hadn't happened in months. Hell, he'd been the only guy in the Vegas strip club not to see stars when a woman sat on his lap, grinding herself against him and rubbing her boobs in his face.

That he'd just got hard didn't bother him as much as the fact it had happened because of a woman who'd attacked him and won. He shuddered at the hit his masculinity had taken and hated that he'd still got aroused. He didn't want to be one of those sick bastards who got off on being dominated. It wasn't him. Never had been and never would be. No, he was chalking it up as a pain-induced aberration. Thank God he was a long way from home and his brothers would never hear that he'd been flattened by a girl who was shorter and weighed less than him. He'd never live it down.

So what if they did find out? This is nothing compared with what Lexie did to you and you're never going to live that down.

For months he'd done a good job not thinking about Lexie and now, twice in a few hours, she'd invaded his thoughts. It had to stop. The whole point of this road trip was not to think about Lexie.

Holding his right arm close to his body, he managed to sit up and rest against the back of the couch. The scent of expensive leather surrounded him. Over the past nine months there'd been times when he'd found himself in some real fleabag dives but not once had he ever been attacked. Obviously luxury was dangerous.

He wanted to stand but his head spun and he couldn't risk falling over. He hurt like hell already without causing another injury, or even worse, more humiliation. Whatever-her-name-was, sure knew how to inflict some damage. It hadn't escaped his notice that first Red had given him a hard time and now a redheaded woman had added injury to the list. He should have known from the start that a town that celebrated weddings had to mean trouble.

As if the act of thinking about her had summoned her, the woman reappeared. Her tight, spiral curls played around her peaches-and-cream face, giving her an innocent if slightly deranged look—a kind of Shirley Temple on meth. It wasn't helped by her crumpled black skirt and soiled blouse, which she'd mis-buttoned to cover what he knew to be deliciously ample breasts.

Stop it. He reminded his wayward body that not only was he on a hiatus from all women, this one had done a number on him and seriously dented his ego and his shoulder.

"Did you miss laundry day?" he said.

She jerked her chin up and crossed her arms over her breasts. "I've had an extremely difficult day, a very long drive, and although it's nothing to do with you, my clothes are still in my car."

Even in his befuddled state, her clipped words didn't make a whole lot of sense. "So you celebrated your arrival here by running around the house naked?"

"No, of course not," she snapped, her plump lips flattening into a disapproving line. "I was in the tub when I heard you arrived. You gave me the fright of my life."

"Oh, right, and you didn't scare me one little bit?" His brain ached. "Why would you have a bath before you unpacked?"

"None of this is relevant," she said in a tone that hinted she was used to quickly dispatching things she didn't want to discuss. "I looked up dislocated shoulders on my phone and you need a sling. I thought we could use this pillowcase."

"Thanks." The automatic response came out despite him not wanting to be anywhere close to being grateful to her. After all, she'd created the need for a sling. "Do you know how to put it on?"

"How hard can it be?" She kneeled down next to him and leaned in, her spiral curls brushing his face as she pressed the cut material against his chest.

The sweet and exotic smell of ripe, luscious mangoes rushed him, instantly taking him back to his childhood in Queensland and the taste of sweet decadence. He and his brothers would climb the mango trees in the backyard, pluck the ripe fruit straight from the branch and bite into them. The juice would dribble down his chin and the velvety pulp would float on his tongue before sliding down his throat and filling him with bliss. It was his first erotic experience, happening years before he had any idea that the taste and feel of a woman was even better.

He found himself taking a deep, deep breath. His tongue flicked out over his lips.

What are you doing?

Shocked, he stopped himself millimeters away from licking her ear.

Her hands fumbled with the makeshift sling and she bumped his shoulder.

Pain flared. "Shit! Be careful."

She stiffened. "I'm doing my best but I never said I had any medical training."

A small part of him conceded that he was pissed she'd attacked him. Even more of him was pissed at his reaction to her. *Keep your distance.* "So what do you do when you're not dislocating shoulders?"

"I'm a..." she seemed to hesitate, "...I'm a lawyer."

"Are you sure about that? You don't sound very certain."

With a jerk, she tightened the knot she'd just tied at his neck and said with equal crispness, "Does that feel better?"

The material took the weight of his arm, diminishing his level of pain from ten to five. "It does," he said grudgingly.

"You're welcome." She leaned back and studied him with a wary and serious gaze. "I'm Amy, by the way." She stuck out her hand.

He flicked his gaze from her round face and intense gray eyes, down to her hand and back again. "Ben Armytage. Forgive me but I won't be shaking your hand."

Her brow creased in an insulted frown and then a bright red flush started at her pale throat before rushing to her cheeks. Her hand shot back by her side. "Sorry. Automatic action. Where are you from, Ben?"

"Australia."

"Oh, wow. You're a long way from home."

For the first time since he'd met her, her voice didn't sound quite so clipped. She even smiled.

"When I was a kid," she continued, "there was this advertisement on the television with some Aussie guy on a beach saying, 'Throw another shrimp on the barbie.' His accent always made me and my sisters laugh. Ever since then, I've always wanted to visit Australia."

The dimples in her cheeks gave her a look of utter ingenuousness which was at odds with her obvious skills of ball busting. "I'm sure they'd give you a job in homeland security keeping out the undesirables."

She rolled her eyes. "Very funny. You may not believe me but I don't make a habit of hitting people. You're the first."

"Lucky me," he muttered.

With a quick and decisive movement, she stood and extended her left hand. "I'll help you up."

He'd never wanted anyone's help and he didn't intend to start now. "I'd pull you over."

She gave a harsh laugh. "I doubt that."

He didn't know what she meant but her tone made him wary. "I'll be fine but I'll take that offer of whiskey now."

"Oh...right." She did a slow turn, paused and then quickly crossed the room to the liquor cabinet.

He rolled to his knees, his breathing hissing as his shoulder objected to the movement. If he hurt this much now, he hated to think how he'd feel in the morning. Hauling himself up onto the couch, he called out, "Bring the bottle."

She returned with two glasses in one hand and a bottle of top-shelf whiskey in the other. It was a brand he'd only ever seen in a store behind glass and tagged at a price he'd never been prepared to pay. Perhaps there were some advantages to being injured in a rich woman's house after all.

She generously filled the glasses and handed him one.

"Cheers." He drained it in one hit, the heat hitting his stomach and spreading through his veins like molasses. He held the glass out toward her. "Again."

Her eyes opened so wide they looked like two silvery gray moons and her back straightened. "Do you think that's wise?"

He'd never seen a woman with such huge eyes but he was familiar with the sort of disapproval that burned there. Although she'd phrased it as a question, what she'd actually said was, "Don't do it."

He'd never responded well to being told what to do. "I think it's going to anesthetize my shoulder, and right now that's all I care about."

Amy didn't like the challenging look in Ben's eyes and she clutched the bottle determined to keep control of the situation. Control and making hard decisions was what she'd forged a career on.

Until today.

She shut out the voice and firmed up her resolve to finish the most out-of-control day of her life on top. "I'm going to drive you to the emergency room." *And leave you there.*

Even with one arm out of action, Ben Armytage unnerved her. There was something about him that made it impossible for her to relax—that was enough of a reason to want him gone.

He sighed. "No, you're not. All they'll do is x-ray my shoulder and put it in a sling. Half the job is done. The rest can wait 'til morning."

Morning? No, no, no. He had to leave tonight. "How do you know that? Are you a doctor?"

"It's an old sporting injury. It's happened before."

"Even so," she said in her best take-charge voice, "you need it all checked out tonight and documented in case it causes you problems in the future."

He slowly put down his glass on the coffee table and turned to face her with one eyebrow quirked. "That sounds a lot like lawyer talk. Worried I'm going to sue you?"

The thought had crossed her mind when she was upstairs pulling on her dirty clothes and checking out the first-aid instructions. She pressed her sweaty palms against her skirt and smoothed it down.

"I think we've established it was all a misunderstanding," she said in the exact tone she used in mediation.

"A misunderstanding?"

He leaned in toward her, his mouth tilted and his green eyes shimmering and hypnotic.

Leather, whiskey and the scent of something essentially male swirled around her, intoxicatingly dangerous and utterly compelling. Instead of automatically leaning back to reestablish her personal space, she had to force herself not to lean forward.

"Yes." Just when she wanted to sound firm and look like she was the one calling the shots, a wayward curl fell into her eyes. She whooshed out a breath to blow the hair away.

"That's a very interesting way of describing it." The tips of his fingers brushed her hair behind her ear and the touch sent tingling cascades shimmering through her.

This is not happening. But her body relaxed in mockery of her protest and her hand loosened on the bottle of whiskey.

She cleared her throat. "It's accurate."

He crossed his left hand over his body, and it brushed her thigh on the way. She gasped as the tingles turned into a ball of heat. His gaze suddenly became calculating.

"Is that your apology, Amy?"

The word *apology* kick-started her brain but not before he'd snatched the whiskey bottle out of her limp grip. *Damn it.*

"It's a statement of fact," she said.

He gave a bark of laugher as he poured another large glass. "You really are a lawyer." He didn't make it sound like a good thing.

"Of course I'm a lawyer," she snapped.

Indignation surged and she couldn't tell if it was because of his jibe at her profession or the fact that on his way to stealing the whiskey, his barely perceptible touch had turned her into mush. Either way, her annoyance doused the irrational sparks of attraction and for that she was grateful. She didn't have time for nonsense like this, especially given the fallout of the last time she'd given in to her emotions. That should be enough to have her avoiding men for the rest of her life.

He took a small sip of his drink. "Where do you work?"

"In Chicago and this is the first day of *my* vacation." The lie sounded so loud in her head she almost put her hands over her ears.

She hated the way he was looking at her—a long, lazy snakelike look that brushed her from head to toe, saying, *I've seen you naked.* She swallowed and frantically tried to think of a way to wrestle back control of the conversation and the situation. She could hardly get him into the car if he didn't want to go, although the thought of dragging him by the hair had some appeal. She gave him her best penetrating stare.

"Why do you have a set of keys to the house?" she said.

"The town's booked solid and I needed a place for the night and two hours ago I would have said I came by the keys as a stroke of good luck. Now I think luck's stretching it." His mouth twitched wryly. "Your mechanic said your family was in Chicago and I could stay here.

Obviously no one told him you were back, otherwise I wouldn't have come."

My mechanic? For a moment she wondered what he was talking about and then she remembered. He thought this was her house so in his mind she had the rights to the property. She had to stifle the whoop of joy that wanted to fly from her lips.

"Believe me," he continued, "I'd leave right now if I could. I'll make other arrangements in the morning."

She relaxed for the first time since he'd arrived. His declaration of departure plans was a balm to her desire to get him out of the house as soon as possible. As he was leaving in the morning, the least she could do was let him stay the night. It would appease her guilt at having attacked an innocent man, and come noon tomorrow, she'd have the house to herself and the space she needed to sort out her life. It was win-win all round.

Assuming the mantle of someone who was utterly familiar with the house, she purposely rose to her feet despite having no clue of the downstairs layout. She thought about bedrooms upstairs. "I'll prepare a room for you in the east wing, shall I?"

He nailed her with his penetrating gaze. "Is that a long way from where you're sleeping?"

"Yes."

He raised his glass to her with a smile. "That sounds perfect."

Amy retrieved her car, driving it closer to the house before grabbing Ben's backpack from where he'd dropped it. Slinging it over her shoulder, she carried it and her suitcases into the great room and saw that Ben had relocated to another couch, closer to the flat-screen television. He'd taken the whiskey bottle with him.

He was watching the sports channel and muttering something about football not being football. He didn't speak to her when she passed on her way upstairs and that suited her just fine. She wasn't up for chitchat. All she wanted was end this atrocious day by collapsing into that phenomenally comfortable bed.

She explored the east wing and bypassed the first two bedrooms with kids' bunk beds and kept looking until she found one with a double bed. She pulled down the quilt and was relieved to find it was already made up and she didn't have to go searching for the linen. She walked back along the catwalk and downstairs thinking as she went how fit she was going to get living here.

As she hit the bottom stair she called out, "Ben, your room's ready."

The only reply was the sports commentator telling her that the Green Bay Packers had to seriously think about game strategy if they wanted to end the season with a place in the play-offs.

She walked around the couch to find him asleep. "Ben?"

His head shot up and he stared at her out of heavy and unfocused eyes. "That's me."

"How's the pain?"

He blinked at her. "Gone."

Really? Every time she thought of his scream of pain when she'd been pulling his shoulder back into position, it made her nauseous. "That's good. Look, it's late and I want to go to bed so I'll show you to your room."

"Okay." He stood up and swayed.

"Whoa, steady there." She grabbed his uninjured arm as he slumped against her. She immediately widened her stance to stop from falling over.

She glanced at the whiskey bottle and saw the level of liquid was now significantly lower. *Just fabulous.* No wonder he didn't have any pain. She could picture a thousand ways he could hurt himself even more than she'd hurt him and she didn't want to be responsible for that.

"How about I help you up the stairs?" she said.

A spark flared in his eyes and he shook away her arm. "No. I've got this." He started weaving an unsteady path across the room.

She hurried after him but to her surprise and relief, he made his way up without mishap, although it was the slowest trip ever.

"Here you go." She opened the door to his room.

He stared at the canopied cedar-log bed with its acorn carvings and bear paw quilt. He turned back to look at her. "Good to know some netting's going to protect me from a bear attack."

She found herself smiling. "A bear's probably more interested in the fish that's mounted on the wall."

"Hmm." He walked in, sat down on the bed, swung his legs up and lay back against the bank of pillows. Less than a second later, his eyes closed.

"Aren't you going to get undressed?" she asked.

A gentle snore was his only reply.

Just leave him. But the thought of him sleeping the night fully clothed seemed wrong—he'd sweat and be uncomfortable. The least she could do was remove his boots. Gripping the heel, she tugged. Nothing moved. She put some muscle into it and pulled with all her might. The boot shifted and she shot back across the room. She returned and repeated the process, but drew the line at removing his socks.

Now you can go.

She worried her bottom lip as she stared at his leather jacket. If she'd thought things through, she would have taken it off him before putting on the sling. Only, thinking clearly around Ben Armytage seemed difficult. She sighed and picked up the wide tab at the top of the jacket's zipper before carefully pulling it down under his injured arm. When he didn't stir, she tried easing his good arm out of the sleeve. She was greeted by solid biceps bulging out of a T-shirt that read, Beware of Drop Bears.

Before she'd thought it through, she found her fingers tracing a line along his arm, following a thick, blue vein. His heat warmed her and she felt the strength of the toned muscle underneath. Of the very limited number of men she'd dated, none of them had arms like this.

He gave a soft groan and she pulled her hand back fast.

"Ben?" He didn't look very awake.

"Hmm."

"Do you want to take your jacket all the way off?"

Using his left arm to hold his right tight to his body, he leaned forward. His head unexpectedly dropped onto her shoulder. He smelled of whiskey and sweat and she wrinkled her nose, welcoming the evidence that he was drunk and therefore not remotely attractive. Then his hair filled her face and the scent of mint hit her, mocking her with its fresh and clean but oh-so-masculine tang, making her want to breathe deeply.

"Okay then," she said out loud more to rally herself than anything else.

She quickly pushed the jacket away from his back and eased him onto the pillows. "Just get the job done, Amy." She moved his good arm so it supported the injured one from the elbow to the wrist. "Ben, hold your arm here."

Without opening his eyes, he followed the instructions and she undid the sling. He gave a long, low moan as she took off the jacket. She flinched at his pain and retied the sling as fast as possible. Then she stepped back, trying hard not to notice how well his chest filled the thin, cotton T-shirt.

"That should help you sleep," she said.

He murmured something unintelligible that sounded like, *Red*, and then he swung his legs over the side of the bed and stood up.

He was six feet two inches of lurching unpredictability and she rushed back, closing the gap between them. "What are you doing?"

"Tight." He put his hand on the snap of his pants and undid them. A moment later they were midthigh.

She could just imagine the disaster of him trying to kick off his pants or taking them down one-handed when he was semiconscious. He'd more than likely fall face-first and fracture his skull.

"Let me help," she said.

She sat him back on the bed and then kneeled between his legs. As she pulled the leathers down, she noticed the hairs on his legs were the same sun-kissed honey-brown as his hair. *Not relevant, no need to look.*

"That better?" she said, pulling her gaze away and glancing up at him as she spoke. She came face-to-face with a pair of black low-rise boxer briefs, whose stretch-cotton technically covered the contents but in reality, hid nothing.

Oh. My. God.

She closed her eyes then immediately opened them for another look at the impressive outline, justifying that it wasn't voyeurism because he'd seen far more of her earlier in the evening.

With a grunt, he suddenly swung his legs back toward the bed and she had to duck to avoid being hit. He seemed to fall instantly asleep.

She quickly pulled the quilt up and over him, tucking it under his chin. If it didn't risk suffocation, she would have pulled it over his head so she didn't have to be tempted to look at any part of his buff, toned body. No one should look that gorgeous in briefs and a T-shirt. She knew she certainly didn't.

She wrenched open the door. "I'm going now," she said firmly as if she was the one needing the instruction to leave.

He didn't reply.

Just as she was closing the door she heard him say, "Night, Red."

CHAPTER FIVE

THE FULL IMPACT of what Amy had done to him hit Ben at six o'clock the following morning when he tried to put on his pants. It had fast been followed by the realization that if he couldn't even get his trousers on, he sure as hell couldn't ride the chopper and leave.

"Shit." He rubbed his face with his hand, feeling the stubble scraping his palm. The idea of a shower taunted him but he knew he'd be hard-pressed to get his T-shirt off on his own, let alone manage the rest.

His head throbbed after last night's self-medication. He couldn't remember getting into bed but obviously he had because his pants were missing. The only person who could have removed them was Amy.

Amy with the face of a cherub and a Rubenesque body that said, *baby, I'm 100% woman, bury yourself here*, but had the disapproving tartness of a skinny puritan. She looked good until she opened her mouth and shattered the illusion. No way was he asking her for any more help.

He'd made a pact with himself nine months ago that he was never asking another woman for anything, and right up until last night he'd honored it. Now it seemed the gods were taunting his recent success in the cruelest of ways. He needed a plan.

He glanced down at his bare legs. Step 1. Put on his pants. Step 2. Check the bathroom for ibuprofen. Step 3. Hitch a ride into Whitetail.

He hated that step one was probably going to be the hardest thing on the list.

The low hum of an engine behind him made Ben smile with hope and he turned and stuck out his thumb. The car came to a halt and the driver wound down the window. Ben's hopes immediately turned to dust.

"You're hitchhiking?" Amy stared at him, her expression incredulous. "I thought you were in bed fast asleep."

Her accusatory words provided the only heat in the chilly morning air. Ben couldn't believe his lack of luck that the only car to pass him on this quiet road belonged to the one person he didn't wanted to avoid. He kept walking.

"Aren't you up early for someone on vacation?" he said.

She drove slowly alongside him. "I'm on my way to buy breakfast and then I was going to drive you to the hospital." She sounded cross that he hadn't fallen in adroitly with her plans.

"I wasn't hungry." His stomach growled mocking his protest and the drugs he'd taken made him nauseous.

"Get in the car," Amy said.

"Given what happened last night, I think it's safer if I walk."

Guilt streaked across her face. "Please get in the car before you freeze."

He'd stuck his good arm into his jacket and pulled the right side over his shoulder but he couldn't do it up. The frigid air was eating easily through his thin T-shirt but he wasn't certain that being warm was worth sharing a car with her. He glanced down the road, willing traffic to appear but it was empty in both directions.

You didn't ask her for help. She offered.

He knew it was semantics but with an hour's walk ahead of him, he'd take it. He slid into the seat and for the first time noticed what she was wearing. Again, it screamed corporate office wear but this time it wasn't crushed and soiled. From what he'd seen of Whitetail, and when he added in the fact she was visiting her family's vacation house, her clothes seemed out of place.

"I didn't realize there was a dress code for the E.R," he said.

A flicker of what may have been awkwardness crossed her rosy cheeks, although knowing Amy, it was probably disapproval. She flicked a look at his unkempt appearance and quickly looked away.

"One of us has to look presentable," she said.

Granted, he looked a wreck but she was partly to blame for his lack of a shower and a shave. And hell, he was on vacation so he had no need of a suit. Come to think of it, he rarely had need of a suit. His work clothes back in Australia had only involved a jacket and tie when he was visiting corporate, but he'd been raised right—he knew all about dressing in appropriate clothing to fit the occasion.

Perhaps it was Amy's scratchy and uptight demeanor but he had the overwhelming need to press her buttons. "Most women—" he ignored the thought of Lexie, "—are more interested in getting my clothes off me than admiring them on me."

He grinned at her. "You'd know all about that."

Her sharp intake of breath was loud in the confines of the car and her knuckles whitened on the wheel. Predictably, she pursed her lovely lips. "I should have let you sweat under the quilt in those damn leather pants."

He laughed and settled back into his seat, happy to let the rest of the trip pass in relative silence listening to the local radio. Apparently it was time to harvest soybeans.

Amy delivered him safely to the to the doors of the E.R. The moment he was out of her car, she drove off without a backward glance, which suited him perfectly. It was a surprise then, some thirty minutes later, when he came he returned from radiology to find her in the waiting area with coffee and doughnuts.

"Breakfast," she said without preamble, setting the cups in front of him with some sugar packets and a stirring stick on the cup's lid. "Any news?"

"They're studying the X-ray now." He usually ate muesli and fruit for breakfast and avoided all the sweet, sugary offerings, but with hunger eating through his stomach lining, he bit greedily into an iced doughnut. The sugar rush hit him with addictive vigor.

She sipped her coffee but her gaze kept flicking between the door and his chest. Finally she said, "What's a drop bear?"

He stifled the desire to smile. He'd won the T-shirt as part of an advertising promotion for Australia's most popular rum and every time he wore it someone asked him the same question.

"They're related to the koala," he said, knowing Americans always added bear to the word Koala.

Her face lit up and her dimples danced. "Koala bears are so cute, but why do you have to beware of drop bears?"

He kept his voice serious. "Because they're Australia's most dangerous and vicious marsupial."

As her eyes became gray pools of surprise, he warmed to his tall tale, loving how whenever he spun this yarn, the Americans always believed him. "They kill their prey by dropping out of trees and landing on them before mauling them to death."

Amy shuddered. "Can they kill humans?"

"There's never been a human death reported. Not yet anyway, but they give really nasty bites. I reckon if your immune system was weak, the venom could take you out. Bush walkers have to be really careful."

Her cheeks pinked up with horror. "I had no idea."

"And that's the problem," he nodded gravely, trying not to laugh. "Australia's a dangerous place and tourists die every year from snake, shark and spider bites."

He felt a smile trying to break across his face and he dropped his head to hide it. Reaching toward the table, he concentrated on trying to pop the lid off the coffee with one hand so he could add the sugar.

"Mr. Armytage, good news," the doctor said, reappearing and holding up the X-ray. "No broken bones so you're good to go. Be sure to do those exercises we discussed to strengthen the surrounding muscles."

"Will do," Ben said. "How long until I can ride my bike?"

The doctor signed his chart. "I'd give it four weeks."

"Four weeks?" He heard his voice sounding overly loud in the quiet waiting area but he couldn't believe he was going to be stuck in this town for twenty-eight days. "Surely it won't be that long?"

The doctor looked skeptical. "You must avoid anything strenuous that risks popping your shoulder out again." Then without skipping a beat, he turned to Amy. "He's going to be sore for a few days so, no matter what he says, he must wear the sling. Don't let him do anything arduous with that arm."

"I doubt he'll listen to me," Amy said, sounding like the injured party. "He isn't very good at doing what he's told. I wanted him to come to the hospital last night."

"No need to be a hero, Ben," the doctor said kindly. "Now's the time to sit back and let this lovely young woman pamper you."

Amy made a choking sound.

"I don't need pampering," Ben spluttered, horrified at the thought. He jerked at the recalcitrant coffee lid and brown liquid spilled, burning the back of his hand. "Damn it."

The doctor raised a brow. "You can't even get the lid off of your coffee so how are you planning on showering, dressing and cooking?"

"I'll..."

But he came up blank. He couldn't sleep in the tent because he couldn't pitch it and he couldn't even lie down flat yet without it hurting like hell. He couldn't ride his bike or drive a car and he'd be hard-pressed to open a can of beans. Jeez, he'd even avoided a shower this morning because he didn't want to ask Amy to help remove his clothes. God, he really didn't have a choice.

"Thought so," the doctor said, giving Ben a man-to-man wink. "I say enjoy being taken care of while you can."

"We're not really together," Amy heard herself squeak, completely aghast at where this was conversation was heading. "And I'm on vacation so..."

Her voice trailed off as the doctor glared at her as if she was a disobedient child. His expression reminded her of her father's reaction when she'd done something he disapproved of or when she hadn't done something he believed she should have.

"You were enjoying being together last night when he slammed into the doorjamb," he said, folding his arms across his white coat.

Doorjamb? She blinked. Why hadn't Ben told him that she'd been the one to hit him with a flashlight? She caught Ben's eye and he tilted his head as if to say, *just agree.* "Ah, I guess."

"No need to be embarrassed," the doctor said. "These things happen but as I told Ben, his arm's not going to be strong enough for sex up against a wall for quite some time."

She stared slack-jawed at the doctor, but he kept right on talking.

"Casual sex is all very well but we have to take responsibility for our actions. You were both involved in this accident and this isn't Chicago or New York," he said, giving her business suit a scorching look. "We're not self-centered out here in the country and we look after each other. You're on vacation so you have the time to take care of Ben, and he's a foreigner who needs your help. Think of it as your contribution to international community service."

Up against all of that, Amy had nothing. As much as she hated it, she'd just got served.

CHAPTER SIX

SOMEHOW, Amy managed to hold on to her temper until she and Ben were out on the street and then a mixture of incredulousness and anger burst out of her.

"You told the doctor we had sex?"

Ben's good shoulder rose and fell. "He asked me how I injured my shoulder. Did you really want me to tell him you attacked me? He would have called the police and they'd ask a lot of awkward questions. Besides, I thought lawyers avoided scandal like cats avoid swimming."

Scandal. She thought about what Jonathon had said to her yesterday before he'd fired her, and shivered. "Yes, but—"

"You're welcome." The facets of green in Ben's eyes sparkled. "Personally, I thought it was a pretty inventive story."

A picture formed in her head—one of her having her legs wrapped around his waist and being held up against a wall by his strong and work-toned arms. Her knees wobbled. She locked them hard.

"Of course you thought it was a good idea," she spluttered." It sounded so much more macho than 'a girl hit me.'"

His leather jacket squared up on one side and his T-shirt stretched even more tightly across his chest. He looked one hundred percent raw male and as grumpy as hell. "If it bothers you so much, I'll go back and ask them to amend the records," he said.

No. She couldn't risk any hint of impropriety outside of her career given what had just happened inside of it.

"I'm sorry," she made herself say. "I do appreciate that you didn't tell them what really happened even if it means I can never enter the Whitetail E.R."

"Why not?"

"I'd die of embarrassment. I'll be known as the overweight woman who broke your shoulder."

He frowned. "You're not overweight."

Yeah, right. You've seen me naked and you said I'm not your type.

"Did it ever occur to you, Amy, that perhaps the staff were impressed by what we did?"

"We didn't do anything!"

Her hands shot out in front of her, waving wildly. God, they were talking about fictitious sex, the sort of in-the-moment sex she'd never experienced in her life, and yet she had crazy sensations dancing between her thighs.

He shot her a withering look. "Next time you do something stupid and I have to make up a story to save your butt, I'll be certain it involves you being uptight and puritanical. Hell, I won't even have to lie."

She wanted to yell, *I'm not uptight.* Forget that, she wanted to be anywhere but here arguing with the most frustrating guy she'd ever met. The only companionable conversation they'd managed was the one about drop bears. She made a mental note to ask him about Australia as much as possible.

"Look," she said, appealing for a truce. "I think we're both agreed that we don't have to like each other, but we do have to get by until you're able to ride that god-awful noisy motorcycle out of here. Then we never have to see each other again."

"You won't get an argument from me."

"Well, that would be a first."

He smiled then and, just as she'd predicted last night, deep creases scored his thickening stubble and raced to his eyes. Even unshaven and unwashed, he radiated a charisma that made her feel both out of control and equally inexperienced. She hated it. She'd spent years fighting these sort feelings and she refused to allow him or anyone else to make her feel this way. Her life was ordered, planned and goal-oriented.

Right now your life is way out of control and all your plans are shredded.

No. It. Is. Not. Taking charge, she her phone from her purse and brought up a note. "I think we need to set some ground rules."

He crooked one brow and shot her the same *I don't think so* look he gave her every time she suggested he do something.

She pushed on. "I was thinking of drawing up a schedule along the lines of who does what. Obviously you're going to get out of dish detail and wood chopping."

His lazy gaze rolled over her. "I figured you do everything and I'd watch."

Again the same prickle of awareness tingled at the base of her spine, stealing her concentration. No man had ever done that to her, not even Jonathon. Especially not Jonathon.

Stay focused. "We need to go grocery shopping so we'll do that now before driving back to the house."

He looked at her as if she'd suggested they eat slime. "*You* do the grocery shopping. I'm going to see Red."

"Who's Red?"

"My bike."

She rubbed the bridge of her nose. "But your motorcycle's back at the house."

"That one was loaned to me. Red's at the mechanic's waiting for repairs. Pick me up there when you're ready."

Before she could object or offer up a different arrangement that didn't mean she was his domestic slave and at his beck and call, he was walking up the street. The straightness of his spine made it absolutely clear there was no invitation for her to join him.

Shoving her phone back into her purse, she decided that the groceries could wait. If Ben could take off and do what he wanted, so could she. Right now she had a hankering to reacquaint herself with Whitetail.

It was a short walk from the hospital to Main Street. Baskets of brightly colored flowers hung from the old-fashioned lampposts and flags printed with the photo of a young couple gazing at each other fluttered in the light breeze. As she'd seen the banner welcoming the Uebelacker wedding, she figured the photo on the flags must belong to the bride and groom. The town looked fresher than she remembered, with stores adorned with bright, new canvas awnings and most had a personalized greeting for the happy couple in their window.

The town was busy but unlike when she'd been a child, and the sidewalk had been filled with vacationers in flip-flops, today there was a hustle and bustle of women dressed in pretty frocks and men in suits. She overheard someone asking, "What time do we have to be at the church?"

Amy wondered at the choice of a morning wedding. Up until recently, she'd always thought a late-afternoon wedding followed by an evening reception would be what she'd choose should she ever marry. Her plan—devised on that long ago vacation in Whitetail—had been *not* to marry before thirty. She'd achieved that far more easily than her teenage self might have imagined.

She passed Whitetail's Market and DVD and Whitetail's Bait, Tackle and Beer, laughing at the combinations that made up each business. Even the funeral home had a sign that read, Keys Cut Here. She paused outside the Northern Lights Boutique, her gaze instantly caught by the gorgeous winter coat on display. She needed a new coat and this one—vivid watermelon with large funky buttons and a crossover collar—might just be it. It looked like wool and her fingers itched to touch the fabric and savor the feel.

A skitter of excitement spun through her. In her frugal teen and student days, she'd made a lot of her own clothes and had always loved choosing the fabric and the exhilaration of making the first cut. It had been years since she'd done any sewing, having stopped the moment she'd got her first job as a lawyer and an accompanying income.

You're out of a job now. You shouldn't be spending money.

But after the soul-destroying events of yesterday she needed to treat herself . Besides, she had vacation and severance pay so she was hardly destitute—not yet, anyway. Pulling open the door, she stepped inside and heard a gut-wrenching wail.

"This is supposed to be my special day and just look at me." A woman in a bridal gown sobbed as she pulled at the sagging bodice. "I'm going to kill Chad."

A woman, who Amy assumed was the bride's mother, held another gown in her hands, ineffectually dabbing at what looked like a black ink stain. "It was an accident, darling."

"I know it was," the bride said resignedly, "but why did it have to happen today?"

Another woman, who looked to be in her thirties, appeared from the back of the store holding two transparent dress bags across her arms. "I've got two more dresses you can try on, Brianna, only they're the same size as the one you're wearing."

"But that's no help," the bride moaned. "They'll be too big as well."

Amy had just reached the coat rack as the worried-looking sales associate said to her, "Are you okay to browse? It's just we have a crisis here and I won't be able to assist you for a while."

"That's okay. I'm not in a hurry." Amy realized with a jolt she'd not uttered those words in years. She'd been in a hurry since she was fourteen.

You still need to be in a hurry. You have to sort out your job. Your life.

And she would. Just not today.

As she riffled through the racks, she couldn't help overhearing the drama-filled conversation about the bridal gown.

"Surely there's a dressmaker in town who could help us, Melissa?" the mother of the bride asked the sales associate.

Melissa wrung her hands. "Annette's out of town at the moment visiting her daughter in Oshkosh."

"Oh, God." The bride's breathing suddenly got faster and shallower, the little gasps audible in the small space. "This is so unfair. I had the perfect dress and now..." Tears poured down her face. "Look at me. I look like I'm playing dress-up in someone else's gown." Her voice rose to a quivering howl. "I have to be at the church in an hour."

Melissa thrust a box of tissues into the bride's hands and patted her back.

"What if we pulled up the organza and used a material rose to cover the stain?" the bride's mother suggested, not sounding hopeful.

"Mom, it's gone right through to the silk."

Amy had long stopped looking at coats, now totally tuned in to the fraught conversation. She studied the slim bride who was wearing a gown with a stunningly beaded and ruched bodice. A full skirt of Thai silk fell from her hips and the top layer was gathered up on the right and held in place with organza flowers.

She ran an out-of-practice eye over the options. "I might be able to help."

The bride swung around to her, surprise and hope clear on her face. "Really? Are you a dressmaker?"

"Actually, I'm a lawyer but I used to make a lot of my own clothes. Granted, it's been a while but—" she fingered the silk, "—this skirt's so full, if I gathered it here and relocated one of those organza flowers no one is going to notice."

She turned the bride around. "A padded bra will fill the bodice and—" she flicked the shoulder straps off Brianna's shoulders so that they rested against the tops of her arms. The crystal beads glinted under the lights as if saying, look at all this beautiful smooth and tanned skin. "—if you wear the straps like this, I can hide a tuck with beads to make it fit. What do you think?"

Brianna's expression was half hope and half despair. "I don't know but at this point I'm willing to try anything."

"Do you have a sewing machine here?" Amy asked the sales associate.

"Yes, in the back room. Annette often works from here doing alterations for me. I've also got bridal lingerie so while you're working on the dress, I'll get Brianna fitted with the bra." Pure relief skated across her face. "I'm Melissa, by the way, and I own the shop. Thank you so much for helping."

"No problem. I'm Amy."

As Amy concentrated on pinning a gather, another woman wearing a similar black suit to Amy's rushed in holding what looked like a toolbox in one hand and a bottle of champagne in the other.

"I came as soon as I got your message, Brianna. I have every stain-removal product under the sun and, oh—" She stopped short.

"This is Nicole," Melissa said by way of introduction. "She's our wedding planner, our hair and makeup expert, and general troubleshooter." She turned to Nicole. "Amy just happened to be in the store and she thinks she can adjust this gown to fit which is just as well because the other dress is ruined."

Nicole visibly relaxed. "That's wonderful. What can I do to help?"

Amy took the pins out of her mouth. "I'm fine but I think Brianna needs some TLC, a glass of champagne and a makeup do-over."

"Brianna, we'll have you looking glowing and gorgeous again in no time," Nicole said.

"But what if Amy can't make it work?" Brianna worried her engagement ring. "No offense but..."

Amy understood. "None taken. I have a bit of a perfectionist streak so I wouldn't have offered if I didn't think I could do it. You're going to look gorgeous and sexy as every bride should."

Brianna stepped out of the dress and quickly slid her arms into the robe Nicole held up. "My wedding day wasn't supposed to be like this."

Nicole patted her shoulder. "It's going to be fine. When I married

Tony, he and every guy under seventy arrived late to the church. All of them were dirty and grimy, having rushed straight from battling a big fire out at the mill. We got married and Tony was too scared to touch me in case he made my dress dirty."

She got a dreamy expression on her face. "I didn't care. The photos are of the most unusual wedding party ever and I love them. It's kinda cool having a wedding no one will forget." She poured two glasses of champagne and handed them to the bride and her mother. "Even if Dylan has to wait a little longer than he expected, he'll be in awe of how beautiful you are."

"And at how I've gone up a bra size." Brianna gave a brittle laugh as she looked at the padded and lift bra Melissa was holding up.

"Honey, he's going to love the cleavage this bra gives you, not to mention the added benefit of all that see-through lace," Melissa said.

Brianna's mother raised her champagne glass. "And there's your silver lining."

"Mom!" Brianna flushed bright pink.

Amy hid her smile behind the acres of silk and followed Melissa into the back room and the sewing machine. She wanted to kiss the absent Annette when she saw the vast array of threads. Pulling out the chair, she got to work.

"Oh. My. God." Brianna stared at herself in the mirror while Amy quickly hand-stitched an organza flower in place. "You're a miracle worker."

Amy couldn't help the wide smile that split her face as she smoothed down the gown. Brianna looked amazing. Nicole had redone her makeup and the super-lift bra had done its job and then some. Combined with the come-hither off-the-shoulder look, Brianna looked both demure and sexy.

"You look amazing," Amy said. "Your groom will think you're totally worth the wait."

"We really need to leave now," Brianna's mother said, hurrying her daughter. "Your dad's waiting in the carriage."

Everyone walked outside and a man dressed in a coachman's

uniform and wearing a top hat, gave a low bow. "I'm Al and it's an honor to escort such a beautiful bride to her wedding.'

He handed Brianna up into the carriage next to her father and then Amy gathered the full skirt and train, tucking it safely inside the carriage away from the large wheels.

"Good luck," she said, feeling both exhilarated and slightly sad that the drama was over. She'd enjoyed using her hands to create something beautiful rather than typing up contracts.

"Thank you so much!" Brianna waved goodbye as Al instructed the horses to, "move on."

Melissa opened the door of the store. "Amy, come in and have a thank-you glass of champagne."

Amy automatically looked at her watch, slightly askance. "But it's only eleven."

Melissa laughed. "I could give you coffee but as you just saved Whitetail's Weddings That Wow's reputation, you deserve to celebrate. I have waffles so we can call it brunch if that's less horrifying, but I have to say, champagne is good at any time of the day or night."

For the past few years, Amy had spent Saturdays working and the idea of champagne before noon seemed decadent.

Try it. It's not like you have anything to lose seeing you've lost everything anyway.

"Sure. Why not?" Amy stepped into the store.

After eating waffles and an indecent amount of divine Wisconsin cream, Amy tried on the coat and purchased it. As Melissa wrapped it in tissue paper, Amy picked up Brianna's ruined dress, running the acres of fine organza through her fingers.

"This is the most beautiful gown."

"It is. Brianna had it made in Minneapolis, but as it turned out she would have been better organizing the dress through me. I keep them safe and far far away from two-year-olds with permanent markers. I'm trying to build the wedding gown part of my business but many brides believe they can get a cheaper dress from China."

Melissa sighed. "When the dress arrives half-finished or not fitting properly, then they jump on the phone and beg me for help in getting it fixed or they end up buying a gown from me. I've taken to advertising that I have a dressmaker on hand for any last-minute hiccups as an added incentive for brides to buy through me. Thank goodness you were in town today to save the day."

Amy smiled remembering how much fun she'd had despite the stress. "I was happy to help."

"Would you be able to help out again if needed?"

"I'm not a qualified dressmaker and I don't even know how long I'm going to be in town."

"Please?" Melissa begged. "Just as a backup while Annette's away."

It's not like you've got anything else to do with your time.

Excuse me, but you have a new job to find.

The idea of finding a new job terrified her because it would beg the question from future employers: Why did you leave M.M. Enterprises?

"Sure, why not," Amy heard herself saying.

Seriously? You really should—

Amy pulled the damaged wedding gown up against her to shut out the argument in her head, gazing at it in the full-length mirror. The thought of being a bride hadn't really crossed her radar in years. She'd been far too busy climbing the career ladder with the intention of shattering the glass ceiling. Now that ceiling had fallen in on her.

And don't forget that one small issue that men don't find you attractive.

The glimmer of reality pierced and deflated the delicious champagne buzz she had going on.

"You okay?" Melissa asked with a frown of concern.

Amy's throat started working against a massive lump as her alcohol high took a rapid plummet toward maudlin, reminding her of her utter folly that had resulted in yesterday's flight to Whitetail. The backs of her eyes burned. *I will not cry. I cannot cry.*

"I'm fine," she said.

Melissa didn't look convinced. "You don't look fine. You look like your dog just died but I know what will cheer you up," she said with a smile. "Try on the dress."

"Oh, I couldn't do that." Amy hastily set the gown over the back of the couch.

"Why not? I try on every wedding gown that comes into the store."

"Why?"

Melissa shrugged. "It's hard to explain." She looked a bit self-conscious then moved across the store, selected a gown and unzipped the protective bag. "This is your size. Try it on and you'll either understand what I mean or you won't. Either way it doesn't matter."

"I'd feel silly," Amy said. "I'm not even in a relationship, let alone thinking about getting married."

"That doesn't matter."

A spectacular soft-white chiffon gown hung on a padded satin coat hanger, dangling from Melissa's French-manicured nails. It called to Amy like the sirens called to the sailors and she couldn't understand why. But then again, she'd been flung out of her normal life and nothing in the past twenty-four hours was remotely familiar. She'd lost her job, attacked and dislocated a motorcyclist's shoulder, undressed the handsomest and most exasperating man she'd ever met and now she was buzzed on champagne in the middle of the day. Why not add in trying on a wedding gown?

"Okay." She kicked off her shoes.

Melissa zipped her into the gown, instructing her to keep her eyes closed. "Okay now."

Amy opened her eyes and stared into the mirror. The gown only had one shoulder strap, which was embroidered with a thousand tiny seed pearls that wound down in a floral pattern over her bust to finish at her waist. The A-line cut of the gown and the soft drape of the chiffon hugged and accentuated her curves, highlighting them in a way none of her work clothes ever did.

She hardly recognized herself. She looked...attractive. Pretty almost. Like the fairy princess in the stories her sisters had always loved to have read to them when they were kids. Stories she'd hated.

"Oh, my God," she breathed out.

Melissa nodded, understanding perfectly. "It's magic, right? Best pick-me-up ever."

Amy laughed. "And it's not even addictive."

An odd look crossed Melissa's face. "It's safer than cocaine for sure."

Amy picked up the church train and twirled a few times, imagining dancing across a parquet floor. The image of Ben, his broad shoulders filling a black tuxedo jacket and with her arms in his as they spun around the room, pinged into her mind. It was instantly followed by his supercilious green gaze locking with hers.

Ben! She'd totally forgotten all about him. He was at the mechanics waiting for her to drive him back to the house.

CHAPTER SEVEN

BEN STARED at the pile of white towels, his neatly folded clean jeans and T-shirt, and a fresh bar of soap, all of which Amy had laid out in the bathroom as if he was a guest at a hotel. The moment he'd put off for most of the day could be delayed no longer. It was time for a shower.

He was finally back at the lake house after spending a large part of the day at Al's workshop. When he'd arrived, the sign on the door had read, Driving Bride and Groom around Town. For the next three hours, no one had wandered in. Either the townsfolk knew Al was busy on a wedding day or everyone else was too.

Not that he'd minded the time. He loved the smell of grease and he'd been happy to have the place to himself. He'd checked out Al's eclectic collection of old cars and bikes and texted his father some photos of the T-model Ford and the Mustang. Then he'd pulled a well-thumbed novel out of Red's saddlebag and read. Spending time alone wasn't an issue—it was the whole reason for this year away. But as the hours had ticked past, he'd realized that Amy was probably paying him back for his refusal to shop with her and do everything her way. If this was her idea of punishing him, he had no complaints at all.

His phone had only rung once and it had been a supplier in Madison telling him that Red's top-end oiler kit, which he needed to fix the bike's mechanical problem, would be dispatched on Monday. Yesterday that would have annoyed the hell out of him. Today, it made scant difference to his life when the thing was shipped. Hell, he couldn't even fit it with one arm out of action.

He'd been using his left hand and scrawling a probably unreadable note to Al when Amy had arrived at the garage all breathless and pink cheeked with her gray eyes sparkling and her tight curls dancing around her face. She'd looked as if someone had just shown her the moon and the stars for the very first time.

She'd looked like a woman who'd just been laid and his gut had rolled and his blood had pounded just that bit harder with the same ridiculous pull of attraction that he'd got last night. It made no sense. He didn't want to be attracted to any woman—he didn't want a woman in his life, period. But he couldn't deny his body was reacting to her and that confused the hell out of him. Surely, if his dormant sex drive was going to wake up, he'd be attracted to the same physical type that had always caught his eye.

He thought of Lexie with her short-cropped hair and athletic build, which she toned daily with a punishing workout regime. He instantly wondered if this unwanted and unexpected attraction to Amy was because she was the total physical opposite of Lexie. The thought instantly reassured him and he relaxed. This odd pull wasn't attraction—it was what his sister-in-law, the therapist, would call overcompensation. He'd call it bullshit at the very least or his body getting sick of the longest sexual dry spell it had experienced in a decade. Either way, he was in the clear and more importantly, he wasn't going crazy.

In the garage, Amy had also looked happy for the first time since he'd met her. But now as she lingered in the doorway of the bathroom, she didn't look happy at all.

"So how do you want to do this?" she asked, chewing on her knuckle.

Her usual take-charge attitude seemed to have slipped and she wore an air of vulnerability he didn't want to acknowledge. Remembering her reaction earlier in the day when she'd found out that he'd told the doctor how he'd hurt his arm, he knew exactly how to get her back to her irritating, outraged self. *That* Amy he could cope with.

"I figured you'd strip me naked and I'd take a shower," he said.

Her eyes widened and her face instantly flamed as red as her hair. "I'll do no such thing," she snapped in her best martinet voice.

He grinned, loving how irate she was. "Why not? You did it last night."

"We've been through this. I did not strip you."

He raised his brows.

Her bee-stung lips pursed. "If you recall, your shirt stayed on. The *only* reason I took off your leather pants was because you were so drunk you couldn't do it yourself."

"Semantics."

"No, facts. Today, I'm prepared to remove your shirt and your boots." She flung her arm out, her ringless fingers pointing in the direction of a chair. "I brought that in so you can sit while you take off your pants."

He could see that working and he appreciated her forethought, not that he was going to tell her given she'd put him in this position. Even so, as good a suggestion as it was, it still didn't make him totally independent and he resented that.

"As much as neither of us want this," he said. "I'm going to need your help getting dressed."

She tugged at her suit jacket as if she was preparing to face the Spanish Inquisition. "When you've showered, use that bath sheet to cover yourself then call me."

"Yes, ma'am." He gave her a mock salute with his good arm.

"Everything's a joke to you, isn't it?"

He wasn't certain if her tone was censuring or wistful. He thought about his past year, which was as far removed from a joke as possible, but she didn't need to know that. "Pretty much."

She stepped in and started untying his sling, her fingers brushing the back of his neck. "Is that an Aussie thing?"

Trickles of warmth stole through him. "What?"

"Being laid-back?"

If she thought she knew him after less than twenty-four hours, he wasn't going to disabuse her of the notion. "Yep. It's part of our DNA."

"Hold your arm," she instructed, then slid the sling away. After that fingers were on the hem of his shirt, the soft pads caressing his chest as she raised the material up.

Silver spots danced behind his eyes, mocking his quip that he wanted her to strip him naked. At this point, still fully dressed, he was going to be hard-pressed not to embarrass himself. *Hard-pressed?* God, what the hell was wrong with him.

"Ben?"

He tried to concentrate. "Hmm?"

"I'm not your slave and I can't do everything for you. You need to help out by pulling your good arm through the sleeve."

Her impatient tone thankfully centered him and he did what he was asked. The next moment, she tugged the shirt over his head and then she slid it down his arm.

"Thanks." His voice sounded rusty.

"No problem." She swallowed. "Um...can you...um..." She glanced away as if she didn't want to look at him and he noticed the tips of her ears were tinged pink.

"Can I what?" he asked, fairly certain he knew what she was going to say but wanting her to say it anyway. It probably made him a total jerk but her acute embarrassment was surprisingly enjoyable. Plus, if his teasing could make her feel uncomfortable then she'd do the absolute bare minimum to help him, which was what he needed if the brush of her fingers on his back made spots dance before his eyes.

She tilted her chin and blurted out, "Manage the snap on your pants."

He grinned. "Probably, but you can always help if you want," he said, knowing full well she wouldn't touch his jeans with a ten-foot pole.

The next moment her right hand shot out gripping his waistband with a jerk and pulling his pants up hard against his crotch. The backs of the fingers of her left hand brushed his belly and his butt cheeks clenched as blood shot to his groin.

She flicked open the snap and then her fingers thankfully leaped away as if the metal had burned her. "The water's extremely hot so you'll need to add cold," she said as her heels clacked against the tiles, heading fast toward the door.

It slammed shut behind her and Ben sat down hard on the chair, closing his eyes and gulping in a breath. *Fan-bloody-tastic.* At this rate he was going to need a cold shower today and every day until he got the use of his arm back and no longer needed Amy's assistance. That day couldn't come fast enough.

"Amy!"

The volume of Ben's frustrated shout almost split the wood on the bathroom door. *Oh, God.* She sucked in a steadying breath, knowing that when she stepped back in there, she wouldn't know where to look. Why did he have to have a body that every woman desired and every man envied? Every muscle and tendon was delineated and screamed strength and beauty. Just looking at him made her feel even more dumpy and frumpy in comparison and she hated that. Yet his body was hypnotic—she wanted to gaze at him in open admiration just as she'd gazed at Michelangelo's David in Florence all those years earlier when she was a college student with her whole life in front of her.

You can do this, she told herself sternly. *Just don't stare. Do. Not. Stare.* She straightened her shoulders, placed her hand on the doorknob and turned it.

"What do you n...?" Her mouth dried as her eyes decoded blue cotton underwear stretched across the tightest male ass she'd even seen. Her eyeballs melded to the glorious sight like they'd been super-glued and she had to close them to break the bond.

Angry at herself for feeling so hot, aroused and out of her depth, and angry at Ben for making her feel that way, she flicked the bath sheet off the rail and said to his back, "I asked you to cover yourself with a towel."

"Yeah, well you try tying a towel with one hand," he said with a deep growl of frustration.

Thankfully he didn't turn around. "Here," she said, flipping out the towel and passing it around his front and knotting it at his hip.

"Jeez, you're one uptight chick. I did my best to protect your poor, fragile sensibilities by putting on my jocks. Anyone would think you'd never seen a naked man before."

She felt the slow flush of heat starting at her neck and knew it was fast crawling over her face. She hated that she blushed so easily but it was the unwanted legacy of some distant Scottish genes, which gave her pale skin, red hair and a propensity to color up.

"Of course I've seen naked men," she snapped, hoping he didn't demand to know exactly how many because the incredibly low figure would give him even more to tease her about. "But unlike Australians, who seem so free and easy with putting their bodies on display in front of virtual strangers, here in the Midwest we're more—"

"Prudish? Repressed?"

Sex with you was so boring I barely stayed awake.

"No," she spluttered against the sneering memory of Jonathon's voice.

Ben turned to face her, his left hand gripping the edge of the vanity. "What then?"

But the bright red trail of blood running down his cheek stalled her reply. "You've cut yourself."

He grimaced. "It appears you need two hands to shave well."

She grabbed some toilet paper, wadded it and pressed it firmly against his cheek, stemming the flow. He smelled of coconut body wash and the image of him running along a beach fringed with palm trees socked her hard. Her body urged her to lean in and see if his clean and burnished skin tasted of coconut too, and it took everything she had to lean back from him. It was then she noticed how extremely pale his face had become.

"Ben?" She pulled the chair toward him. "Sit down before you fall down."

To her surprise he actually obeyed her and sat down heavily.

She tried not to smile. "Yesterday when I put your shoulder back into position you coped with excruciating pain, but today you nearly faint at the sight of a minimal amount of your own blood? What's with that?"

He gave her a half smile. "Survival."

She didn't understand. "How is fainting at seeing blood survival?"

He rubbed his unshaved cheek. "They reckon if a caveman fainted at the sight of his own blood, his opponent walked away thinking he was dead."

"Well, I think you're going to live this time." She checked the nick had stopped bleeding.

"I'm sure as hell not shaving again until I can lift both arms," he said.

She laughed.

"What's so funny?"

"You look like the Yin and Yang symbol with one cheek white and the other brownish-black."

"I'm glad my misfortune entertains you."

For the first time he looked ill at ease—sulky almost—which surprised her. "I guess I could shave you."

His honey-brown brows shot to his hairline. "Have you shaved anyone before?"

"I've shaved my legs plenty of times." She stood and picked up the shaving cream and twirled the razor.

His eyes darkened to the color of moss that grew on the rocks by the lake. "You're enjoying this, aren't you?"

She grinned, realizing that she was but not understanding why, unless it was because for the first time since she'd met him he seemed uncertain. Prior to the moment when he'd almost fainted, he'd been this perfect specimen of manhood—confident and secure about everything. It was the complete opposite to how she felt about her own life. How she always felt in the company of men. But right now, sitting here, Ben seemed as fallible as herself.

"I am enjoying it," she said, "but not as much as if it was a straight razor."

"It's 'The Man From Ironbark' revisited," he muttered as she approached him.

"The man from where?" She rubbed shaving cream into his unshaven skin, enjoying the feel of his prickly stubble against her fingertips.

"It's an Australian poem about how flowing beards became popular after one man's ill-fated shave."

"Tilt your head back."

His eyes took on a steely look. "Be careful."

She smiled at him as she scraped the safety razor through the cream, watching his smooth skin appear. "Perhaps you're not as laid-back as I thought you were."

"And what? You'd be totally at ease if I had you on a chair half-naked with your hands tied and I was brandishing a razor?"

A throb of pleasure pulsed through her at the image, half horrifying her and half exciting her. She pressed her thighs together to stop it. "I've hardly tied you down."

"No, you've just reduced me to needing help with basic hygiene."

She sighed. "How long are you going to milk that cow?"

His gaze held hers. "For as long as I think it's going to work for me."

"We agreed it was an accident." She carefully scraped the razor along his jaw, trying to remain detached like nurses must be with their patients. "Lie back and enjoy this. After all, it's only temporary. Some people need help their entire lives."

She thought about a family she knew who had a child with severe muscular dystrophy. The charity she'd founded at M.M. Enterprises had helped them purchase a special bathroom hoist.

A lump formed in her throat. That rat bastard Jonathon had even claimed Kids Plus as his own.

"Steady, Amy."

She realized her hand was shaking and she instantly went on the offensive hoping to cover her momentary lapse. "You're the one freaking me out because you think I'm going to cut you."

"Prove me wrong," he said, his gaze catching hers with a combative glint.

She rinsed the razor and did another three sweeps before using the washcloth to remove the remains of the cream. Then she opened the vanity and picked up a tube of men's facial cream she'd noticed earlier. She flicked open the lid and squeezed some into her hand.

Cupping his cheeks, she rubbed the moisturizer gently into his skin, trying not to acknowledge how good he felt under her hands.

His entire body stiffened. "What are you doing?"

"Moisturizing your skin."

A horrified look crossed his face. "I'm a bloke."

"And what? Your gender means you don't get dry skin?"

"Jesus. My skin just is—okay? I'm don't need a regime of lotions and potions like your boyfriend."

She frowned. "My boyfriend?"

He didn't seem to notice her confusion. "Or your brother or whoever else this stuff belongs to."

Concentrate, Amy! He thinks this is your house, remember?

"At least they're not threatened by the fact that they take some care in their appearance," she said.

"I don't get any complaints about my appearance," he said, sounding delightfully grumpy.

I'm sure you don't. She quickly splashed some cologne on her hands and patted his face.

"Bloody hell!"

His yelp of pain made her jump. "What now?" she said, surprise making her tone clipped.

"That stings like no tomorrow."

"Sorry."

She'd forgotten about the cut. God, she was so bad at all of this helping stuff. She quickly used the washcloth to remove any of the remaining cologne and covered her mistake with a brisk, motherlike, "There you go, all better now." Without thinking she dropped a kiss onto his cheek as if he were her little nephew.

The moment her lips touched his smooth, warm skin she stilled, shocked into immobility by what she'd just done. What she was still doing. She saw the moment surprise hit him, making the vivid green of his eyes vanish under a pool of shimmering black.

Pull away!

But his heat fused her mouth to his skin, his fresh, clean scent filled her with an intoxicating need to keep breathing him in and some strands of his hair softly caressed her face. Half of her wanted to run from acute embarrassment and the other half of her wanted to stay.

She tried desperately to think of a clever and witty retort to cover what she'd just done—was doing—but her mind was beyond blank. His cheek moved under her lips.

Oh, God, I've left it too long. He's pulling away. I will die of embarrassment.

The texture of his skin suddenly changed and his lips were grazing hers—the touch so soft that she momentarily thought she was imagining it. But then she felt the slight touch of moisture on her lips, the hint of peppermint toothpaste and the flare of heat.

Then it vanished.

"Thanks." He rose abruptly to his feet. "You did a fair job but I think it's best for both of us if I skip shaving until I can manage it myself."

"Good idea." She took the out he'd just offered her with both hands and ran with. "I suck at this sort of thing anyway."

She hurried from the warm bathroom, her heart thundering as fast as galloping horses. What the hell was wrong with her? Wasn't her life already a disaster without making a complete fool of herself by kissing Ben? She didn't even like him. More importantly, men like him never gave women like her a second glance so kiss made her look needy and she hated that. It took her back to her teen years when boys had called her Ginger and used a friendship with her to date her pretty best friend.

The kiss reminded her of every mistake she'd made with Jonathon.

It was just one more piece of evidence that her life was a smoking wreck.

It was time to take charge and crawl back control. Amy knew exactly how to do that—she'd been doing it for years.

Her twenty-four hours of chaos and feeling sorry for herself ended now. She was making a to-do list and tomorrow things would be very different.

CHAPTER EIGHT

"So here we are again—Saturday night," Melissa said out loud to her empty sitting room. She noticed a giant cobweb hanging off her light fixture. "You, me and nothing to do but dust."

Her lack of a social life hadn't been quite so obvious to her over the busy summer wedding season, but with fall's arrival there were fewer weddings and today's had been a daytime function, leaving her with an empty evening. She picked up the phone planning to call Emily, her fellow single sidekick, and arrange to meet her at the Udder Bar. She immediately set it down—her friend had left town straight after delivering the wedding flowers and wouldn't return until Monday.

She checked her calendar, ever hopeful that she'd forgotten it was one of Lindsay and Keith Leiderman's themed movie nights at the cinema, but no, that was still a few weeks away. Maybe she could just go eat at Sven's Swedish Smörgåsbord. After all, she knew everyone in town so if she wanted company she just had to step outside her front door. The thing was, there was company and then there was *company*.

The dating pool in Whitetail was limited and if she was honest with herself it was nonexistent. At thirty-four, with her ovaries shriveling daily, she didn't have time to waste on men who didn't want to commit, or on men with emotional baggage and difficult ex-wives, on men whose behavior indicated that their genetic makeup should never be passed on to future generations and on men too old to be good father material. It had been a sad day when she'd had to cross Luke Anderson off her list. He had the genes to make beautiful babies, he'd been the right age and there wasn't an ex-wife in sight. Sadly, the moment Erin Davis had swept into town with her camera and can-do attitude, Luke had suddenly gone from avoiding commitment like the plague to embracing it like a second skin.

Melissa sighed again and picked up her keys. She refused to be a woman who stayed home and dusted on a Saturday night. That was too tragic. Besides, she and Emily had made a pact on New Year's Eve that this was going to be *the* year that both of them got married. With that end in mind, they'd determined that every wedding weekend they'd hit the Udder Bar no matter what because those were the days when there was a bigger chance of meeting a guy from out of town. Sure, dating apps offered the chance to meet out-of-towners at any moment of the day or night, but Melissa had been burned a few too many times. She preferred sizing up guys in real life—at least you knew if they were the right age and had their own teeth.

But the thought of walking into the bar without Emily made her resolve waver. She could stay in and do the accounts for the store. *Staying in won't get you a husband or a baby.*

The urge to have a child had gotten so strong lately that it had become a permanent ache in her chest. Technically, she supposed she could go ahead and have a child on her own but she didn't want to do that. She had firsthand experience watching her sister struggle with single parenthood. Call her old-fashioned, but she wanted to raise a child in a loving family with both parents living in the same house, just the way she'd grown up. That wasn't going to happen if she didn't meet someone, and she couldn't meet someone if she didn't leave the house.

Tonight might be the night, she told herself, slipping her arms into her fall coat. She pulled open the front door and marched down the street.

As she lived behind her boutique, it was a very short walk to the Udder Bar, which was both a brew pub and a restaurant. The chef made the best sweet potato tots and waffle fries she'd ever tasted and over the summer with the long and busy hours, she'd been eating there a lot. Pulling open the bar's inner door, she was immediately struck by the lack of noise emanating from inside. Her heart sank. She'd forgotten that Brianna's wedding had a lunchtime reception so people had already left Whitetail to drive west to Minneapolis.

"May I help you?"

She glanced up with a start to find a bespectacled and unfamiliar man standing behind the bar. "Where's Johan?"

"He's out back tapping a keg but I assure you, I can pour beer or wine just as well," he said mildly as if he'd heard the same question quite a few times already.

"Sorry. It's just Johan's been behind that bar for as long as I can remember." She put her purse on the bar and extended her hand. "I'm Melissa Bergeron and I own the boutique five stores down."

"Scott Knapp. Good to meet you." His large but narrow hand enveloped hers with a firm, dry shake. "What can I get you to drink?"

"I'm planning on eating so..." She glanced around, scanning the tables and booths hoping to spot someone she could share a meal with.

Erin and Luke Anderson were dining with Nicole and Tony Lascio and they all gave her a wave but Melissa had learned long ago that dining with couples only worked if she had a date. She saw Lance Peters motion her over but she ignored him. He'd gotten into the habit of proposing to her every time they were alone, regardless of the fact she'd said no on at least five separate occasions. Despite hitting a lot of essential points on her list of what she wanted in a husband—single, no ex-wife, mid-thirties, own business—Lance still lived with his mother and Mrs. Peters had never loosened the apron strings. Melissa knew if she married Lance, Hettie would be right there in bed with them.

John Ackerman and his wife were sharing a table with Mrs. Norell, Al and a few others, obviously informally debriefing the day's wedding as they loved to do. She should probably go over and add her contribution but as a formal meeting would be held on Monday, she'd wait until then.

There was a group of twenty-one-year-olds loudly celebrating a birthday but she instantly ruled out joining them. She had no intentions of being a cougar or—in what she knew would be a lot closer to the mark—a second mother to them. She sighed. She really should have stayed at home and done the accounts.

"I can arrange for you to eat a meal at the bar if that suits you better?" Scott said behind her.

She turned back to see him flicking a cloth over his shoulder and handing her a menu. His hazel eyes met her gaze full on, their depths filled with a question and something else she couldn't quite decipher. She wasn't certain if he was helping her out of a dilemma or feeling sorry for her that she was dining along. It sent a ripple of irritation through her.

"I'll have the grilled salmon with salad, a side of waffle fries and a glass of the honey-sunflower beer, please."

He didn't comment on her choice, just tucked the menu back into place, dexterously poured her beer, slapped down a coaster and set her glass in front of her before producing a bag of nuts. Then he tapped her order into the computer, sending it direct to the kitchen and set about clearing some dirty glasses and wiping down the bar.

For some reason she found herself noticing that he had really long fingers and neatly clipped nails. He moved with remarkable grace and his fluid actions spoke of years of experience in bar work.

"You've done this before?"

He smiled at her again, a professional smile that neither gave nor took. "Just a bit. I put myself through college pulling beer."

As he looked slightly older than her, college hadn't been in the past year or ten. "So why are you still doing it?" The words blurted out before she thought to censor them and she immediately recanted. "I'm sorry, that was rude."

He tilted his head as if he could read her most intimate thoughts and she squirmed on the bar stool. "I get the feeling you don't see working in hospitality as a career," he said.

She did not but she also didn't like the way read her so easily. "I...well...no...unless of course you owned the bar," she finished quickly, feeling distinctly uncomfortable and wishing she'd ignored his question.

He continued making up the drinks order a waitress had just handed him. "Owned the bar or owned the debt?"

"True, there is an element of that." She thought about the bank loan on her store. "But at the end of each day wouldn't you prefer to be working for more than tips?"

"There's more to life than money," he said quietly.

She took a moment to study him. He wasn't overly tall but then again he certainly wasn't short. His shoulders didn't declare he worked out but they weren't thin or slumped. He wore the distinctive Udder Bar polo shirt—black, white and with a splash of pink—which he'd tucked into the belted waistband of clean jeans. His chocolate-brown hair was cut neatly in a way that hinted at it being barber-styled rather than unisex salon and his glasses gave him a serious, professor look.

He wasn't the type of man she ever gave a second glance, but habit made her look at his ring finger on his left hand. Was that a faint white line? Not that she needed to know because he'd already failed at least five "must-haves" on her "What I'm looking for in a guy" list without adding in an ex-wife. She knew what she wanted in a man and she was determined to hold out for the perfect guy and avoid the nightmare her older sister had fallen into of marrying down both financially and intellectually.

It hadn't ended well. Years of dating experience had taught Melissa that men who told her there was more to life than money usually didn't have any. "What do you love most about bar work?" she asked.

He turned and dispensed whiskey from the bottles behind him. "The flexibility of the job suits me."

She fiddled with her coaster and gave a nervous laugh. This

surprised her but for some reason Scott made her feel uncomfortable. "Next you'll be telling me you're just doing the job until your band gets its big break," she quipped, trying to make a joke.

Again his intense gaze hooked hers, the hazel depths filled with an almost somber look that made her feel superficial and frivolous. "Actually, that's already happened," he said.

Was he deadpanning her? He was far too clean-cut and boring to be a rock star. It frustrated her that she couldn't work him out. Taking a long slug of her beer, she quickly scanned the room, hoping someone had left to give her an escape route from this fraught conversation.

Lance waved to her again.

"Melissa," Johan's booming voice hailed her attention. "How's my favorite customer?"

She swung back. "Fine, thanks." *Better now you're back behind the bar.*

Johan beamed and said to Scott, "Melissa's in here a lot."

The words sprayed her with a reputation she didn't want to own. "I don't think it's all that often, Johan. I—"

"I see you've met my nephew, Scott." Johan continued ignoring her attempts at an explanation. "He's just moved to Whitetail and he's gonna be helping me run front of house while I concentrate on the back-end of the business. I hope you've given him the Whitetail welcome we're legendary for."

The beer she'd drunk tried returning to her mouth.

"She certainly has, Uncle Jo." Scott raised a shot glass in her direction. "We've been shooting the breeze and getting along like a house on fire. Turns out we've got a bunch of stuff in common."

Right then she knew Mr. Clean-Cut had just given her the metaphorical finger. Although a part of her knew she deserved it, she didn't like it one little bit.

CHAPTER NINE

"Sorry to call you on a Sunday, Beth." Amy gripped her cell phone so hard the edges cut into her palm. "But I need you to—"

"Amy, you no longer work for M.M. Enterprises and I'm not your personal assistant anymore."

The stoniness of her ex P.A.'s voice slammed into Amy, almost winding her. "I do realize that, Beth, but as I left the building so quickly on Friday I need the Kids Plus Foundation files and my personal folder so I can start applying for jobs. Can you please email them to me at—"

"I can't do that, Amy."

"Why not?" she asked, working hard to keep her voice even while infusing some polite authority into it. "They're my files."

As her P.A., Beth had been her right hand for three years and in that time they'd become close. They'd exchanged Christmas and birthday gifts, had numerous wine-filled evenings discussing the lack of men in their life and they'd even flirted with a gym membership, although Beth had been much better at attending than Amy. Just last weekend, when Amy had been struck down with stomach flu, Beth had stopped by her apartment with chicken soup and filled her in on all the details of the Kids Plus ball which Amy had organized and then missed due to being unwell.

How could things have changed so fast in seven days?

Beth still hadn't replied and Amy could hear the rumble of a male voice in the background. "Beth?"

"Jonathon says those files belong to the company."

Jonathon. Amy's chest tightened so fast it was hard to move air. "He's there? At your apartment?"

"Of course he is," Beth said airily. "We've been together for a month now."

The duplicity socked Amy hard and she scrambled to stay calm and think. "Put him on the line," she ground out through clenched teeth.

She didn't expect Beth to comply but the next moment she heard Jonathon's smooth yet vindictive voice. "Amy, you have to accept that we're over."

Oh, we are so over, buddy, you have no idea how over we are. She refused to let him draw her down the personal path. This was all about work and nothing to do with an ill-thought-out relationship. "I want my files."

"I don't think so."

"You know Kids Plus is my baby, not yours."

"Everything's mine now, Amy. The promotion you wanted, your P.A. and your little charity. That trip to Ohio was very fortuitous."

His words rained down on her like acid, burning her resolve not to get personal. "If I hadn't caught a stomach bug, you would never have got near Ohio."

"I was always going to take that meeting."

His quiet yet cutting words sliced into her, eliciting a memory and making her think of how he'd unexpectedly offered to cook supper for her the night before she was due to catch her Ohio-bound flight. "You poisoned me?" Her voice squeaked with incredulity.

"Don't be overdramatic. You're fine. You were just indisposed long enough for me to get the job done. Besides, I sent Beth to look after you."

Anger and deceit almost knocked her off her feet. "You bastard. I'll tell the board what you did."

"Will you, Amy? We talked about this on Friday and now, this phone call, which Beth is witnessing, will just add to the texts and the file of evidence I already have against you. Let it go. Go do something else with your life."

The line went dead.

Amy slumped onto the sand and gazed out at the lake, tears threatening. She tried breathing through the pain in her chest but it burned so hot and vicious that she couldn't sit up straight. Step one of her plan to get her life back on track and a new job in corporate law had just been blocked by a very real threat.

Her phone rang and she automatically answered it with a very wobbly, "Amy Sagar."

"Sweetie, are you okay? You don't sound yourself."

Oh, God. She should have checked caller ID. "Mom," she said, trying frantically to lower the register of her voice. "I'm fine. I..." *Think.* "I just saw that advertisement with the puppies and you know it always makes me tear up." She blew out a breath and sucked in another. "So, what's up?"

"Oh, not a lot. Your sisters are coming over for Sunday lunch today and I just wanted to check what time you're arriving?"

Guilt speared her. Her mom had left a message on Thursday night and with all the drama, she'd totally forgotten to return the call. "I'm sorry, Mom. Work's been frantic and...um...you know how it is."

Her mother gave a half laugh, half sigh. "I don't understand how a company can expect you to work Sundays."

Her mom had finished high school and nine months later given birth to Amy. She'd gone on to have three more daughters and now she worked part-time in a drugstore.

"If I want to be a V.P., this is what I have to do," Amy said.

You are so far from being a V.P. it's not funny.

"We'll miss you, honey. The last time we were all together was the fourth." Her mother paused for a moment. "How about Daddy and I drive up one night this week and meet you for supper?"

Kill this idea now! "It's a long way after you've both worked all day. I don't want to wear you out."

"I'm just fifty, honey, not eighty-five," her mother said briskly as if Amy had just insulted her.

"I'm sorry, Mom." Her brain bounced in her head searching for a plausible excuse to stop her parents visiting her in Chicago when she wasn't actually there.

"I've just remembered that my Ohio trip's been rescheduled," she said in a rush. *Really? Of all the excuses you could have come up with you chose that one?* "I promise, Mom. I'll come visit really soon."

I'll visit when I've got a new job, which I will tell you about without ever mentioning the real reason for it. "Have a lovely lunch, say hi to everyone and give my gorgeous baby nephew a hug."

Amy ended the call before her mother could say another word.

The massive size of the house meant Ben could pretty much avoid seeing Amy. He was taking that as a win given he'd kissed her last night. *Idiot!* The fact he'd turned his head and brushed her lips with his still shocked him. He had no clue why he'd done it, especially as she'd been doing a no-nonsense Mary Poppins impersonation, which was about as sexy as an old lady without teeth.

He'd decided his out-of-character kiss was due to his body finally rebelling against the months of self-imposed celibacy. It was the only answer that made any sense. Why else would he have got an overwhelming urge to taste her the moment her soft lips had touched his cheek? And she'd tasted the complete opposite to how she so often sounded. Instead of tart lemons, he'd caught a hint of sweet cherry.

Fortunately, sanity had prevailed and he'd moved his mouth or she'd pulled away. He wasn't certain of the order but the look on her face had told him that she shared his opinion. The kiss—it could barely be called a kiss; it was more like the momentarily sweep of lips—had been a mistake. A big mistake. Since then, he'd only seen Amy on three separate occasions. All of them thankfully brief—helping him get his T-shirt off last night, on again this morning, and then at dinner. That is, if you could call the meal she'd produced last night, dinner.

He'd been taking advantage of the only plus of being stuck in Whitetail—this house came with everything and then some—and he'd been watching a movie in the home theater when she'd appeared and thrust a brown paper bag at him. The curly writing on the outside proclaimed Del's Diner and inside was a burger, fries and a chocolate shake. Before he'd had time to respond, she'd said, "Put your dirty washing in the chute and breakfast's at nine." Then she'd abruptly left the room.

Now his stomach rumbled, reminding him it was past noon and he was starving. When he'd come down for breakfast at nine, there'd been no sign of Amy but she'd stuck a note on the coffee machine telling him there were Danish pastries in the fridge. More sweet, sticky food that didn't come close to being called breakfast. Not only was it loaded in fat and sugar, it didn't last a damn in killing his hunger.

For the first time, he regretted not going grocery shopping with her. At this point, he'd kill for fruit. Hell, he'd kill for some unprocessed food but sadly he needed her help to get it. Now he stood in the center of the great room and yelled, "Amy."

Silence greeted him.

He really needed to get her cell number because finding her in this house could take days. He walked onto the veranda that ran across the front of the house and the cool autumn wind whipped him in greeting. He looked down toward the beach and thought he could make out someone huddled on the sand as if trying to reduce their wind exposure. Surely it wasn't Amy? She had acres of house to sit in, which was a damn sight warmer.

He yelled her name again.

A flash of red crossed his vision and then Amy was on her feet, trudging slowly back toward the house looking as if she had the weight of the world on her shoulders. As she got closer he noticed she was wearing sweatpants, which she'd teamed with the same blouse and suit jacket she'd worn yesterday. What the hell was with her clothing choices? Given this house, she'd obviously grown up with money and yet she lurched between corporate attire and mismatched homeless grunge.

Amy met Ben on the path back from the beach. His green eyes crinkled at the edges as he took in what she was wearing. "Interesting fashion choice."

Every morning Amy bemoaned the way she'd packed—flinging random clothes into her suitcases without any thought for how they'd coordinate. Or to be more precise, how they wouldn't coordinate at all.

"I packed quickly," she said.

"I would have thought you'd have an entire vacation wardrobe down here permanently."

"I stored my clothes at the end of summer and with all the stuff going on with *you*—" she deliberately hit the word with extra emphasis to take the spotlight off her, "—I haven't gotten round to unpacking them."

Liar, liar, pants on fire. It's scary how good at this you're getting.

She shut out the voice by concentrating on Ben, who'd thankfully interrupted her pity party on the beach or who knew how long she'd have sat there rocking back and forth on the sand. The wind was picking up his hair and the longer strands fell across his eyes, giving him a boyish look which was at complete odds with the leather-wearing biker that he was.

"So," she said briskly, "you yelled?"

"Can we do lunch? I'm starving." His plaintive words added to the image.

She laughed. "Oh you poor malnourished thing. I'll get my keys and we'll go eat in town."

He shook his head hard. "I want a home-cooked meal."

Her stomach plummeted to her feet. She was a good lawyer but she didn't cook. Feeling out of her depth, she tried to cover. "I'm doing your laundry and helping you with your..." The image of his golden skin slick with water dried her mouth.

"Showering?"

"Yes," she said, hating the way he managed to raise one brow and make her feel like a silly, inexperienced schoolgirl—although that wasn't too far from the truth. "I don't want to have to cook and clean as well. After all, it's my house. Surely I get some say."

Oh, God, now she sounded like a disgruntled wife and she braced herself for his expected comeback that she'd put him in this situation.

An unexpected conciliatory look crossed his face. "How about we make an omelet together and I'll help as much as I can? As for cleaning up, we can pretty much throw everything into the dishwasher."

"An omelet?" She knew she sounded like an echo but it came out before she could stop it. She had no clue how to cook an omelet.

"Yeah, I saw eggs in the fridge."

She sighed and decided to confess. "I know how to boil an egg," she said with a slightly embarrassed shrug as they walked back inside, "but I've never made an omelet."

"I lived on them when I was working on the mines in Western Australia. I'm happy to tell you what to do and I'm sure a state-of-the-art kitchen like yours will have an omelet pan which will make it even easier."

"You need a special pan?"

He laughed at her incredulousness. "I gather you're not a foodie."

She'd never been able to understand the fascination people had for food, television cooking shows or collecting cookbooks. Food was fuel. She needed it to ease hunger pangs and sometimes she was known to eat it when she wasn't hungry to ease other pangs, but that tended to be foods filled with salt or sugar or fat, none of which was ever gourmet.

"I can make coffee, fry eggs and bacon, and everything else I buy," she said. "Chinese, pizza, burgers, burritos, whatever. My loft apartment in Chicago doesn't have an oven."

A horrified expression crossed his face and she couldn't stifle a laugh. "You're a biker. Surely you don't cook?"

"Of course I cook." He stomped into the kitchen as if she'd just insulted him. "Do you think I'd be in this shape if I'd eaten takeaway crap for the last two hundred and eighty days?"

She assumed *takeaway* was Australian for *takeout* and she'd seen the evidence that his body was indeed in good shape. Gloriously beautiful shape. God, he even had a six-pack while all she could offer up was a muffin top.

Two hundred and eighty days? The fact-loving part of her brain cut through her momentary lust fest and she did a quick calculation. She came up with a figure she didn't trust.

"You can't have been traveling for nine months?"

He pushed up from the open cupboard clutching a gleaming silver pan—thinner and smaller than the average frying pan. "I can and I have."

He put the pan down on the stove and got eggs out of the refrigerator. "Do you have anything green like a capsicum?"

He must have seen her confused look. "Sorry, I think you call them bell peppers. Or maybe you have shallots? Scallions? Green onions? Lettuce even?"

She stared at him, stunned. "How can you not work for nine months?"

He closed the fridge with a sigh. "I'll take that as a no to anything green. The moment we've eaten this omelet, we're going shopping and fruit and vegetables top the list."

"Nine months without working?" she repeated, trying to get her head around the enormous amount of time. The idea was not only a foreign concept to her, it was anathema.

"You're sounding like a cracked record," he said.

"If I took that amount of time off it would be career suicide."

"I doubt that."

"Oh, no, it would be." She thought about her lack of a job and how ideally she needed to be employed again within the month to hold her standing. The longer she was out of corporate law, the harder it would be to get back in. "Do you have a career?"

He rolled his eyes as if a career wasn't important. "Right now I'm a hungry engineer. You start dicing this onion and the bacon and I'll tell you about my road trip."

An engineer. The news surprised her. She'd assumed he'd have a trade qualification of some sort like her dad.

"Amy?"

"Sorry." She started opening cupboards and drawers, looking for the cutting boards.

"You really don't cook much do you?" he said.

Caught in his bewildered stare, she laughed, thankful that her confession was coming in handy to hide the fact she had no idea about the layout of the kitchen. "Well, this is a vacation house."

He nodded as if he understood. "And you probably have a cook. How come she isn't here with you now?"

Fortunately she had her head in a cupboard and he couldn't see the flush blasting across her face. "This trip was a spur-of-the-moment decision. She'll be here at Thanksgiving though."

Who knew you could learn to lie so easily and so quickly, her conscience admonished her.

He's here for a short time and then he's gone for good, so what does it matter?

She stood up, brandishing the cutting board then located the knife block. "You're telling me about your road trip."

"I shipped Red—"

"Your motorcycle?"

"My 1950s *vintage* bike." He sounded very proud of this fact. "I shipped her to Chile and then we headed south, crisscrossing in out and out of Argentina and through the Andes. By the end of the first month I'd forgotten what blacktop was."

Ben smiled, the memories clear in his eyes. "I learned fast how to keep both me and Red going with thin air with my lungs and her engine clogged with dust."

"Did you get to Tierra del Fuego?" she asked, remembering her seventh-grade project on the archipelago off South America's southernmost tip.

He expertly cracked eggs single-handedly into a bowl. "I did. I left Red there for fourteen days and headed farther south to the Antarctic."

Amazement spun through her. "What was it like?"

"There's a bit of ice and a lot of wildlife," he said with typical Aussie understatement. "Oh, and wind."

She was fascinated. "Did you see penguins?"

"Emperor, Adélie, chinstrap, gentoo, macaroni and rockhoppers. I thought women could multitask."

"We can," she said, slightly taken aback at the abrupt change of topic.

He shot her a grin that lit up his face. "Then start dicing that onion you're holding or I'll stop answering questions."

She peeled the onion. "Are you always this grumpy when you're hungry?"

One brow rose. "Aren't you?"

She couldn't argue that and her knife sliced through the layers of onion, the first vapors immediately stinging her eyes. "I've never met anyone who's been to Antarctica. It's like the last frontier. So where did you go after that?"

"I headed north. Argentina, Uruguay, Ecuador, Peru, the Galápagos Islands—"

"Oh, the blue-footed ducks," she said, smiling at the thought. "I've always wanted to see them."

"Yeah, they're crazy to look at. You seem to know a bit about South American wildlife."

"Not really. Only what I've picked up after years of watching wildlife documentaries with my dad." She was suddenly struck by a thought. "With your vintage bike, were you trying to replicate *The Motorcycle Diaries?*"

His shoulders tensed. "'Che' Guevara rode a 1939 Norton, not a Harley."

She laughed. "What? Just because the bikes are different that means you're not doing the same trip?"

He shot her a look that seemed to combine pity at her lack of motorcycle knowledge along with something else that was a lot less clear. Not that she could see anything much through her now-stinging eyes. She blinked rapidly but it wasn't enough to stop the burn and she squeezed them shut tightly against the onion tears.

"Argh, this is why I don't cook."

Ben laughed and passed her some tissues. "You need a whizzer."

She mopped her eyes, which she knew would now be rimmed bright red. Such an attractive look.

It doesn't matter. You're not trying to impress him, remember?

"What's a whizzer?"

"A kitchen appliance that dices and chops and purees."

He held out a slab of butter and she cut where he indicated. He flicked it into the pan and then turned on the stove, watching the melting butter. "Okay, so now you sauté the onion."

She did as she was instructed and ten minutes later she was sitting at the large, wooden table, sighing as she tasted the light, fluffy and slightly golden omelet.

"How can something this simple taste so good?"

Ben laughed as if she was clueless. "Fresh ingredients and you're eating it straight out of the pan. Oh, and butter." He winked at her. "Butter makes everything taste better."

She smiled at him, utterly intrigued by this seemingly macho, leather-wearing, bike-riding Australian engineer who knew his way around a kitchen and was fussy about food.

In her mind none of those things went together. Who blew off years of study and hard work at college to ride a motorcycle? No one she knew.

You've seen him naked. He doesn't even have a tattoo. How can he be a biker without a tattoo?

The thought rocked her and it instantly begged the question: Exactly who was Ben Armytage?

CHAPTER TEN

BEN WAS SUITABLY IMPRESSED by the range of locally grown organic vegetables at Whitetail Market and Video. "Look at how glossy those zucchini are?" he said to Amy who was pushing the cart. "When I see fresh vegetables stacked like this, I always think they look sexy."

"That's an oxymoron." Amy's cheeks instantly bloomed pink and she stumbled, clipping his ankles with the cart.

"Ouch." He side-stepped out of the way.

"Sorry." But she didn't look sorry at all. Her curls bounced indignantly around her face and her intriguing gray eyes flashed. "You enjoy making me flustered, don't you?" she said.

He did, and she made it all too easy, which fascinated him. The women he knew were confident in their own skin and never backward in coming forward when it came to men—they took what they wanted.

Perhaps female engineers needed to be self-assured to survive in a very male-dominated industry. He thought about some of the off-color jokes the construction workers still cracked despite workplace education. Amy wouldn't last an hour in that environment—she'd self-combust from blushing in about three minutes flat. Obviously the law was a far more rarified atmosphere.

Lexie, on the other hand, had thrived in the rough and tumble mining world. One day, yellow hard hat on her head and red dust rising from her booted heels, she'd marched up to him on-site and demanded a date. She'd been the one to initiate sex that night, although in retrospect it hadn't been quite the gift he'd thought it was at the time.

He shoved the unwanted memory away and focused on Amy who always looked pretty when she blushed. "I'm just trying to put some color into your pale cheeks," he teased.

"Oh, gee, thanks." Her red lips pouted.

He instantly remembered the soft, warm touch of them against his own. His body reacted with an increasingly familiar surge of heat and he moved to distract himself with vegetables.

"Look at the brightness of the colors. The orange of the carrots, the yellow of the squash, the red of the tomatoes, the purple of the eggplants, the cream of the cauliflowers—it's nature's palate. Can't you feel it calling to you and saying, *ratatouille?*"

Amy gave him a long look as if she thought he'd taken more than just a hit to the shoulder. "Ah, no," she said, a resigned tone in her voice. "But I have a strong feeling I'm about to learn all about it."

He grinned. "There's nothing like ratatouille with fresh, crusty bread and a hearty Cabernet Sauvignon."

"If you say so."

"I do, and you'll find out when you cook it."

"You do remember that I struggle to boil water?"

It was the first time since he'd met her that she'd cracked a joke mocking herself. He liked it because it reminded him of the Aussie self-deprecating humor. Perhaps there was a chance after all that they might get along during this enforced time together.

She walked toward the checkout, hips swinging and he silently groaned, remembering his unobstructed view of her sweet ass the night he'd arrived. How plump and curvy and alabaster-white it was, just like a Ruben's painting. She shouldn't be hiding it behind those god-awful sweatpants. Did she even know how sexy she was when she walked?

She spun around then and planted a hand on her hip. "Come on, hurry up. We've got a list a mile long and at this rate we're never going to get everything done. You still have to do your shoulder exercises."

Right then, he remembered every reason why they were *never* going to get along.

Mondays at the Northern Lights Boutique were quiet from a customer point of view but busy in every other way. Although Melissa dusted and vacuumed the store each trading day, she did a thorough clean on Mondays. It was also the time she did her stock audit and perused the catalogs. Right now, she was ordering wedding gowns for spring weddings.

She had three brides who'd chosen to take appointments with her after their initial Whitetail tour. She and Nicole always conducted the tours, which included champagne, a carriage ride and the opportunity to try on a gown or as many as the bride wished. Melissa had come up with that idea right from the start, but it had been Erin Davis who'd suggested take a photo of the prospective bride in a gown and text it to the prospective customer. The idea was that when the bride-to-be got home, she'd gaze at the photo on her phone and not only choose Whitetail as her wedding venue but call Melissa and order the gown. She'd had some success with this but, as she'd told Amy, she wanted more sales.

Her phone rang. "Northern Lights Boutique."

"Hi, Melissa, it's Janey Holzworth."

"Janey, hi." She flicked open her large, alphabetized wedding notebook at *H*. Annette was making her dress and just last week, the bride had approved the second toile. The wedding was six months away and Annette was planning to stitch the gown during the long, cold Wisconsin winter. "How can I help?"

"I've just found out I'm pregnant, which is so exciting but we're moving the wedding forward so I can still look like a bride."

Melissa heard her cell phone beeping wildly with the tune she'd assigned to Nicole. Obviously Janey had called her first.

"Congratulations," Melissa said, trying not to skip a beat despite her gut plummeting and her brain shifting into overdrive. "So when are you getting married?"

"Three weeks from Saturday."

Noooooooooo. Annette was away for the entire month. "Janey, your gown isn't even made."

"I know but Annette has the pattern and the material so I was hoping she could throw it together for me."

Throw it together? A wedding gown wasn't a summer dress with two side seams and not much else. Melissa wanted to bang her head hard on her desk. She loved working with brides but sometimes they were clueless.

"I'm sorry, Janey, but Annette's not available."

"Oh, I never thought that would be a problem. I guess I could try and find someone else..."

"No," Melissa said resolutely, thinking about the hours of work she and Annette had already put in to this project only to lose it all at the very last minute. "There's someone else in town who might be able to do it."

Crossing her fingers, she said, "I'll call her now and see if she can squeeze you in but you'll need to work around her schedule for fittings."

"No problem. Thanks, Melissa, you're amazing."

No, she wasn't. She was just desperate not to lose money on this wedding. "I'll call you by seven tonight."

Janey rang off and Melissa immediately called Amy but it went straight to voice mail. She left a message and tried to return to her ordering but she couldn't focus. What if Amy couldn't help? What then?

After taping a sign on the door that read, Back at 10:30, Melissa headed out the door to find Nicole. On her way to Affairs with Hair, she passed the town hall and was surprised to hear the sound of a piano floating through an open window. Although the beautiful Richardsonian Romanesque building gave the impression of greatness, the town had never quite grown to match the vision of its Swedish founders. The town hall certainly wasn't used for recitals. In fact, the old grand piano had been moved out of the main room and into a smaller one years ago and Melissa couldn't remember the last time she'd heard it played. She was surprised it was even in tune, but going by the beautiful music, it was very much on pitch.

Curious, she walked inside and stopped abruptly at the first doorway. Scott Knapp, the bartender, sat behind the glossy black piano, his face a study in intense concentration. His entire body moved as his long, graceful fingers raced up and down the keys. Melissa watched mesmerized as the music seemed to flow from him. The beautifully poetic sounds washed over her, sounding almost sad but just as a lump formed in her throat, the music changed into a strident, jangling, discordant noise. It stopped abruptly.

Scott pressed the bridge of his glasses upward, adjusting them on his nose before his clear and direct gaze landed on her. "Melissa?"

His expression was neither open nor hostile but she suddenly felt like she was intruding. "Hi. I didn't mean to interrupt. I just followed the music."

He grimaced as he stood then hauled the dust sheet back over the piano. "It was Rachmaninoff, not that you'd notice. I'm a bit rusty."

Was he kidding her? "If that's you being rusty, you must have been a concert pianist."

"That was the aim." He slung a satchel over his shoulder before walking toward the exit.

Intrigued, she hurried after him. "And it's not anymore?"

He stepped back and allowed her to walk out onto the street ahead of him. She knew that as an independent woman she shouldn't be affected by this display of good manners but despite the rational thought, she still got a crazy zip as if she'd been singled out for preferential treatment.

He joined her on the sidewalk. "I'm a bit old for all of that now and what do they say? Those who can, do, and those who can't, teach."

The words should have sounded bitter but instead his melodic voice made them very matter-of-fact. All of it confused her. "But you're working at the Udder Bar."

"Shocking, isn't it?" His face broke into a teasing smile that stripped away his Mr. Clean-Cut-serious-and-boring to expose a wicked sense of humor. One that was making fun of her.

An unexpected tingle of sensation whizzed through her, surprising her, and she gripped her purse.

"I also teach piano." He handed her a business card with his name and cell number printed above a piano keyboard. "If you know anyone who wants to learn, perhaps you can give them my number?"

"Sure. I'd be happy to put some on display in the store, if you have more."

This time surprise crossed his face as an offer of help was the last thing he'd expected. "Thanks."

His surprise made her self-conscious about their conversation at the bar when she'd jumped to the conclusion that he lacked career ambitions. Not that working in a bar and teaching piano counted as a career per se but she was always ready to help out a fellow Whitetail businessperson. She thought about her own piano that her mother had insisted Melissa take when she'd downsized the family home and moved into a smaller place. It taunted her with unfulfilled dreams every time she passed it.

"Actually, I have a piano gathering dust and could do with some lessons."

He tilted his head, studying her as if he wasn't certain if she was being serious. "I'd expect you to practice."

"Why do you think I wouldn't practice?" Indignation flared, despite the memory of past teachers saying, "Melissa could do better if she applied herself."

"Just putting the expectation out there," Scott said, his mouth quirking up.

This time the rogue tingle intensified and shot straight to the apex of her thighs. She stifled a moan. It wasn't that she didn't love the feeling—she did. She loved sex, but she'd made a pact with herself at the start of the year not to waste any time on men who didn't have the qualities she wanted in a husband. The qualities she'd spent countless hours quantifying on her list.

She'd been absolutely true to her pact and, sadly, that meant the only action she'd had was with her bright purple vibrator and, really, it had been quite a few weeks since she'd used it. Given the streak of pleasure tangoing deep down inside her right now, it was obviously time to get it out again. In fact it was absolutely necessary, because there was no way she was ever slaking any urges with Scott. The only point on her list he came close to hitting was the fact he was male.

Scott paused outside the Udder Bar, his hand on the door. "Call me."

"I'm not interested in dating."

"Me neither. I'm talking about piano lessons."

Idiot! "Oh, right." She wished she could vanish on the spot.

He gave her a smile—a combination of smugness and open delight. "Catch you later, Missy."

"Melissa," she called to his retreating back and instantly hating herself for having done so.

Damn it. She shouldn't be bothered by what he called her. He was just some guy new to town without an income stream worth a damn, and if she did take piano lessons, she'd be the one helping him out.

So why did the fact he so didn't want to date her bother her so much?

CHAPTER ELEVEN

DESPITE THE SIZE of the house, Ben had cabin fever. For months he'd been living outdoors, spending his days on Red, camping under the stars and only checking into a motel or B and B on Sundays so he could do laundry and kick back in a comfortable bed.

It was his third day of sitting around and he was climbing the walls. After the sixth movie, the attraction of the home theater had worn off and he'd watched so much sports he knew more than he ever needed to about Canadian curling and unicycle polo. He needed exercise and for some reason he wanted conversation too. He found Amy on the veranda staring at her phone.

Today she wore shorts, a knit top decorated with intricate beading that looked suspiciously like evening wear and to offset it all, hiking boots clad her feet. As outlandish as it was, he had to admit she looked good. The shorts showed off her long legs, which were in pretty good shape, and the scoop neck of the top revealed the first glimpse of the breasts he'd seen since the night they met. He enjoyed the reunion more than he cared to admit.

"Great, you're sort of dressed for a walk," he said. "Let's go and explore that trail that leads off the beach path."

"Okay."

Her easy agreement surprised him. "You're in a good mood."

"I am."

With sparkling eyes, and excitement dancing on her cheeks and bouncing her curls, she slid her phone into her pocket and almost skipped down the steps. Her cheery body language was in stark contrast to the tense and edgy demeanor of the last few days.

He followed her, enjoying the view and they entered a grove of birch and beech trees. The slight breeze created a confetti of autumn leaves. "I just got a job," Amy said.

"I thought you had a job?"

Her eyes widened for a fraction of a second. "I do...I...um...I mean a vacation job."

Nothing about Amy was clear-cut and he guessed he should have known from her general uptightness that she was a workaholic. "Correct me if I'm wrong, but doesn't the word *vacation* mean taking a break from work? Not taking on pro bono."

"I don't mean as a lawyer. I've been asked to make a wedding gown."

His intake of breath caught at the back of his throat and he started coughing.

"Are you okay? "Did you swallow a bug?"

She thumped him on the back with bruising force, which ricocheted across to his shoulder.

He gasped at the pain but it stopped the coughing. As it faded, he managed to steady his breathing.

"No. I'm fine."

She didn't look convinced. "You've gone white just like the time you cut yourself."

"That's because your excellent first aid hurt like buggery."

He hated how observant she was. There was no way was he admitting that the words *wedding gown* were enough to make him choke. "You should come with a general warning that says, 'beware all men: avoid at all costs,'" he joked, keeping the conversation well away from weddings.

She stiffened and all the joy drained from her face, quickly replaced by a look that actually made him ache.

"Hey." He reached out his left hand, skimming his palm along her upper arm, wanting to banish the desolation lingering in her eyes. "I was just teasing, Amy."

Her brows rose, disappearing under auburn curls. "Many a true word is spoken in jest."

"Don't quote Chaucer at me." He tucked a recalcitrant curl behind her ear. "Of course men don't need to avoid you. Hell, you were supposed to slap a hand on your hip, slice me with one of those quelling looks you specialize in and say, 'if you can't hack getting physical, don't waste my time.'"

A gorgeous blush pinked her face and her right hand flew to her mouth. She looked delightfully innocent, slightly shocked and deliciously sexy.

"As if I could say that." Her tone combined critical assessment and naughty wonder.

His fingers didn't want to leave her hair and he toyed with the curls that brushed her nape. "I dare you," he said softly.

Her eyes widened to black pools. Then, ever so slowly, she tilted her chin and fixed her gaze on his. "If...if you..." She swallowed.

Mesmerized, he followed the movement down her alabaster throat.

Her tongue flicked out, moistening her lips and then the words came in a rush. "If you can't hack getting physical, don't waste my time."

Like the strike of lightning on sun-parched grass, her husky words lit through him, igniting need. Primal need he'd suppressed for months. It tore through him, torching all reason and he leaned into her. His lips brushed against hers and he groaned at the decadent softness that greeted him again like a long-lost friend. Her tropical mango scent swirled around him, binding him to her like silk ties and enticing him to stay. Then he tasted chocolate. Not the heady taste of exotic dark chocolate, which would have matched her scent, but the surprisingly sweet, ingenue flavor of milk chocolate.

Sweet Jesus, he wanted more.

She stilled, rigid under his touch and for a brief moment he almost pulled back but then the tip of her tongue caressed his top lip. It was the barest stroke, a minimalist touch but it was all the encouragement he needed. She wanted this kiss as much as he did.

He captured her mouth with his, inhaling her taste, her heat and every contradictory thing about her.

Jonathon's betrayal started with a kiss, Amy's mind screamed at her, but she already knew Ben was nothing like that snake in the grass. Just moments ago he'd been so kind and she used that knowledge to silence her concerns.

She opened her mouth under Ben's delicious onslaught, welcoming him in. God, he tasted amazing. As his fingers splayed across her scalp, holding her head firmly so he had easy access to her mouth, she wanted to say, "it's okay, I'm not going anywhere."

Are you insane? Talking would break this incredible kiss.

She gloried in the heat rushing through her as his tongue gently explored her mouth. His caressing touch showered her in addictive tingles that shimmered in wondrous starbursts starting at the tips of her hair and finishing in her toes. Each one built on the last until she was quivering yet still she craved more. She couldn't get enough of his touch and his divine kisses.

Her knees threatened to buckle and she moved into him, gripping his good shoulder for support. The solidness of his chest pressed against her and she immediately felt his injured arm between them and his hand pressing against her breast. Her nipples peaked with a sizzling bolt of sensation and she groaned, wishing the material could just vanish so she could feel his skin against hers. Feel his fingers working the magic she instinctively knew they could.

His mouth was playing hers like a bow against strings and she loved it. She could stay here for hours, passively receiving his touch but she wanted to explore his mouth, his body. Him. Using her tongue, she deepened the kiss.

His shudder thudded through her and then cool air streaked between them, shocking her. She opened her eyes to see him pulling away.

His chest heaved as fast as hers and with a grimace, he ran his good hand through his hair. "My shoulder's not quite up to this."

But he wasn't gripping his upper arm like he usually did when it caused him pain. And he wasn't looking at her.

Sex with you was a huge disappointment.

Jonathon's voice instantly taunted her. God, maybe it wasn't just sex she sucked at. Now it seemed she had the evidence in front of her that she couldn't kiss worth a damn either. The moment she'd actively entered the kiss had been the moment Ben had pulled away.

"I think I'll head back," he said without an invitation for her to join him.

Mutely, she nodded then watched him walk away, feeling part of her shrivel. She pulled her phone out of her pocket and called Melissa.

"Can you bring everything I need to make this gown over to the house now?"

After this humiliating experience with Ben, the only way to survive sharing a house with him to keep herself busy. So busy, she wouldn't have time to think about the fact he'd walked away.

Al was reversing down his driveway when he saw Ella Norell lugging a cooler out to her car. He threw the truck into Park and jumped out. "Let me get that for you, Ella."

"Thanks, Al." She popped the lid of the trunk for him.

He'd known Ella Norell for forty years, having met her and her husband, Ron, the day he and Alice had arrived from Minnesota as newlyweds. They'd gone on to be firm friends. Their kids had all grown up together and each summer they'd treated both the Norell and Swenson homes as one, moving easily between the two. He still missed the noise since they'd grown and moved away to college then established their lives farther south in Madison and west in Saint Paul. This past weekend, with his family visiting, had been fun but once again, the house was quiet and empty.

Ella had co-mothered his kids and had been a good friend when Alice had died suddenly from a heart attack five years earlier. When Ron finally lost his long battle with cancer, Al had tried to return the favor but Ella didn't make it easy.

He swung the cooler into the trunk. "So who are you feeding this time, Ella?"

"Amy Sagar."

The name wasn't familiar. "Who?"

"I'm not sure you know her. Years ago, she and her family used to rent our lake cottage. You know, the one Ron bought as an investment but all it did was drain his time."

"Ron was never happier than when he had a project flipping houses."

Ella laughed. "And yet he was never as keen to fix up ours. Anyway, Amy arrived the other night looking bedraggled and worn out. Like she needed a good vacation."

"Oh yeah? And of course you're gonna feed her, eh?"

Ella fed everyone. Well, almost everyone. "You know, Ellie," he said, giving her a wink, "you could always feed me."

She clicked her tongue in disapproval. "You're quite capable of cooking for yourself, Al Swenson."

"That I am." He swallowed a sigh. The fact he'd been looking after himself for five years didn't lessen the fact that he enjoyed being cared for every now and then. He slammed the trunk closed. "You drive safe."

"I will." She glanced at his tow truck and tapped her forehead. "What with the weekend's wedding, I keep forgetting to tell you. If you're heading out by the Rasmussens' to service their vehicles, Amy's staying there."

He stared at her in surprise. "Since when?"

"Friday."

"I gave my set of keys to a young Aussie on Friday night when the town was booked solid." He laughed. "No wonder he hasn't been at me about fixing his bike or returned my chopper."

Ella's eyes danced. "Is he a good-looking young man?"

"Not a patch on me."

She rolled her eyes. "You're sixty-five years old, Al, and a grandfather of five."

"That's right, Ella, but I'm not dead." He leaned into her car and popped her trunk.

"What are you doing?" The pink tips on her short, spiky hair bristled as did the rest of her.

He sighed. Trying to help Ella Norell was often an impossible task. "I was just on my way out to the lake house to find out what was going on with my chopper so I'll take out your casseroles, eh? Save you a trip."

"Oh, no, I'm coming with. I want to meet your Aussie."

"He's thirty years too young for you, Ella."

"Just drive, Al."

"Yes, ma'am."

CHAPTER TWELVE

AN HOUR after Ben had kissed Amy, he was clumsily polishing the intricately decorated gas tank of Al's chopper, wishing he could just jump on the bike and ride. Ride long, far and fast, letting the wind and the road take him far away from this town, this house and Amy.

Gorgeous, frustrating, and sexy Amy.

He groaned. He'd successfully stayed immune to women for months but he'd come undone with Amy of the fathomless gray eyes, lush bee-stung lips, pillow breasts and curves that would have earned pinup status back in the day when his grandfather served. She'd felt so deliciously soft and pliant against him and he'd consumed her mouth like a starving man rips into food. It had felt amazing right up until the moment she'd kiss him back. Kissed him like she, was starving too and that had been enough to freak him out.

Goddamn it, Lexie. Leave me alone.

He threw the rag to the ground and picked up the spray bottle of wax, squirting it jerkily. He hated that Lexie was still in his head when he was nine months and ten thousand miles away from her. The whole point of this trip was to get as far away as possible from her, forget her and everything he'd believed to be real about them as a couple, and move on.

What sort of screwed-up son of a bitch did this make him if he'd allowed thoughts of Lexie to invade a kiss with another woman? He wasn't that guy. He hated the very idea of being that guy.

The crunch of gravel thankfully broke up his thoughts and he glanced up to see Al's truck slowing on the circular drive. He gave a wave and waited for Al and his passenger to get out.

Al's gaze took in the sling. "Hell, son, what did you do to yourself, eh?"

Ben gave a wry smile. "Had a bit of an accident when I arrived on Friday night."

"On the chopper?" Al's eyes shot straight to his precious bike just as Ben's would have done.

The bright-eyed woman standing next to him clicked her tongue. "Dangerous machines, motorcycles."

"Not that sort of accident." Ben patted the gas tank. "She's fine. I was just polishing her up for you. I left you a note on your workbench on Saturday, explaining things."

"That chicken scrawl?" Al shook his head. "I had no clue what it said."

The woman gave Ben an endearing smile. "You poor boy. You probably injured your writing hand."

It had been a long time since Ben had been called a boy, but there was something about this woman that reminded him of his mother so it seemed perfectly natural. Come to think of it, Al, with his collection of junk and love of engines, shared a lot in common with his father. He smiled, thinking about his parents. How odd to cross the world and meet parental doppelgängers.

"I'm fast learning how to use my left hand, though, Mrs. Swenson."

She quickly shook her head. "I'm not Mrs. Swenson, dear. I'm Ella Norell."

"Ella's my neighbor," Al said with a warm look in his eyes, "and she likes to feed people. Apparently, she gave a set of keys to a young woman on Friday who's staying here too, eh?"

Ben looked between the two of them. "Isn't Amy the daughter of your client?"

Ella laughed. "Oh, no, dear. She's not a Rasmussen."

Surprise dumped all over him and yet, it felt like pieces of a puzzle were falling into their rightful place.

It's my house. Yet she seemed completely ignorant of where anything was kept in the kitchen.

I packed quickly. Her crazy wardrobe combinations when she should have had clothes here.

Ella continued, "She arrived in town unexpectedly late on Friday and looking like she desperately needed a vacation. I didn't know Al had given you keys. I hope neither of you got too much of a surprise."

The memory of Amy's naked body sprawled out in front of him returned in stunning 3-D. He cleared his throat. "Not too much of a surprise, no."

But did he have a surprise for Ms. This-is-my-house Amy who'd lied to him. Lying meant she was hiding something. He'd allowed Lexie to lie to him and, damn it, he was never letting another woman do that to him again.

He smiled at Ella and Al. "Please come inside. I just know Amy will be thrilled to see you."

Amy was checking out potential sewing rooms downstairs when she heard voices. Had Melissa arrived already? She excitedly made her way to the great room only to stop short just inside.

Ben must have heard her footsteps because he turned and said, "Here she is now. Amy, you know Ella and this is Al Swenson."

Mrs. Norell stared at her momentarily stunned as if trying to assimilate evening wear with hiking boots, and then rushed forward with arms open wide. "Amy, dear, you look like you're getting into the vacation spirit."

"That's one way of putting it," Ben mumbled.

Amy, her body utterly rigid, let Ella hug her, all the while frantically trying to think how she could avoid Ben finding out that this wasn't actually her house.

Does it really matter?

Yes! The man wielded enough charismatic power over her when he thought he was a guest in her house. Without that caveat, he'd feel he owned equal rights. Oh, God, he might even stay longer.

A ridiculous skip of anticipation shot through her.

What is wrong with you? One kiss was enough for him to make it clear he doesn't want us. Besides, we need to be here on our own to re-strategize.

"I brought you some casseroles which Ben has kindly put in the freezer," Ella said, "and I'm sorry about the confusion on Friday. But it sounds like the two of you are getting along famously."

"I really fell on my feet, Ella," Ben said.

Amy's ears heard mocking sarcasm in his delectable melodic voice, but it was lost on Ella. Going by the expression on her face, she was utterly captivated by his sexy accent and good looks.

"Not only is Amy an excellent caregiver," Ben continued, his lovely green eyes suddenly sharp and piercing, "she's also an excellent cook. Why don't you and Al stay for tea...I mean supper? You'll be amazed by her ratatouille."

An odd squeak involuntarily left Amy's mouth as her stomach plummeted to her toes. Ben knew she had no clue how to make ratatouille, which meant he'd been told this wasn't her house.

Standing by the fireplace, all model good looks and easygoing charm, he raised one sardonic, honey-brown brow in her direction. The look seared her with its potency but it wasn't sexual. If anything, it resembled pain.

That makes no sense. She discarded the thought. He was just pissed at her so he planned to embarrass the hell out of her. She pursed her lips. Two could play at this game. Earlier this afternoon when he'd teased her, he'd thought she should have teased him back so who was she to disappoint him now.

"Supper's a great idea, Ben." She smiled sweetly, meeting his mocking expression head-on and taking great delight in the slight frown that scored his forehead.

That's right, buddy. Be afraid, be very afraid.

She addressed Ella and Al. "We'd love for you both to stay especially as you so kindly arranged for us to spend time in this lovely house, but..." She shrugged her shoulders in her best pleading way—a skill she'd learned in mediation. "It's just I'm going to need a little bit of help."

"What do you need me to do, dear?" Ella said.

"Ben needs help getting undressed and showering and as I'm cooking supper..."

"Oh, no problem." Ella clapped her hands together, smiling at Ben. "I was a nurse so there's nothing I don't know about showering and shaving a man."

Al grunted, his face suddenly scowling.

Ben paled. "I really don't want to impose and—"

"Nonsense." Ella walked toward him. "We'll have you all freshened up in no time."

"Give in now, son," Al said with weary resignation. "Once Ella gets an idea into her head, there's no talking her out of it."

Ben shot Amy a deadly look that said, *I will so get you back for this,* but instead of making her anxious, she felt the now-familiar zip of sexy anticipation. That worried her far more. She didn't want to feel this way about him when he was so far out of her league. When she sucked so badly at anything to do with men.

But despite her anxieties, when Ella marched Ben up the stairs, all the while talking nonstop about the importance of male hygiene, Amy burst into laughter.

"Private joke?" Al gave her a look that saw far too much.

"Just a tiny bit of payback. I don't suppose you know how to make ratatouille?"

"I'm more a meat-and-potatoes guy, but isn't ratatouille just a whole heap of vegetables cooked up in a pan?"

"Is it? Well, in that case I can probably handle it."

He glanced up the stairs as if he wanted to follow, but Ben and Ella had already disappeared from view. "Tell you what. I'm happy to be your kitchen hand in exchange for a beer, eh?"

She gave him a grateful smile. "Deal."

Amy turned on the dishwasher and then poured herself a glass of Merlot before glancing around the kitchen. It was clean, tidy and ordered, which was exactly the way she liked things. For the first time since Friday, she had a sense of control.

This isn't control. This is just the wine. Plus, you didn't clean up.

Ella had done most of the after-dinner cleaning and tidying, insisting that Amy just sit and rest as she'd done all the meal preparation.

Amy had felt slightly guilty given that Al had done most of the cooking and all she'd done was follow his instructions, but as Al and Ben had conveniently gone outside to lovingly gaze at the chopper, she'd acquiesced. The evening had been unexpectedly fun despite the fact Ben now knew she wasn't who she'd led him to believe. Not that he'd said anything about it to her or to the others. Throughout supper, he'd been very entertaining, telling Al and Ella about drop bears, deadly snakes and sharks, and not once had he mentioned that she'd been the one to injure him. Amy wasn't certain if that was because he was protecting himself from ridicule or if he was protecting her.

Why would he protect you? Apart from Daddy, no man ever has.

"So, Amy..."

She started at Ben's smooth, bass voice behind her, which seemed deeper than usual. She turned slowly to face him. Ella and Al had left and she could no longer hide behind their presence.

Ben was leaning up against the doorway wearing jeans and a light wool sweater that clung to him, outlining his deliciously toned and lean torso. Someone who'd not met him before would say he was relaxed. Amy knew better. His green eyes flickered with predatory intent—a look she'd not seen on him before—and she gave an involuntary shiver. She knew he wouldn't hurt her but he looked coolly angry. Restrained. As if it wouldn't take much to unleash his fury in a torrent of words.

She took a gulp of the wine. "So, Ben, did you manage to wheel the trash can to the road?"

"I did. I survived that task just like I survived Ella's ministrations and her no-nonsense advice on the care of certain body parts I don't usually discuss with anyone."

Amy sucked in her lips, desperately trying not to laugh. "So I heard."

"And it entertained you more than it did me."

He pushed off the doorjamb, his long legs quickly covering the distance between them and stopping just inside what she considered her personal space. Her heart skipped a beat. He was so close and his heat radiated into her in delicious waves.

He slowly lifted his left arm so it skated as close to her as it could without touching and then he slid a wineglass out of the rack above her head.

She was staring straight into his armpit. Her nose caught the whiff of sports deodorant and the hint of masculine sweat. Every part of her wanted to lean in, bury her face and inhale deeply.

His armpit? Isn't that totally gross?

But her body overruled her mind.

He stepped back and her body whimpered.

Stop it now. He walked away from the kiss, remember. This is just a power play because I buried the truth.

He flipped the glass in his hand, placing it down on the counter before picking up the wine bottle and filling the glass with the velvet maroon contents. Then he took a sip, closed his eyes for a moment and when he opened them he said, "So, Amy, who are you?"

Oh, no. I'm not doing this. "I'm Amy, just like I told you."

His brows rose in an *I don't believe you* action. "The night I arrived you seemed very hesitant about what you did. Are you even a lawyer?"

"Yes, I'm a lawyer," she said briskly, silencing the cawing crows that declared hourly that currently she was not.

He pulled out a chair and spun it around before sitting and leaning his good arm over the top. "So what's with the crazy clothing?"

Don't let him get too close. "Like I told you already, I packed quickly."

"Because?"

She made herself meet his suddenly penetrating gaze and swallowed hard. How could she have thought this guy was laid-back?

"I don't believe I agreed to be in the witness box, Ben."

"You put yourself there when you lied to me."

It was harshest tone she'd ever heard him use so exactly what was going on here? His lovely eyes, which could be so warm and full of fun, had developed a hard edge.

"I withheld the truth," she said.

"That's still lying in my book."

His gaze made her feel small and she felt a waver in her resolve never to tell anyone she'd lost her job. "We barely know each other and I haven't interrogated you."

His body tensed. "I don't like being lied to."

Again, she had to fight the pull of feeling to tell him the truth, only this time it was because she thought it might remove the look of desolation from his eyes. "In the grand scheme of things, Ben, we're just strangers forced to share a house for a short time before we go our separate ways."

Her hand had wandered to her mouth and she pushed it back by her side. "I'm sure you've got secrets too."

He flinched.

Bull's-eye. She instantly wanted to know what they were.

He stood and set his glass down and by the time he glanced again in her direction, humor had returned to his eyes. "Can you at least promise me you're not running from the law? That you've not buried a dead body in the garden? I really don't want to be charged as an inadvertent accessory to a crime."

She thought how she daydreamed hourly about emasculating Jonathon but that only made her stomach clench at what the rat bastard was holding over her. She forced a laugh.

"Like you said, we lawyers like to avoid scandal."

He moved and once again he was standing close to her but this time the predatory anger was gone. This time he was gazing down into her eyes as if he was seeing right through her.

She shivered again, fighting every impulse to reach out and touch him.

"Are you okay?" he asked gently, concern clear on his face.

His question stunned her. "Yes, of course. I'm fine."

He frowned and wound one of her curls around a finger. "I think you're far from fine and sometimes, it's easier telling a stranger what's going on than family. I'm happy to listen."

She didn't know if it was the concern in his eyes, the heat of his body, which was making coherent thought impossible, or the fact he was a stranger, but suddenly she craved some relief from the pain that had pressed down on her for days. She dropped her head onto his chest.

"I got fired."

Ben heard Amy's muffled voice but he couldn't decipher the words. He wanted to cup her cheeks and lift her head but with only one hand, all he could do was tilt her chin.

"What did you say?"

Her lovely mouth wobbled for a moment before firming into a tight line. "I said, I got fired."

He didn't know what he'd been expecting but that wasn't it. Amy seemed so competent and organized. Sure, there were times she was bossy and as irritating as get out but professionals with high standards often were. Hell, there'd been times close to project deadlines when he'd totally lost his cool.

"I'm sorry." He dropped his fingers from her chin before he was tempted to slide them down her neck and play in the small but seductive hollow.

Her chin shot up, her look determined and steely—clearly refusing to accept any sympathy. But it was the black smudges under her eyes and her unfamiliar aura of fragility that were doing his head in. All of it was the juxtaposition that was Amy.

He wanted to hold her tight and tell her that things would improve, but that was totally insane on two fronts. Holding her would make him want to kiss her and he had no clue if her situation could be improved.

"I gather you didn't see it coming?" he said.

"That's possibly the understatement of the year." She picked up her wine and walked quickly out of the kitchen.

He followed and took a seat next to her on the couch by the fire. Al had lit it earlier and the embers now glowed orange as small red flames with blue tips raced between the logs.

"And?" Ben looked at Amy expectantly, wanting to know the full story.

"And nothing. I got fired I thought coming up here to get away was a good idea."

He was sure what had happened fell a long way short of nothing. "Do you know why they fired you?"

She stared into her glass. "The guy who got promoted over me and installed in my dream job decided I didn't bring what he needed to the team."

"Ouch."

"You have no idea." She drained her glass.

He could understand why she'd sought the peace and tranquility of the lake. "So you're taking a few weeks' break up here to regroup and do some sewing?"

She shook her head. "The wedding gown job was unexpected. It's just something to keep me busy while I put out feelers for a new position."

"In Chicago?" A thought snagged him. "Unless of course that was a lie too and you don't live in Chicago?"

"The truth seems very important to you." She gave him an unexpectedly long look which made him squirm. He wondered if she'd ever used her sweet and angelic looks to hoodwink a jury or a judge into underestimating her razor-sharp mind.

Well, he wasn't playing ball—she didn't get to ask him questions. He lobbed her statement straight back at her. "The truth should be important to everyone. Especially lawyers."

Her smile was wry. "Let the record reflect that apart from allowing you to think this was my house and that I was on vacation, everything else I've ever told you, like not being able to cook and living in Chicago, is true. I just need to find another job at a Fortune 500 company."

"Why one of those in particular?"

Her gray eyes glowed with the silver of steel. "My expertise is corporate law and I want a company with a career path that leads me to the top. Fortunately, there are another twenty-six of them in the Chicago area."

"Knowing what you want is half the battle." He thought about the career path she'd just been pushed off. "So how does it work getting a good reference from the company you've just been asked to leave?"

She straightened, her shoulders squaring. "What happened was just a clash of personalities. One personality in particular. I was well regarded by everyone else so getting references from others in the department won't be a problem. Tomorrow, I'm starting the serious job hunt."

He hoped for her sake she was right about the chances of positive recommendations. "It's all good then."

"You're right," she said.

"Always," he quipped, surprised she'd concede something like that.

She rolled her eyes at him and he grinned, feeling an easy camaraderie.

"Let me quantify that. I meant you were right about it being easier telling you about losing my job than telling my parents." She interlaced her fingers like a child playing the steeple game and then she turned them over before pressing them into her lap. "They...they wouldn't understand."

He thought about his own supportive his family and how he'd run from their suffocating understanding. "Sometimes we have to sort things out on our own."

She sighed, leaning back on the couch. "Amen to that."

He badly wanted to put his arm around her, draw her close and bury his face in her hair but he didn't trust himself not to go any further—not to kiss her. And he didn't trust himself not to pull away from her again.

Silently, they both stared into the fire.

CHAPTER THIRTEEN

SCOTT GLANCED AT HIS DAUGHTER, Lily, who was struggling to connect two building blocks before returning his gaze back to the preschool teacher. "She'll get there in the end."

"Of course she will." Nancy van Lanen smiled reassuringly. "Lily's not the first child with Down syndrome to attend our preschool and she won't be the last. How's her health?"

The dark days of worry and the long nights of fear were thankfully over. "Since her heart surgery three years ago, she's been fantastic."

"That's great. Anything else I should know? Problems with hearing, eyesight, potty training?"

Scott pulled out a copy of Lily's medical history. "She's seeing a speech therapist and I practice with her at home. It would be great if you could remind her to keep her tongue inside her mouth. She's getting a lot better at that but winter's coming and I don't want her to get an ulcerated tongue."

Nancy nodded and made some notes before standing up and walking around to Lily. "Would you like to come and do some drawing, Lily? Meet the other children?"

Lily looked at Scott, her almond-shaped, up-slanting eyes

automatically checking that this was an okay thing to do. They'd been a team of two for so long.

Scott smiled at her encouragingly, trying hard to hide the anxiety that never really left him and was especially strong when Lily met a new group of kids. "That sounds like fun, Lily."

"I draw houth," Lily said, taking Nancy's extended hand.

Scott watched them both disappear through the door into the preschool room, hearing the noise of kids busy at work and play. The door shut behind them and silence barreled into him. He knew this was his cue to leave but he couldn't quite manage it. Instead, he sneaked a peek into the room, watching Nancy settle Lily next to a little girl at a round table filled with crayons, scissors, colored paper and glue.

His heart cramped. Would the other children welcome Lily? Would they taunt her? Would she cope with preschool?

Would he?

Telling himself he was doing the right thing, he forced his legs move and he left the squat, brightly painted building and turned in the direction of home. By now, he should be an expert at leaving Lily, but it never got easier. Whenever she started a new program or therapy, he felt cast adrift for an hour or so. The idea of returning to an empty house wasn't enticing and neither was the pile of dirty laundry that waited or the detritus of the breakfast dishes. He needed to do something different so he detoured to the Whitetail market and the coffee cart.

As he entered the store and joined the line, he immediately recognized the blonde woman in front of him. To be more precise, he recognized the back of her. The way her hair fell in a perfectly smooth bob that finished just above her collar line. The way her cropped jacket fitted her like a glove and tantalizingly brushed her hips when she moved saying, *hold me here and hold me now.*

He closed his hand against an itch to touch her as he took in how her black trousers curved over her cute behind. The soft material fell to the tops of her high-heeled black ankle boots and he immediately blocked the thought of what that footwear brought to mind.

Melissa.

Melissa of the calculating blue eyes. With one flick of her gaze, she assessed people and he reckoned she usually found them wanting. She'd clearly assessed him on Saturday night and he should have found it insulting but instead, he'd found it incredibly erotic.

For his own sanity, he probably should avoid her. Hell, she'd already told him firmly that she wasn't interested in dating him and he sure wasn't interested in dating anyone. His life was complicated enough and it was going to take a very special woman for him to drop his guard and invite her into his and Lily's life. Melissa Bergeron, with her judging gaze, didn't come close.

He remembered her indignant protest at his abbreviating of her name and he couldn't resist tapping her on the shoulder. "Hey, Missy."

She spun around, surprise and chagrin bright in her blue eyes. "Scottie."

He smiled. "That's what my family calls me. You on the other hand didn't call." He hadn't been surprised. "Given up on the idea of music lessons already?"

She brandished her phone at him as if it was a sword. "You're on my to-do list."

Yes, please.

He told his body to heel. "And here I am in person, giving you the chance to cross something off your list," he said.

"I guess I can." She didn't sound thrilled at the idea.

"You two having your usual?" John Ackerman called out cheerfully.

"Yes."

They spoke at the same time, their words rolling over each other and Scott instantly heard the harmonies of bass and soprano. He wondered if she sang.

You don't need reluctant students or snarky ones with attitude.

I need the income. "So what times work best for you?" he said.

She scrunched up her nose in thought. "I open the shop at ten during the week, nine on Saturdays and noon on Sundays. I close at six so that probably won't work out with your schedule. Never mind. It was probably a dumb idea anyway."

"What about now?" he asked, thinking about his bank balance.

She blinked at him. "Now?"

"Sure. We can do a half-hour lesson and be done by nine-thirty, giving you plenty of time to get to the store and be open by ten."

As they accepted their coffees and walked over to the cream and sugar counter, Melissa still hadn't said a word. He sighed, suddenly realizing he may have let his need for paying students override his ability to read people.

"Just tell me now if you were blowing smoke about the lessons and we'll drop the subject," he said.

She quickly stirred sugar into her coffee and met his gaze head-on, hair swinging. "I don't blow smoke, Scott. In fact, ask anyone in town and they'll tell you I'm known for saying what I think. What's your address?"

Crap. He'd forgotten all about the mess in his house that he'd walked out on. Not that his piano was in the kitchen or the laundry room, but still, he didn't want Melissa or any other adult in Whitetail to see his domestic situation under anything less than pristine conditions. Usually the house was under control—his personal statement that as a single father he was more than capable—but this morning's stress of Lily's first day at a new preschool had sent all his routines out the window. And there was something about Melissa that made him even more protective about Lily than usual.

"How about we use the grand at the town hall?"

A horrified expression crossed her face. "We can't do that."

"Of course we can. All pianos need to be played and that one's crying out for some love and attention."

She sucked in her lips as if she was steeling herself for something. *Interesting.* Did the confident Ms. Bergeron actually have some insecurities?

"I'm not very good," she finally blurted out.

It was an honesty he hadn't expected from her and it tangled uncomfortably with his ideas of the woman he thought she was. "With lessons and practice, you'll get so much better," he said.

She jammed the lid onto her coffee. "It's kind of public and people will hear my mistakes."

He found himself giving her a reassuring smile. "We'll close the windows and the doors making it relatively soundproof and totally private."

Her bright blue eyes suddenly darkened and for an infinitesimal moment he caught an unexpected but unmistakable flare of heat.

His blood swooped to his groin. He slugged down some coffee fast, trying to shock his body back to order. The last thing he'd ever expected was that Melissa Bergeron would be attracted to him.

He suddenly started to hum.

Amy paced back and forth across her bedroom, pressing her cell hard against her ear while waiting for the person on the other end of the line to pick up.

She'd woken on this beautiful sunny morning determined that today was the day she would get a job. Telling Ben last night that she'd been let go from M.M. Enterprises had been remarkably freeing and his empathy unexpected.

You didn't tell him the whole story.

I told him enough.

"David Randall." The disembodied voice of the man she'd been calling rumbled down the line.

"Hey, David, it's Amy Sagar. How are things?"

"Amy?" She heard the surprise in his voice and she tried not to let it unnerve her. Sure, she hadn't spoken to the man in two years but they'd worked together in her early years.

"Things are fine." David sounded busy. Distracted.

"Great." *Keep going.* "I'm thinking of making a change and leaving M.M and I was wondering—" she crossed her fingers, "—if there were any openings over at Lewsons?" There was a long silence and her breakfast doughnut lurched in her stomach. "David?"

"Amy, I heard you were let go."

The doughnut reached the back of her throat. *Please don't say you've heard anything more.* "It was just a reshuffle." She hoped she sounded both firm and resigned without a trace of panic. "We both know this sort of thing happens all the time in our business."

His sigh reverberated down the line. "Sorry, Amy, there's nothing for you here. Good luck," he said in a tone that suggested she was going to need it.

The sound of a disconnected call beeped in her ear.

She blinked rapidly as she struck a line through David's name on her list and then she blew her nose.

Did you really think the first cold call would get you a job?

David is hardly a cold call, and yes.

She huffed out a breath and checked the next number. Lucy Makanski. Perhaps she'd have better luck with a woman.

Ben had spent the morning in Whitetail with Al watching him service Red. He'd thought he'd hate it or at the very least find it frustrating knowing someone else had their hands all over his bike but it hadn't been like that at all. Al loved an engine as much as Ben did and they'd discussed how innovative the Harley-Davidson Panhead engine had been for its time.

While Al fitted the new oiler kit, Ben had answered a few customer calls on the garage's phone and, with his shoulder giving him less pain, he'd been able to write messages using his right hand. He'd even given some advice on a car battery problem.

"So how long's this shoulder going to be giving you grief, son?" Al asked as he wiped his greasy hands on a rag.

"The doctor said I couldn't ride for a few weeks."

Al's face took on a thoughtful look. "If you've got nothing better to do, I could use a helping hand around here, eh?"

The request surprised and delighted Ben. "It would literally be one hand. What did you have in mind?"

"Answering the phone for a start. Polishing the Rolls-Royce for the next wedding."

Excitement jittered along Ben's veins. "You have a Rolls-Royce?"

"Vintage 1934." Al grinned. "She was a wreck when I found her and it took me a couple of years to restore her to her former glory but she's a sight to behold now, eh?"

Ben was slowly learning that the "eh?" Al tacked on to the end of most sentences didn't always mean he was asking a question. "I bet it was a labor of love, just like me and Red."

Al scratched his beard thoughtfully. "She got me through some tough times for sure after Alice...my wife died."

"Sorry to hear that," Ben offered up, never quite knowing what to say when someone mentioned their loss.

"It was five years ago now. You slowly get used to being on your own but when you've lived with someone for thirty-eight years, you'll always miss them. So," he gave himself a shake, "you up for some light duties?"

Spending time in the workshop with or without Al was no hardship. "I think I am."

Al grinned. "Good. You can start by going to the coffee cart."

Three hours later, Al dropped Ben home. He'd been to the market he walked directly to the kitchen and lowered the bag filled with the fresh ingredients for dinner onto the counter.

Amy was sitting at the huge wooden table surrounded by the remains of what looked like bright orange macaroni, chocolate brownies and one lone bag of potato chips. Her spiral curls lacked

bounce and looked suspiciously like bed hair, her T-shirt, declared I
Love Cookies and screamed pajama top and she was back wearing
those awful sweatpants.

Shit. "Job hunting not going so well?"

Her head shot up, eyes flashing. "This is lunch."

The stubbornness in her eyes did something crazy to his libido,
pulsing desire into every crevice of his body. She looked like a train
wreck and yet he wanted her so badly he ached all over. Hating that
his body was betraying him, he took it out on her.

"God, Amy, how can you eat this crap?"

Her mouth developed a tart line. "One bite at a time."

The image of nibbling and gently biting her exploded in his head
and he quickly dug into his cloth bag. "Here." He tossed a rosy-red
apple at her as if it was a cricket ball.

Her hand shot up and she caught it remarkably easily, hinting at
some hidden athletic ability. She took a large, crunching bite. "Thanks,
Mom. Happy now?"

At least that's what he thought she'd mumbled around the fruit.
She looked like a sulky teen and with that pouty, ruby bottom lip,
incredibly sexy.

He wanted to pull her into him and kiss her senseless. Explore all
her soft, smooth skin and bury his face in her breasts, but that wasn't
going to happen so he came up with a different plan. He needed to do
something physical to wear himself out and nuke this unwanted
attraction and Amy needed to get outdoors into the fresh air to get out
of her own head.

"You're welcome, honey." He matched her mocking tone. "Now be
a good girl and go put on some shorts and your hiking boots."

Her gray eyes went as round as her face but they still held wariness
and skepticism. "Why?"

"Because, Amy," he said, setting aside all teasing, "it's a beautiful
day and we're going for a walk."

"I don't want to. I'm going to watch a movie."

Sit in the dark on a beautiful day. He recognized the signs of depression because he'd been there. "I'm not giving you a choice. If I could ride Red, I'd take you out so you could feel the rush of the wind and the exhilarating power of tearing up a road, but I can't so it's a walk. You need the endorphins of exercise. You need the sunshine on your skin and you need the tranquility of the lake." *And I need to exhaust myself.*

"You'd take me out on your motorcycle?" She sounded slightly incredulous and a little bit awestruck.

He grinned at her, ridiculously pleased, because right up to this point, she'd seemed less than impressed by the fact he rode a bike. *A vintage bike.* It was usually a point of interest for most women.

"The moment my arm's strong enough, I'll take you out."

Just before you leave town, right?

One hour before.

CHAPTER FOURTEEN

SWEAT POURED into Amy's eyes and her hair stuck to her face as she puffed and panted, struggling to keep up with Ben. "Slow down."

"No." He strode just ahead of her at a speed reminiscent of power walking rather than a gentle stroll. "Keep up."

Bastard. Only he wasn't a bastard at all. She was sure in his mind he was being kind and supportive despite the fact he was treating this hike like boot camp. Once again, he'd surprised her with his kindness. Not that he'd ever been really horrible to her but she wasn't used to men, other than her dad, being especially nice to her. Given the fallout of her ill-fated liaison with Jonathon that had turned into blackmail, she was particularly wary.

She'd had a shitty morning, drawing blanks on almost every contact she had. Not one person had wanted to meet with her, let alone discuss job possibilities. Part of her thought Jonathon must have made good with his threat to tell all, except she knew that if he had, not one person would have accepted her calls. Everyone on her list had spoken to her but all they'd offered up was, "Good luck."

She didn't need luck, damn it; she needed a job. By the time Ben had come home, she'd given wholly and utterly into self-pity. He'd insisted on this hike to haul her out of her blue funk and it wasn't his fault she'd let herself get so unfit. How could she have convinced herself that those thirty minutes on a treadmill once or twice a week were comparable to hiking up an escarpment?

As penance for her physical laziness, she had to walk behind him. The delectable sight of his tight ass in faded jeans hovered slightly above her on the trail, tantalizing her with the way it moved. The way he moved. Meanwhile, she was so out of shape she could barely see, let alone enjoy the view.

Her foot hit a loose rock and gravel and soil slid away off the side of the trail. She flung her hand out, grabbing at a pine tree to steady herself.

Ben turned around. "You okay?"

"No."

Concern crossed his face. "Are you hurt?"

"I can't breathe and my calves are about to explode."

"Oh, is that all?" he said, devoid of any sympathy. "I thought you'd twisted an ankle. Come on, we can't be far from the top. That last sign we passed said a quarter of a mile."

She pressed her palms to her thighs, dragging in gulps of air. "I'm dying here, Ben."

"No, you're not." A hint of exasperation had crept into his voice, which up until now had been positively upbeat and cheerful. Infuriatingly cheerful. "Believe me, Amy, you're going to feel so much better once you see the view."

"How do you know?" she said, feeling fractious and exhausted all at once. "You've never even seen the damn view."

His rich laughter reminded her of decadent chocolate fondue and it rolled over her as he took off again. His large feet bounced easily off the rocks as if this hike was a Sunday stroll through the park. How did he have such good balance when one arm was strapped to his side?

He's in shape. You're not. Get over yourself.

She scrambled after him, annoyed with him, annoyed with herself and feeling demoralizingly inadequate as she often did outside of work. Muttering curses at Jonathon, the hike trail, Ben and herself, she stumbled and staggered up what she hoped was the last incline. Suddenly, she was at the top being greeted by Ben's wide smile. A smile that raced through his stubble and lit up his eyes.

She instantly felt light-headed and not just because of the hike.

He flung out his good arm. "Look at that view and tell me it wasn't worth it."

He looked amazing. Tan, relaxed and happy. Everything she wasn't. "I'm blind from oxygen deprivation," she said with snark, sinking slowly onto the pink rocks. Her heart slammed so hard against her ribs she thought it might well fly out of her chest and over the cliff.

He sat next to her and handed her a water bottle. "Here, drink this." As she put her hand around it, he moved his and spun the top off with a crack.

It wasn't the first time she'd noticed his manners. She chugged the water down her parched throat, loving the coolness. It took her a moment before she realized he was probably sharing it with her. She wiped the top of the bottle on her T-shirt and passed it back. "Thanks."

He smiled. "No worries."

He took a slug and she sneaked a peek at the way his throat worked —his Adam's apple moving up and down seductively. She ripped her gaze away and stared at the view. The lake shimmered blue below them, framed by the fall colors of the trees on one side and an impressive rocky outcrop on the other.

"Oh, wow," she breathed out as she took it all in.

"I told you." Ben took a photo before handing her a small baggie of soft candy.

She looked between him and the bag. "I thought you didn't approve of sugary things."

"Not as a mainstay of your diet. But you're hiking and burning up energy so you need some glucose or you'll find it hard going on the way down. I don't want you falling, especially when I can't carry you."

The snarky teenager with the self-esteem issues took control. "Is that code for Amy, you're fat and unfit?"

He frowned, his expression startled. "It's not code for anything but given how hard you found the climb, you know you could be fitter."

She sighed. "I so want to argue that with you but the evidence is all too obvious."

"Do you want to be in better shape?"

"I want this hike to have been easier so, yes, I suppose I do."

He nodded, understanding in his eyes. "So use this unexpected time at the lake to get fitter. I'm happy to be your walking buddy. I love hiking and running."

"Running, ugh." She dropped her head between her knees just thinking about it.

He laughed. "What sort of exercise do you enjoy?"

Not much at all. She thought of what she liked doing best. "Reading. Lying in bed."

He made an odd sound and she raised her head, meeting his gaze, which had darkened to moss. A throb of pleasure pulsed deep inside her.

He broke the eye contact and stared off in the distance, his jaw tight and tension clinging to every part of him. She'd swear that he'd felt the zing of attraction that had just arced between them as powerfully as she had. Then again, given her track record, she could be imagining the entire thing.

She'd thought there'd been attraction between her and Jonathon when in reality there'd only been scheming and sabotage. And she'd known Jonathon—at least she thought she had. All she knew about Ben was that he was Australian, an engineer with an obsession with vintage motorcycles and he was on a road trip. For all of his generally easygoing personality, he hadn't given away much information about himself at all. Not in words anyway. She remembered his tension last night when she'd said, "We all have secrets."

"Ben, why did you decide to take this trip?"

As he turned back to her, she saw the shutters on his eyes close down tight. "For views like this." He stood and stretched out his good arm toward her. "Come on. We need to be down before the sun sets."

She looked up at all stunning six feet of him, knowing he'd just deflected her question with expert ease. "Slave driver."

"Couch potato."

"Boring fitness junkie."

He grinned. "I'm taking that one as a compliment."

"You have the weirdest sense of humor. I bet your healthy-living fetish drove the last woman you lived with far, far away."

"Actually, Lexie was far fitter than I was."

He pulled her abruptly to her feet, dropped her hand and started off down the trail line.

Lexie? She followed, her mind buzzing with even more questions.

Amy excitedly opened the front door to her guests. Janey Holzworth, the pregnant bride, and Melissa had driven out to meet with her to discuss Janey's wedding gown. "Hi. Come in."

Janey stepped into the lake house with a smile. "On our way here we passed a guy with his arm in a sling who looked like he'd come out of your gate."

"That's Ben. He's staying here while his arm heals." The fact that Janey had noticed Ben probably wasn't unusual. Amy was pretty certain that women around the world noticed him wherever he went.

"Well, Ben's one cute-looking guy," Janey said.

"Janey Holzworth," Melissa teased, "you're pregnant and about to be married. The only cute guy you should be noticing is Rick."

The bride laughed. "And I love Rick to bits but there's nothing wrong with window-shopping. My mom's an expert at that and she and Dad have been married for thirty-one years."

While Amy settled them onto one of the couches in the great room, poured coffees and handed around home-style cookies, she wondered how she was going to tactfully raise her concerns about Janey's wedding gown.

As the bride and Melissa chatted about the wedding plans, Amy's gaze slid to the toile—the mock-up garment Annette had made to test the pattern of the gown and determine the perfect fit. It had been stitched in jersey to mimic the flow of the divine and expensive delustered satin that the real gown would be made from. Based on her own experience, Amy knew the mirror hid nothing and she decided she'd let it show her doubts rather than speaking them and risk upsetting Janey. The young woman was only going to expand between now and the wedding and her dress of choice was definitely designed for a model-thin woman.

"Janey, can you please try on the toile so I can check everything's good to go?" Amy said.

"Sure thing. Where can I change?" Janey rose to her feet.

"There's a powder room through that door, first on the left."

"Great. I'll be back soon." Janey scooped up the dress and left the room.

Melissa sipped her coffee. "I love this house. It's a shame the Rasmussens aren't here. They throw the best parties."

Amy laughed. "If they were here, I wouldn't be."

"I take it all back, then." Melissa sat forward. "I really need you for this wedding and I can't thank you enough for giving up your precious vacation."

She felt uncomfortable that Melissa thought she was being generous with her time and she recalled what Ben had said about the company of strangers. "Actually, Melissa, I'm not technically on vacation. I just lost my job so really, you're helping me out."

"Oh, I'm sorry to hear that." Genuine sympathy wove across her face. "But I'm thrilled you're here. Us girls need to stick together. We should grab a meal together sometime."

"Thank you. I'd like that."

Melissa smiled. "I can't promise too much in the way of nightlife or available men though. It's Whitetails one drawback."

"That suits me fine. I'm not looking for either of those things."

Melissa gave her an assessing glance. "Is that because you and eye-candy-on-a-stick Ben are together?"

"God, no," Amy spluttered as her coffee caught in the back of her throat.

"You make it sound like being with him would be the worst thing in the world. Is there something wrong with him?"

No, just with me. Amy cleared her throat and laced her fingers, trying to sound composed. "Not at all but we only met six days ago."

Melissa laughed, the sound incredulous. "And that's holding you back? After losing your job, honey, you should be treating yourself."

"He's got an injured shoulder," Amy said briskly, hating that whenever she talked about sex she got nervous and it made her sound snappy.

"Last time I checked, Amy, that wasn't the body part used during sex," Melissa teased.

She felt the heat of her flush start the climb from her neck to her hairline. "Can we get back to talking about Janey's wedding, please?"

"I've embarrassed you. I'm sorry." Melissa sounded contrite. "It's just I don't know many women in your position who wouldn't want to jump into bed with him."

"Amy," Ben's distinctive accent sounded from across the great room, "I can't find my— Oh, sorry." Ben came to an abrupt halt. "I didn't realize you had a visitor."

Before Amy could speak, Melissa was on her feet looking trim and perfectly turned out in the latest fall style. With her blond hair swinging and her blue eyes sparkling, she swept an all-encompassing and assessing tip-to-toe look at Ben.

"Please, don't apologize," Melissa said.

A bristle of something unfamiliar, but with a definite green tinge, ran up Amy's spine. "Ben, this is Melissa Bergeron, who owns the boutique in Whitetail."

"G'day." Ben greeted Melissa with a friendly nod. "Please don't try and change Amy's fashion style too much, will you? I reckon she's on to a winner with her workout wear meets cocktail chic."

Melissa glanced between the two of them with a bemused smile and Amy felt another blush race up her face and settle in the roots of her hair. She shot Ben a look she hoped would seriously hurt him.

"Forgive Ben," she said. "He's Australian."

Instead of looking like he was offended at the zing, he grinned at her—the relaxed and easy smile he always wore when he was teasing her. Only this time it seemed to be saying, *well done.*

"Australian?" Melissa sounded disappointed as she sat down hard on the couch. "So you're just here on vacation?"

"I am, although with this arm, I'm going to be in Whitetail a bit longer than I'd intended." Ben slid a cookie off the plate.

Melissa's gaze was fixed firmly on his chest. "What's a drop bear?"

"They're related to the koala," Amy said, suddenly realizing it was odd she'd never heard of them given how many wildlife documentaries she'd watched with her dad.

"Amy's quite correct." Ben poured himself a coffee and proceeded to tell Melissa about the dangerous creatures.

"Melissa! Amy!" Janey's worried voice suddenly cut across Ben's as she walked into the room wearing the toile. The white jersey clung to her like a second skin, exactly as it was designed to do.

"Someone sounds upset," Ben said, turning around. "Shit."

The next moment Amy felt the burn of coffee on her leg as Ben's cup hit the floor, bounced and sent the hot liquid flying into the air before snaking along the floorboards. "Ouch."

As she reached for a napkin, she expected Ben to at least apologize or help her clean up the mess, but he stood fixed to the spot, staring at Janey like he was seeing a ghost.

"Ben?" She put her hand on his arm.

He shrugged her off with a jerky movement. "I'll get a sponge."

"No need. I've got it with the napkins."

But he left the room anyway, only instead of heading for the kitchen, he exited onto the veranda and disappeared outside.

What the...? But she was too busy righting the mug and stemming the flow of coffee to work out what was going on with him.

Melissa seemed oblivious to Ben's odd behavior—all her attention was centered on her distressed client. "I'm sure Amy will be able to fix this," she said, with a desperate and pleading look in her direction.

"I hope so," Janey sobbed, "because that guy took one look at me and left the building. I love that I'm pregnant, I really do, it's just I always pictured myself as a bride."

"Don't worry about Ben. He's on painkillers and a bit out of it," Amy said trying to reassure the bride.

Part of her gave thanks Ben was out of the room and couldn't hear the lie, which was dumb because in this instance the white lie helped. But she couldn't shake the memory of how upset he'd been when he believed she'd lied to him about the house.

"You're going to be a beautiful bride, Janey. In a stunning gown that will flow over and around you, masking your beautiful, pregnant belly. I've done some sketches to explain what I mean." She showed Janey the Empire line dress with swathes of embroidered organza that fell in waterfall layers.

Janey sniffed as she studied the drawings. "Do we have enough time for you to make this?"

Amy thought about her lack of job interviews, the series of company doors slamming in her face and she stifled a sigh. "My entire focus between now and your wedding is your gown."

When Melissa and Janey finally left, the sun was setting and golden rays poured into the great room, lighting up the earthy tones of the rocks in the fireplace and the enormous wooden beams. Amy held the Italian silk charmeuse in her hands and gazed out the prow window, watching the play of light on the water. The view tempted her to think life was simple when really, it was anything but.

The luxurious material trailed through her fingers reminding her of her task. She wondered if Janey could sell it online and recover the cost because no matter which angle she came at it, the clingy nature of the material precluded it from being used in the new gown.

Ben walked in holding a six-pack with four bottles remaining and his expression stony. "This house has twenty-five rooms, Amy. You need to keep all your sewing crap somewhere else because this room is shared space. I have the right to quiet enjoyment of the property."

Before she could respond to his use of legalese, which was part of every tenancy agreement, and tell him that she was not his landlord, he'd sat down, grabbed the remote and turned on the TV. The actions screamed end of discussion.

It doesn't work that way, buddy.

She wanted to ask him what was going on and why he'd left so abruptly earlier but even with her limited experience with men, she felt sure he wouldn't give her a real answer. Even so, she wasn't letting him get away with issuing orders. She walked over and stood between him and the television.

"You scared my bride."

"I scared her?" he said incredulously. "How the hell could I have done that?"

"She's self-conscious about her pregnancy and you staring at her didn't help."

"Tough." He wedged a longneck between his legs and spun the cap off with his left hand. "If she wants to be a bride she's going have to get used to people staring. That's the whole bloody point of a wedding, isn't it?"

The latent romantic in her spoke. "I thought it was a public declaration of love."

"Oh, yeah, it's a public declaration of something all right," he mumbled, before taking a long slug of beer. His gaze met hers, sparking like flint. "Move. I can't see the TV."

His lack of the word *please* caught her attention—he was usually so polite. Even when he'd been in a great deal of pain he'd still managed to thank her when she'd fashioned the makeshift sling.

She glanced at the screen and then back at him. "It's ice hockey and you're Australian."

"So? It's your fault I can't chop wood or ride my bike so I have to resort to some vicarious violence." He took another long draw of his beer.

The only other time she'd seen him drink to excess was the night he'd arrived and that had been to drown out the pain of his shoulder. She did a quick study of him. He wasn't holding his shoulder rigid but the lines around his eyes had deepened and his jaw was so tight that a ball could bounce off of it. His shoulder might not be causing him pain but something was.

She swiped the remote, switched off the TV and sat down next to him. "What's going on, Ben?"

"Nothing seeing as you just turned off the game."

She pressed on. "When you saw Janey, you looked..." *How, exactly?* "...shocked."

"Yeah, well I was hardly expecting a bride to be standing in the middle of the room." Avoiding her gaze, he opened another longneck but instead of offering it to her, he started drinking it himself.

Something inside her ached for him. "It's my experience that brides don't tend to have that effect on people. Usually they make everyone around them feel happy and positive."

His head swung around fast, his eyes flashing. "So you're a wedding expert, are you?"

His hostility sliced into her and she had to work at not leaning back. "I've been a guest at a few weddings, yes. I also remember a few years back how the royal wedding made millions of people around the world feel very happy and positive for the future."

"Ah, Amy." His sharp gaze softened as he reached out his hand, winding a curl around his finger. "So deliciously innocent and naive."

The gently spoken words tumbled over her like mist. He was so close that she could see the individual lashes fringing his emerald eyes, smell the sunshine on his skin and feel the delicious tingling touch of his finger against her cheek. The featherlike caress turned everything inside her to mush, including her mind, and she forgot everything.

His lips met hers but unlike the soft and gentle kiss in the woods this one was scorching hot—like the dry heat of a fire on summer-brown grass. His tongue raided her mouth—gulping her down like a parched man drinks water.

In the midst of her surprise at the intensity of the kiss, she tried keeping up with him but it swamped her. It wasn't that she didn't like it, she did, but she'd never been kissed quite like this before in her life and her senses melted in overload.

Stunned, she pulled back to grab a breath and as she did she glimpsed raw and ragged pain in his eyes. Then it was gone. "Ben, I—"

"Romance isn't all it's cracked up to be, is it now, Amy?" he said, picking up his beer again. "It can be ugly and nasty."

She stood up on wobbly legs, feeling like he'd just used her to prove a point himself. It buried her desire to help him. "You're drunk."

"Oh, baby," he said harshly, raising his bottle to her in a mocking salute. "Not nearly enough."

CHAPTER FIFTEEN

THERE HADN'T BEEN many moments in Ben's life when he loathed himself, but this morning was one of them. On his early morning walk along the lake trail, he'd rationalized that if he wasn't stuck in Whitetail, if Amy hadn't decked him with that bloody torch, if he hadn't been ambushed by that bride, if he could have ridden Red or chopped wood, he would never have behaved so appallingly as he had last night.

Only you can take responsibility for your actions, son.

"Gee, thanks, Dad." He spoke so loudly he frightened a chipmunk who scurried away. He might be ten thousand miles away from home but he could never outrun the wisdom of his father.

Which was why he was now in the kitchen setting a tray complete with a pretty daisy he'd found on his walk. His arm was coping with light duties and he'd managed to oven-bake Canadian bacon, make pancakes and cut up some fruit. The gurgle and beep of the coffee machine said the latte was ready and he placed it on the tray. Now he just had to get it all upstairs without dropping it. Amy was going to eat breakfast in bed and he was going to eat humble pie.

Despite the blow to his shoulder, he made it up the stairs without mishap and knocked on Amy's door.

"Are you decent?" he asked.

He heard a groan and took that as a yes. Walking into the darkened room, he set the tray down on the dressing table and then threw open the curtains. "Good morning."

"Go away," Amy's muffled voice sounded from under the covers. "I'm not going on an early morning walk with you."

"I brought you breakfast."

The bump under the quilt moved and then auburn curls springing at crazy angles appeared followed by her round face and sleep-flushed cheeks. She sat up and one cheek had a pillow crease. She looked warm and soft and delectable, except for the scowl that marred her face.

A streak of remorse reminded him why he was here. "I'll grab you another pillow," he said as he placed the breakfast tray across her lap.

She stared at him nonplussed. "You made me breakfast?"

"Yeah."

Her scowl got deeper. "Put your arm back in the sling. The doctor said three weeks."

"It's allowed to be out for short periods as long as I don't overuse it." Her bossy tone didn't bother him like it would have a week ago. He'd slowly worked out that Amy was at her most tart and organizing when she was nervous.

Good. He was nervous too.

She surveyed the contents of the tray. "You've made me unhealthy stuff like pancakes and bacon?"

He gave what he hoped was a self-deprecating smile. "There's fruit salad too."

"Of course there is," she said waspishly. She flipped out the napkin and cut into the maple-syrup-covered pancakes.

He watched her carefully as she slowly chewed then caught the fleeting look of delight cross her face when the combination of the light pancakes and the decadent syrup hit her tongue. At least he'd got that right. Finally, she raised her gray eyes to his.

"Guilt-induced cooking, is it, Ben?"

He opened his hands in supplication. "Peace offering."

She blinked as if she didn't quite believe him. "*Why* is it a peace offering, Ben?"

He ran his right hand through his hair then winced as a shot of pain reminded him that lifting his arm wasn't on the agenda yet. He slid it back into the sling. He might have made the decision to tell her the less-complicated version of the story that was Lexie, but that didn't make it easier.

He blew out a breath. "I should never have kissed you."

She slumped for a moment as if he'd hit her and then storm clouds scudded across her eyes complete with flashes of lightning. "Well, you're not the first guy who's said that to me, and I doubt you'll be the last. I'd throw breakfast at you but then I'd only have to clean up the mess."

Her words lashed him. "No. Shit, Amy, that's not what I meant. I shouldn't have kissed you the way I did."

She savagely speared a piece of bacon. "Would that be the first or the second time you kissed me?"

He understood her anger at him. He'd anticipated it, but it was her unexpected well of hurt which confused him. Every part of him wanted to leave the room, run from this sort of emotional angst which he didn't deal with well, but he'd caused part of it and he had to fix it. She didn't deserve what he'd done.

He sat down next to her on the bed, careful not to touch her, partly because he didn't want to upset her any more and because he didn't trust himself. When she looked at him with those enormous gray eyes, all he wanted to do was pull her into his arms and kiss her senseless.

"Amy, I don't want to sound like one of those wanky self-help books but in this situation, what happened both times I kissed you, was way more about me than it was about you."

She stared at him over the rim of her coffee cup, disbelief clear in her eyes. "Now that's a new excuse. Usually the guy says, 'it's you, not me.'"

He frowned. "What sort of idiots do you date?"

She flinched. "You're apologizing to me, remember?"

"Yeah. Sorry." He sighed. "Yesterday when you said I looked shocked after seeing that woman in her wedding dress—"

"Actually, it was the toile; a mock-up of the gown."

"Jeez, Amy, now isn't the time for semantics. It looked like a bloody wedding dress to me."

"Sorry." She sucked in her lips indicating she would remain silent until he'd finished.

"The last time I saw a woman in a wedding dress..." he scrubbed his face with his hand, "...it was at my wedding. A wedding that didn't happen."

Amy didn't know what she'd been expecting to hear but it wasn't this. Stunned she said, "She left you at the altar? But—" She bit off the words, *you're gorgeous. You're sex-on-a-stick.*

"Yeah," he said wearily, "she did."

"I'm sorry." Amy hated whoever-she-was on principle. "This woman, was she the one who was fitter than you?" *And a hell of a lot fitter than me.*

He nodded. "Lexie."

Lexie. Things fell into place. "So that's why you're on this road trip and traveling for so long? You're running away."

"I'm *not* running away."

She raised her brows at his curt tone.

His green eyes narrowed. "If I'm running away, then so are you."

"No, I'm not." She justified to herself that she'd made calls, trying to set up job interviews.

"Amy, you're a long way from Chicago where all the big law jobs are. Meanwhile, you're here making some woman's wedding dress."

"Gown," she corrected, hating how succinctly he'd just articulated her current situation. Instantly, she realized what she'd done. "Sorry."

He shook his head at her but his expression was oddly indulgent. "So you're not hiding out in Whitetail?"

Her stomach rolled as she thought about how she'd not told her parents she'd lost her job or left Chicago, or the reasons why. "I'm not hiding, I'm regrouping."

This time he raised his brows implying, *I do not believe you one little bit.* He also looked incredibly sexy.

Sexy and unavailable.

Not that he'd ever been available to her. Those kisses were all about his ex-fiancée and nothing at all to do with her. "I'm guessing the fact you flipped out yesterday means you still love her?" she said.

He shrugged, his face twisting. "Not really. It's complicated."

She supposed it must be, although how he could still love someone who obviously didn't want him was beyond her. She couldn't get her head around the fact that a woman wouldn't want Ben. Apart from last night and the time he'd got all bent out of shape about being lied to—and now all of that made sense—he was a good guy. A bit anal about eating healthy all of the time but then again, everyone had their quirks. And if Lexie had been in better shape than him then she would have been just as obsessive about exercise.

The more she thought about it, the less sense it made that Lexie would jilt him.

"So here we both are."

Ben's voice broke into her thoughts. "Excuse me?" she said.

"You and me. Not hiding out in Whitetail," he said, winking at her.

"That's right." She crossed her arms against the tingles dancing inside her. "I have a job."

"So do I."

Surprise whipped her. "Really? Doing what?"

"Helping Al a few hours a day with one-handed tasks. It'll make the days shorter. I'm not very good at standing still."

She knew all about that. "You really miss your motorcycle, don't you?"

"You have no idea." He picked up her tray. "So are we going for that walk before we both go to work?"

She groaned and sank back onto the pillows, every part of her rebelling at the thought.

"Come on, you know you want to."

His words sounded almost like a caress and she fought the dizzy feeling, knowing that she was imagining something that didn't exist. "Why are you badgering me?"

He looked offended. "I'm not. You said the other day you wanted to get in shape. I'm just trying to be a good house mate and friend, and give you some support."

She studied his face for a hidden agenda but could only see genuineness. "The other day you said we were strangers."

"We were, but given we've both seen each other naked and we've traded sorry stories about our current life situations, I think we're a step up from strangers."

"I've never had a friend who was a guy." She heard the doubt in her voice.

His laugh sounded strained. "There's a first time for everything. I'll meet you downstairs in five."

He departed with the tray and she got up and went into the bathroom. After splashing her face with water, she examined herself in the mirror and groaned. Her hair resembled a bird's nest, she had a zit coming up from the chocolate brownie binge and her pajama top hung like a sack, making her look like a marshmallow. No wonder Ben was suggesting friendship. She was simply resistible.

CHAPTER SIXTEEN

MELISSA MET Amy at the Udder Bar on Saturday night, pleased to have some company. Once again, Emily had gone to Madison to visit friends. She'd been very cagey about the visit so Melissa was wondering if she'd met someone, although if she had, she couldn't understand why she hadn't told her about it. They usually shared all their guy stories—the good, the bad and, sadly on occasions, the ugly.

"Did you and Janey manage to find material for the gown?" she asked Amy while surreptitiously checking out the nearest tables for possible male talent.

"We did." Amy's curls bounced and her face wreathed in a wide smile. "It took a lot less time than I expected, which is why I got back in time for supper. I'd thought I might have to stay over in Minneapolis." She picked up the menu. "So what's good?"

"Everything. The chef here is great."

While Amy studied the menu, Melissa scanned the room more widely but once again, now the height of wedding season was over, the only men she could see were locals. As she swung her head back toward Amy, her gaze met Scott's serious one framed by his glasses. Glasses that gave him a sexy gravitas.

No they do not.

But her body disagreed with her, tingling deliciously as the brown in his hazel eyes reminded her of hot caramel sauce.

She crossed her legs, giving herself a lecture of all the reasons why Scott Knapp was not for her. He was, however, her piano teacher and seeing him reminded her that she really needed to practice before her next class.

"Hello, ladies."

Melissa looked up to see Ben standing by their table with dusty boots and a streak of grease on his sling.

"Sorry I haven't dressed for dinner, but my ride stopped in here for a beer and now Al looks pretty settled in that bar stool. May I join you both?"

"Sure." Amy gave his dirty sling a disapproving glance and pushed out a chair. "Have you been breaking doctor's orders again and working on Red?"

"Would I do that?" he said with the look of a kid caught with his hand in the candy jar.

"Beyond all reasonable doubt, yes," Amy said briskly, sounding as if she was a grandmother rather than Ben's contemporary. "You do realize the more you try and rush things, the longer it's going to take to heal."

"She's a bossy housemate," Ben said to Melissa, only he didn't sound at all ticked off. If anything there was a hint of affection in his voice.

"So how are you two getting along sharing that house?" Melissa asked.

"It's interesting."

Their identical words rolled over each other and then they were both laughing. Melissa swore the sound held a private joke. She was about to ask what it was when the waitress arrived to take their order.

Ben and Amy argued about what constituted the healthiest meal on the menu and gave the most complicated order Melissa had heard in a long time. It included them sharing wedges and asking for the salad dressing to be served on the side.

Amy rolled her eyes. "For a biker, Ben's disgustingly healthy."

Ben raised his brows. "Amy's palate is adjusting to the subtle but unadorned flavors of an organic salad."

Were they flirting? "If you want organic food, I'll introduce you to Keith and Lindsay after supper," Melissa offered. "All the vegetables they grow on their farm are organic and they have a bunch of great recipes."

Ben grinned. "Oh, recipes. Now Amy, you'd love that, wouldn't you?"

Amy gave him a sweet smile. "I would, although perhaps not quite as much as you'll enjoy visiting with Ella Norell tomorrow. Sadly I can't come to lunch because I have to work, so she's going to pick you up. I'm sure you'll have a lovely chat about all sorts of things."

The sexual electricity arcing between the two of them was so high-voltage it zinged and Melissa wondered why Amy hadn't acted on it. Until recently, if a good-looking guy like Ben had been flirting with her like that, no way would she be holding out.

Ben said he'd "shout them a round," which Melissa worked out meant he was paying for their drinks. Scott arrived with two beer sampler trays, which he set down in front of Ben and Amy. Then he placed a single glass in front of her.

His gaze sought hers. "I thought you might like to be one of the first to enjoy Johan's newest brew, the Kaiser's Kiss."

Surprise and excitement flowed through her. Johan had been talking about this new beer for weeks. "I thought it wasn't going to be available until next Saturday?"

"It's a sneak peek." He smiled at her, his face creasing into well-worn lines that made him look younger and slightly less serious. Then he winked at her. "I have connections, you know."

Not even crossed legs and pressed thighs could stop the blitz of unwanted arousal that hummed through her as if she was an animal in heat.

I am not missing sex. I am not missing sex. I am no—

Oh, God, who was she kidding? She hadn't realized how much she'd needed the weekend sex with those potential Mr. Rights until it had stopped. Scott was so *not* Mr. Right but her body didn't seem to care.

"Thanks," she finally managed to say.

"You're welcome." Tucking the tray under his arm he returned to the bar.

Just their meals arrived, the band started playing which made conversation difficult so they ate in relative silence. Melissa's eyes kept straying to Scott. He moved around the room with unhurried grace, collecting dirty glasses and pausing now and then to chat with people when the bar was quiet.

"Attention, everyone," Keith's voice soddenly boomed down the microphone and Melissa's gaze snapped to the stage. "Just a reminder that old-time movie night's coming up. This time the theme's the roaring twenties so get out your flapper dresses and gangster suits."

Woots and catcalls bounced around the room and Melissa leaned toward Amy and Ben. "It's awesome of fun. You two should come."

"What's the movie?" someone called out.

"It's the silent movie *Gold Rush*, staring Charlie Chaplin," Keith said. "And...drumroll please."

Lance obliged and then finished with a *boom-tish* on the cymbal.

"Scott's going to play the score on the piano for us," Keith said.

Cheers ensured and Scott gave a flourishing bow, complete with the flick of a bar towel.

"And now back to regular programming." Keith stepped off the stage and took Lindsay's hand before walking over.

Melissa introduced the couple to Amy and Ben and the conversation immediately turned to vegetables. It wasn't that Melissa had anything against produce, it's just she'd rather talk about fashion or just about anything else. That and she'd been feeling a bit like a third wheel all evening with Ben and Amy and now she was surrounded by couples. Excusing herself, she walked to the bar with her now-empty beer glass.

"So what did you think?" Scott asked without preamble.

She slid onto a bar stool. "It's a stout, right?"

"It sure is. And?" His expression was expectant.

"And it seems wrong but I can taste coffee and a hint of chocolate."

"You're absolutely correct, Ms. Bergeron." He raised his hand for a high five. "Who knew you had a beer taster's tongue?"

She met his gaze. "Are you saying I spend too much time here?"

"I'm the bartender so I wouldn't dare." Only going by the way his baritone rumbled over the words, it was one hundred percent a dare.

Unasked, he poured her another beer and she sat watching people drift onto the dance floor as the band cranked out the tunes. It was another Saturday night and she was alone in a crowded room.

"Penny for them?" Scott asked.

She swung back to him, not having heard his question. "Excuse me?"

"You seemed far away watching the dancers. Do you like to dance?"

"I do." She smiled, remembering all the way back to her prom where she and her friends had ditched the guys and just danced until they were wet with sweat.

"So do I." Scott's expression became thoughtful. "It's been a while though."

"Me too." She studied him, seeking clues, but he didn't give away much. She found herself wondering why he was so serious most of the time and yet humor and fun broke out when she least expected it. "Do you want to dance?"

One brow rose. "Are you asking me, Missy?"

Was she? "Only if you want to dance for the joy of dancing and you don't read anything else into it."

"Like dating?"

She remembered what she'd said the other day. "Exactly."

He paused in his wiping down of the bar. "You coming out of a nasty breakup?"

"No, it's just there's no one in Whitetail who..." She let her voice trail off, not wanting to say anything else and offend him. Yet again, she wished she hadn't even started answering his question.

"No one who meets your high expectations?" he said mildly, giving her a look that said, *I can read you like a book.*

Irritation meshed with embarrassment and she tilted her chin. "Is there something wrong with having standards?"

"Technically, no. But in real life, sometimes you need to be more flexible." He set down the bar towel and smiled. "This conversation's getting far too deep and meaningful and you wanted to dance. Come on, let's burn up the floor for the joy of it."

He hauled her to her feet and led her out onto the compact dance floor where people were paying homage to John Travolta and the Bee Gees in a retro set. He spun her out into a partnered hustle, moving to the music with a style and fluidity she should have expected given his musicality.

As the song came to an end, Henry Letterman called out, "Enid and I want to waltz." The band obligingly changed tempo.

Melissa turned to thank Scott, intending to leave the floor but he pulled her into the waltz position with the regulation amount of space between them. He steered her with ease around the floor and she didn't need to worry for her toes or her new shoes.

Lost in the movement and the music, she was suddenly bumped from behind and found herself splayed against Scott's chest, her face buried just under his shoulder.

The firmness of his chest against hers was like a spark to gunpowder and her body exploded. Her breath dropped to short, ragged jerks and she had the overwhelming urge to wrap her arms around his neck and kiss him senseless.

Holy crap.

"You okay?" He was looking down at her, his eyes darkening into honey-caramel. "You look like you've had the wind knocked out of you."

She stepped back quickly, trying to slow her racing heart and sound like her normal self. "Thanks, that was fun. I'll see you around."

"You'll see me on Monday, Missy."

His quiet voice washed over her, setting off another round of delicious shimmers she didn't want to be feeling. She slapped a hand on her hip and shot him a killer look. "Where I'll be paying you so you'll have to call me Melissa."

"Yes, ma'am," he said, his tone serious.

It should have given her some relief. Instead she just felt prickly and uncomfortable and hellishly confused.

As Amy crawled around on the floor carefully cutting out the pattern for Janey's gown, almost every muscle in her body ached. This was an improvement on how she'd felt four days ago when she'd just ached, period. Previously, it had been a taunting, burning ache, reminding her of how unfit she'd allowed herself to become. Now it was more like a "things are improving" ache. She was gradually gaining fitness, although thankfully due to Ben's injury he was forced to walk not run or she'd never been able to keep up. His power walking was her jogging speed.

She couldn't say that she loved getting up early to jog or that she didn't roll over with a groan when the alarm went off. In fact, the sound of the alarm set off one hundred excuses in her head as to why she should delay or avoid but then Ben would pound on the door. If she was slow to appear he wasn't above coming in and pulling the quilt off her. So despite her innate dislike of exercise, she knew she was better off for it.

You enjoy that time with Ben.

She did. She'd stopped trying to tell herself she didn't. He was good company. He made her laugh and he did genuinely seem to want her to improve her fitness. She'd never experienced a supportive relationship with a guy. Not that this was a relationship but being friends with Ben was one of the easiest and hardest things she'd ever done. She knew neither of them was in a place in their lives where a relationship was wise but her body still craved him. Sitting next to him in the Udder Bar on Saturday night, she'd gone hot and cold so often she thought she'd caught a cold.

Her phone rang, the vibrations sending it spinning on the table. She reached up, grabbed it and saw who was calling, prevaricating for a moment on whether or not to answer it. *Avoiding it only delays the inevitable.*

"Hi, Mom."

"Amy, honey, how are you?"

Her mom's voice sounded strained and Amy bit on her knuckle before replying. "Great. Busy, you know, the usual."

"How was Ohio?"

"Ohio?"

"Your *business* trip."

Her heart took off faster than when she was jogging. *Shit, shit, shit.* She remembered too late that she'd told her mom she couldn't meet her last week because she was going to Ohio. *If you're going to lie, at least learn how.*

She tried for a joke. "What can anyone say about Ohio?"

"I believe they're very proud of their Rock and Roll Hall of Fame," her mom said with a trace of reproach.

"I didn't see much outside of my hotel room and the business center." *Change the topic now.* "How are you and Daddy?" She walked outside, needing to see the lake for a much-needed shot of tranquility.

"We're thinking of taking a trip," her mom said.

Ben appeared on the lake path giving her a wave and a smile. Her already racing heart flipped and her mind blanked, leaving her mother's statement hanging.

"Amy, are you still there?"

"*Um, yes, Mom. What had her mother been saying? Talking about her grandson?* "How's Aiden?"

Ben glanced down at his feet then bent over to pick up whatever he'd just seen. Amy didn't even try not to stare. Ben was like an exclusive store window display—beautiful, tempting and completely out of reach. Watching him was all that was available to her.

"Growing fast. You sound distracted, honey. Did I catch you at a bad time?"

Take the chance. "Sorry, Mom, it's a little crazy."

"Okay then, I'll say goodbye. See you soon." The line went dead.

Amy stared at her phone slightly discombobulated. Her mother usually never got off the phone without having asked many more questions. Questions which varied around the themes of work, friends and possible men in her life. But the one that was always asked without fail was "when are we going to see you next?" Today, her mom hadn't said it.

Take it for the win.

Relief trickled through her that she hadn't lied again to her mother about why she couldn't meet her in Chicago or come for Sunday lunch in Bloomington, where her parents lived. Where she'd grown up. She was about to slide her phone into her pocket when she noticed Ben and his drop bear T-shirt had disappeared from sight.

It reminded her that ever since he'd first told her about drop bears, she'd been meaning to look them up. Bringing up a browser on her phone, she typed *drop bears* into the search engine and clicked on the first suggestion. The Australian Museum page opened with a brief introduction and the following information was much the same as Ben had told her.

As she continued scrolling, she came across a distribution map that showed in red where in Australia drop bears could be found. There was almost continuous red coloring up the eastern seaboard and then, in the middle of the map of Australia, which she knew was desert, there was a combination of red-and-white splotches. She looked at it twice before she recognized the configuration of colors formed the shape of a koala's head.

She half laughed and half moaned. There was no way this distribution map was real and she didn't need to continue reading the information that advised Vegemite smeared behind the ears or the wearing of a fork in the hair warded off drop bears to know that they didn't exist. Ben had scammed her.

Her and no doubt a bunch of other easy-to-fool Americans. She'd asked all sorts of questions and the whole time he'd been yanking her chain, telling her the Aussie version of a tall tale like Paul Bunyan. She blushed at her gullibility. She was a lawyer for heaven's sake—she should have spotted his game.

Why? It didn't stop you missing what Jonathon was up to. He got you and your job.

The half-formed scab over that particular wound peeled back fast. She waited for the protective balm of anger and regret to hit her like it did whenever she recalled how she'd allowed Jonathon to undermine her. Ben had tricked her, damn it.

Only anger didn't come—just a dribble of self-righteous embarrassment. She dug deep, wanting to be furious with him but all she found was laughter at herself. Unlike Jonathon, this was a bit of harmless fun.

Fun. It had been a long time since she'd behaved like a child and had fun. Maybe it was because she was at the lake but she suddenly remembered something she and her sisters had done to an annoying cousin. She grinned and walked directly to the kitchen.

Ben Armytage was toast.

CHAPTER SEVENTEEN

BEN WAS HAVING some geological fun studying all the different rocks around the lake when his phone beeped.

Amy
I've made you tea.

He smiled and two minutes later he found her in the kitchen with two steaming mugs on the counter. She was wearing shorts that were covered in white fluff and the button-up blouse she'd worn with her business suit the day she'd taken him to the E.R. He instantly noticed that she'd left the top two buttons undone. Sadly, despite his best efforts, he couldn't see even a hint of creamy breast. He'd gotten used to her zany, mismatched clothes but today, even with a pen stuck in her chaotic hair and held in place by a tight curl, she looked different.

"What?" She glanced down at herself. "Am I more of a mess than usual?"

"You're much the same. Are you planning on doing some clothes shopping any time soon?"

She shook her head. "I'm unemployed, remember. Besides, I'm sort of on vacation and I've decided it's fun not having to always be dressed in corporate work clothes."

And that's when he worked out the difference. For the first time since he'd met her, she looked relaxed.

"So, how's the..." Why had he even brought up the subject of the damn wedding dress? "...the project coming along?"

She gave a wry smile. "I'm getting close to the scary bit."

"Everything to do with weddings is scary." He saw the unasked question hovering brightly in her eyes. *Why did Lexie jilt you?* Even if she asked, he wasn't prepared to tell her.

She blew a curl out of her eyes. "I'm talking about the moment I cut into the incredibly expensive silk and organza. It's terrifying."

He knew what she meant. "It's like pouring the foundations of a big project. Everything has to be right or the rest—"

"Is a nightmare. Exactly. Although you have far more at stake with a bridge or a building than I do with material."

"But as well as being scary, it's also exhilarating, right?"

"It totally is." She sipped her tea. "Oh, I meant to tell you, while I was working, I was listening to the radio and I heard a news report from Australia."

"Yeah?" It had to be a mass murder or an election to make the American news services.

She nodded. "A drop bear mauled a man and he's fighting for his life."

He scanned her face looking for laughter but her big, gray eyes held only concern. He wondered if the joke had crossed the Pacific on Twitter given it had been picked up by the news. Who was he to ruin a good story?

"It was probably a tourist." He shook his head in fake despair. "You tell people about the dangers, you put up signs but do they listen?"

"Actually, they said on the radio he was an Australian."

"I doubt that," he said firmly. "Avoiding drop bears is the first thing they teach us at school, fast followed by how to ward off croc attacks.

The guy must have been drunk. Drop bears can't stand the smell of booze."

"You mean rum, right?"

This time he was pretty sure he saw her eyes sparkle. "Especially rum. It makes them go troppo. Sends them into a rage."

She shivered and brought her hand up to her mouth, biting her knuckle in the exact same way she did when she was anxious. "Stories like this make me glad that we don't have things that drop out of nowhere here."

She looked truly relieved so maybe he'd just imagined that she was in on the joke. "Well, you don't have to worry about me." He grinned. "I know to always look up."

"I'm glad." Rinsing out her mug, she placed it in the dishwasher before turning back. "Can you get me some flour out of the pantry, please?"

"Flour?"

She nodded and indicated the sugar and eggs she already had out on the counter. "I thought I'd make you an angel food cake."

He laughed. "That involves you turning on the oven, Amy. Do you even know how?"

"I'll have you know that back in the day at summer camp, I learned how to make this one cake, but if you don't want to try some quintessential American cooking..." She shrugged her shoulders as if he'd just offended her.

He put his hands up in faux surrender. "Sorry to have doubted you. I'll get you the flour. What sort? Self-raising? Plain?"

She frowned. "Flour is flour."

"Not where I come from but if you say so." As he pulled open the pantry door, he thought he heard her counting backward from five.

Poof! The next minute he was wearing and tasting flour as the white dust settled in his hair, his eyes, his nose, his mouth and everywhere else. He wheeled around to find her bent over, laughing and with tears pouring down her face. "Amy!"

"Oh, dear, did something *drop* on you?"

He blew flour out of his mouth. "You think you can tangle with a drop bear expert and live to tell the tale?"

She tossed her curls, her face shining with delight. "Word."

"Right." He reached for her.

She dodged out of his reach and shot around the counter, her hands gripping the smaller side of the rectangle. He tilted his shoulders left as if he was going to move in that direction and then immediately took off the other way. He caught the back of her blouse as she turned too late, having fallen for the ruse.

"Gotcha." He pulled her into him, clamping her against him with his good arm and using his fingers to tickle her between the ribs.

Shrieking and gasping, she wriggled against him, trying to get away and in the process rubbing her butt back and forth against his groin. He was hard in a second. *You didn't think this through.* "Don't mess with the master."

"I...give...in," she spluttered and turned to face him. Her hands immediately went for his ribs.

"Unlike you, I'm not ticklish." He grinned and recommenced his tickling,

Squirming and laughing, she said, "If I hurt your arm it's not my fault."

"It's all good and I can do this all day." He dug his fingers in a bit harder and she squealed. "Are you ready to plea bargain, Counselor?"

"Never." She whipped her hand up to his armpit.

He slammed his arm down hard against it, trapping it and then he caught her other hand with his. Shaking his head slowly back and forth, he made flour rain down on her. "I do believe you're trapped."

Her eyes sparkled silver like water in sunshine, her cheeks glowed pink and her plump, kissable lips taunted him. So did the touch of her panting chest as her breasts rose and fell against him. All the strain that had dogged her since he met her had vanished. She looked happy.

And sexy. Undeniably sexy.

He lifted her hand that he held to his mouth and kissed the tip of her middle finger. Then he sucked it into his mouth.

Her eyes widened so much he could have tumbled into them. God, she was amazing. Forget friendship, he wanted to taste her, touch her; hell, he wanted her. 'Can I kiss you?'

'Please.'

He lowered his mouth and kissed her gently. She tasted of peppermint tea and the freshness drove into him, urging him on. He pressed kisses along her top and bottom lip and then traced their outline with his tongue. She sighed against his mouth then opened hers, allowing him in.

He fell into heaven as her flavor and heat rushed him. He explored her mouth slowly, taking his time with long, strokes of his tongue, not wanting to miss any part of this cavern of delight. She made a mewling sound in her throat and his blood ran so hot, he thought he might explode on the spot.

She pressed against him, her body molding to his as if they'd been designed to fit and then she raised her arms around the back of his neck. She cautiously deepened the kiss.

Her hesitancy burned him. He knew he was the cause of her uncertainty after pulling away last time and he needed her to know that was the last thing he wanted now. He stepped her toward the counter until her hips rested against it and then he pushed his left hand gently under her blouse. Running his fingertips along her spine, he savored the amazing feeling of her warm, soft skin until he reached the clasp on her bra. Had he been able to use his right arm, he would have had the bra undone in a second but it took him two flicks with his left hand to unhook it. Warm, round, heavy flesh filled his palm. *Oh, yeah.*

He brushed her erect nipple with his thumb and she gasped, sagging against him. He staggered slightly, widening his stance to hold her, loving how responsive she was. Breaking the kiss for a moment, he turned them around so he now had the support of the counter.

"As much as I want to be spontaneous and have sex on the kitchen counter or up against the wall, I can't do it," he said. "Doctor's orders."

She gazed up at him with a jumbled array of emotions in her expressive eyes. "I understand."

Something about the way she said it sent a shiver through him. "I'm talking about us having sex in a bed, Amy. What are you talking about?"

She bit her knuckle and he captured her hand again, pulling it away from her mouth. "What is it?"

She sucked in a long breath. "Are you really sure you want to have sex with me?" Her words tumbled over themselves. "It's just I'd rather you stop now before you freak out on me again when you remember I'm not Lexie."

He tried not to flinch at the memories that name evoked. "It's wonderful that you're not Lexie or anything like her."

"Still..." All the tension that so often cloaked her had returned.

He stroked her cheek. "Tell me what you're worried about?"

"That you'll regret it because I'm not very good at any of this."

He thought of how she'd just kissed him. "Believe me, Amy, you're more than good."

Two worry lines scored the bridge of her nose. "Others would disagree."

A surge of anger for the faceless men who'd preceded him made him pull her even closer. "Amy, it's totally up to you but I have to ask. Do you want to have sex with me in one of the many beds in this house, right now?"

CHAPTER EIGHTEEN

AMY STARED AT BEN, her knees barely able to hold her upright after his scorching kisses. Did she want to have sex with sex-on-a-stick Ben? *Does the Pope have an art collection?*

"Yes, please."

He grinned, kissing her again and liquid silver streamed through her. The man was a kissing legend and he'd told her there was nothing wrong with her kisses. She was working really hard on trying to believe him.

"Excellent." He suddenly frowned. "Do you have condoms?"

She felt the blush hit her and imagined she was fifty shades of pink. "No. Why would I have condoms?"

His sigh was tempered by the indulgent expression on his face. "You're the most unusual woman I've ever met."

"Oh, right, I'm unusual? I can't say I have men falling at my feet but you, you're the guy every woman looks at twice. Besides, I thought all guys had a condom in their wallets from age sixteen."

His face twisted briefly. "Yeah, well it's been a while."

Oh, God. She'd just brought his ex-fiancée into the room for a second time in two minutes. She needed to get better at all of this. Fast. "Sorry."

He ran his hand through his hair. "Don't be sorry. There are seven bathrooms in this house," he said, his voice full of strain. "Surely one of them has to have a packet of condoms?"

"You've gotta hope." She moved up on her toes and kissed him, loving the way his arms instantly tightened around her. Loving the feel of his erection hard against her—proof she really did turn him on. She pulled away from him. "Race you for it."

Knowing there were no condoms in the vanity in her or Ben's bathroom, she tried the powder room, the bathroom next to her sewing room and the spa room bathroom before running upstairs to check out the bathrooms in the opposite upstairs wing.

Tampons, razors, aftershave, antifungal cream, shampoo and economy packs of ibuprofen tumbled out, pulled forward by her frantic fingers but no condoms. "Oh, come on!"

She had a hunky guy—a guy she really liked—and miracle of miracles, he wanted to have sex with her and there wasn't a goddamn condom to be found in this mansion. She waved her fist at whatever deity was mocking her. What was wrong with the Rasmussens? Was their wealth better than sex?

Undeterred, she kept looking but when she'd totally emptied the cabinet, her breath froze in her throat. What if this delay made Ben come to his senses and realize what he was doing? She didn't even want to think about it.

"Amy!"

She ran to the catwalk and stared down at Ben who was standing at the base of the stairs.

"Any luck?" he called up.

She shook her head. "Nothing. You?"

He grinned and slid a strip of foil squares out of his sling.

She clapped her hands. "Where did you find them?"

"The carriage house. Seems that the guests party more than the Rasmussens."

"So we're playing to type?"

"Damn straight." He took the stairs two at a time until he was standing next to her and pulling her close. "Your room or mine?"

The deep rumble of his voice set off a delicious raft of tingles. "How about the first one we find?" Grabbing his left hand she tugged him into the nearest bedroom.

He laughed. "I like the way you think."

Emboldened by his words, she whipped up his T-shirt, easing it over his injured arm like she'd done twice a day for ten days, only this time she had carte blanche to stare and touch his chest in open admiration.

She splayed her fingers against his ribs and pressed an awe-filled kiss to each of his nipples.

He stiffened against her. "And yet you said you weren't any good at this."

His husky voice wrapped around her and she raised her head to meet his now-velvet-green eyes, which were ablaze with need for her. It deafened the past. "I'm making it up as I go along."

He kissed her again and when he broke away he said, "I suppose I could risk my shoulder and undo those buttons on your blouse."

Feeling safe, she slowly popped the bottom button on her blouse. "I wouldn't want you to risk further injury."

He grinned, his gaze glued to her. "You're all heart."

She undid the next few buttons until the only one closed was the one over her already-undone bra. She walked him back to the bed and then put both her hands on his hips and gently pushed until he was sitting on the bed, his face level with her breasts.

He snuggled his face against the material and sighed. Then his hands were on her waist and in one quick movement he tugged her shorts to her ankles. She stepped out of them and then realized that the only thing covering her jelly belly was her blouse and it was about to come off and expose all.

Panic filled her. What the hell was she thinking trying to be a sexy siren in front of a perfectly proportioned, buff and totally toned guy when she really needed to lose five or ten pounds? She stepped back, tugging the edges of the blouse together.

"Amy?" His hand touched the one clutching her blouse. "What's wrong? You've gone white."

"I...you're..." His heat flowed into her, addling her brain and making her body pant. "Me naked is not a pretty sight."

He stood and tilted her chin so she had no choice but to look him straight in the eye. "The first time I met you, you were naked. Believe me, you're more than pretty."

She bit her lip wanting to believe him but she clearly remembered that encounter. "You told me I wasn't your type."

"I lied. You've had me going hot and hard from the moment I met you."

Surprise and relief tumbled into each other. "Same."

He kissed her but not hard and fast like the last few kisses, but gently as if she was going to break in his arms.

A sob rose to the back of her throat and she fought to stop it escaping. His tongue darted into her mouth, blanking her mind, and her body took over. She returned the kiss, dueling with him until, his breathing was ragged and he pulled away.

"So are you going to slip off that blouse or will I tug it off with my teeth?"

She shrugged it off her shoulders, letting it fall at her feet and then she leaned forward and the bra straps slid down her arms until they slipped off her hands.

"Look up, Amy."

Oh, Lord, this is it. With her bottom lip caught between her teeth, she lifted her head.

"Atta girl. Now I want to explore every gorgeous inch of you."

This time he sat her on the bed before kneeling between her legs as if he was paying homage to her and then he did. His mouth played over hers in an erotic kiss as his hands fondled her breasts with soft, enticing touches that made her body ache for more. Slowly, his mouth moved from hers, trailing down her jaw, across her collarbone and then, kiss by kiss, he traversed her breastbone until he'd buried his face in her cleavage.

She dropped her face into his hair, breathing in the mint and pine scent, letting it wash through her and convince her that this was really happening.

His mouth closed over her nipple, sucking it in, abrading it with his tongue and she yelled out in pleasure as a flood of sensations she'd never known before exploded inside her. Her hands gripped his head as she writhed under the delicious assault of his tongue.

"Amy." His voice was muffled. "I can't move."

"Sorry." She quickly dropped her hands, not knowing quite where to put them. She wanted to touch him but she didn't know where because she didn't want to get in the way of him doing what he was doing. She never wanted him to stop doing that.

He raised his head, his face split with a grin. "I'm hearing and feeling that you liked that."

Her face was on fire. She'd never had so much conversation during sex. "I did. I do."

"Good, because there's more where that came from." He turned his attention to her other breast and she felt like her body was floating on a wave of sensation. Then his mouth was on her belly, his tongue drawing a moist, tingling line directly down.

It was like fireworks on the Fourth of July—every nerve ending exploded, releasing pleasure into her veins that raced and caught more pleasure until it built into a living, breathing thing that demanded more.

"Amy, lie back."

She did as he asked, realizing with a jolt of surprise she would have done anything if it meant feeling like this. She lifted her hips and quickly discarded her panties.

The next moment, his lips were grazing her thighs. Feeling utterly amazing, she instinctively pulled her legs up and let them fall open so Ben could have free and easy access.

"You're beautiful." He breathed out the words and then kissed her where no man had ever kissed her before.

"Oh, God, that's..."

But she lost the power of speech as his tongue found the perfect spot. Her head thrashed back and forth as the intoxicating spiral of need that promised release and yet at the same time demanded she let go of everything and climb with it, caught her in a swirl that spun her so fast she could barely breathe.

Her muscles quickened, pulling up and craving something to grip. "Ben...I...want...you."

"This one's for you." He slipped two fingers inside her.

She cried out in a combination of relief and disappointment and all the while his tongue kept doing that amazing thing. She lost track of where she was and the pressure of the mattress underneath her fell away. All she knew was that this was the most delicious pain she'd ever known and it was taunting her that there was more. Her body begged her to let go and follow it. , Feeling safe with Ben, she surrendered to it.

Her body twitched and writhed as pleasure exploded, raining down on her in streamers of silver and gold before pouring through her fast and then slow, until every single cell was sated. Slowly her vision came back into focus and her breathing slowed and she lifted her head to see Ben's smiling face leaning over her.

"That was... I... Words can't explain it," she said breathlessly. "Thank you."

He grinned at her. "You're welcome."

"No, really, thank you." She felt the heat of her blush wash over her but she didn't care. "That's...ah...never happened to me before."

He suddenly looked worried. "But you've had sex before, right?"

"Yes, just not very often."

His jaw dropped. "This was your first orgasm?"

She pressed her hand to his cheek, wanting to hide the disbelief that scored it. "I thought I might have had one before but you just very effectively disproved that theory."

His expression was a combination of sadness and unadulterated pride. "Obviously, Australian men make better lovers."

She laughed. "Apparently so. I can't promise I'll be any good at returning the favor, but I can try." She reached for the snap on his jeans.

His gaze burned hers with pure desire and his hand caught hers, trapping it. "If it's okay with you, I'd rather come buried deep inside you than in your hand."

Embarrassment and an odd sort of relief tangoed at his straight talking. "I'd like that too." She tugged at his pants, just like she'd done the night she met him, only this time she didn't have to imagine what was under the soft cotton of his boxer briefs. This time she could see him in all his glory.

His erection sprung free and she stared at it in delighted fascination.

Up until today, sex had been more of a wham-bam affair of fumbling in the dark and definitely devoid of gazing. "You're not circumcised," she said without thinking.

He laughed, pressing the condom packet into her hand. "It was out of fashion thirty years ago."

"Oh." She stared at the foil and then back at him, once again feeling out of her depth. *Just say it.* "Today's a day of firsts for me, Ben. I've never put a condom on a guy before and you're going to have to talk me through this."

He smiled at her but there was no trace of pity in his eyes at all. In fact, she saw the glitter of excitement.

"I'm starting to see definite advantages to having sex with an inexperienced woman."

"Really?" She couldn't see how that was remotely a turn-on. "All the women's magazines tell me that men like sexually adventurous women who take charge."

He flinched and she wondered if he'd bumped his shoulder.

"Don't believe everything you read" He kissed her quickly and thoroughly. "Ready for lesson one?"

"Yes, sir."

"Now we're talking."

He told her how to open the condom packet at the little tear and how to squeeze the air out of the tip.

"Oh, it's so slippery." She laughed as she touched the latex.

"All the better to slide into you," he said, his eyes darkening.

Her heart rate picked up and with a slightly trembling hand, she rolled the condom over him, amazed at how hard and smooth he was and how wonderful he felt against her palm. "There you go."

"You make it sound like you just put on a bandage," he said giving her a bemused look.

She laughed. "More like a raincoat, really."

"That's enough talking." His voice was raspier than ever. "Now straddle me."

"Excuse me?"

He sighed. "I'd love nothing more than to have you under me with your legs wrapped high around my back, but I can't support my weight with this bloody shoulder. I'd suggest doggie style but I want to be able to see your face so you're going to have to ride me."

Doggie style? Ride him. Oh, God, the most adventurous she'd ever got was— Not now. Don't think about that now.

"I've never been on top. I might not know how."

"Sweetheart, you'll be great." His face filled with encouragement. "There's no right or wrong here. Tell me what feels good and what doesn't and we'll find our rhythm. Remember to listen to your body and the rest will be amazing."

She stared down at him and realized that for the first time ever she was having sex with a man who had faith in her. A man who wanted her to have as much of a good time as he was planning on having.

She leaned down and kissed him before moving over him. Using her hand to guide him into her, she felt herself slowly opening until she was fully impaled on him in the most glorious way. "Oh."

"Oh, indeed." He winked at her as his hand fondled her breast.

Shards of delight speared directly to her core and she instantly tightened around him.

"That's the way." Both his hands gripped her hips and he pushed up into her.

She moved, surprised at how much she could feel and how amazing it was. She met him stroke for stroke and caught the moment his eyes glazed and his breath got ragged. She wanted to watch him shatter but he was taking her with him. Her body was controlling her and pulling her mind up and out of herself toward the ball of bliss.

Gasping, he shuddered under her and a moment later she screamed his name as she was flung into a place she'd never been before. A place she instantly wanted to revisit.

With limp limbs, she rolled off Ben, knocking his shoulder.

"Ouch, wrong side."

"Sorry." She rolled back and he pulled her in against him, holding her there with his good arm.

"How did that work for you?" His eyes searched her face.

She grinned like a crazy person. "Words can't touch it." But worry instantly filled her. "And you?"

He kissed her on the nose. "It's good to be back in the game."

It is what it is, she reminded herself. A game. Sex between two people passing through Whitetail and sharing this massive house.

As much as she wanted to stay snuggled up next to Ben and listening to the steady *lub-dub* of his heart, she'd read enough to know that cuddling wasn't something that happened after casual sex. For once, she wasn't going to be the one left in the bed. She gave him her best attempt at a scorching kiss and then swung her legs over the edge of the bed and fished up her panties with her feet, blushing at how fast she'd whipped them off earlier.

Ben's fingers walked up her spine. "Bathroom visit?"

"Ah, no. I should get back to the project," she said, adopting his euphemism for the wedding gown.

"That's a shame. I've just been lying here working out how many bedrooms there are in this house."

A shiver of anticipation shot through her as she found her bra. "How many?"

"Nine plus the carriage house."

"That's a lot of sets of sheets to wash." She threw his jeans at him. "Especially as it's hard to make beds with one arm."

"I guess that makes me the romantic in this situation." He dangled the jeans and pulled them up over one leg.

"Do you need a hand?"

"I'd prefer not to have to put them on at all."

Oh dear lord, he was a gift she still couldn't quite believe was real.

He pulled her to him and pressed a kiss to her belly. "I can't wait until this arm is stronger and I'm working at full capacity."

Ben at full capacity boggled her mind.

A calculating glint entered his eyes. "I was thinking that seeing as you dumped flour all over me, you should probably get in the shower with me and wash me."

Yes, please. "There's more room in the downstairs spa."

He caressed her hair. "I like the way you think."

She spun out of his arms. "First one there gets to be washed first."

As she ran out of the room she heard his cry of "no fair" and the sound of him jumping up and down to get his other leg into his jeans.

Laughing, she was halfway down the stairs when she heard, "Oh, there you are."

She froze like a deer caught in headlights, only she had been caught shirtless in the surprised gaze of her parents.

Her hands instantly crossed her chest in an X as her mouth dried so fast her tongue stuck to the roof. "Mom? Daddy?" The words came out barely above a whisper. "Wh...what are you doing here?"

"We've come to ask you that very same question," her mother said.

"But...but how...how did you even know I was here?" She'd been so careful not to drop any hints that anything about her life had changed.

"Your sisters said there were some photos on Instagram that had you tagged as being in Whitetail."

"Instagram?" Her gut dropped to her toes. Although she

deliberately hadn't posted on any social media since leaving Chicago, it had never occurred to her that Melissa or Janey might tag her.

Her mother suddenly looked up and beyond her.

The creaking sound on the staircase told her that Ben was behind her. *Oh, God, oh, God, oh, God.* She was thirty-two years old but she felt like she was sixteen and in huge trouble for sneaking around with a boy. Suddenly his hands were on her and her blouse was being clumsily put around her shoulders.

He whispered against her ear, "I thought you might need this."

Mortified, she shoved her arms into the shirt, and as her trembling fingers tried to button it up, she noticed her mother was giving Ben a wide and joyous smile.

"This is an amazing house, Jonathon."

Right there and then, Amy wished her life was a fantasy novel and she had the power to evaporate on the spot.

Jonathon. Ben filed that name away for a future discussion with Amy. Right now he wasn't certain exactly what was going on but given the similarity in hair coloring between Amy and the older man, he'd bet his bottom dollar that she was talking to her parents. He wanted to take his cues from Amy only she seemed glued to the spot and rendered mute. Obviously, she hadn't been expecting her folks.

He moved past her and walked toward her parents, sliding his arm out of his sling so he could shake their hands. "G'day. I'm Ben. Ben Armytage."

"Todd and Lisa Sagar." Amy's father gave Ben a look that said, *you hurt my daughter in any way and I'll hurt you so bad you'll need more than that sling.*

Ben appreciated the sentiment even if it did put him at risk. "I'll put the kettle on, shall I? Looks like everyone could do with a cuppa or would you prefer something stronger?"

"It's five o'clock somewhere, right?" Todd said gruffly, looking like he could do with a stiff drink. "Is that flour in your hair?"

"I don't understand." Lisa between Ben and Amy. "Where's Jonathon?"

Amy was whiter than alabaster and her shocked expression jolted his memory. She hadn't told her parents she'd lost her job and obviously they were expecting a different guy—a guy she'd failed to mention to him. He wished she'd say something, give him a clue on how she wanted to play this.

"It's a funny story, isn't it, Amy?" he said encouragingly, hoping to kick-start her into speech.

She nodded, her curls bouncing perkily despite her quiet desperation. "Hysterical," she said weakly, catching his gaze, her eyes pleading.

"This is David Brandenburg's vacation home." At her mother's blank look Amy added, "One of the senior partners."

Okay then. Ben guessed Amy must have her reasons for lying but he wasn't happy about it. "And it's a hell of a house," he said. "Would you like a tour?"

Lisa's eyes narrowed as her gaze zeroed in on him. "So you work for M.M. Enterprises too?"

He shook his head. "No, I'm—"

"Ben's an Australian friend of the Brandenburgs," Amy said firmly, finally moving off the stairs. "Only David's secretary double booked the house and I thought he was breaking in. This is the sort of funny part."

"She hit me with her torch." Ben immediately translated Australian to American. "Flashlight."

"And I dislocated his shoulder." Amy gave a tight laugh. "Ben's staying here until he's able to ride his motorcycle out of town."

"And he's sleeping with you?"

"Mom!"

"I'll go get those drinks." Ben decided it was definitely time to exit.

"I'll come with you," Todd said firmly, flanking him all the way to the kitchen.

Life on the open road just got complicated.

CHAPTER NINETEEN

"Mom, what is wrong with you?"

Amy stomped over to the fireplace and picked up the fire poker, shoving it jerkily at the logs.

Her mother, who was usually so circumspect, glared at her. "I could ask you the very same question."

"I'm fine."

"Really?" Her mother wrapped her arms around her in a hug before drawing back. "We've been worried sick about you, Amy. You've always scheduled us into your busy life but you've missed our last two lunches and you haven't sounded like your usual self over the phone. Are you having some sort of breakdown?"

Amy bit her knuckle, appreciating her mother's concern but not prepared to risk seeing disappointment in her eyes if she told her the truth. "No, Mom, I'm not having a breakdown."

Lisa tilted her head. "Honey, you told us you were in Ohio."

Shit. It was hard enough keeping track of her lies without social media complicating things. "I was and after that we came up here because the client has a vacation house nearby. Everyone's gone back to the office, but I'm staying on here a while longer to work on the project because it's quieter."

"And Jonathon?"

At least she didn't have to lie to her mother about this. "We broke up."

"Ah."

"What do you mean, 'ah'?"

Her mother's smile was tinged with worried understanding. "That would explain the scruffy-looking Australian. Honey, be careful. You've always been so serious and driven about your life and Jonathon might have broken your heart but—"

"Mom," she stabbed the fire so hard a log rolled out, "Jonathon did not break my heart."

"If you say so." Her mother's expression said she didn't believe her.

Ben walked in behind her father who was holding a tray of drinks. His gaze immediately sought hers and she could feel him asking her, "Are you okay?"

Her heart did a crazy flip that in some odd way he cared. Was she okay? Her parents had arrived unannounced and had found her half-undressed with a bare-chested man in tow and now they a hundred questions. Okay seemed way too high on the positive scale.

She shrugged and he gave her what seemed to be an apologetic smile. That confused her. Why would he be apologizing?

Her father handed out the coffees and when he reached her, he said, "Ben and I have had a chat."

"Oh?" She hadn't heard her father sound quite so patriarchal since her youngest sister was fifteen and she'd been caught trying to sneak out of the house to meet a boy. Amy took a sip of her drink.

"I was telling him it's been years since we visited up this way and Ben insisted we stay awhile," Todd said.

The unexpected burn of the whiskey in her coffee hit the back of her throat at the exact moment she decoded her father's words. She coughed violently.

Ben immediately rubbed her back. "Sorry. I should have warned you it was Irish coffee."

Gulping in deep breaths, she finally found her voice. "That's great, Daddy, but are you sure you can spare the time from work?"

"I'm owed vacation time."

"What about you, Mom?" She prayed her mother's schedule at the drugstore would kill this idea fast. "Between work and helping Cindy and Heidi with the babies—"

"I deserve some vacation time too."

Panic simmered in her veins. She could hardly plead there was no room for them when the house had nine bedrooms. "Just as long as you know that I'm on a deadline so I can't drop everything and vacation too."

Ben's fingers squeezed her shoulders. "This house has everything you need for a relaxing holiday," he said, "and the carriage house is all set up if you want to move your gear in there. While you're getting settled, Amy and I will start getting dinner ready. How does seven o'clock sound?"

As her parents murmured their agreement, Amy's brain spun out in blind panic. How the hell was she going to keep her lack of a job and the making of a wedding gown hidden from her parents?

"How could you?"

Amy's fury hit Ben full throttle the moment they walked into the kitchen.

"How could I what?" he said

She slammed a chopping board onto the counter with a loud *thwack*. "Invite my parents to stay!"

"Hey," he said indignantly, "your father invited himself. By the way, when you were a teen did he used to scare all your boyfriends away with that evil-eye look he's got going on?"

She hacked into a lettuce. "I didn't have any boyfriends to scare away."

"That makes sense."

She wielded around banishing the cook's knife. "What? That no guy would ask me out because I had crazy red hair, summer freckles and a body type that was more pear than straight? Thanks a lot."

"No. Hey." He slid the knife out of her hand and pulled her to him, kissing her and trying to banish what he figured were deep past hurts. Convince her that she was beautiful.

"What makes sense is that as you haven't had many boyfriends your dad isn't used to meeting one of your lovers. It explains why he's gone all caveman parenting on me."

She gazed up at him, her gray eyes filled with torment, surprise and desire. "You're my lover?"

He stroked her cheek. "Well, I was this afternoon and had plans to do it again if you're up for it."

Her head fell against his chest and he heard a muffled, "I'm thirty-two and my life sucks."

Smiling, he kissed her hair. "Is that a yes or a no?"

She raised her head. "How can I have sex with you when my parents are in the house?"

"First up, they're in the carriage house. Second, they already know we've had sex so it's not like you need to hide *that* from them." He couldn't stop the criticism entering his voice. He didn't like secrets. He had personal experience that they tore life apart.

"So now that they're here, you're going to tell them about your job, right?" he said.

She shook her head. "Ben, this is my family and you don't know them." Her earnest tone spun around him. "Trust me. Doing things my way is best."

He wasn't happy about it but there was something about the plea in her voice that made him decide not to push it. "Okay but I'm not your parents so other than the fact you've lost your job and you apparently had a boyfriend called Jonathon, is there anything else I should know so I don't put my foot in it?"

Her expression flickered with guilt and determination. "Don't mention the wedding gown."

He grimaced. "Yeah, right, like I'd do that."

She rose on her toes and kissed him briefly, a combination of thanks and quiet desperation.

He played with her hair at the back of her neck, hating himself for what he was about to ask but needing to anyway. "So this Jonathon. Was he the guy who never made you orgasm?"

She dropped her gaze, moved out of his arms and returned her attention to the salad.

A slither of unease ran through Ben. He seriously hated lies and she'd told him she didn't have very much experience. Would she make up a man to appease her family too?

"Amy, was this guy real?"

The knife split open a cabbage. "Oh yes, he was real."

"But your parents never met him?"

"No."

He knew she was hiding something from him. "And?"

"I don't want to talk about it."

"Why not?"

She narrowed her now-flinty-gray eyes at him—her gaze slicing through him as surely as if it was the knife in her hand. "Do you want to tell me all about Lexie?"

Hell, no.

She slid the cabbage into a bowl with the same brisk actions she always used when she was fighting for control. "Didn't think so. Can you go check the barbecue has propane so you can cook the steaks?"

"I can do that." He left her dicing and chopping with ferocious intensity and headed toward the deck. The idea of sitting down to dinner with the three Sagars and all that associated tension was right up there with an hour in the dentist's chair.

He pulled his cell out of his pocket and made a call.

Ella was putting the finishing touches on the gum paste calla lilies she'd been working on all afternoon, pleased with how they'd turned out. They were part of a cascade of flowers that would wind its way around Janey Holzworth's five-tiered, butter cream wedding cake.

"Ellie," Al's voice called, as the screen door to her kitchen squeaked open. "You need oil on this."

She bristled. Just lately, every time Al came over he commented on something that needed fixing. "It's on my list."

"I could do it for you now, eh?"

"Thanks, Al, but as Ron never oiled a hinge in this house, I've been taking care of the screen door for a lot of years. I don't see any reason to stop now."

A flicker of something close to hurt crossed his face and she regretted her tone. Al was a good man and a dear friend, but she didn't want him getting any ideas into his head about needing to take care of her. She didn't need taking care of and she didn't want him thinking she might want to take care of him. She'd spent years caring for Ron and although she missed him, she didn't miss the lifestyle of caring for a sick and dying man.

"So anyway," Al continued, "I just got a call from Ben. He's inviting us over to the house for supper. Says he's cooking steaks."

Ella glanced around at the sugary mess that was her kitchen and thought about the piece of salmon in her fridge ready to cook for her supper. "It's short notice."

"He said it's impromptu because Amy's parents just arrived, but it's real casual." Al pulled at his beard. "It sounds crazy but he sounded kinda like he needed us to come."

She laughed. "Poor boy. He probably doesn't want the third degree from Lisa and Todd. They were always very protective of Amy. She doesn't have the same easygoing nature as her sisters."

"So you'll take off that apron and come, eh?"

"Sure, why not. Doing spontaneous things keeps me young."

Al grinned. "Good to hear. Talking spontaneous, I'm taking on my chopper."

Had the man lost his mind? "I'm a grandmother, Al Swenson, and there is no way on God's green earth that I'm getting on that noisy and dangerous machine with you."

He sighed. "Have I ever had a motorcycle accident, Ella?"

She cast back her mind. "Well, not that I recall, but it's the other drivers I worry about."

"It's a weeknight in October in Whitetail. There's no traffic." His pale eyes suddenly twinkled in a tempting and coaxing way. "Come on, Ellie, live a little."

Live a little. Isn't that what she'd craved during the last year of Ron's life? She'd loved him dearly but his illness had tied her to him. For a tiny moment she actually contemplated what it would be like to ride on that powerful machine and then her common sense thankfully asserted itself.

"I feel like I just got my life back, Al. I'm not going to risk losing it by riding with you on that damn bike."

An intransigent look crossed his face. "Suit yourself. I'll meet you there."

His reply startled her. "Aren't you going to drive me in the truck?"

"Nope. I'm taking the chopper." He strode out of her kitchen and the squeaky screen door slammed shut loudly behind him.

She stared at it. She'd fully expected Al to concede on the bike but now he seemed to have taken offense at her refusal to ride with him. Why was he so touchy about it? In her memory, she never recalled Alice getting on the bike so why would he expect her to?

Men. Fine, she'd drive herself. It was no big deal. She drove herself most everywhere anyway. She was fine doing things on her own. Hanging the apron behind the door, she stomped toward the bathroom, annoyed with Al for being so ungentlemanly and annoyed with herself for letting it bother her.

CHAPTER TWENTY

"So, Mom, are you and Daddy going to take up Al's offer to use his boat for a day on the lake?" Amy asked hopefully as she glanced outside at glorious fall sunshine.

"We thought we might," her mother said, "for the morning at least. I was hoping if we left you to work alone this morning, then you could spend time with us this afternoon."

She thought about the amount of work she had to do on Janey's gown but if she said no to her mother's request, it risked too many questions. "That sounds like fun."

Her mother looked at her peculiarly. "I thought we could go clothes shopping."

Amy glanced down at her faded jeans and a baggy Whitetail polo shirt she'd found in the woods on a jog with Ben. She'd brought it home, shaken out the dirt and laundered it. She'd deliberately worn this combination today so as not to draw attention to herself, because apart from her white blouse and black business suit, it was as close to normal as her wardrobe got.

Shopping was currently out of the question due to the rent due on her apartment in Chicago and because of the distinct silence from the two employment agencies she'd contacted after all her own leads had frozen.

"I'd rather hike up to the bluff," she said. "The view's amazing."

Her mother laughed. "Honey, do you remember the time we wanted you to hike up the bluff with us and you said no because you were reading *Gone with the Wind?*"

"I was fifteen, Mom."

"I know, but you've never been one to hike. Even last year on Mackinac Island, you read while the rest of us hiked to Fort Holmes."

"I was on vacation," she said irritably, wondering when her mother had gotten so observant.

Lisa fiddled with a place mat. "Ben seems very athletic."

"He is and he's a bit OCD about healthy food."

"Amy," her mother said softly, "any relationship is doomed if you try to be someone you're not."

The words whipped up every insecurity she'd ever known to be true about herself and men. "What's that supposed to mean? That you don't want me to be healthier and drop some weight? Or that no handsome guy could possibly find me attractive?"

Her mother looked askance. "That's not what I meant at all and you know it. It's just you've always been so serious and focused, striving for what you want." She leaned forward. "Daddy tells me that Ben is on an extended trip from Australia with no real plans. He just doesn't sound like your sort of guy."

"Oh and with my vast experience with men, I have a particular type of guy?" Amy used sarcasm, trying to cover the fact that her mother's words reflected her own beliefs but for very different reasons. "Can't I just have a fling?"

Her mother shuddered. "You never have before and I don't think you're wired that way. Are you sure everything's okay?"

"Yes! Why do you keep asking me that?"

Her mother's lips firmed into a thin line. "Because right now you sound just like your sisters did when they were seventeen."

"When I was seventeen don't you mean?"

Lisa shook her head. "No. You never sounded like that. You never rebelled or caused us a moment's grief. You worked hard at school, you got good grades and we were so proud of you the day you called us up with your bar exams results. Do you remember what you said?"

So very clearly. "I'm the first lawyer in the history of the Sagar family."

"And now you're on track to being a department head. Daddy's not above bragging about you at the plant, you know." Lisa smiled widely. "You've done what he and I only ever dreamed about."

The words turned like a knife in Amy's chest. Her parents had never had a college education—they'd been too busy working hard and putting food on the table for their young family and pouring their hopes and dreams into their daughters.

And I just lost it all with one stupid mistake.

"Talking about work, I need to start so we can take that hike this afternoon,' Amy said quickly. "Have a fun time on the lake." She kissed her mom and left the room.

Melissa cringed as she hit yet another wrong note on the simple tune that Scott had given her. *Stupid piano.*

It was their second lesson and this time Scott had come to her house because Melissa felt far too intimidated playing the grand in the rehearsal room. For some reason, Scott hadn't offered his place even though she knew he taught kids there. She readjusted her hands and started over but came undone again in the seventh bar just as she always did. Frustrated, she glanced up and met his steady gaze.

"Before you say anything at all, yes, damn it, I did practice."

"I know you did," he said quietly, his hazel eyes free of judgment.

Surprise rocked her. She wasn't expecting him to have believed her given the mess she was making of "Greensleeves." "How do you know I practiced?"

"Because you're trying too hard."

"Too hard? How can I be trying too hard? I thought that was the point!" She banged her hands against the keys in frustration, the music lessons of the past resurfacing to haunt her.

He passed her a glass of water. "Take a sip then some deep breaths."

"I don't need a drink."

"Yeah, you do." The glass hovered between them, his long fingers wrapped around it.

With a sigh, she accepted the it and took a few sips.

"Now the breathing," he said.

"I am breathing," she said tartly. "If I wasn't I'd be dead."

He laughed and the sound washed over her, calling her to join him but she fought it. "I'm glad I'm entertaining you."

"Always, but that's immaterial. Why do you want to learn the piano, Melissa?"

Because you teach it.

That is so not the reason.

Come on, it's one reason. "Why does anyone want to?" she said stiffly.

"For as many people who learn an instrument, you'll find as many different reasons."

"That's very Zen."

He gave a wistful smile. "Oh yeah, that's me, totally Zen. But we're back to you. You said you wanted piano lessons, so why do you want them?"

She chewed her lip.

"There's no right or wrong answer, Melissa."

Yet even in her head it sounded cliché but she sensed he wasn't going to give up so she told him. "I want to be able to play Pachelbel's 'Canon in D.'"

"Great," he said, sounding like he meant it. "You've got a goal and we'll work toward you learning a simplified version sooner rather than a more complicated one later."

She thought about her requests to the piano teachers of her

childhood—ones that had always fallen on deaf ears. "You'll really do that?"

He looked taken aback. "Melissa, the teacher-student relationship is a team."

This time she laughed. "Since when? All I remember is subservience and dominance."

His eyes darkened for a moment and she suddenly felt very hot and very aware of him sitting so close to her. The brush of his jeans felt like the lick of flames.

"Some piano teachers have a lot to answer for," Scott said, clearing his throat, "which is why you're tense, forgetting to breathe and letting your head get in the way of your hands. Can I put my hands on your shoulders to demonstrate something?"

"Um, okay."

He stood and then she felt his palms resting passively on her shoulders—his heat passing easily through the silk of her shell. Instinctively, her shoulders rose up to meet them. *Stop, not a good idea.* But it had been too long since a man had touched her and it appeared her body was seizing control.

"Now take in a deep breath and then blow it all the way out," Scott said.

Melissa did as she was instructed. As her breath rolled out of her, her shoulders drooped and the pressure of his hands lessened.

Her body did a pouty sob.

"That's the way." His finger and thumbs moved in a circular motion across her shoulders—digging and rolling into muscle and easing tendon over bone.

"Oh," she breathed out, her head automatically tilting back, "that feels absolutely amazing." Suddenly she was looking straight up into his face.

A current arced between them, lighting up his eyes and stripping her body of strength in the most delicious way possible. Slowly, his head lowered, dropping down toward her and closing the gap in what seemed like a time-delay sequence.

He was going to kiss her.

Oh, yes, please. She didn't care that he wasn't list material. She just wanted the touch of a man. Once. To slake a craving that had surfaced after months of no sex.

He quickly pulled back and then his hands dropped away.

"Now try playing," he said huskily.

Good grief. Her body was panting so hard for his she couldn't see straight, let alone read music, and he wanted her to play?

Get a grip! This time as she laid her fingers on the cool keys she automatically blew out a breath. The metronome clicked out the rhythm and she closed her eyes for a moment, letting the sound take hold of her. She started to play. Her right hand established the simple tune, her fingers dancing on the keys as her left hand entered, building the melody. The music swelled as her hands worked as a team, answering each other in musical conversation. Before she knew it, she'd read the final bar and come to the end of the piece.

She turned to Scott, stunned. "I can't believe it. I got past bar seven. I've never got past bar seven."

He grinned at her, delight and pleasure on his face. "Good for you."

"Good? It's a freakin' miracle." Joy bounced through her and she leaned her shoulder against his, giving him a gentle bump. "Thank you."

"You're welcome."

He bumped her back and then she was staring into his eyes, which burned for her behind his glasses.

She leaned forward, wanting him to kiss her just like he'd been about to do five minutes earlier before he'd pulled back. Had it been teacher ethics? The look in his eyes had definitely been one of need. Well, she'd never been slow in asking for what she wanted.

"I think I want to kiss you," she said.

"Go right ahead, as long as you're not going to regret it later and give up lessons."

"I have a funny feeling it's going to improve my piano."

His eyes twinkled. "Who am I to stand in the way of that?"

Her hands pulled his head down and her lips met his. He was warm and solid under her palms and the stubble on his top lip prickled against her mouth. He tasted like Christmas candy—fresh and sweet but with a musky undertone that was all male.

Oh, how she'd missed this.

She sighed as his hands tightened around her waist and he returned the kiss, exploring her mouth exactly how she liked it with a balance of delicacy and control. With each flick of his tongue, her body craved him just that little bit more until she was a heaving mess of need.

Who would have thought a bespectacled and serious musician could kiss like this? But, oh, could he kiss, which led directly to the supposition that if he could kiss like this, he was probably amazing in bed.

He pulled back and she swallowed a moan. She opened her eyes to see his serious gaze fixed firmly on her.

"Where are we going with this, Melissa? Are we stopping at kissing?"

Please, no. "What's your stance on casual sex?"

He pulled her to her feet, his fingers playing with the hem of her silk shell. "Define casual."

Her fingers started undoing his belt. "Consenting sex between two adults when they both want it."

"No dating, no expectations." He lifted her shell over her head and undid her bra.

"Definitely no relationship. Just sex." She freed him from his jeans, loving the sound of his groan as her hand closed around him. Oh how she'd missed this.

"Piano lessons and sex. He reached for her nipples, tweaking them with just the right about of pressure.

Spots danced in front of her eyes as she went wet with need. "Sex and piano lessons."

"Deal." He pulled her against him, kissing her until she could barely stand.

"I've got condoms in my nightstand," she said.

"Thank God."

Still kissing him, she walked them to her bedroom. Shucking each other's pants, they finally fell onto the bed. Cushions cascaded onto them.

"What the hell?" Scott started pitching cushions and pillows off the bed. "I never get the point of this. You throw 'em on the floor and then you put 'em back so you can throw them on the floor again?"

She laughed. "They're pretty."

"They're in the way." He whipped back the covers.

"So next time we go utilitarian at your house."

He stilled, a frown line creasing his forehead. "I guess I can deal with a few cushions."

Before she could wonder at his frown, he'd rolled her underneath him. "Now, exactly where were we before the great cushion attack?"

"Before you started whining, you mean?" She reached for him.

He slid back, just out of her reach. "Oh yeah, I remember now." He lowered his mouth to her toes, sucking each one of them in turn.

The sweet sensations she missed came rushing back. He kissed her feet and then his hands massaged and caressed them until she was trembling. "God, where did you learn to do that?"

He grinned at her. "Pianists have very strong hands."

She remembered his shoulder rub. "So I'm coming to appreciate."

"Appreciate this." He lowered his mouth over her breasts and she bucked against him as deliciously painful pleasure speared through her. Every muscle twitched. Every part of her wanted him right now.

Her legs wrapped around him. "Consider yourself appreciated. Can I do some appreciating myself?"

"What did you have in mind?"

She handed him the condom.

"Now? I thought women liked foreplay?"

"We do. Mostly. Thing is, I haven't had sex in a very long time and although the pregame entertainment is amazing, it's not the sole reason I'm here."

He moved his head back and forth very slowly, a smile crawling across his face. "You like things your own way, don't you?"

"Not necessarily." She reached up to slide his glasses off his face. "I just know what I like and what I want."

His hand stopped hers. "I want to be able to see you come."

How could she argue with that? "Keep talking like that and it will happen faster than you think."

He quickly rolled the condom on and with slow thrusts he entered her inch by tantalizing inch until he filled her. Then he put his hands behind her knees and lifted her.

"Oh my, that's it."

"No, Missy, this is it."

He moved against her, meeting each of her thrusts with one of his own until bone and muscle ceased to be and all that existed was blessed sensation. She shattered with a scream, her hands gripping his arms.

Panting hard, he followed a moment later. Hovering above her, he leaned down and kissed her gently before rolling to the side. "Thank you."

She rolled to face him. "And you."

CHAPTER TWENTY-ONE

BEN TOSSED his book aside and stared at the mounted head of a black bear in his bedroom. He immediately wondered what the Australian equivalent would be in taxidermy circles. The native animals like wombats and Tasmanian devils were protected and farmers considered kangaroos and foxes vermin. That left fish. Although Ben was more of a catch-and-release kind of guy, he recalled a mate from university whose father had a huge marlin mounted on the wall of his bar.

He picked up his phone and texted Amy.

> Am feeling in need of protection from bears.
> Come rescue me.

Since her parents had arrived, Amy had been like a cat on a hot tin roof and he'd hardly seen her. The dinner on the first night would have been excruciating if Al and Ella hadn't been there to tell entertaining stories about Whitetail and genially squabble over inconsequential details.

Amy had taken to getting up really early to work, and this morning Ben had met her coming back from a jog just as he was heading out.

Between locking herself in the office and doing things with her folks, and his work at the garage, he hadn't seen much of her the past two days. He glanced at his phone, willing it to beep with a return text. It was silent.

He'd get up and go find her except he wasn't certain if Todd and Lisa were in the house. Although he and Amy were adults and had been for years, Todd still saw Amy as his little girl. Ben could do without the, *what are your intentions, son?* glare, especially as his intentions involved getting his daughter naked as soon as possible.

Still the phone didn't beep and he couldn't deny his disappointment. He knew Amy didn't have a heap of sexual experience but she'd been willing to try new things with him the other day when he'd needed her to be on top. He'd thought she'd be quick to get into the spirit of a bit of text flirting. He tried again, keeping on with the theme of bears.

> I'm bear-chested for your convenience.

He wasn't, but now that he could undress himself, he'd happily divest all of his clothes for her the moment she walked in the door. Or let her undress him if she'd prefer. He glanced at the clock. Ten-thirty p.m. Surely, her parents had gone to bed? Todd had been yawning at dinner after a day out on the lake not catching fish.

Perhaps words weren't enough. Feeling slightly stupid—but then again being horny did that to a guy—he pulled off his shirt, put one arm up behind his head and took a photo of himself, all the while trying to silence the voice that said, douche bag. He typed again.

> Your wardrobe could do with updating. Come
> try me on.

Forty seconds later, he heard rapid footsteps and thankfully, his door flew open. Amy stepped in.

She quickly shut the door behind her and turned to face him, her cheeks bright red. "What are you doing?"

Her hair looked as if she'd been electrocuted and there was something about the crazy look in her eyes that made him think that the redness wasn't only her tendency to blush whenever he flirted with her.

He swung his legs off the bed and reached out his arm. "Getting you here."

She held up her phone. "You could have just said, I need to see you."

"Well, yeah, I *could* have." He grinned at her. "But where's the fun in that?"

"Fun?" She started frantically deleting his texts from her phone, her fingers jabbing wildly at the screen. "What if my parents saw this? What if I lost my phone and people saw stuff like this on it?"

"They'd think isn't Amy Sagar lucky." He wrapped his arm around her leaned in to kiss her.

She planted her palms against his chest, her face now pale under the red hot spots. "Ben, please don't sext me again."

He stared down at her wondering why she was acting so crazy about this. "It was hardly sexting. I was dressed and making bad bear puns."

"Please." She bit her lip. "It makes me really uncomfortable."

He sighed, hearing her plea but not understanding why. She'd been so open to ideas when she was naked but now she was freaking out over some innocuous texts.

"Okay, but can we at least come up with a text code for let's have sex?" he said.

"What about, let's work out together?"

"Oh, right, and like that's not open to interpretation? We may as well send emojis of egg plants cucumbers, cherries and melons."

She hit him playfully on his left shoulder. "Let's leave fruit and vegetables out of it, shall we?"

"I don't know. I told you eating healthy was fun." He ran his hand up the back of her neck, burying his fingers in her thick tumble of hair, loving the feel of her against him. "Would *call me* suit your sensibilities, Ms. Sagar?"

Gratefulness filled her eyes and she rose on her toes and kissed him. "Thank you."

"No worries." He lay back on the bed, bringing her with him and slinging his good arm around her so she had little choice but to snuggle into him. "So how are you holding up?"

Her entire body slumped. "I can't believe my parents are planning on staying the whole week or longer. Thank goodness they haven't thought to invite my sisters."

The thought of even more Sagars in the house distracting Amy churned his gut. "Exactly how many sisters do you have?"

"Three."

"I have two brothers, but I'm the youngest."

"I'm the big sister, but they're all married with children."

He kissed the top of her head. "So you're Auntie Amy?"

"Aunt Amy, that's me."

He wasn't sure if she sounded happy or just resigned. He wasn't an uncle and his parents were probably a good ten years older than Lisa and Todd. "Your folks are pretty young to be grandparents."

Amy sighed. "Mom was barely eighteen and just out of high school and Dad was twenty and at college when they got the..." she waggled her fingers, "...surprising news that I was on the way. Dad dropped out of school and got a job at the nut plant and they married. Dad still works there."

"You make that sound like a bad thing?"

She raised her head to look at him. "He lost the opportunity to become an engineer and he's had to work under guys he's more talented than for years. I don't know how many times growing up my mom told me that college would change my life." She wriggled her nose.

"What?"

"Oh, I was just thinking about one of the biggest ironies of my life. At sixteen, Mom insisted I start taking the contraceptive pill..." she waggled her fingers again, "...just in case. She was paranoid I'd get pregnant like she did except, unlike Mom and my sisters, I didn't exactly have guys flocking around me. I was the geeky girl with my head always stuck in a book while Cindy, Heidi and Sally were into cheerleading and sports."

"And obviously, you went to college."

"I did but it was a bit like the contraception. I felt that I didn't really have a choice."

He stroked her cheek. "But you wanted to go, right?"

"To a place that honored books? Absolutely. I loved my liberal arts college and besides, how could I not go when Mom and Dad had scrimped and saved and gone without so we could have the opportunity they'd missed out on?"

She didn't say, *because of me* but she didn't have to. He suddenly had a picture of a studious and earnest teen who wanted to please her parents. He recognized the remnants of her in the organized, yet at times, confidence-battered women. He didn't agree with her that her parents hadn't had opportunities for education but he wasn't about to say so. Families were a complicated beast.

A few days earlier, he'd seen some of her discarded sketches of the wedding gown in the trash. Despite knowing that everything to do with weddings made him break out in a cold sweat, he'd smoothed out the papers. They'd been good.

"So why law and not art and design?" he asked.

Her brow furrowed as if he'd asked an unintelligent question. "I needed a career not a hobby. Most people in the creative arts don't earn a living wage from their art. They either work two jobs, marry money or find a benefactor."

"So you don't miss being creative?" He stroked her back. "It's just you seem to be having fun with this dress project."

"Gown," she corrected, bringing her knuckle up to her mouth before sharply pushing it away. "And no, I don't miss it. I don't have any time to miss it."

Her voice took on her brisk take-no-prisoners tone. "I might be between jobs but I'm a damn good lawyer."

He held up his hands in mock surrender. "Hey, I was just asking."

She blew out a breath. "Sorry. I guess I'm finding the job hunting harder than expected. The thing is, I'm only making Janey's gown to keep busy and, talking about Janey, can you help me out?"

Warning lights flashed in his head. "Maybe."

"Can you take my parents out somewhere when Janey comes for a fitting?"

He sighed. "Why not just tell them you're between jobs and that you're making the damn dress?"

A horrified look streaked across her face. "No way. It's easier this way."

"Really? Sneaking around and lying is easier?"

"Fine. Don't help." She pushed away from him.

Cool air rushed in between them, replacing her cozy heat with disappointment that rammed him so hard it hurt. Did it matter if she was keeping secrets from her parents? *Yes.*

If you push this you're not going to have sex with her again.

Call him shallow, but he wanted to have sex with her. He justified it was only vacation sex so surely he could help her out even if it went against his better judgment.

"Al mentioned a classic car and quilt event over at Hayward. If you think your mum and dad would enjoy that, I'll play the 'can you drive me' card and get them out of the house that way."

Her eyes lit up, shinning with appreciation. "They'd love it. Thank you."

She threw her arms around his neck and he had the craziest sensation of feeling like a king. "Careful of the shoulder, Amy."

She dropped a kiss on it. "Better?"

He grinned. "I think the other one's feeling left out."

"We can't have that then."

She kissed it and then for the first time she got adventurous all on her own. Her mouth explored his chest, taking a very decided trajectory downward. Despite not wanting to, he tensed and she glanced up at him, questions in her eyes.

"Am I hurting you?"

Not in the way you think. "How about we try this?"

He sat up and pulled her onto his lap and kissed her, his tongue working her mouth the way he knew made her sigh with delight.

She instantly slackened against him and her mewl of bliss carried relief into every part of him. He gave up a vote of thanks for her sexual inexperience, knowing she'd let him lead the play. It was the only way to keep the ghosts of Lexie firmly locked away.

Melissa was in a meeting with Nicole and a prospective bride and groom but her mind kept wandering to what she and Scott had been doing in her bedroom less than an hour ago. Three days earlier when they'd had sex for the first time, it had been electric. This morning had aced it. Who knew that sex at nine in the morning was the most amazing way to start the day? Why had she always had sex at night?

"...don't you agree, Melissa?"

Nicole's voice broke into her thoughts and she realized she'd totally lost track of the conversation. "I do," she said, pulling her concentration back to the here and now and giving thanks that she and Nicole generally agreed on most things connected with weddings.

"Great." Nicole turned to the prospective bride. "Do you have any questions for either of us?"

"We'll get back to you." The groom's tone that indicated they wouldn't be using Whitetail as their wedding destination.

"We'll discuss it," his fiancée said firmly as she picked up the information package Nicole and Melissa had tailored for them. "Can you hold the date for twenty-four hours?"

Melissa predicted a long argument on the drive back to Madison.

After they'd said goodbye to the couple, Nicole washed the coffee cups. "So, what's up?"

Sex, glorious sex. Melissa picked up the dish towel and took moment so she'd sound like her normal self. "Not much. Same old, same old. You?"

Nicole laughed. "I don't believe a word. Your body might have been in the meeting but your head sure wasn't. If I didn't know better, I'd say you've met someone."

"May I remind you that you and Erin snapped up the last two eligible men in this town," she teased in an attempt to distract her. Nicole wouldn't approve of the deal she had going on with Scott so she didn't plan to tell her.

She played her trump card to guarantee a fast change in topic. "So how's Max feeling about the idea of a baby brother or sister?"

Nicole gasped. "How do you know? We haven't even told my parents."

Melissa didn't want to admit to wanting a baby of her own so badly that she'd read a book on pregnancy—it would only make her look tragic.

"Too easy. You're a coffee addict and today you passed."

"I can't believe the scent of coffee is making me feel sick," Nicole moaned. "That didn't happen with Max, but this time I have a horrible metallic taste in my mouth all the time."

Melissa had read about that too. She tried hard to squish the wave of jealousy that blindsided her at the confirmation that Nicole was pregnant. Her friend had experienced a crappy few years and she deserved this, but it didn't stop the little voice deep down inside her from saying, *I deserve it too.*

"I'm so excited for you. I promise I won't say a word until Ella Norell tells me that she heard from Mrs. Ackerman who heard from Donna that you're expecting."

Nicole laughed. "You left out half of the gossip chain, but thank you. Tony and I appreciate your discretion. God knows, there's not much of it in a town this size." She threw Melissa a questioning look. "I saw you dancing with Scott."

"Don't even go there, Nicole. The only thing Scott and I share in common is that we both like to dance." *And to burn up the sheets.*

Nicole opened her mouth as if she wanted to say something but closed it again. They locked up the office and drove the short trip back to Main Street.

"Can you spare five more minutes?" Nicole asked. "I was feeling so sick this morning that I totally forgot to pack Max's lunch. I promised to bring it to him at school."

"Sure, why not? I haven't been to Whitetail Elementary in years. Do they still hang the kids' art in the corridor?"

"They do. And Mrs. Lindem is still teaching fourth grade too, so you better be careful."

Melissa grimaced. "She wasn't my biggest fan and then I got Mr. L at middle school so of course he never believed anything I said."

Nicole pulled into the school parking lot, which was located between the elementary and middle schools. At the far end, in stark contrast to the other utilitarian, brown brick buildings, was the preschool and kindergarten campus with its brightly painted fence, adventure garden and play equipment.

"Are you coming in?" Nicole said.

"And risking the wrath of Mrs. Lindem? I think I'll stay here."

"Okay, I'll be back in five." Nicole walked quickly toward the double doors of the elementary school.

Melissa checked her phone for messages and found three. Amy had texted to say she might have to put back the first planned fitting by forty-eight hours. Emily wanted her to water her house plants because she was staying in Madison longer, and a supplier had dispatched the two wedding gowns Melissa had ordered to add to her slowly growing collection for future brides.

Her eye traveled to the text sent at 8:45 this morning.

Scott
How do you take your coffee?

A shimmer of bliss ran through her as she remembered how he'd arrived at her door ten minutes later with coffee and a kiss that had led to her almost being late for her meeting. He'd mentioned he was working tonight but the bar closed early on a Tuesday so she wondered if he might want her to bring him over some pizza and beer. Or wine. Did he drink wine?

She shook her head, realizing how little she knew about him and then promptly reminded herself that she knew enough to know she didn't need to know more. He was Johan's single nephew, an unemployed classical musician working two jobs to meet rent like most of the people who failed to make it in the arts. All of it added up to him being a bed buddy only. In that respect. he checked all the boxes and then some.

She glanced up from her phone and noticed the preschool and kindergarten children were out playing. They looked so cute and the increasingly familiar pang she got whenever she saw babies and little children burned her. As her gaze moved along the fence, she noticed the high security gate opening and a child wearing jeans and a sweater ran out. From the distance, it was hard to tell if it was a little girl or a boy.

A man hurried out, catching the child around the waist. He swung them up in the air, both stopping the kid from running away and creating delight at the same time. A moment later, he lowered the child to the ground and with a firm hold of their hand, started walking toward the sidewalk.

Melissa's breath stalled. She blinked three times but nothing changed the image—she'd recognize that fluid gait anywhere. Dressed in his Udder Bar polo shirt and jeans, Scott Knapp was collecting a child from preschool.

Her mind lurched from point to point like a drunk trying to absorb and translate the messages being fed from her eyes. Maybe he was helping Johan? She instantly ruled out that idea—Johan's grandchildren weren't old enough for preschool. She squinted, trying to see the child's face but they'd moved farther away not closer. As they reached the curb, Scott stopped and bent down as if he was instructing the child on road safety. As his head touched the child's she saw the identical chocolate-brown match.

A hundred different emotions hit her at once making her nauseous and dizzy. The guy she was having no-strings-attached sex with was a father.

CHAPTER TWENTY-TWO

WHEN THE LAST customer said good-night at a conveniently early ten-thirty, Scott was pleased. As tonight's shift had been unexpected due to staff illness, it meant his high school babysitter could get home before eleven and her parents wouldn't be calling him saying they didn't approve of her working for him midweek. It also meant an earlier night for him. Back in the day when he'd last done bar work, he hadn't been a dad so he'd been able to sleep late the next morning. No such luck now. In fact, he had a load of washing waiting because this morning he'd allowed himself to get deliciously distracted with Melissa.

Melissa. What an unexpected gift she'd turned out to be. There weren't many gorgeous women out there who just wanted him for sex, but when he'd pulled the no-dating card on her, relief had danced across her cheeks. Uncomplicated sex was usually an oxymoron, but this thing with Melissa seemed to be the real deal—as straightforward as the agreement they'd made. She wanted sex but not a relationship—it was a perfect match and who was he to argue?

Starting with the interior door, he commenced the locking-up process just in case someone decided they'd try to stop by for that one last late beer while he was still tidying up. As he flicked the latch he heard tapping on the outside door. Surprise and delight whipped through him—Melissa stood on the stoop, wearing a tightly sashed mid-length trench coat, sheer stockings and high-heeled shoes.

Oh baby. She was a fantasy come true. He quickly opened both doors and pulled her in against him. "Perfect timing, Missy."

He kissed her neck. "I hope you're naked under that coat."

"No." Her chilly blue eyes matched her tone.

The last time he'd seen her, those eyes had been slightly unfocused and full of post-sex euphoria. She pressed her palms firmly against his forearms and pushed him away.

"We need to talk," she said.

"Okaaay." In his experience, when a woman spoke those four words it was never a good thing. He walked directly back behind the bar. "Do you want to argue with me with or without a drink?"

"You're a father?"

Her rising infliction bounced around the empty bar loud, incredulous and accusatory, slamming into him with the velocity of a bullet. Uncomplicated sex? Who was he kidding?

He poured a finger of whiskey into two glasses and pushed one toward her. "I am."

"Are you married?"

He raised his glass to her as fury simmered deep down inside him. "And thank you so much for the vote of confidence in my moral compass."

She slammed her purse on the bar. "You don't get to be self-righteous, Scott. I would never have had sex with you if I'd known you were married."

There was no point doing anything other than telling the truth. "I'm divorced." He drained his glass and poured another one.

Relief crossed her face but then her shoulders straightened even more. "I don't get it. Why not tell me you're a single dad?"

Where to start? "It isn't relevant to us."

"Relevant?" Her brows shot to her hairline. "This is a small town. Did you really think you could just hide your child away?"

She's an embarrassment. Margaret's words burned him and he slammed his fist on the bar. "Hell no. I didn't tell you about Lily because you're *never* going to meet her."

She stared at him as if she didn't recognize him then gulped down the whiskey and stood, clutching her purse close to her body.

"Thank you for making it perfectly clear that I'm good enough to screw when the need hits, but I'm not worthy enough to meet your daughter. Goodbye, Scott."

Fuck! He heard the pain in her voice—pain he knew he'd put there. All the reasons why he knew he should never have given in to the chemistry that swirled between them raced home to roost.

"Melissa, wait."

She kept walking. He strode out from behind the bar and caught her arm. "I'm sorry. It's complicated, is all."

She stood perfectly still, her shoulders rigid, but she didn't turn or say a word.

This was his worst nightmare. This was why he hadn't mentioned Lily. "Lily's special."

She turned and her mouth, which that morning had kissed him so thoroughly, was now rigidly tight. "All children are special, Scott."

He sucked in a breath and spoke the words that always hurt. "Lily's got Down syndrome."

He watched for the expected judgment, distaste and pity to shine in her eyes but instead he got speared by blue-and-silver anger.

"You really don't think very much of me, do you? What did you think I was going to do if I ever ran into the two of you on the street? Cross to the other side?"

Weariness flooded him and he sighed. "This isn't about you, Melissa. This is about Lily."

Scott's quiet words, heavy with resignation and grief, shattered Melissa's anger like a hammer against china. "I get that you're protecting her but I would have liked to have known she existed."

His jaw jutted and he brought his fingers up to make quotation marks. "'Definitely no relationship' were your words, remember?"

"Yes, of course I remember, but, God! She's your child. A huge part of your life. Even if I never meet her, don't you want to talk about her? I mean, if I had a kid I think I'd be boring everyone stupid with stories."

He closed his eyes for a brief moment. "It's not quite the same when your beautiful little girl doesn't fit neatly into the normal bragging box. When I get excited that she built a four-block tower, it usually evokes sympathy not celebration."

Melissa realized that some of the lines around his eyes must have been put there by sorrow and heartache. "Next time Lily does something you want to celebrate, tell me. I'll high-five it."

He stared at her as if he didn't recognize her and then he quickly pushed his glasses up to the bridge of his nose. "I have to get home and relieve the babysitter."

He sounded isolated and tired and she didn't want him to go home alone. "I'll walk with you."

He rolled his eyes. "In those shoes?"

She opened her purse and pulled out ballet flats, quickly exchanging them for her heels.

He ran his hand through his hair. "I won't be inviting you in, Melissa."

The fact he'd used her full name underlined how serious he was. "I don't expect you to, but it's a clear, crisp night out and I can do with a walk to blow away the head of steam I've worked up over the day."

"How did you find out?" he asked.

"It was an accident. Nicole was dropping off Max's lunch and I was waiting in the car. I saw you come out of the preschool."

He flicked off the lights and opened the door for her. "Lily's five."

She walked past him, catching the scent of beer and laundry powder. "Pretty name."

"I think so." He locked the door behind them. "Nancy thought she'd do better in kindergarten if she took an extra year in preschool."

The moon shone on the dewy sidewalk. "Sounds sensible."

There was so much she wanted to ask, like who and where was Lily's mother? How long had he been doing this sole parenting gig? But she knew enough that if she peppered him with questions, he'd tighten up faster than a Maine clam. She let the silence roll even though it almost killed her.

Scott broke it as they turned into his street. "How's your piano practice going?"

"I've been playing straight after breakfast each morning, only today I was interrupted." She elbowed him playfully in the ribs.

He elbowed her back. "You need to get your priorities sorted if you want to reach your goal."

"I promise I'll practice as soon as I get home tonight."

"Or in the morning." He shoved his hands in his pockets. "I'm guessing our deal is off?"

Disappointment rolled her gut. "I'm sorry I got all bent out of shape. It was mostly the idea of you still being married that did my head in."

"Yeah." He rocked back and forth on his heels. "I can see how that would be a sticking point. I promise you, there's nothing else. What you see is me. Divorced classical pianist, music teacher, bartender, Lily's dad and home renter."

Excess baggage in every shape and form. The sort of baggage that had destroyed her sister's marriage. Melissa pictured the massive line of red Xs marked in every box on her—then again, she'd known that from the start.

She met his gaze and the moonlight cast shadows on his face, only not all of them were caused by the moon. Some were part of him and now she knew why. It accounted for his mostly serious demeanor.

Except when he's flirting with you. Except when he's in bed with you.

Scott was the single dad of a special-needs child. Fun probably didn't feature much in his life. And even though he wasn't the guy for her, he was a great lover. After her self-imposed celibacy since the new year, she wasn't about to walk away from it just yet.

"Up until I bit your head off were you having fun?" she asked.

He brought his hand up to her cheek. "The most fun I've had in a very long time."

She smiled at him, oddly glad that she lightened his load in some small way. "As long as we're both really clear on what we want and what we don't want, I can't see the harm in keeping the deal on the table."

She turned her mouth into his hand and flicked her tongue out, drawing a wet and lazy circle on his palm.

He groaned and she grinned, stepping quickly away from him. "Sleep well, Scottie."

"Very funny, Missy."

"See you around."

He pulled her back in against him. "See you in the morning?"

"Yes, please."

CHAPTER TWENTY-THREE

"I wonder if all Australian young men are as thoughtful as Ben," Ella said to Al as they waited by the truck. "If I was thirty years younger..."

They'd spent the afternoon at the quilt and car fair and now Ben had gone to find Lisa and Todd so they could head back to Whitetail.

Al crossed his arms. "You wouldn't have given him a second glance because he rides a bike and they're far too dangerous for you."

She crossed her arms right back at him. "I can't believe you're still going on about that, Al Swenson."

"I can't believe you won't even give it a try. I've ridden it every day this week without incident, just like the last forty years."

"I know you've ridden it," she said testily, thinking of how the noise had woken her with a start every morning, racing her heart and leaving her feeling both alive and terrified all at the same time. "Exactly why you feel the need to kick-start it outside of my house escapes me."

"Just giving you the chance to change your mind."

"That's not going to happen anytime soon." She waved to Ben who was walking back with Amy's parents.

"All good to go, eh?" Al opened the truck doors.

They all piled in and the men started talking engines, each one of them as enthusiastic as the other as they waxed lyrical about the simplicity of the Model Ts. Ella had noticed it was the only time Todd seemed warm toward Ben. She caught Lisa's eye.

"I have to hand it to Hayward," Ella said grudgingly. "The organizers sure knew what they were doing staging the quilt show at the same time as the vintage car fair. They got double the attendance because of it."

Lisa laughed. "That's true. I know it made me want to get out my quilt board again and do some fussy cutting."

Ella nodded, thinking the same thing. "I've been so busy with wedding cakes I haven't done any quilting in a long time. Did Amy get her sewing talent from you?"

Lisa looked surprised. "I suppose but she hasn't sewn anything in years."

"But she's—"

"My mother's a keen quilter," Ben offered, suddenly breaking away from the engine conversation. "Although today she would have been torn between the quilts and the cars. She met Dad when her Beetle ran out of petrol...gas...and she'd forgotten to close off the emergency tank. He gave her a ride on the back of his motorbike and they've been together ever since."

"See, Ella, some women ride bikes, eh?" Al said pointedly, his eyes finding hers in the rearview mirror.

Ella pursed her lips. "I imagine Ben's mother wasn't in her sixties."

"She is now," Ben said cheerfully. "She and Dad have graduated to a Gold Wing, which is really luxurious. My brothers and I give them heaps because it's not a Harley. Dad just laughs and says he and Mum are growing old disgracefully and busy spending our inheritance. I think it's great."

"Actually, Todd and I bought a motorcycle this summer," Lisa said with a quiet smile.

Ella didn't understand the attraction at all. "Why?"

Todd chimed in to the conversation. "We had our kids pretty young so we're catching up on the things we didn't do in our twenties."

"You can borrow Red if you like," Ben offered, then seeing Lisa's confusion added, "my vintage Harley."

"Weather's looking good for the next few days. Maybe we could take it up the rustic road by Lost Lake, eh?" Al suggested. "It's a real pretty ride with the fall colors. I've seen wolf packs up there."

"Oh, I'd love that." Lisa leaned forward enthusiastically and put her hand on Todd's shoulder.

Todd turned to face the backseat, giving Ben a quizzical look. "Are you certain you're okay with us riding your bike?"

Ben tapped his injured arm. "Someone should be riding her. I'll run through the whole kick-start process. Apart from that, the only other thing you need to know is she's thunderously noisy so I'm not sure you'll see any wolves."

"I think I'll trade wolves for riding a vintage Harley." Todd grinned. "What do you think, Lisa?"

"I'm all for it."

Al turned the steering wheel, taking the right fork in the road. "So that's three then, eh? Excellent. We can have a picnic."

"You're not able to come?" Lisa asked Ella.

"Oh, Ella can come. She just won't," Al said before she could open her mouth. "She thinks bikes are noisy and dangerous so she'll stay home and do something real safe like climb on her roof and clean out her gutters."

"You do that?" Lisa asked in a stunned tone. "I think riding a motorcycle is a lot safer than climbing on a roof. It's definitely way more fun."

Ella glared at the back of Al's head, furious at him for making her look like a killjoy in front of the others. "I'll come but only because Al's picnic food will probably poison you."

Al gave a good-natured laugh. "Hell, I was going to buy lunch but if you're offering to make your beef subs, Ellie, that's even better."

Right then and there she knew Al Swenson had just played her like a bow.

It was Saturday night and Amy had never seen Whitetail so busy. Although the trucks and cars that filled all the parking spaces on Main Street looked familiarly modern, the people walking on the sidewalk did not. Everyone had gotten into the spirit of the evening and it was like taking a step back in time to the roaring '20s. Lindsay and Keith had even set up a mock speakeasy in the foyer of the movie theater, serving drinks in teacups and asking people to cloak their guns.

She was looking around for Ben, who'd texted her earlier saying there'd been a problem at the garage and he was staying longer to help out Al. He'd promised to meet her in the foyer. His height usually made him easy to find but tonight, in the small and crowded space she couldn't see him anywhere.

"Amy!"

Melissa waved and made her way over, looking very glamorous in a red beaded flapper's dress and holding a long, black cigarette holder between her fingers. "Doesn't everyone look wicked awesome?"

Amy noticed Melissa's gaze linger on Scott who was talking to Keith. "Wow, who knew Scott could look so debonair out of jeans and a polo shirt?"

"Hmm," Melissa murmured before seeming to shake herself. "He's just getting into character. The movie pianist always wore white tie and tails."

Amy glanced down self-consciously at the costume she'd patched together using a combination of her own clothes, a shirt of her father's and some bits and pieces she'd found in the Rasmussens' cloakroom.

"With my parents visiting and Janey's gown, I didn't have time to make a dress."

Melissa smiled. "I think what you've done is very inventive. Very Marlene Dietrich. You look great."

"Thanks." She just wished her curls weren't constantly trying to dislodge her fedora.

Keith's voice boomed through the speakers, cutting across the chatter in the foyer. "Ladies and gentlemen, it's time to take your seats but don't worry, the usherettes..." He paused while Lindsay and another woman wearing a short skirt and balancing a big tray, curtsied. "...will be coming around selling ice cream cones, popcorn and candy cigarettes."

People moved into the cinema, all talking excitedly about the upcoming silent movie but Amy still couldn't see Ben anywhere. She checked her phone for a message. Nothing.

"Are you coming Amy?" Melissa was drifting toward the doors with the crowd.

"You go in. I'll be there soon."

Amy cut back through the crowd and out onto the sidewalk, looking up and down and across the street for Ben. She saw two couples hurrying toward her but no one else. Disappointment sat on the top of her gut like oil on water.

She had the evening all planned. They were going to snuggle up in the very back row of the old cinema in the seats everyone had told her to avoid because they were really uncomfortable. Then, under the cover of darkness, they were going to make out. She was determined there'd be some fondling involved. Her fondling Ben to be exact, because up until now, that had never happened. Whenever they were having sex and she got close to experiencing the sensation of holding him, let alone getting her mouth to him, he always changed positions and she lost the chance. Sure she slid the condom on him but the moment it was on, he caught her hand in his.

She knew she probably should tell him what she wanted—or to be more precise, what she thought she wanted because she'd never actually given a guy a hand job or a blow job. Since meeting Ben, she'd come a long way sexually, and he seemed to get a kick out of her relative inexperience, but she still wasn't comfortable initiating a discussion.

Just thinking about it made her all quivery, agitated and excited but nothing could happen unless Ben arrived. She took another glance along the street before stepping back inside. Should she just take a seat and tell Lindsay where she was sitting? After all, that would give the usherette a chance to use her flashlight and direct Ben to her just like in the old days. No, that wouldn't work. Lindsay would just direct her to the seats farther down the front.

Come on, Ben. As she checked her phone again, she heard Keith say, "You bet, Ben. I guess you were looking for a flapper but Amy's standing right over there."

She turned around and there was Ben, wearing a white open-neck shirt, a chocolate V-neck sweater, jodhpurs and long leather boots. A felt cap sat on his head and a pair of goggles rested around his neck along with the obligatory sling.

"Oh, how fantastic!" She clapped her delight. "You're a 1920s biker!"

Emboldened by the fun of being in character, she pulled out a silver hip flask with one hand and stretched out her other to Ben. "Hey, bad boy, do you wanna come make out in the back row?"

He didn't move and she realized he was staring at her. "What?" Her fingers automatically brushed her cheeks. "Do I have a smudge on my face?"

His usually smiling eyes narrowed to slits. "What the hell are you wearing?"

His words poured over her like the hit of icy water and floated all her insecurities to the surface. Fighting to keep them at bay, she tilted her chin and snapped her suspenders.

"I'm a gangster."

"Every other woman in that cinema is dressed like a woman."

His low voice sent an uneasy shiver through her and chagrin flared. "This is my costume, Ben. Melissa thought I was very Marlene Dietrich."

"Exactly my point." He hustled her outside.

Shocked at his rough-arm tactics, she tried to pull away. "What is wrong with you?"

"Nothing," he ground out between clenched teeth.

"This isn't nothing. We're supposed to be having a lovely evening and you've pushed me outside."

"There's no way I'm making out with you dressed like that."

"Fine." She crossed her arms against her hammering heart that was overflowing with confusion and hurt. Memories of similar comments by other boys and men who'd been dismissive of her looks and clothes, slugged her. "We'll just go and watch the film."

He shook his head so hard, his cap slid off. "You don't get it. I'm not going anywhere with you dressed like a man."

She stared at him slack-mouthed. "Have you been inhaling gas fumes this afternoon?"

Without a word, he spun on his booted heel and strode down the street.

"Ben!"

He kept walking so she ran after him and this time she grabbed him by the arm. "What's gotten into you?"

"I'm going home."

"You're walking five miles because I'm not wearing a flapper's dress? Can you hear how crazy that sounds?"

"Whatever." He tried to shrug her hand away.

She held fast, pulling back. "It's not whatever. Even when I hit you with a flashlight you made more sense than you do right now."

"Let it go, Amy."

The threat in his voice wasn't lost on her but neither was the pain that vibrated behind it. "You've just ruined what was supposed to be a lovely evening and I don't understand why."

The streetlamp illuminated the planes of his face, making them appear stark and hard when she knew they could be soft and tender. He let out a sigh. "I'm not stopping you from enjoying the film."

"Oh right, you tell me I'm unattractive and you refuse to be seen with me, but I'm to go watch the movie anyway? Can you hear how crazy that is?"

Ben hated the catch in Amy's voice and, worse still, he hated the fact that he'd been the one to put it there. Seeing her in that suit had brought the past back so fast he had whiplash, but that wasn't her fault. Now she was standing in front of him like a vulnerable child and it was all his fault.

Shit. What a mess. He tried to appease her. "You're beautiful, Amy, you know that."

Her enormous eyes stared at him, filled with hurt and anger. "The thing is, Ben, most of the time I don't know that, and just when I dare to believe it something like this happens."

He wanted to touch her, hold her but that fucking outfit was doing his head in. "I'm sorry. Of course I'm happy to be seen with you."

She threw her hands up in the air. "Ben, I have an IQ of one-twenty and I can understand most things but you are not making any sense."

"It makes sense to me and that's all that matters. It's my issue, not yours." He walked away.

Red curls bounced everywhere as she marched beside him. "Oh, no. You don't get to play that card again. Strike two and you're out."

Hell. He immediately remembered saying something similar back when he'd first kissed her to silence a question. "I think that's strike three and you're out."

"You're Australian," she said accusingly, "you're not supposed to know about baseball. Stop changing the subject."

"Just pointing out a fact. I thought facts were important to lawyers."

"It's not going to work, Ben. You won't distract me."

He saw the in-control lawyer—the woman who was sure-footed in her area of expertise—and knew he could no longer avoid telling her. Before now, he hadn't told anyone. Granted, his family and friends knew but he hadn't told them either—he hadn't needed to. They'd been there to witness the implosion of his wedding. More than anything, he wanted to hop onto Red and get out of town, ride away from this like he'd been doing for months but he couldn't even start the damn bike, let alone ride it.

They'd reached her car and using her key lock she beeped it open before facing him. "This is what's going to happen, Ben. We're going to drive to a place of your choosing and then you're going to tell me what it is about this costume that has upset you so much."

"You're going to have to take it off first."

"I'm serious."

A long sigh shuddered out of him. "So am I."

CHAPTER TWENTY-FOUR

AMY SAT on a couch in the master bedroom watching Ben pace back and forth in front of the bay window. He'd been silent on the drive home and she hadn't pushed him to talk. She'd kept her end of the bargain—she'd changed out of her costume—and now it was time for him to keep his.

"Ready when you are," she said.

Ben stopped abruptly and stared at her through hooded eyes. "I'm never going to be ready."

"So choose a place to start. What was it about the suit that set you off? Was it the color?"

He ran his hand through his hair. "Black isn't a color. It's a tone."

She decided not to respond to that because he only wanted to distract her. Instead she tucked her legs up and under her then pulled a throw rug over her to ward against the chilly evening air.

With his back to her, he gazed out into the starry night. "Lexie borrowed my suit occasionally and wore it to costume parties. I used to tease her that she looked better in it than I did."

Her heart ached for him and for herself. "I'm sorry. I didn't mean to remind you of her."

"You don't remind me of Lexie in any way at all, which is what I need, but that fucking suit did." He turned around, his face taut and strained.

For a moment she wondered if she should pursue this if it was causing him so much pain. He pulled at his hair.

"I hate that I managed to live with a woman for months and have no clue she was gay," he finally said.

Amy heard the shame and embarrassment in his tone and it took her a moment to digest the actual words. "She's a lesbian?"

Ben nodded slowly, his eyes filled with shadows. "She says she's bi, but she's more attracted to women than men."

Of all the scenarios she'd run through in her head over the past couple of weeks as to why Lexie would have broken off the engagement, she'd never got anywhere near close to the truth. "And that's why she stood you up at the wedding?"

"Yeah." He shoved his hands into his pockets. "It was hell of day all around. One I've spent the past year forgetting."

Her heart ached for him. "Except it keeps coming back, doesn't it?"

"When I least expect it." His green eyes flickered with hurt and pain. "What really gets me is that I'd have been happy to get hitched in a registry office and go to the pub afterwards but Lexie insisted she wanted the full-catastrophe white wedding with all the bells and whistles. She kept saying, 'let's make it count. Let's show everyone how amazing we are together. Let them dream about what gorgeous children we're going to make.'

So there we all were, one hundred and fifty people in the Melbourne Botanical Gardens on a beautiful autumn March day, sitting in white chairs listening to a string quartet and waiting for the bride."

Amy pictured Ben standing in his tuxedo in front of an expectant crowd and she bit her lip. "And she didn't show?"

"Oh, she showed," he said bitterly. "She arrived wearing a black suit. Her bridesmaid wore the wedding dress."

A blast of fury blew through Amy that almost laid her flat. It had absolutely nothing to do with Lexie being gay and everything to do with the way she'd humiliated Ben.

"But that's horrible. Why would she do that to you?"

He scrubbed his cheeks with his palms. "She swears she didn't set out to do it, and over time I've come to believe her, but when it happened it was... Honestly, there are no words to describe it. For a moment I thought it was another one of her crazy pranks. Instead, it was the culmination of what I now know was always going to be a train wreck. At least that's what I've been telling myself for months, needing to believe it, because it's all so fucking complicated. As soon as I think I have it straight in my head and understand it, the next second I don't."

His voice deepened, filled with something close to acrimony. "I blame Sian for the very public way Lexie came out. I swear it was her idea."

"Sian?"

"The bridesmaid. Or to be precise, the bride."

His bitterness slammed Amy so hard she rocked. She wanted to rush over, hold him tight and tell him— What? She had no clue what to say because a thousand questions spun in her head so fast she felt dizzy.

"I don't understand," she said. "If Lexie thought or knew she was gay, why did she even accept your marriage proposal?"

He flinched. "She didn't. I accepted her proposal to me."

"Oh."

Amy was struggling to keep up with his story. She couldn't imagine having the guts to risk asking any guy to marry her when there was a devastating chance of hearing no way.

Ben gave her a wry smile tinged with resignation. "Lexie's tenacious and she usually gets what she wants, and she decided she wanted me. Or at least she thought she wanted me but it turns out it was for all the wrong reasons."

Amy had the distinct feeling she was sliding down a slippery slope. Every time she thought she understood, it slid from her grasp. She could only imagine how Ben must have felt—still be feeling.

"How did you meet her?" she asked.

He blew out a long, protracted sigh. "Lexie's an engineer like me and we met at an iron ore mine out in the Pilbara in Western Australia. It's in the middle of nowhere, surrounded by blistering heat and red dust, and ninety-nine percent of the staff is male. I loved the work but it's not something you want to do forever. I had a close mate, Mark, who was working up there with me and we'd both decided at the end of the contract, we were heading back east."

He seemed to stare off into space for a moment before clearing his throat. "Four days after that conversation, Mark died in a freak accident. He lost his footing on a mining truck and fell the equivalent of two stories."

Her hand flew to her mouth. "That horrendous. I'm so sorry."

"Yeah. You're not supposed to die at twenty-nine. That's the age you're starting to think about settling down. Making a commitment to someone and moving forward with your life. Hell, that had been the plan and Mark lost the chance."

Ben open and closed his hands a few times. "Three weeks after Mark died, Lexie walked onto the site with a bright yellow hard hat on her head, dust rising from her heels, and she made a beeline for me. She said, 'G'day, we're having dinner together in the mess tonight.'

"I laughed but like I said, Lexie's nothing if not determined. And she was fun. She changed my life at the mine and turned it on its head. We did some crazy and outrageous things and she lifted my grief. When she proposed six weeks later, I accepted. 'Why wait,' she said, so the wedding was planned for eight weeks after that. There was just enough time for my stunned parents to help us organize it from four thousand kilometers away."

His emerald eyes implored her to understand. "I know it was fast but it seemed like a good idea at the time. I was starting my grown-up life with a woman who made me laugh, wanted marriage, kids, the whole nine yards. I kept thinking how lucky I was that what I wanted had fallen into my lap."

Amy thought about his dead friend. "You were doing what you and Mark talked about. Honoring him?" she asked softly.

He blinked at her in surprise. "That's what my sister-in-law the therapist said."

"Did you..." *Just ask him.* She sucked in a breath. "Did you love her?"

"I thought I did." He slumped onto the window seat as if telling the story had drained him of energy. "Now I don't know. Believe me, I've asked myself the same question a million times but everything about me and Lexie was so fucked up I can't separate the real from the fake. I had no clue that our entire relationship was based on a lie and she was using me to fight her demons. I didn't guess that the occasionally crazy, risk-taking stuff she did was part of her problem. She was in denial, trying so hard to live a straight life—a life everyone expected her to live and part of her wanted to live, while the rest of her shuddered at the thought."

Amy thought about the fallout that would engulf her and her life if she stood up to Jonathon and a wave of sympathy for the unknown Lexie rolled through her. Part of her understood why she'd struggled and resisted coming out.

"So no one knew she was gay?"

He grimaced. "One person. Sian. I didn't meet her until we came back to Melbourne, two weeks before the wedding. Sian wasn't my biggest fan," he said with ironic understatement. "She hated me. After a few attempts to find some common ground with her and getting nothing, I gave up. Lexie visited her without me and I didn't give it a second thought because, shit, women do stuff together all the time, don't they?"

Amy heard and saw his appeal for confirmation. She didn't really have girlfriends and she was still burned from Beth's betrayal, but she had sisters and she knew what he meant. "Girls' night out, weekends away?"

"Yeah, all of that. As the wedding got closer, Lexie was spending full days with Sian and I just thought it was wedding stuff. It turns out they'd been in a relationship before I'd met Lexie, and Sian had been pressuring her to come out then. Lexie was scared and confused, and she broke it off, came north and chose me to be her attempt at living straight. I had no clue about any of it. I was just the pathetic bastard who got caught up in the middle of a fucking mess."

"You're not pathetic."

Amy shot to her feet and sat next to him on the window seat, putting her hand on his back. The muscles were so tight they almost pushed her fingers away. "You were grieving for a friend and Lexie only showed you the person she wanted to see. The person she was trying to be, not the person she was fighting. You had no reason to suspect she was gay."

"I should have realized. Everyone betrays themselves in some way." He shot to his feet and opened the minibar. "Booze in the bedroom? The rich think of everything, don't they?" He poured himself a scotch and offered her one.

She shook her head. "Do you really need that?"

He immediately put the glass down and pulled her to her feet. "I'd rather have you."

He kissed her like he always did—taking charge and reducing her to a delicious, quivering mess.

But he was hurting and this time she was determined to give back. She undid his shirt and pulled it out of his pants before pressing kisses to his chest. Her hands kneaded his back until they reached his hips and then she brought them around to his front. She could feel his erection straining against the button fly of his jodhpurs and she quickly undid the buttons and dropped to her knees.

"No." The harshness of his voice whipped her as both his hands gripped her head hard. "Get up. Now." He hauled her to her feet and immediately turned away from her, downing the whiskey.

Mortification burned her cheeks as anger, embarrassment and abject sadness pummeled her so hard she swayed. She'd thought it would help him, be something he might enjoy. Would she ever get this sex thing right?

It's not you, it's me.

The thought stopped her automatic spiral into self-doubt and loathing. *Examine the facts. He's always the playmaker in sex but you haven't minded because it's all new anyway. He's never let you touch him except to roll on a condom.* She'd always put it down to her inexperience and sexual timidity but the more she thought about it the more she realized it was because he didn't want to be touched.

Everyone betrays themselves in some way. I should have realized.

She sat down on the bed. "I refuse to let you make me feel bad. If we're going to keep having sex, I need you to tell me what you like and what you don't like so we don't end up here again."

Ben saw the determination in Amy's eyes and he knew he had a choice. He could refuse and instantly end this thing between them or he could give her the last piece of information of the debacle that was him and Lexie. The one thing he'd held so close to his chest that he'd never told anyone. Not the therapist he'd seen once or his caring sister-in-law, and definitely not his brothers. It was the answer to the question, how could you live with her, sleep with her and not realize she was gay? The question he'd seen in everyone's eyes at the wedding and in the days that followed. The question that implied his own stupidity and it had driven him out of Australia and on this road trip.

It was the missing piece in the jigsaw that represented his blindness and his denial that everything had happened too fast and that there were some problems between him and Lexie. The one niggling thing he'd always papered over with excuses.

"Ben?" Amy spoke his name so softly, so hesitantly that he barely heard it.

It broke him. He sat down next to her and picked up her hand. "I'm sorry. It's just that sex with Lexie was mostly oral. She said she was saving herself for me, to make the wedding night special, and fool that I was I believed her and didn't push her on it. It was the *one* clue she gave me and I ignored it."

"You're not a fool. You're a guy who respects women." Empathy shone in her eyes and she squeezed his hand. "I understand that me wanting to..." She cleared her throat. "Anyway, don't worry because I'm not sure how I feel about...." the tips of her ears glowed fire-red "...oral sex." She grinned at him. "It might all be a bit too messy."

She'd just made his issue all about her and he almost cried at her thoughtfulness. "Thank you."

"You're welcome." She rested her head on his shoulder, her curls brushing her face. "Can we keep doing the other stuff, though, because I really liked all of it."

He laughed. "We can do that."

"Now?"

He pulled her down onto the bed with him and kissed her.

CHAPTER TWENTY-FIVE

"My party." Lily pointed to the invitation on the fridge.

"No, that was Eva's party, Scott served the pasta casserole he'd made for their supper. "Remember, we went on Tuesday and you gave her the jigsaw puzzle. It's all done now. You can take the invitation down and put it in the trash."

Lily shook her head. "Lily party."

Lily had been embraced by the parents of the kindergarteners and she'd been to three birthday parties in quick succession. "You went to Eva's, Kaylee's and Sydney's parties." He set her plate down in front of her and poured a glass of milk.

Lily's mouth formed a mulish line. "Lily party. My cake."

His hand stilled on the salad servers. "You want to have a birthday party?"

Lily bounced in her chair. "Blow out the candle."

Her birthday had occurred during the move. He'd been too overwhelmed by setting up the house and getting Lily settled into school so he'd let it slide with the intention of doing something special a bit later, like a trip to the Minnesota Zoo. Now she was asking for a birthday party like any normal five-year-old. His throat tightened.

"Okay, Lily, you can have a birthday party."

Her eyes lit up. "Now?"

He shook his head, half laughing, half groaning. "No, we have to count sleeps."

"Okay," she said happily and started eating her supper.

Slowly the joy of having his little girl ask for something so normal started to fade. He'd never thrown a kid's party in his life. Where the hell did he start?

Melissa finished the piano piece she was playing with a flourish, thrilled she'd only made one mistake. She waited for Scott's praise but ten seconds ticked past.

"Wow, Melissa," she said, "that was amazing. You deserve a special treat for working so hard."

Scott stared silently into space and she snapped her fingers in front of his eyes. "Hello, earth to Scott, I've finished."

"Great. Good job," he said distractedly.

"You didn't hear a thing, did you?"

A sheepish expression crossed his face. "Sorry."

"And you even missed the hint about sex so whatever it is you're thinking about must be pretty big."

He sighed. "In a moment of insanity I promised Lily a birthday party."

Surprise rolled through her. It was the first time he'd ever volunteered any information about his daughter. "And?"

"Do you have any idea what's involved in a party?" He looked at her, his hazel eyes bright with terror. "God, I thought it was cake and candles then send them home with a goody bag, but on the children's party websites it says I need a theme, a magician or a visiting fairy."

Melissa laughed. "They're only five. Just blow up some balloons."

"I can do balloons."

"There you go. One problem solved."

"Do you have any other suggestions?"

"Um..." His question surprised her and she thought about her middle sister's children who always had birthday parties. "Games are easy and they love them. Play pin the tail on the donkey and musical chairs. Then you can feed them, sing 'Happy Birthday,' blow out the candles and send them home."

He pushed up his glasses. "You make it sound so easy."

She studied him. "So you've never thrown her a party?"

"No, and I want this one to be good. It's hard enough for her not being as developed as the other kids without her dad throwing her a crap party."

Melissa's heart rolled. "If all else fails, just play your piano. Little girls love to dance."

Anxiety wove across his face. "It's just I can't split myself five ways, heating food, running games, keeping the girls under control and making sure Lily's coping." He looked at her, a battle clearly raging in his eyes, and then he huffed out a breath. "If I get everything organized, could you help me out on the day? Be my party wingman?"

Her heart did a crazy flip like it had never done before and she rubbed her sternum. "Sure."

"Thanks, Missy."

He smiled at her—a warm, quiet smile that added to the odd sensations that had taken up residence. Sensations that scared her. She steeled herself and wrestled back some control. "My terms are this. The party needs to be on a Sunday and you have to call me Melissa."

"Absolutely, Missy. How about you play that piece one more time and I promise to give you all of my attention." He dropped a kiss onto her hair—one that was all to do with affection and absolutely nothing at all to do with sex.

The kiss sent the already-simmering panic inside her spilling over and she grabbed his hand, determined to reset all her feelings about him. "I've got six minutes. Give me your undivided attention in bed."

Amy was in Whitetail having told her parents she was collecting Ben from the garage. It was the truth but she'd come into town early so she could make calls without the risk of being overheard. Despite the size of the house, with her parents in residence, it was suddenly too small.

For the seventh time in an hour she was making a call which basically started with, "Hi, I'm Amy Sagar and I'm just touching base in regards to the advertised position..." then she filled in the blanks based on the notes on her yellow legal pad. The agencies she'd signed with hadn't produced any interviews so she was back combing the internet for jobs.

"We have your résumé, Ms. Sagar, and we'll be in touch," the brusque woman at the end of the line said, using the exact same tone as every other P.A. who'd taken her call.

It told her nothing and failed to give her any hope. She thanked the woman put a red strike through the last number on her list as misery washed through her. Time was rushing and she wasn't any closer to a job. As much as she was enjoying making Janey's wedding gown, it wasn't a job-job. She missed working, she missed her charity, Kids Plus, and she missed the families who benefitted from it. Her only consolation was that the Foundation had a prestigious reputation so Jonathon wouldn't tamper with it because he'd want the associated glory.

She glanced at her watch. She still had thirty minutes before Ben was ready to leave. Ever since Ben had told her about Lexie, she'd been thinking about the whole awful story. Awful for both Ben and his ex-fiancée. She thought he was being way too hard on himself for not realizing Lexie was gay. She'd even done a bit of internet research, reading stories from both men and women whose partners had come out. They all shared the same stunned disbelief that Ben had talked about.

People had a thousand sides and they chose the ones they wanted to display to the world and the ones they wanted to hide. She thought about Jonathon and her jobless state and how she hadn't told her parents anything. *You haven't told Ben the full story either.* Her mind leaped away from that like fingers from fire. It wasn't like they were engaged. Ben didn't need to know.

The cold nipped at her ankles in the darkening park and sitting here wasn't going to make her feel any better about her life. She could go and hang out in the garage while Ben finished up but he'd only ask how the job hunting was going. She didn't want to have that conversation, thank you very much. She preferred it when she and Ben were exercising or having sex, and he was too busy to ask her the hard questions. Shoving her hands into her coat pockets, she crossed the road and admired the new window display in the Northern Lights Boutique.

She suddenly got an idea to cheer herself up and stepped inside. It was near closing time and Melissa was alone in the store. She looked up from steaming a jacket and smiled.

"Hi, Amy."

"Hey, Melissa." She ran her hand along a rack of long-sleeved blouses whose shades covered the full gamut of fall colors, suddenly feeling embarrassed by what she'd come in to ask.

Melissa switched off the steamer, her face welcoming if slightly confused. "I wasn't expecting you. Are there problems with Janey's gown?"

"No, it's coming along just fine."

"That's great."

"Yeah."

"The coat looks good on you." Melissa moved to a display of scarves and picked one up. "This came in the other day and I thought it would really suit you."

"It sure is pretty."

Melissa wound it around Amy's neck. "There you go. Perfect."

Amy thought about her bank account, which was healthy but without a regular income it may not stay that way for too long. "How much is it?"

Melissa waved her hand. "It's my treat as thanks for helping me out with Janey, unless of course you'd like something else?"

"Actually..." She felt the burn in her cheeks.

"Just ask, Amy. I can give you a discount to the value of the scarf on another item if you'd like it more."

"It's not that... I feel stupid asking but I've had a pretty crap day on the job-hunting front and I was wondering if I could try on a wedding dress?"

Melissa's face broke into a wide smile. "Heck, yes, you can do that. After all, it's wine o'clock." She locked the store door and turned the sign to Closed. "Which one do you want to try on?"

"The one with the sweetheart neckline, the beautifully beaded bodice and the full circle tulle skirt," Amy said without a moment's hesitation.

"Oh, great choice," Melissa said approvingly. "I love that gown." She retrieved it off the rack and unzipped the protective bag.

Both of them sighed with delight, looked at each other and laughed.

"Will you try one on too?" Amy asked. "I feel bad for taking up your time."

"It's fine and I'm always happy to try on clothes. Seeing as you're here and can do up forty-five buttons, I think I'm in the mood for a bit of 1930s vintage style." Melissa quickly located the gown she wanted. "You try yours on first and then you can help me get into mine."

Ten minutes later they were both wearing a wedding gown and alternated between twirling and standing still while staring into the large mirror.

"Oh, my God, I have no clue why this makes me feel giddy with joy," Amy said, "but it's amazing."

"That dress really suits you." Melissa handed her a glass of champagne. "You should remember this style when your time comes."

"Don't hold your breath." Amy clinked Melissa's glass. "I have to get a job first."

"Job or no job, you and Ben seem cozy?"

"I could say the same about you and Scott," Amy said quickly, not wanting to discuss Ben even though he was hands-down the best man who'd ever been in her bed.

In your life.

Melissa laughed. "Scott is all about sex and nothing about marriage."

"So you love wedding gowns but you don't want to get married?"

Melissa took a long slug of her drink. "Oh, I want to get married and I have my gown all picked out. I just need a single man in his thirties who doesn't live at home, isn't divorced, has a well-paying job, doesn't have commitment-issues and wants to have babies straightaway."

"Are you ordering him from a catalog?" Amy thought about Ben who'd clearly wanted to get married once but after the trauma of Lexie, she doubted he did now.

"I wish," Melissa said. "But I'm determined to avoid the heartache and financial problems my eldest sister's facing. My friend Emily and I made a pact to find two perfect guys by Christmas."

"That's not so far away."

"I know it." Melissa sighed and drained her glass. "Here's to finding a good man."

Amy wondered if she'd already found one.

CHAPTER TWENTY-SIX

SCOTT TOUSLED Lily's hair before collapsing next to Melissa on the couch. The party was over, the guests had left and the house was blessedly quiet.

"Man, I'm exhausted," he said.

Melissa laughed. "Five-year-olds have more energy and stamina than I thought." Her gaze drifted to Lily who was looking at a picture book. "Lily's got your sense of rhythm. She's a great little dancer."

The compliment was unexpected and it warmed him. "Thanks. She likes to sing too, but sadly with her speech impediment singing in the shower's going to be as close as that gets to a career."

Melissa frowned. "I know you've mixed with the crème of musical talent, but most of us who like to sing don't have the ability to be soloists, Scott. Doesn't stop us singing."

Her words set him back slightly. He loved Lily to the point of pain and he wanted the best for her but part of him always went first to what she'd never be. "I guess I hadn't thought about it in those terms."

Melissa gave a wry smile. "Besides, if they allowed me to sing in the school choir, they'll let Lily join in the future."

"I've never heard you sing."

"And you're never going to."

Her emphatic tone was an instant dare as well as a test. "Hey, Lily, do you want to hear Missy sing?"

His daughter jumped up, a wide smile on her face and her brown eyes sparkling from behind her glasses. "Hot potato?"

Melissa tensed and for a moment Scott thought she was going to give an excuse.

"You're a sly fox, Scott Knapp," she muttered as Lily stood in front of her clapping with expectation. Then all her attention was fixed on his daughter. "Lily, I don't know that song so you need to teach me. You sing it while your daddy plays the music."

Before Scott had reached the piano, Lily had started singing and dancing. She was kicking out her jean-clad legs with enthusiastic fervor and giving her own interpretation to the dance actions she'd learned from watching *The Wiggles* over and over and over.

Melissa watched Lily intently before standing up and smoothing down her bright green pants with rigid hands. "I'll try but I'm not sure my dancing's going to be as good as yours."

She formed two fists and stacked them on top of each other. Then, in a delightfully husky, but definitely off-key voice, she sang, "Hot potato, hot potato."

She hadn't been exaggerating—she really couldn't sing—and yet she kept going, moving on to the next verse of *cold spaghetti* and flinging her arms out as wildly as Lily. After a rousing version of *mashed banana* she fell onto the couch with a giggling Lily. She shot him a death stare.

"Happy now?" she said.

"Definitely amused." He was in awe that she'd stepped way out of her comfort zone so as not to disappoint Lily. He wanted to haul her into his arms and kiss her.

She pointed two fingers at him as if they were a handgun. "You tell anyone what you just heard and you're a dead man."

"Noted." But he'd just seen past the facade of the well-dressed, perfectly made-up woman who didn't take any crap from anyone. She was like crème brûlée—once you cracked the hard topping, she was all soft inside.

"Come on, Lil." He scooped up his tired daughter. "Time for a bath and bed."

Melissa watched Lily snuggle into Scott's chest and rubbed her sternum, trying to move the heavy feeling that had settled there. If Scott had thanked her once for helping him out today, he'd thanked her ten times but it was unnecessary—she'd loved being in the thick of the party action with the little girls. There'd been a couple of challenging moments when she'd needed to remind one of the guests it was Lily's party, and she'd had to think on her feet when Eva Sorenson had asked why Lily talked funny and why she wasn't wearing a party dress. Apart from that it had been lots of fun but now it was over and Lily was heading to bed, which was her cue to depart.

She drained her glass of wine and stood. "I'll leave you to it."

"You don't have to," Scott said quickly, sounding like he really meant it. "I was hoping you'd stay for a thank-you supper. I've made a beef stew and I have a nice Zinfandel to go with."

She thought about going home to her empty house. All that waited for her there was dusting and dishes. "I guess I have to eat so why not?"

"Great." He got a sheepish look. "How would you feel about reheating the stew and peeling the potatoes?"

"Hot potato," Lily sang sleepily, not even lifting her head off Scott's shoulder.

The heavy feeling in her chest gained another pound. "I suppose I could do that."

"Thanks. I'll be about twenty minutes." He looked down at Lily. "Say good-night to Missy."

"Ni-ni, Miffy."

"Sleep tight, Lily."

She watched Scott's retreating back for a few seconds before entering the tiny kitchen and turning on Scott's MP3 player. A classical piano piece swelled in the cramped space and she cleared away the remains of the party so she could find counter space to peel the potatoes. Just as she was opening the oven, a jarring rap song came on and she almost dropped the casserole dish. *Rap?* She wondered what else he had on his playlist.

When she'd finished her jobs she opened the wine and took a wander around the small living room looking at photos, picking them up and setting them back down. There were a few of Scott and Lily together—at the park, at the zoo, with a Christmas tree—one with Lily and a man who looked like an older version of Scott and a larger group photo that she assumed was Scott's extended family. She found herself looking for a photo of Lily's mother and wondered if the picture she had in her hand was it.

"That's my adopted sister."

Scott's quiet voice surprised her and she set the photo down before turning around feeling caught red-handed. "She needs a dust."

"We all need a dust." He poured himself a glass of wine.

"Will Lily sleep after all the excitement?"

"She's a great eater and sleeper." He gave her a crooked grin. "Now *that* I got to brag about at playgroup."

If he'd taken Lily to playgroup then he'd probably been raising her alone for a long time. Screw waiting to be told, she'd just ask. "Does Lily see much of her mom?"

"She doesn't see her at all," he said curtly before walking into the kitchen.

Melissa followed and leaned against the counter watching him slam the masher into the cooked potatoes, the muscles of his forearms bunching. He whipped butter and milk into the mash with a fraught energy she'd never associated with him.

As she set the table with silverware and trivets for the hot dishes, she wondered about the woman who could dent Scott's usually calm aura.

He brought over the stew, the mashed potatoes and a green salad and they served themselves from the center of the table. When they were both seated with steaming food on their plates, she continued from where she'd left off.

"Why doesn't Lily see her mother?"

"Because it's better this way."

He sounded so resolute. So hard. It struck her as being utterly out of character with the gentle and caring guy she was getting to know. She wasn't certain she agreed with him on this parenting point—she had friends who'd been separated from one of their parents by the other and it hadn't worked in their favor.

"How is it better? I don't know any kid who wouldn't prefer to have both parents in their life."

He put down his fork with a clatter. "I know you have strong opinions on just about everything, Melissa, but this time you don't have enough information to form one."

She refilled his wineglass then met his ire-filled gaze. "So tell me so I do."

His mouth tightened. "It's pretty simple really. Margaret doesn't want to be part of Lily's life."

Melissa didn't know what to say.

He raised his brows. "You weren't expecting that, were you?"

"No." She pushed a piece of beef around her plate. "How can a mother not want her child?"

"That's the exact question I asked myself for two years but now I'm over it." He fiddled with the stem of his wineglass. "Sure, I worry for Lily, but answer me this. Isn't it better to have no mother than one who can't hide her distaste and disappointment in you?"

An ache throbbed deep down inside her. "Your ex-wife couldn't love Lily because of her Down syndrome?"

He shrugged. "Margaret's a perfectionist. She'd be hard-pressed to love a normal child."

"Then why did she have one in the first place?" Melissa's words shot out with unexpected anger that was tied to her own lack of a child.

Scott pushed his glasses up the bridge of his nose. "We weren't married when Margaret got pregnant. She'd just been accepted into the Ann Arbor symphony orchestra, second desk, which was step one of her plan to become first violin in an orchestra somewhere, preferably Boston or Chicago. Ironically, going on the dates, Lily was probably conceived the night we celebrated that success."

Melissa's stomach cramped. "So Lily wasn't planned?"

"No. She was a total surprise and we got married. It wasn't an easy pregnancy or an easy time. Margaret was stressing how she was going to keep up her practice, deal with touring and a baby. I couldn't get her to see that between the two of us, we could balance our careers and one child. God, I remember saying, 'You're being a drama queen. How hard can one baby be?'"

Irony twisted his mouth. "When Lily was born needing far more help than the average baby, Margaret didn't cope."

"I can imagine it would have been a huge shock." Melissa hooked his gaze with hers. "I don't think anyone goes into parenthood thinking they're going to have a child with a disability."

"You got that right. Especially a woman who'd barely come around to the idea of being a mother, period, let alone the mother of a child who isn't perfect."

He sighed, his eyes filling with memories. "She went on antidepressants so she could attempt to function and I picked up the slack. When Lily was six weeks old, Margaret's doctor suggested she return to work hoping it would help lift the depression. My next concert tour dates hadn't been scheduled and my agent was arguing with venues so I took over at home."

He rubbed his face and slowly shook his head. "I didn't know what hit me. I had a wife who barely spoke to me, a baby with a heart condition that scared me shitless and a daily schedule of early intervention programs that exhausted both me and Lily. On top of all of that was the normal baby stuff like bottles and diapers."

It was nothing like what Melissa imagined being the parent of a newborn would be and her heart went out to all three of them. "It sounds like a tough, tough time."

He met her gaze. "I've had better days."

She wondered if he'd been the one to pull the pin on the marriage. "How old was Lily when you separated?"

"We didn't make it to her first birthday. When Lily was eleven months, Margaret got on a Tuesday-morning flight to go audition for the Boston Symphony Orchestra. Lily and I waved her off from Detroit with a promise to meet her plane on Thursday. She never came back."

Never came back. "But she's seen Lily since then, right?"

He shook his head. "Margaret's life is all about Margaret. Believe me, things are better this way. Lily needs to know she's loved and adored and I love her to bits. She's my joy and my delight. She makes me laugh and she teaches me more than I teach her."

His love for his daughter rolled into her and she gave his hand a quick squeeze, hating how she'd been so quick to jump to conclusions about him the first night she'd met him. "And I'm guessing you haven't had another concert tour?"

"Hey, I've played to many an appreciative playgroup."

His irony downplayed the seriousness of his career-ending decision to raise his child. She thought about how much Lily had enjoyed her first party even though she'd often been a beat behind the other little girls. The glow of delight on her face when she blew out her birthday candles had stayed with Melissa. "You're the most amazing man I think I've ever met. You gave up your career for Lily."

"Lily needs me."

And there it was. The simple and yet heartbreaking truth. Sometimes life totally sucked. She stood and sat on his lap, wrapping her arms around his neck, wanting to touch him. "So exactly how heavy a sleeper is Lily?"

He grinned up at her. "Very."

"Good, but I won't stay the night."

"Thank you."

His words should have reassured her. They almost did.

CHAPTER TWENTY-SEVEN

Boneless and panting, Amy eased herself gently off Ben, kissed him and then rolled in next to him. "That was a perfect afternoon delight," she said. "Thank you."

He grinned, tangling his hand gently in her hair. "Anytime."

She drew small circles on his chest, loving being cuddled up next to him. "It was especially thoughtful of you to lend my parents your bike so they were gone all day."

"That's me. Mr. Generosity." He stroked her cheek. "I'm just trying to get in sweet with your dad so it doesn't feel like Antarctic temperatures whenever we meet in the great room."

Her heart trembled at his thoughtfulness and she had to work hard to ignore it. "It was nice of Ella and Al to invite them to supper too. It gives me a few more hours to work on Janey's gown so I'm ready for the final fitting."

His green eyes hooked her gaze and took no prisoners. "You need to tell your folks about your job and the dress."

She tensed, not wanting to have this conversation again. "I've told you why I can't do that."

"I know and I don't agree. Besides, you haven't factored in the fact that Ella knows about the dress."

Horrified, she sat up fast. "Ella knows?"

"Well I think she does. Last week I jumped into a conversation when Ella mentioned your sewing skills."

"Last week?" She heard the screech in her voice. "And you've only just thought to tell me now?"

He held up his hands in surrender. "Hey, don't shoot the messenger. You know how I feel about lying."

"I'm not lying. I'm just not mentioning it."

"Lexie didn't mention her sexuality and it totally screwed me up. Tell your parents before they find out and everything is ten times worse."

She pictured talking to her parents. *Mom, Dad, I lost my prestigious job that makes you so proud of me and makes up for the fact I've hardly ever had a boyfriend and my personal life sucks. Oh, and I'm also being blackmailed by Jonathon and I can't get an interview anywhere.*

Nothing could be worse than that.

She bit her knuckle thinking about the lie Ben had unwittingly lived and the fallout of it. "I'll tell them about the dress. Happy?"

Reproach scudded through his eyes.

If she'd wanted absolution from him on that point, she didn't get it.

"You ready, eh?" Al sat astride the monstrous bike with a grin on his face the width of Texas.

"My picnic will be squished as flat as a bug in those saddlebags." Ella clutched both her basket and at straws, looking for a way to get out of this ride. "I'll take the car and meet you there."

"Oh, no. You promised." Al got off the bike with an ease that belied his age. "I guarantee you there'll be no squished subs." He relieved her of the basket and carefully packed the sandwiches and drinks.

Ella held her hand out for the empty basket but he ignored her and instead strode up to her porch, denying her the excuse of retreating with it. As he bent over, safely depositing it under a chair, she couldn't help but notice how good he looked in black leather pants.

She'd known Al Swenson for most of her adult life but she'd never noticed his butt before. She immediately gave herself a shake. Today wasn't the time to start noticing things like that.

He walked back to her. "Let's rock 'n' roll."

The idea of rolling made her more anxious than ever. "Where's my helmet?"

"Aw, Ella, you'll enjoy it more without one."

"I'll barely enjoy it with one."

He unclipped the helmet from the saddlebag and placed it on her head, his fingers brushing her chin as he adjusted the strap. He leaned in. "Is it comfortable?"

Surprisingly, it was. "Yes. Where do I sit?"

"There." He pointed to a very small seat. Given the size of the driver's seat, it seemed tacked on as afterthought.

"You have got to be kidding me?"

He laughed. "You're tiny, Ella, so you'll be fine."

He got on the bike, kicked down and suddenly the engine roared to life. She jumped. Even with the padding of the helmet over her ears, the roar of the engine was deafening.

Al turned to her with a grin. "Put your hand on my shoulder and get on," he yelled as he pointed downward to the exhaust. "Don't burn your leg."

"Burn my leg?"

Her rising fear almost choked her. Gripping his shoulder like it was the only thing between her and certain death, she managed to throw her leg over the bike. Al pointed to where she should put her feet and she gripped his waist, feeling like she was perched rather than sitting on the pillion seat. She was petrified she was going to fall off. Powerful vibrations ran up and down her legs and unlike in a car, she felt like the bike was part of her. She didn't know if she liked the sensation or not.

And then they were moving slowly down the street. She didn't dare move in case she made the bike wobble and she'd barely got used to not having the security of a car around her when Al turned onto the county road. The bike took off, the increased speed sending her backward—she almost vomited in her mouth. Trees whipped past so close and so fast that everything was a green blur. She closed her eyes.

Bad idea. Unable to see anything, she felt nauseous and more likely to fall off any second so she opened her eyes again. She yelled, "Slow down," and heard her words whipped away from her.

The bike raced down the blacktop, going so fast that the white lines of the road seemed to join into one continuous line. She moved her gaze back to the trees. Nope, it didn't help so she stared at Al's back, seeing a steady, blur-free black. She was just about to tell him she wanted to go home when he slowed and turned onto the rustic dirt road.

They hit a pothole and she screamed.

Al said something but she couldn't hear it over the engine and the pounding dread in her ears. Suddenly and blessedly, the beast stopped moving and Al turned around.

"Ella, you gotta relax or you're gonna tip us both off the bike."

"Relax?" She stared at him gob smacked. "How can I relax when I'm terrified?"

"The more you fight the bike, the more you're gonna hate it. Riding a bike's like dancing and you're a fabulous dancer, Ella."

She ignored the compliment that spun traitorously through her making her giddy. She sharply reminded herself she was no longer a girl. "This is nothing like dancing."

"Sure it is. You move with the rhythm of the bike. Lean into the bends instead of fighting them."

"I want to go back."

"Ella, what the hell is wrong with you?" Al growled. "You're one of the most resilient women I know. You raised three kids; hell, you organized Ron for over thirty years, you pushed Whitetail to get this wedding business up and running, and not once in all the time you nursed Ron did I hear you say you wanted to quit. So why are you quitting on this?"

"None of that scared me like this does."

Only she knew it wasn't the bike that scared her. It was Al. He'd been acting different lately and she didn't want things to change.

"Come on," he soothed. "Lisa and Todd are expecting us. Tell you what? I'll go slow and you lean into the bends."

Before she could object or argue, he started off. This time the trees stayed in focus and she didn't have the same sense that she might fall. The sunshine warmed her face and leaves floated down around them on the breeze, their message loud and clear—winter was coming. The fresh scent of pine mixed with marsh mud and although she couldn't hear the birdsong, she could see them. A flock of Canada geese flew overhead and she followed their flight path, her view unobstructed.

She was right in the middle of nature rather than boxed out of it like in a car.

The bike sped up some but it didn't bother her. She was too busy wondering what the red flowers were they'd just passed. Al's right shoulder moved against her as if to say, *look* and she glanced up, seeing the bend up ahead. Fighting every urge to stay rigid, she pressed her body against Al's broad and comforting back and moved with him.

The weight of the bike shifted and she followed it.

It felt like freedom and she wanted to feel it again.

Amy dug into the tub of popcorn that her father passed her, loving the way salt and butter conspired to make it taste so damn good. The two of them were in the home theater watching a documentary on Australian marsupials that Todd had found in the Rasmussens' vast DVD collection.

"This is just like the old days." Todd gave her shoulder a squeeze.

Amy laughed. "Our couch and TV weren't quite in the same league as this though."

"True enough but there's money to be made in the law it seems. You've got yourself a job in a good firm. I'm so proud of you."

Guilt tumbled through her and she shoved another handful of popcorn into her mouth.

"Funny how this show hasn't mentioned drop bears," Todd said with a grin.

She shot him a sideways glance. "What's Ben told you about drop bears?"

"That you believed him for a bit but then you got him good with the flour the day we arrived. That's my girl." He sipped his soda. "I didn't expect to like him, Amy, but he's okay."

Damned with faint praise. She laughed tightly. "You're only saying that because he bribed you into liking him by letting you and Mom ride his bike."

"Well, there is that." Todd smiled before sobering. "Even so, he's educated, well-mannered and the only thing I can hold against him is this extended vacation thing. There's something not quite right about it."

"There you two are," Lisa said from the doorway.

She took a seat next to Amy as her father said, "We were just chatting about Ben."

Amy caught the look pass between her parents and realized way too late she was suddenly sandwiched between them and all exits had just slammed shut. This wasn't a DVD viewing, it was an ambush.

"His arm's a lot better and Al's loaned him a car," Amy said, trying to keep the focus away from her.

"He'd be unwise to ride his bike too soon," Lisa said. "I guess he'll be staying here longer than you. Surely the office needs you back?"

Her heart rate picked up. "Actually, I've taken some vacation."

"Oh, Amy." Her mother's look of disappointment slugged her. "Vacation to be with Ben? This really isn't like you. I'm worried you're going to get hurt."

"I didn't take vacation time because of Ben, Mom." She could hear Ben's voice in the back of her mind. "I took it because I'm making a wedding gown for a Whitetail bride, and to spend extra time with you and Daddy."

Tell me lies... crooned the voice in head.

Her father looked askance. "A wedding gown? Why?"

She couldn't tell him the whole truth but she gave him something she'd learned from making Janey's gown. "It was just one of those things of being in the right place at the right time. I was able to help them out and I'm really enjoying it. Remember how I sewed all the time when I was at high school and college?"

"But it's just a vacation thing, right?" Her father sounded worried she was going to ditch the law for dressmaking.

"Totally." She rubbed his arm to reassure him. To reassure herself.

Lisa didn't look reassured at all. "Sweetie, I've been doing some reading. I think you're having a quarter-life crisis."

Amy wanted to duck to avoid her mother's penetrating gaze. "Mom, I'm thirty-two. I'm way passed my quarter life."

"Yes, but your life's all about work. I guess we were hoping that things with that lawyer, Jonathon, you've talked about over the last few months were going to develop into something more serious."

Oh it's pretty serious, Mom. Just not how you think.

"Mom, you really need to stop reading the self-help guides. Not every woman needs a man in their life full-time."

"Most want one."

Her mother's bald words hung between them, dripping with the truth she'd spent her life denying. She went on the attack. "I can't win, Mom. You're not happy when I'm single and you're not happy about this thing with Ben."

"Thing?" Her mother winced. "See, that's exactly the problem. I just want you to be happy."

"Of course she's happy," Todd said firmly. "Being a lawyer is all she ever talked about and she's good at what she does."

"But it's not a balanced life," Lisa argued back.

Amy's stomach clenched so hard that it moved the popcorn upward until it sat mid-chest in a hard lump. Even when her parents thought she was a successful lawyer, they still talked about her life with a pitying look in their eyes. And sadly they had good reason—a reason she was never going to confess to them or anyone else.

"I'm sitting right here, Mom, Dad. I'm not twenty anymore. I'm all grown up. It's my life so stop discussing it. Please."

Amy hit the volume on the remote, bringing up the dulcet tones of the narrator who was explaining the reproductive cycle of the kangaroo. Hiding out in a pouch for eight months sounded awesome.

CHAPTER TWENTY-EIGHT

SCOTT LOVINGLY WATCHED Lily as she ran ahead of him and Melissa on the trail, her yellow rubber boots kicking at piles of fallen leaves. "She's never happier than when she's playing with leaves."

"There's nothing better." Melissa's blue eyes sparkled. "Especially when someone's just finished raking them into a big pile."

"I bet you were a handful when you were a kid."

She laughed. "My mother tells me that when I have a child of my own I will know exactly how much grief I gave her."

Lily turned around and pointed to a big pile of leaves on the side of the trail. "Miffy, look."

"Now that *is* a big pile." Melissa leather boots sprayed leaves everywhere.

Lily joined her with a squeal of delight.

They were on their way back to the car after choosing a Halloween pumpkin from Keith and Lindsay's farm. Scott had seen a poster up in town and he'd asked Melissa about the pumpkin train one morning after what had become regular yet amazing sex at her place.

She'd told him Keith was a keen train enthusiast and that he had a mile of 7 ½-inch gauge miniature railway track in his field. Every year he turned it into a pumpkin patch. She'd said all the local kids loved it and Lily would too. Scott had found himself inviting her to come along.

It was the third time he'd invited her on one of his and Lily's outings and, just like at the party, Melissa had been relaxed with Lily without talking down to her. Today on the train, Lily had snuggled up with him in her loving way as they'd chugged to the pumpkin patch, but she'd wanted to sit next to Melissa on the way back. Scott had been left sitting behind them holding the pumpkin.

Not that she'd snuggled in with Melissa but, with her face shining, she'd giggled at things Melissa had said. He'd sat watching Lily, filled with absolute happiness, tinged with regret. He couldn't work out if the regret was to do with Margaret's abandonment of Lily or if he was finding it hard to share his daughter with another person.

They'd been a team of two for so long and seeing her laugh like that had unsettled him. He'd spent so many years focusing on just getting through one day at a time—learning how to be a dad to Lily, dealing with her health scares, managing all her therapies and protecting her from hurt—that he'd never entertained the possibility of settling down again. Never expected to find someone who might love Lily as much as he did.

The drive home was filled with off-key singing that made him and his perfect pitch shudder, but he smiled anyway. When they arrived at the house and Lily had chosen exactly where on the stoop to put the pumpkin, he invited Melissa in for some spiced coffee to round out the fall afternoon.

"Would you mind if I gave Lily a present?" Melissa asked while they waited for the coffee to brew.

The question surprised him. "Um, I guess that depends what it is. What did you have in mind?"

She pulled a package out of a tote bag. "It's a dress."

A ripple of impatience washed through him. "We're not all slaves to fashion, Melissa. Thanks anyway, but she doesn't need a dress."

"Yes, she does," Melissa said firmly. "You're a fantastic father,

Scott, but you're dressing Lily like a boy."

"No, I'm not." His voice sounded unusually loud and defensive. "She's got jeans with pink on them."

Melissa tilted her head, her smooth bob moving to brush her chin. "She has practical clothes and I get it. They're easy to wash and they don't need ironing but she needs a pretty dress or two and ribbons in her hair."

"Ribbons? Jeez, Melissa, I've got more to worry about every day than damn ribbons in her hair."

Her face filled with understanding but her gaze was determined. "How about we let Lily decide if she wants the dress or not?"

"She's five with the intellectual abilities of a three-year-old."

"She's a little girl first," Melissa said quietly.

Her words punched him hard, making it hard to breathe and he crossed the kitchen so he could see Lily who was dancing to a DVD. She wore a hand-knitted sweater that his mom had sent her and jeans. With her short, easy-to-manage hair, it was hard to tell at first glance if she was a boy or a girl.

Nausea rolled his stomach. He'd spent five years fighting for his daughter to have the same opportunities as every other child. Was he culpable of the same sin he accused others of? Of seeing the Down syndrome first and the person second?

Hell no! But Melissa had a point. He'd prided himself on dressing Lily androgynously, but truth be told, far more boy than girl.

He turned back to Melissa, running a hand through his hair. "I guess I feel uncomfortable with all that girly stuff so I've avoided it."

"Well, you are a guy." Melissa gave him an indulgent smile. "I'm happy to give you little-girl fashion tips."

"How do I even tie a ribbon?" The thought bewildered him.

She laughed. "I'll show you, but I suggest you practice on a doll before you try it out on a squirming Lily."

His heart swelled with something so much more than gratitude and appreciation that it took him a moment before he recognized it. He was falling in love with her.

He waited for the thought to scare him rigid but it didn't. It was warm and soft and wonderful. He reached for her, pulling her into him, loving the way she fitted against him and he pressed a kiss to her forehead.

"You're the most surprising woman, Miffy."

She cuffed him lightly on the shoulder. "Only Lily's allowed to call me that."

He grinned down at her. "You're nothing like the person I took you for the day I met you."

Her eyes flickered with something unreadable. "Neither are you."

Ben walked around Red three times, squeezing his injured shoulder as he went. Since Todd had ridden Red, she'd been garaged at the house and Ben tinkered with her constantly but he was yet to take her out for a spin. He was into his third week since the accident and he'd managed to drive automatic cars without any drama. Mind you, they had power steering and the roads out here were pretty straight. Red lacked the gentle touch on the body that a modern bike offered, and as much as he wanted to ride her, he didn't want to skid into an embankment at the first bend because his shoulder gave out.

"Ben!"

He turned to see Amy jogging over the gravel wearing jeans and a jacket, with a pretty scarf around her neck. Her legs looked good. Not that they hadn't looked good when he'd first met her but the running had toned them up. He wanted to tell her that but it was dangerous territory. A bit like the question, *does my bum look big in this?* There was no right answer whichever way you came at it. He wished she could see herself through his eyes.

She arrived next to him, eyes sparkling and pink cheeked from the chill in the air. "So this is Red?"

"This is Red. Red, meet Red."

She shot him a look. "You've never called me Red."

"I do all the time in my head. It's what I call my two favorite girls."

"Oh." Her cheeks got pinker. "I've never had a nickname before."

She was a conundrum to him. Naive in so many ways and worldly in others. He couldn't work her out.

"You're not planning on riding her, are you?" she asked, her tone bossy-lawyer-esque.

"I was thinking about it."

Her brows rose. "She looks heavy like me."

"Jeez, Amy, you're not heavy." She winced at his sharp tone and he sucked in a steadying breath. "You're healthy. There's a difference. You have to start seeing that or you're never going to be happy."

He expected her to decry his statement but she gave him a wry smile. "I hate the fact that the exercise is working."

Now he really didn't understand her. "Why?"

"Because it means you were right and I've got no excuses not to do it."

He put his arm around her waist. "I was right? Can you text me that so I have it on my phone to show everyone?"

Instead of telling him where to get off, she spun abruptly out of his arms and drew circles in the gravel with her shoe. "So tomorrow's the Holzworth wedding and I'm on duty until after the photos so I was thinking maybe we could do something today. Like a fall picnic or go fishing?"

He liked the sound of that. "Good idea. Should we invite your parents seeing as they're leaving on Sunday?"

The sound of car tires on gravel made them both look up. Amy made a sound at the back of her throat that was half squeal and half groan. Before he could ask, the cars came to a halt and doors opened.

"Amy!"

Three women rushed toward her, arms wide open.

Amy managed a strangled, "Hi," before receiving and giving hugs.

Meanwhile, three guys were unbuckling children from car seats. Todd and Lisa ran from the house, their faces wreathed in smiles.

"Girls, you made it," Lisa said, hugging each one in turn.

All three women had long, straight brown hair with blond streaks, and trim up and down bodies that lacked Amy's lush curves. Close in age, they could have passed for triplets and all of them looked like younger versions of Lisa. None of them looked anything like Amy.

"How was the drive up, Cindy?" Todd asked.

"Long. Traveling with a baby is hard work. Holy crap, look at the size of this place."

Amy's large, gray eyes were the size of saucers, filled with a mixture of pleasure and dread. "What are you all doing up here?"

"Mom invited us."

"Mom?" Amy swung her gaze to Lisa. "Why did you do this without mentioning it to me?"

"Don't go all lawyer interrogation," Cindy said with a smile. "Relax, you're on vacation."

Lisa took the baby from one of her sons-in-law and bounced him in her arms. "I didn't mention it because you have that wedding tomorrow and I thought you'd say no. I didn't think it was enough of a reason not to take advantage of having us all here together for the weekend, and besides," Lisa hooked Amy with a look, "can you promise me you'll be home for Thanksgiving?"

Ben watched Amy squirm. For the thousandth time, he wished she'd tell her family about her lack of a job.

"I promise to try, Mom," Amy said.

"Wow, Amy," said another sister as a toddler pulled at her dress. "This is your boss's house? I guess it might make up for all those crazy hours you work. Man, I probably should have finished graduate school."

One of the men slipped an arm around her waist and kissed her indulgently. "Heidi, you'd have hated working for a corporation."

She picked up the toddler. "True. I just need more people to buy my nursing blouses so we can have a house like this."

"You look different, Ames," said the third sister who looked slightly younger than the others. "Good different. I like that scarf."

"Thanks, Sally," Amy said weakly. "Hi, Corey, Zac, Dan."

"Hey, Amy." Her brothers-in-law all gave a wave as they unloaded bags from the trunk.

"Does it have an indoor pool?" Heidi asked hopefully.

Amy, who'd lurched from indignant to passively accepting, seemed at a loss so Ben said, "No, but it does have a large spa."

Six sets of questioning eyes suddenly swung toward him. He imagined he felt much the same as a kangaroo caught in the glare of headlights.

"Who are you?" Sally asked, her brown eyes full of intrigue.

"This is Ben," Amy said quietly.

"You're Ben?" Cindy said on a rising inflection as she exchanged a look with Heidi and Lisa.

Something made Ben sling his arm around Amy's shoulders as if she needed protecting. "That's me."

"You're not quite who we were expecting," Heidi said.

"Sorry about that. What you see is what you get." Ben felt the unintended insult from Heidi was more directed at Amy than himself.

"No wonder you're taking vacation," squealed Sally, punching Amy in the arm.

Amy's cheeks flared from pale pink to fire-engine-red in two-tenths of a second.

"Come inside, everyone," Lisa instructed firmly as if she'd just realized that Amy was under intense sister scrutiny. "Todd will give you a tour."

"Hell, is that a vintage Harley?" Corey asked, noticing Red.

"Ben's a biker," Amy said firmly as if she'd just found her feet, "and that's Red. She's a 1957 Hydra-Glide."

That's my girl. Ben gave the top of her arm a squeeze, not quite able to believe she'd actually remembered.

As everyone walked inside ahead of them, Amy held back. "Ben, I'm so sorry. My mom has this thing about having the four of us under the same roof whenever she can manage it. I've missed a few gatherings recently what with Jon—work and stuff and I guess she saw an opportunity and took it."

He thought about his own family and how his mother probably would have done a similar thing given the opportunity. "No worries. It's just a couple of days."

She bit her knuckle. "I love my sisters but they can be pretty intense when they're in the same space."

"Amy," Sally called from the veranda. "Stop hogging that Aussie hunk and bring him inside so we can grill him Sagar-sister style."

Amy dropped her head onto his shoulder. "Oh, God, I'm sorry. It's just they're not used to seeing me with a..."

He heard the hesitation in her voice and he wrapped his arms around her. "Lover?"

She groaned. "It's more like they're not used to seeing me with a guy, period. I'm Amy the workaholic single sister. The one they love, envy and pity all at the same time. They've never seen me with a lover."

"Well, they're going to today. Let's go show your sisters you're not a woman to be pitied."

"It's going to involve soccer and board games."

"I can do that."

Her gray eyes filled with gratitude. "How come you're so nice?"

The question made him wonder yet again about this guy Jonathon who he'd already tagged as a jerk. "You make it easy."

Her shocked expression said she didn't believe him and he really wished she would. When she'd resolutely told him she was a good lawyer, her self-confidence had sung but it seemed outside of her job, she didn't recognize what she had to offer. It was like there was this needy little girl inside the competent woman.

Not knowing how else to show her, he leaned in and kissed her full on the mouth. Then he walked her into the house and in front of Cindy, Heidi and Sally, he kissed her again.

They cheered.

She blushed.

Todd and Lisa frowned.

CHAPTER TWENTY-NINE

AMY STEPPED into the well-lit Weddings That Wow's warehouse and watched Ben putting the gleaming, vintage 1930s Rolls-Royce to bed. The Holzworth wedding reception was in full swing and both of them were off the clock.

She couldn't believe how sexy he looked in the period chauffeur's uniform and the now-familiar rush filled her. There was definitely something about those brass buttons and a man in a hat.

"How you doing?" she asked.

He looked up with a smile. "Good."

She walked over to him. "Sure?"

"Yes." The word came out flatter than usual and with a definite edge.

She'd been surprised he'd agreed to work the wedding but when she'd questioned him earlier, he'd said Al needed a hand and he was helping out by driving the bridesmaids. Part of her had been secretly relieved that he'd agreed to do it. She hoped it meant he was getting over his own wedding experience. That he was moving beyond the legacy of Lexie. She could forgive the unknown woman her confusion about her sexuality, just not the way Ben had become collateral damage.

She thought about today's bride—the smiling Janey. Swathed in swirling organza with a train streaming out behind her, she'd looked radiant and blissfully happy as she'd stepped out of the church with her newly minted husband on her arm. When Amy had seen her, she'd got a hitch in her chest—a combination of happiness overlaid with pride and a slight disbelief that she'd created the beautiful gown.

"How do you think it all went?" she asked.

Ben pulled a rag out of his pocket and rubbed at a smudge on the hood. "She ran pretty smoothly but there's a knocking noise that needs checking out."

She elbowed him in the ribs. "I wasn't talking about the car. I meant the wedding gown."

His green eyes studied her. "Are you pleased with the way it turned out?"

"Thrilled."

"Then that's what matters." He moved away and polished the fender.

Disappointment slugged her.

Seriously, what did you expect him to say? Great stitching, Amy? Even if he hadn't been jilted at his own wedding, he's a straight guy so he's not going to notice the art of a wedding gown.

She hated that she'd wanted some approbation from him, especially given that her mother and sisters had been so complimentary and Janey and Melissa had been thrilled. She quickly changed the subject.

"I heard the bridesmaids doing some pretty outrageous flirting with you."

He grinned. "Too much champagne."

She stepped in close, wanting to take his mind off weddings and for that matter, bold and forward bridesmaids who'd looked stunning compared to her in her utilitarian black business suit. Battling the blush she felt rising, she said, "I think all the flirting might have something to do with this uniform."

He leaned against the car, taking her with him. "Is that so?"

She loved the gentle way he held her at the waist. Ben had only ever been caring and she trusted him implicitly. "Hmm, it may be. In fact, I might just have to live out my fantasy of the rich girl seducing the chauffeur."

"Now there's an idea." He grinned down at her. "After all, there's a lot of room in the back of the Rolls."

A thrill shot through her and she lost the battle to hold back the blush, feeling her cheeks blaze hot.

He laughed and kissed her tenderly. "You almost did it. Good job, though, on telling me your sexual fantasies. Next level is sexting."

Her mouth dried. "I don't think so."

He tilted his head. "It might be fun."

That's what Jonathon said. "I just graduated to fantasies, Ben. Don't rush me."

He raised his brows at the snappish tone in her voice and panic rippled through her. What if he pushed it? Asked her what was going on?

Thankfully, he wound one of her curls around his finger. "So back to this rich-girl fantasy. Does it start with her finding the chauffeur at the end of his shift?"

She slid his hat off his head and ran her fingers through his thick hair. "As the chauffeur, you're totally at my disposal."

"Yes, miss."

She undid the buttons and slid the jacket off his shoulders. "Open the door for me, Armytage."

He opened it with a flourish and then stood to attention, his knee-high boots shining under the lights. "As you wish."

Westley. Her heart sighed at the memory of *The Princess Bride,* a movie she and her sisters had watched over and over. Amy sat down on the car's wide sea and inhaled the scent of leather.

"Armytage, I need some assistance with my..." *What?* They didn't have seat belts in 1930s cars.

Ben poked his head inside the car. "With the driving rug, miss?"

Driving rug? "Ah, sure, if you say so, Armytage."

He sat down next to her and flicked a woolen rug over her knees. "You don't want to get cold, miss."

"Actually, Armytage, I'm feeling a trifle warm."

His eyes sparkled at her. "May I help you off with your jacket, miss?"

"Yes, please."

He eased it off and started undoing the buttons on her blouse one by one—kissing each bit of exposed skin before moving on to the next. She realized this was the first time he'd ever undressed her.

"Your arm, Armytage," she said, giggling at similarity of the words as she lay back on the seat. "It's um...much improved," she said, trying to stay in character.

"It's working quite well now, miss. Thank you for asking." He pushed her skirt up and pressed a kiss to her inner thigh.

She sighed. "You do that quite well, Armytage."

"I'm glad you think so, miss. I aim to please." He lowered himself over her and kissed her on the mouth just the way she liked it, before turning his attention to her breasts. And her belly. And her thighs.

Her body melted under the delicious onslaught and when she heard the rip of foil, she was hot, panting and oh so ready. He lowered himself over her. With his hands behind her thighs, he pulled her gently forward and entered her. Filling her. She gasped.

He tensed. "Is this okay?"

His caring wrapped around her. "Yes," she half said, half sobbed.

"You sure? You don't sound very certain."

But she was certain. Certain she loved the feel of him inside her, certain he was the most considerate lover she'd ever had and certain he was a good man.

Certain she loved him.

Her heart stuttered in her chest. Oh, God, she loved him.

How had that happened?

He cares.

And there it was. Outside of her father, Ben was the only other man who'd ever truly cared for her and protected her. And he'd done it right from the very start when he'd told the doctor that crazy story rather than the truth that she'd hit him.

"Amy, let's not test my shoulder too much, okay?"

His strained words broke into her thoughts, centering her. "Sorry."

She put her palm to his jaw, leaned up and kissed him hard and fast and then, wrapping her legs around him, she met him thrust for glorious thrust, letting the sensations build, each layer combining with her freshly discovered love for him in new and wondrous ways.

As he tipped her over the edge, she called out his name, engraving it on her heart.

Ella couldn't focus on anything. With the Holzworth wedding over, she should be using Sunday as a day of rest but she was jumpy and unsettled. There were plenty of things she could be doing, like oiling the screen door, but nothing held her attention. She didn't have a wedding cake to make for another week and earlier in the day she'd done a casserole and cream puff delivery to the town's shut-ins. She felt like company but the Sagars were busy with their family and anyway, they were about to leave town. She was missing Todd and Lisa already.

Sunshine streamed through the kitchen window, warming her through the glass, and she thought about how the sun had warmed her the day they'd all gone on the picnic. She thought about that day a lot. The leaves had fallen so fast in the breeze it had been like confetti and each dropped leaf reminded her that sunny days like these were numbered. Winter was nipping at their heels with frosty mornings and soon the first snow would hit and motorcycles would be garaged until spring. And spring came late this far north. The thought made her inexplicably sad.

Admit it. You want another ride.

She did, but she wasn't sure she wanted to see the *I told you so* look on Al's face. With a jerk of surprise, she realized that more than a week had gone by since he'd stopped by for a chat or to offer to fix something or hint that she might like to make him supper.

Her chest tightened. What if he was ill? She hadn't seen him yesterday either and Ben had been driving one of the wedding cars.

She gave herself a shake. If Al was sick someone would have told her. Heck, Al would have told her, wouldn't he?

Of course he would have. For gosh sakes, they'd been friends for years. Still, he'd been acting odd for weeks, badgering her to go for a ride on his bike and now that she had, he'd disappeared. *Men!* She pulled on her coat and stomped outside across the lawn and up the back steps of the Swenson house.

Al sat at his kitchen table, looking tan and relaxed. He had a sandwich on a plate on his left and a coffee on his right and he was reading the paper. "Ellie?" His forehead creased into two worry lines. "Everything okay, eh?"

"Of course everything's okay," she snapped, not liking the strength of relief filling her that Al looked so fit and well. Not that she wished him sick, mind.

"Good to know. Coffee?"

"I don't have time for coffee, Al," she said, trying to cover her reaction. "I was just checking you were okay."

"Why wouldn't I be okay?"

"Well, I haven't really seen you since the picnic."

"I gave you a wave yesterday at the wedding. Not my fault you didn't see." He grinned. "Don't tell me you missed me, Ellie?"

"Don't be ridiculous." She straightened his tablecloth. "I was just checking in, is all." *Liar!*

"Well, thank you but I'm not one of your shut-ins, Ella." He folded up the paper. "Lovely day, eh?"

"It is." She sighed. "Probably one of the last."

"Yep. Weather's going to close in soon enough. Perfect afternoon for a ride on the bike, eh?"

She didn't want to look too eager so she gave a huff. "What about the garage?"

"It's Sunday, Ella. If there's an emergency, they can call Ben. He's got one and a half functioning arms. He may not be a qualified mechanic but what he doesn't know about an engine isn't worth writing about. Figure I use him until he leaves town."

"I'll miss him when he leaves."

Al raised one brow. "You've always had a soft spot for the men under forty."

"Al Swenson, you say the darnedest things. That boy is younger than my Adam."

He folded the paper in half. "I was thinking of going for a ride out by Lakeview Farm. Luke wants me to look at one of his tractors."

"I did promise Erin a jar of my cranberry relish."

Al rubbed his beard. "If you go get it, I'll take it out there for you."

"And risk you breaking it?" She crossed her arms against the zip of excitement tumbling in her chest. "I don't think so."

He nodded slowly. "You're right. Looks like you'll just have to come along then, Ellie."

She smiled. "Looks like I will."

Just after lunch, Amy had told Ben that her entire extended family was going for a walk along the lake before starting their long drive back to Illinois. He'd decided not to join them, giving them some Sagar-only time, so he was surprised to find Todd sitting by the prow window in the great room with a baby monitor next to him.

Since Todd had followed him to the kitchen on the very first day, Ben had generally tried to avoid any alone time with him and he'd succeeded right up until now.

He was about to turn back when Todd glanced up.

"Ben."

He shoved his hands in his pockets. "G'day, Todd. I thought you were out walking with the others?"

"Aiden fell asleep so I offered to stay."

"Grandfather duty?" Ben took a seat and reached for a magazine.

"Once you're a father you're never off duty." Todd's gray eyes, so similar to Amy's, had a flinty edge. "So, Ben, what are your intentions with my daughter?"

"Intentions?" Ben hadn't been interrogated like this since he was fourteen and had let off rocket caps in the school quadrangle.

Todd sighed. "I know Amy's thirty-two but as much as I like you, Ben, you're not the sort of guy she usually dates."

He used what he'd learned. "How would you really know? Amy doesn't date much. In fact, I think I'm guy number three."

Surprise washed over Todd's face. "She told you that?"

"Yes."

"She's aiming for vice president of her department." Worry lines scored the bridge of his nose. "Did she tell you that too?"

Giving Todd the truth still felt like lying. "No."

"Her job's important to her. Always has been."

"Cut to the chase, Todd. What are you saying?"

He leaned forward. "Don't go suggesting she go traveling with you."

Relief rushed him. Despite it being the twenty-first century, he'd been thinking Todd was about to pressure him to marry Amy. "I never intended to ask her, Todd."

"Good." The emphatic answer shot around the room as he leaned back in his chair. "I'm glad that's settled. No hard feelings, Ben. It's just like you said, Amy hasn't dated much and, well, I'm not too old to remember the heady feeling of lust."

Todd ran his hands through his hair. "It can blind you to sensible decisions. We'd hate her to throw away everything she's worked so hard for."

Like you did? "Todd, if I was dating Cindy, Heidi or Sally, would we be having this conversation?"

Something flickered in his eyes. "Amy's special."

"Jeez, you're making her sound disabled."

"What I mean is, we've always worried more about her than her sisters. She's different, very different from them. She takes life far more seriously."

Just like you.

And that's when Ben saw it. While Amy's sisters were very similar to Lisa, Amy was like Todd. Whatever the story, somehow the serious guy had caught the eye of, and fallen for, the pretty cheerleader. As a result his life had changed irrevocably. In Todd's eyes, Ben was the cheerleader and although Amy wasn't a twenty-year-old, Todd was living part of his life vicariously through Amy. If Amy jumped on the bike and left town with Ben, Todd would be losing out for a second time.

Ben finally understood why Amy was avoiding telling Todd and Lisa that she'd lost her job. Not that he thought she should withhold the information, but now he saw the heavy weight of Todd's expectations. Part of Ben wanted to ask Amy to come traveling with him to spite Todd but he wasn't that dumb. He knew Amy wouldn't come and, as much as he loved this time with her, they both knew it had an end date. Still, this Amy-Todd dynamic wasn't healthy.

Ben lurched to his feet. "Amy doesn't like to disappoint people," he said obliquely, hoping Todd would take his point that Amy didn't want to disappoint him.

Todd nodded. "That's true. It's why she works so hard. You know she started a charity for sick children? She spent months convincing the company board it was an important corporate responsibility and now, the way they talk about it, you'd think it was their idea."

Ben didn't know she'd started a charity, but he wasn't surprised because Amy had a huge heart. He stuck out his hand. "It's been interesting, Todd. Have a safe trip back to Bloomington."

Todd shook his hand. "Thanks for the ride on Red."

To hell with being oblique. "Ask Amy about the V.P. position," Ben said. Then he walked out of the room before Todd could ask him why.

CHAPTER THIRTY

MELISSA SWUNG her feet up onto Scott's couch having arrived five minutes earlier. It was just past eight and Lily was in bed. "Hurry up. I'm sure you didn't invite me over on your night off to leave me here all on my own."

"Keep your pants on," Scott said from the kitchen.

She laughed. "I didn't imagine that was your plan."

Scott had texted her mid-afternoon, inviting her over, which had surprised her because apart from that one time after Lily's party, generally their alone time was spent at her house.

"Actually, my plans for you this evening are many and varied." He set down a beer sampler tray from the Udder Bar.

Surprise scudded through her. "You only want me for my well-defined beer taste buds?"

"You fishing for compliments?"

"Always."

"You already know you're good."

Smiling, he leaned down and kissed her and she was glad she was already sitting or her knees might have given way.

She'd expected that using Scott to scratch her itch for sex would have run its course by now, but it hadn't happened. If anything that need had grown stronger—he just had to kiss her and she wanted him, and she thought about him way too much between booty calls. The surprising thing was that when Lily was around and it was a no-touch zone, they still had plenty to talk about. The sex part had got all tangled up with an unexpected friendship, leaving her in a place she'd never found herself before—friends with a lover.

Not wanting to think too much about what that all meant, she studied the color of each beer and breathed in the aroma before sipping it. She closed her eyes as she drank, swishing each beer around her mouth and savoring the distinctive flavors. One tasted of cranberries and malt, another of pumpkin and cinnamon, and the third had a distinctive nutty caramel flavor.

She smiled. "Are you and Johan planning a holiday lineup of beers?"

"Yep. We're hoping the ladies will go wild for the sweeter taste. We thought they were ready but we wanted your take."

"I concur with the brewmaster. So that's the beer, what else?" she said before continuing to sip the cranberry brew.

"Yesterday was grandparents' day at school and Johan stood in for my dad." Scott sat next to her, his leg pressing gently against hers as he brought up a photo of Lily on his phone. The little girl was wearing the dress she'd bought her, clutching Johan's hand and was grinning widely at the camera. "Pretty cute, right?"

"Adorable." She smiled at him. "And go you. You managed ribbon bows."

He laughed. "And they lasted all of five minutes before they fell out but Lily paraded around the kindergarten room as if she owned it. The problem came at bedtime when she wanted to sleep in the dress. To distract her, I showed her that children's clothing catalog you gave me, and now she wants everything in it."

"Girl power." She laughed, wishing Lily was still up so she could high-five her. "A girl knows what a girl likes."

Scott gave her a look that was probably supposed to be critical but came over as indulgent. "Seeing as you've unleashed the fashionista in the five-year-old, can you choose her one dress, one cardigan and a coat and then I'll order them online."

"Sure, I can do that but..."

"But what?"

She hesitated for a moment, not sure how he'd respond to what she was about to say. "Can I choose the clothes with Lily? I can narrow down the field and let her pick from two or three. What do you think?"

He stared at her for a long moment then hauled her into his arms and kissed her like she was about to vanish.

She kissed him back, loving the feel of him against her, but also very aware they were in his house. Although they'd had sex here once, she was still worried that Lily might wake up. As his hand reached her bra strap, she broke the kiss.

His brows drew together. "Problem?"

"What if Lily wakes up?"

He nodded, his face filled with understanding. "I wanted to talk to you about that."

He nestled her between his legs, snuggling her back against his chest and entwining their legs along the length of the couch. He buried his face in her hair. "So this thing between you and me..."

Her breath caught for a moment and all she could hear was the thundering of her heart. Was he ending it? "What about it?"

"I want it to have a future."

The quietly spoken but unexpected words boomed in her ears like an explosion. She pushed up, turned around and faced him. "What did you say?"

His eyes glowed with love. "I want a future with you. You, me and Lily."

She couldn't move air in or out of her lungs. *No. No, no, no, no.* "Scott, I..."

"Shh," he put a finger to her lips, "let me finish. I know we agreed this was just sex and it's been amazing but getting to know you has been even better." He stroked her hair. "The thing is, after Margaret, I never thought I'd want to be with anyone ever again but I was wrong. These last few weeks with you have been the best times of my life and I want more of them. Lots more."

She stared at him, her blood surging through her veins and spreading panic all the way down to the smallest cells. A lump the size of Texas clogged her throat. "I...I don't know what to say."

Yes you do. Say no.

A slow, comprehending smile wove across his face. "We don't have to go fast. In fact, for Lily's sake, we should go slow but I wanted us both to be on the same page. Know this is something special and that we're moving forward together."

He kissed her gently. Reverently. "I love you."

Scott was having trouble reading Melissa's expression, which seemed frozen in an odd smile. Suddenly, her palms were pressing hard against his chest and she lurched to her feet.

"I'm sorry, Scott."

The entreaty in her voice told him he'd stunned her. Hell, he hadn't meant to do that. He rose and took her hands. "There's no need to be sorry. I know I took you by surprise and it's a lot to process."

"You did. It is." Her face had paled, and a tremor ran through her and directly into him. She pulled her hands away and hugged herself. "The thing is, Scott, you're not who I want."

The hit pierced him, slicing through the joy. He thought about everything they'd done together—the laughter, the caring—and couldn't make sense of her words.

"I don't understand," he said. "You can't deny these last few weeks have been more than just sex."

"That's true." Her voice vibrated with reluctance.

He rubbed his jaw as if that would help make sense of her words. "So what did they mean to you?"

"I don't know." She wrung her hands. "I mean, I do know. I really like you, Scott. You're a wonderful man and a great father. It's just..."

Lily? He couldn't believe he'd got it so wrong. "You're rejecting me because of Lily?"

"God, no." She shook her head so hard her hair flew everywhere, jarring the sleek bob.

"What then?"

She blew out a long breath. "I want to get married and have a family."

Relief parachuted in like storm troopers and he smiled. "I didn't want to freak you out by proposing today and maybe I didn't make myself clear but marriage and a family is exactly what I'm offering you."

An agonized look crossed her face. "But you're complicated. I don't want complicated."

Complicated? He didn't understand what she was talking about. He was just like any other guy with a kid, wanting the best for them and working hard to try and provide it.

"How the hell am I complicated?" Her face became pinched as if she was fighting something and she remained silent. "Melissa?"

"You're divorced. You have an ex-wife and a child."

He moved to reassure her. "I already told you, Margaret's unlikely to ever reappear in my life."

"Yes, but you don't know that." Her eyes took on a haunted hue. "One day she might wake up and regret having abandoned Lily and want to be part of her life again."

"That is never going to happen."

"But you can't guarantee that."

"I can't guarantee the world is going to be here tomorrow either but chances are it will be." He put his hands on her shoulders, desperate to convince her she had nothing to worry about.

"My feelings for Margaret died a very long time ago. Even if she did make contact again, and she won't, there isn't a single spark of affection in the ashes of our relationship that could be fanned. I promise you that. It's you I love. You."

She sucked in her lips and raised her gaze to him, her eyes filled with sorrow. "It's not just your ex, Scott. I've seen what happens to marriages when there's not a lot of money. How living in cramped conditions and counting every penny strain love, turning it bitter and hateful. I don't want to risk that."

He looked around at the small house he'd rented, which at the time had seemed fine for him and Lily, and saw it through Melissa's eyes.

"Of course we'll move into a bigger house," he said, going into fix-it mode. "I know it doesn't look like much now because I'm just starting up my music school but it will grow into a solid business and in the meantime, the bar work's regular. Besides, we'd be a two-income family so I'm sure we can find a house you like. What else?"

She closed her eyes and sucked in a deep breath.

His unease returned and immediately doubled.

When she opened her eyes, they were filled with pleading. A pleading to understand. "I want a baby, Scott. My baby. You can barely afford to care for yourself and Lily let alone take on another child."

The glancing blow his heart had taken when he'd thought she'd misunderstood him suddenly deepened into a gushing wound. "Wouldn't that be our baby?"

Her brow furrowed. "Do you really want another child? Would you risk having another child?"

Her words pummeled him as memories sucked him back to the moment the doctor had said, "Mr. Knapp, I'm afraid I have some difficult news," and all his dreams for his baby daughter had shattered.

"I don't know," he said.

"Exactly. You're complicated." Tears ran down her cheeks. "I'm thirty-four, Scott. I don't have time to waste and I can't afford to wait and see if you change your mind. It's not a risk I'm prepared to take."

The slow burn of hurt ignited into anger. "So you've been slumming it with me while you wait for a rich, single guy to walk into your Whitetail life?"

Her shoulders squared. "Please don't cheapen what we've got, Scott. We both agreed this was only supposed to be sex and I know it's far more than that to me too now. But I'm sorry. I really am, but I can't give you more than friendship."

Fuck friendship. He was beyond being calm, reasonable and adult.

"Tell me, Melissa. When Mr. Perfect finally does show up and falls in love with you, are you planning on slapping him with a DNA test?"

She winced and picked up her purse. "That's unfair."

He wrenched open the front door. "There's no such thing as perfect, Melissa, and you're going to die lonely if you think there is."

Melissa turned in the doorway and faced him. She hated that she'd hurt him but she refused to believe him. "You're wrong, Scott. Other people have it."

He shook his head. "You just think they do. You're looking at life like you look at clothes You mix and match so you're perfectly coordinated and color-coded. That's not real."

His words stung like the tail of a whip and she wanted to flee, but if felt like her insides were tearing. "I'll text you about Lily's clothes."

"Don't bother."

"Scott, please don't be like this. I still want to help."

His hazel eyes burned hot and angry. "Lily and I will deal with it on our own. Goodbye, Melissa."

The finality of his words made her fight back. "This is Whitetail. We're going to run into each other."

"I doubt that. Your perfect world is unlikely to intersect with my messy one."

The door slammed shut in her face.

CHAPTER THIRTY-ONE

"G'DAY, GORGEOUS."

A fizz of delight tingled through Amy at the sound of Ben's voice. She glanced up from the text message she was reading and smiled. He had a grease smear on his cheek, one on his long-sleeved T-shirt and his nails were rimmed with black. She laughed and jumped to her feet.

"I can see you had a good day." She kissed his cheek before rubbing it with her thumb. "You're filthy."

He laughed and kissed her neck, working his way up toward her ear. "Come and have a shower with me."

Sensations shimmered between her legs. Since her parents had left, three days earlier, she was reveling in having the house and Ben to herself. They'd made love in the fall sunshine, in the spa and on his canopied bed. Every day she fell in love with him just that little bit more.

"I'd love to," she said, " but I just told Melissa I'd stop by her store."

Frown lines marred his forehead. "It's past closing."

"I know, but she texted me wanting an opinion on a wedding gown."

"I thought the one you made was going to be it," he said with a trace of censure in his tone.

"It was. It is, but if she has a bride who needs an alteration, I can help with that."

Ben gave her a long and penetrating look. "So no news on the job hunt?"

Excitement and sadness tangoed inside her. "Actually, I've just heard. I have a job interview in Chicago next week."

"That's great news." He kissed her on the nose. "My arm's almost at full strength and you're heading back to work so it's good news all round."

Except I love you and we're going in opposite directions. "Why don't you get cleaned up and come meet me in Whitetail for supper."

"I can do that." He kissed her again. "We can celebrate your interview."

Her heart rolled at his support and yet it tore at the same time. She could see and hear how genuinely happy he was for her but part of her wanted to see a sign he was also a bit sad that their time together was fast coming to an end. She wanted to see some of the feelings constantly churning inside of her, mirrored in his eyes.

"Earth to Amy?" He laughed and waved his hand in front of her eyes. "I can see you're already imagining yourself in the job."

"Right," she said faintly. Only he was wrong. She wasn't imagining herself in the job at all and that was the problem.

When Melissa opened the door to Amy's insistent knock wearing a half-buttoned wedding gown, she knew she looked like the bride of Frankenstein. "Thanks for coming over so fast."

Amy stared at her. "You have rivers of mascara running down your face. What's happened?"

"Come in." She stood back while Amy crossed the threshold, then she locked the boutique's door behind her.

"Would you like me to do up the buttons on your gown?" Amy's expression was a mix of unease and concern.

She nodded. "Thanks, that would be great. Then I want you to put on a dress and keep me company."

"Sure." Amy didn't say anything until she'd finished doing up the long line of buttons that wound from the base of Melissa's spine to her neck. "I think I'll try on the ombré tulle. I love the color. It's not ivory but it's not quite apricot either and I could just drown in the fullness of the skirt."

Melissa unzipped the dress bag. "Good choice. I think it will really suit you. White's too stark for your complexion and drains the color from your face."

Amy stepped into the gown. "A bit like you today."

A bit like me for days. Melissa zipped the gown closed against Amy's back then picked up a bottle of champagne. With a wrench of desperation, she twisted at the cork.

"I think I better do that." Amy took the bottle out of her hands. "You don't want to risk spilling any on that amazing gown."

She was past caring about anything but she automatically nodded her thanks. A few moments later, she accepted the proffered glass of the sparkling, straw-colored liquid and took a long gulp.

"No toast today?" Amy asked.

She shook her head. "Scott proposed."

Amy blinked, her gray eyes round with surprise. "And I'm guessing you don't think that's a good thing?"

The lump that had taken up residence in her chest doubled in weight. "It's the worst possible thing that could have happened and now he hates me."

Amy's brow wrinkled in confusion. "So why are we wearing wedding gowns?"

Tears pricked at the backs of her eyes. "Because usually this cheers me up and I desperately need something to do that."

Amy fingered the glorious tulle in the skirt of her gown and her face filled with the wonder that usually enveloped Melissa. The wonder she'd been seeking for three days but it had utterly vanished.

"Is it working?" Amy asked.

"Not so much." She drained the rest of her glass, hoping the bubbles would take the alcohol quickly into her veins to numb the pain.

Amy set down her glass. "When did he propose?"

"A few days ago."

"And you had no clue?"

She smiled wryly at Amy's amazed tone. "Not even a hint. Things had been going great. We'd been having so much fun together and then he went and ruined everything by telling me he loves me." Her voice rose in a wail she couldn't stop. 'And then he proposed."

Amy got an odd look on her face—one that said a wedding proposal was something wonderful and special and then it collided with an expression that lacked comprehension. "Exactly how is Scott telling you he loves you, ruining things?"

"Because I want to be friends and he doesn't." She pulled at her hair, welcoming the discomfort. "I mean, we weren't even supposed to be friends. We agreed it was just about the sex."

This time Amy picked up her glass and drained it with an abrupt gulp. "So what changed?"

"I don't know." She'd been asking herself the same question over and over. "I guess we started talking and then he asked me for help with Lily's party. I met Lily and it just seemed so normal to be hanging out together, doing stuff. Lily's gorgeous and Scott's...Scott. He's calm and steady, which should be as boring as grass growing but somehow it isn't."

"It all sounds...great?" Amy asked uncertainly.

"It was." She picked at the Viennese lace of the gown thinking about the time they'd ridden the pumpkin train. "It was easy and I could be myself with him because there was no pressure."

Two deep lines appeared at the top of Amy's nose. "As opposed to...?"

She gave a long, shuddering sigh. "You know how stressful it is during those first few dates when you're trying to work out if the guy is *the one* or just a douche bag or married even."

"I know all about douche bags."

Something about Amy's tone made her look up and she caught her friend pursing her lips. "Sorry, Amy. Guys can be such pricks. If it helps any, I've had more than my fair share of them too. It's why I made a decision at New Year's to be very selective about who I dated but even then, the whole scene is exhausting. With Scott, there was none of that."

"Because you weren't dating?"

"Exactly."

Amy tilted her head, her curls bouncing and her gaze clear. "Remind me again why you didn't want to date him?"

Melissa took another sip of champagne and wondered how to explain it. "I watched my older sister get involved with a divorced guy. We were all worried about it but she was in love and convinced they could make it work. Neither of them had great jobs and the child support he paid for his kids from his first marriage left him and Ellen struggling financially, not to mention the emotional tornadoes his ex-wife caused every few months. When Ellen gave up work to have their baby things went from bad to worse.

"His past got all tangled up in their present and it ended up so ugly. Now she's raising her kid on her own and it's hard. Really hard. My parents help out and I do too but she's bitter and old before her time. I don't want that sort of struggle. I want what my parents have. I want a comfortable life and Ellen's taught me that sometimes love just isn't enough."

Amy sat up a bit straighter, suddenly looking very much like a lawyer. "But Scott has full custody of Lily, right?"

"He does." She sniffed, holding back tears. "He gave up his solo music career to raise Lily when her mother walked out on them."

Amy drummed her fingers as if it helped her think. "That means it's unlikely he's paying his ex-wife any alimony. You know, Melissa, he sounds like a really special guy."

"He is," she said softly, tears falling fast. "I know at first he seems really serious and quiet but he's not once you get to know him. He's got a dry sense of humor and he makes me laugh. Or he did. I keep going to tell him something funny that happened at work, or I see something I think Lily would like and I go to buy it and then I remember. It's over."

She gulped in a breath. "He ruined everything. I hate that I miss him so much. It's like I've got this big ol' empty hole inside of me and I hate him for putting it there."

Amy refilled their glasses and gave her a long, thoughtful stare. "Melissa, I don't have much experience with relationships, but I wonder if you've fallen in love with him."

"No," she said sharply as her heart rolled over. "That isn't possible. I know what I want in a man. I've known it ever since Ellen and Vince imploded and it's been reinforced by watching my sister living with the fallout of that disastrous marriage."

Amy's gray eyes filled with sympathy. "I can see why you'd make a list of ideal characteristics in a man but it's academic, not real. If there's one thing I've learned this past month, it's that life is messy and confusing."

My life is messy. "Which is exactly why I have my list." Her voice took on a slightly hysterical edge. "I don't want to start my married life with someone else's baggage that will make everything difficult."

"Do you mean Lily?"

Horror streaked through her. "No, I don't mean Lily. She's not baggage. She's a child with a disability."

Amy shrugged. "Some people would say that's a huge amount of baggage. All that therapy, the fact she may need support her whole life depending on how capable she becomes. It's pretty messy. And what about other children? Are you worried if you have a child with Scott it might be disabled?"

"Yes. No. I don't know. Doesn't everyone worry about that to a degree?" She rubbed her face with her palms, hating the whole situation. "I think he's worried about having another special-needs child because he wouldn't commit to having another child and for me, that's huge. I'm desperate to have a baby and I'm fast running out of time to have one."

Amy nailed her with a steely look. "How many guys have you ever met that fit your criteria?"

She dropped her gaze, not wanting to answer that question.

"Melissa, I need an answer."

Irritation flared. "Man, I forgot you were a lawyer."

Amy gave a wry smile. "So?"

She sipped her drink, letting the bubbles float on her tongue, wishing she could avoid the stark truth. "None."

"The problem with imaginary people is they behave exactly as we want them to," Amy said.

"There's no harm in having standards!" Annoyance that Amy wasn't siding with her collied with rising panic. Had she fallen truly and deeply in love with Scott? Is this why she was more miserable than she'd ever been in her life?

Amy's expression was neutral. "Let's look at the facts. On one hand you have a guy who's your friend and your lover, a guy who makes you laugh and is a giving and dedicated father, *and* he wants to spend his life with you. Yes, he's a bit short on cash right now but he's working in a family business, he's building his music school and, who knows, he might even be able to teach in the Whitetail school district one day. Plus, he is isn't paying alimony. Also, unlike your sister, you own your own business which is doing okay so financially it's a totally different ball game. Would you agree?"

"Yes but,—"

"No buts, Melissa." Amy's voice was firm as she picked up the ombré tulle and let it slide through her fingers. "On the other hand you have your yet-to-meet list guy, who's a bit like this dress—beautiful, worth a lot of money but untested on how it will survive what the day may throw at it. Like the permanent marker stain on Brianna's dress. It didn't even make it across the first hurdle. Who knows how the unknown guy will cope with what life might throw at both of you."

There's no such thing as perfect. Scott's words sounded loud and harsh in her head.

She thought about Scott. He'd given up so much for Lily, including his dream job, and yet he didn't seem bitter. He was calm and caring and had a sort of peace with his life. Something she didn't come close to experiencing. Did she have her priorities all tangled up? Was it wrong to want to start a relationship without the fear that the past would intrude?

"It's not that simple," she said.

"I know." Amy squeezed her hand. "But life isn't. My parents had a shotgun wedding and were married at eighteen and twenty. Statistically, it shouldn't have worked. They made it work. Sure, we never had a lot of money but we weren't dirt-poor either."

For weeks Melissa had been the happiest she could remember and for the past few days she'd been desperately sad. Was this love? Feeling like a part of her had been ripped out of her chest.

"I always thought falling in love was supposed to be a happy time." Tears cascaded and her chest heaved with great, hulking sobs. "Oh, Amy, I love him so much but what if he doesn't want to have a child? I think my heart will break."

"Go talk to him," Amy said simply.

And that scared her to death.

CHAPTER THIRTY-TWO

SCOTT'S PHONE buzzed with a text and his eyes shot open. The clock on his nightstand clock read 11:50. He'd been asleep for a total of twelve minutes. *Great.* Still, it was about eight minutes longer than he'd managed over the past few nights.

Fumbling for his glasses, he slid them up his nose and the text came into focus.

> **Melissa**
> Am outside. Can we talk?

It had been four days since he'd slammed the door shut in her face. Four long days of deafening silence that had stretched out between them like a desert after the oasis of weeks of daily talks and texts. When Margaret had left him, it had been a shock but in so many other ways it had been a relief. With Melissa, it was different. She'd pulverized his heart and he'd never felt more sad or lonely.

He hated that. He hated her for that. He was an idiot for having allowed himself to fall in love with her. He'd known what she was like from the first time he'd met her—self-absorbed and fixated on the superficial.

You wouldn't have fallen in love with her if she was really like that.

Shut up.

He heard a soft tapping on his window and then his phone beeped again.

Please, Scott.

Most of him wanted to ignore her request. He wasn't certain there was anything left to say when she'd made herself very clear on the many and varied reasons why he wasn't good enough for her. But the word *please* snagged him. The plea was out of character. Feeling that he was going to regret it, he replied.

Go to front door.

He swung his legs to the floor and padded out to greet her, begrudgingly acknowledging her thoughtfulness at not ringing the doorbell and waking Lily.

He pulled open the door and his jaw dropped. She stood on his mat, her pale face illuminated by the yellow porch light. Her normally sleek bob of hair was in disarray, mascara smudged the skin under her eyes and she looked uncharacteristically unkempt. But it was the perfectly fitted, incredibly intricate, lace wedding gown that stalled his breath in his chest. It fitted like a glove, highlighting her curves—curves he knew by heart and desperately missed.

You're pissed as hell, remember. "Did I miss the invitation to the costume party? What are you? The bride from hell?"

"Probably."

Her unexpected agreement took the wind out of him.

"I'm freezing," she said, sounding more like herself. "Can we talk inside?" Clutching a fistful of papers in one hand, she lifted the skirt of the dress and the train with the other and moved forward.

He stood back, allowing her to enter and as she brushed past him, the lace of the dress ran over his bare feet. For something that looked so beautiful, it was oddly scratchy and rough.

She stood in the center of the room, the material of the dress filling the small space, and she licked her lipstick-free lips as if now that she'd made it inside, she didn't quite know where to start.

"Why are you wearing that dress?" he said.

She dropped her gaze then lifted it to him, embarrassment shining in her eyes. "When I have a bad day, I have a habit of trying on wedding dresses."

He didn't quite know what to say to that. "I guess it's healthier than getting drunk."

"I don't think I can kid myself anymore that it is." She sat down abruptly and was immediately surrounded by a sea of lace. "You see, I'm addicted to this dress."

An aura of vulnerability circled her, calling to him and he quickly reminded himself that she'd rejected him, finding his offer of love and commitment lacking. Finding him lacking. He hardened his heart.

"I'm sure there's a twelve-step program somewhere for you, but I can't help," he said.

She swayed as if he'd hit her. "Scott, I want to explain."

"I think you did a pretty good job explaining when you were last here. I'm not good enough for you. I'd be the thrift-shop purchase in your designer life. I get it. You can leave now."

She lifted her chin with the determined jerk he knew well and then sucked in a breath. "No, thank you."

He sighed wearily. "It's not a choice, Melissa."

She didn't move to stand. Instead she pushed at the lank strands of hair that stuck to her cheek. "It's an allegory."

Don't engage. But he opened his mouth anyway. "What is?"

"The dress." Her empty hand fingered the intricate lace. "I bought it in January as the talisman for my year. I figured that if I had the dress, then I'd meet the guy I'd marry."

Incredulity dumped on him. "Life isn't a fairy tale, Melissa."

She opened her palms in her lap as if she was accepting the criticism. "I know it sounds idiotic and it is. Plus me explaining it to you will probably make it sound even more stupid but I'm thirty-four, Scott and I've got a body clock ticking as loud as a jet engine. On New Year's Day, I decided this would be the year I would silence that roar and replace it with the gurgles and cries of a baby. I just didn't realize that along the way I'd be so focused on what I wanted that I'd lose perspective and, worse than that, throw away the best thing that's ever happened to me."

Hope soared but his protective instincts tempered it. Sitting down on the coffee table, he faced her and tried to read her. "What are you saying?"

"I love you, Scott."

The words—both welcomed and feared—hang between them. More than anything, he wanted to trust her. He ached to, but self-preservation held him back.

"Really? It's not easy to believe you after everything you said."

She bit her lip and heartache filled her face. "I know and I'm so, so sorry. Sorry for what I said and sorry for being so blind and so utterly idiotic. You were right. I had this idea of what I wanted for my life I was blind to what was in front of me. You're so different from any guy I've ever been with that everything snuck up on me. I...I didn't recognize that my feelings for you were—are love."

His heart hammered hard and fast. He was desperate to believe her but he needed to know more. He leaned forward, his knees and feet tangling in the lace. "So what's changed? How do you know it's love?"

Her bluer-than-blue eyes filled with tears. "These last four days have been awful. The most miserable I've ever been and I've missed you and Lily so much it hurts."

"Thank God." He picked up her hand and kissed it, feeling like he'd been raced to the top of the tower ride and filled with elation.

She tugged her hand away, fisting it in her lap.

The ride dropped him fast and wariness pressed in on him like lead weights. "What?"

Silent tears rolled down her cheeks. "Loving you both scares me rigid."

A long sigh shuddered out of him. "You're scared of being Lily's mom?"

"No." She shook her head violently and grabbed his hands. "It's not Lily. Please hear me on this. I love her and I know we'll probably have some heartbreak along the way as we get her to adulthood and beyond, but that doesn't scare me."

He saw her love for him and for Lily in her eyes and his bewilderment tangoed with frustration. "So what scares you? Tell me, because it can't be worse than what I'm already imagining."

"I love you, Scott, and I know I almost lost you by obsessing about things being perfect. That was dumb and I can compromise on a lot of things but I can't compromise on a baby." Her voice cracked. "I want us to have a child together. I want Lily to have the joy and frustration of a sibling. We love each other but that's the easy bit, right?"

The reality of her words dripped fear through him and he rubbed his face with his hands before raising his gaze again to hers. "I've been on my own for so long that until the other day I'd never given any thought to having another child. I love Lily but I'd be lying if I said I'd be happy to have another special-needs child."

Understanding flowed from her and she pressed the papers she'd been holding against his lap. "I know it freaks you out and part of it freaked me out too, so I've done some research."

Surprise slugged him. "Research?"

"Yes. Knowledge is power," she said quietly as she rifled through the pages. "Listen to this." She commenced reading. "'Most cases of Down syndrome are not inherited and the chromosomal abnormality occurs as a random event. The abnormality usually occurs in egg cells and very occasionally in sperm.'"

She looked up. "In other words, if you were having another child with Margaret the risk of having another child with Down syndrome would be a lot higher. With us, the risk's not as high, although the longer we wait, the higher it rises, but it's relatively flat until I turn thirty-seven."

His mouth dried as he forced himself to say, "And if the baby did have Down syndrome?"

"We'd be unlucky but we'd cope." She slid her hand along his cheek. "I think we should talk to a doctor so we have all the facts."

"And what if..." He ran his hand through his hair. "What if I was the 'very occasionally' reason Lily is how she is? You're still willing to take that chance and have a baby with me?"

She smiled wanly. "Someone I respect and love once told me that life isn't perfect. There's a risk attached to everything, Scott, and I don't see this as a big risk. If we're unlucky, we'll deal with it together. I'm not like Margaret. I want this baby. I ache for it."

She reached out her hand. "I want you, Lily and our baby in my life. Will you take a risk on imperfect me and marry me?"

We'll deal with it together. I'm not like Margaret.

And he knew to his core that she wasn't anything like his ex-wife. He'd known that within a couple of weeks of meeting her. She wanted to take this life journey with him and Lily and their yet-to-be-born children. A journey with pitfalls and imperfections, and a whole lot of love. If she was brave enough to try then he'd be a fool to walk away.

He gazed at her—all smudged makeup and disheveled hair—surrounded by yards and yards of lace and she'd never looked so beautiful. Tears pricked the backs of his eyes.

"I couldn't think of anything more wonderful," he said.

Melissa let go of the breath she'd been holding as equal parts relief and joy bowled into her, making her dizzy. She'd been on tenterhooks for so long, completely uncertain of his reaction to the baby idea and her proposal. She still couldn't quite believe her ears. Despite everything, despite her foolishness, he wanted her. He wanted to take a leap of faith and have a child with her. Share Lily with her. She'd never felt so loved in her life.

Needing to touch him, to reassure herself this was all real, she flung herself into his arms, her tears dampening his shoulders. "I thought you'd say no."

He cupped her face in his palms and his gaze overflowed with love. "How could I say no to a bride?"

"No bride should ever look like this." She wiped her face with a tissue. "I'm a complete mess."

"You're a beautiful mess." He kissed her, infusing her with his love and hope for a future neither of them could predict.

A future they'd deal with together. A future she couldn't wait to start.

As his mouth roved over hers, his hands traversed her back and then her front before settling on her waist. "This dress is a fortress. How the hell do I get to you?"

She laughed. "There are forty-five buttons and a corset to undo."

"Seriously? And this was your perfect dress?" He found the hem.

"Well, I can see now that it might have a design fault."

His hands lifted the skirt and his head disappeared as lace cascaded over her head.

His hands touched her thighs and his muffled voice said, "I think I've found a shortcut."

"Can't breathe." She hit him on the back while trying to claw at the lace so she could get some air. "The *Bugle* headline will be, Groom Suffocates Bride with Dress."

He reappeared with a grin on his face. "Can't have that."

He swung her into his arms and carried her to his bedroom. As he carefully undid each button, he whispered all the things he was going to do to her and when the dress finally fell in a puddle of lace at her feet, she was a puddle of need.

She pulled him down onto the bed, wrapping her legs around him and tilting her hips, reveling in the way he filled her body. When her orgasm hit she knew he filled her heart, her mind and her soul. She might have been slow to know the joy of the love of an amazing man, but it had been well worth the wait.

CHAPTER THIRTY-THREE

AMY HAD FILLED a yellow legal pad with as much information as she'd been able to find on Stokes and Bent, the company that was interviewing her the following week. It wasn't a Fortune 500 but it had a growing reputation as being innovative and, as none of the other twenty-six companies had offered her an interview, she was taking this one. She needed this job.

Her phone beeped and she laughed at a photo Cindy had sent her, taken when they'd been playing Twister. Ben, who'd been keeping his right arm out of the action, had still managed to bend backward and balance himself over Heidi to win the game.

> **Cindy**
> Men who play Twister with our family are worth keeping. Ignore Daddy who thinks no guy is ever good enough. Besides, Ben's hot!
> C x

Amy sighed. She knew Ben was worth keeping but how did she keep a guy who didn't want to be kept? She had no clue but ever since the night she'd spent with Melissa, she'd considered telling Ben she loved him. Only every time she got close to telling him, a nagging voice said, *what's the point?* She had this new job and he had—What did he have? More solo traveling? For a guy who sought solitude he certainly wasn't a loner. He was far more at ease in social situations than she was.

Getting no joy from this line of thinking, she tried to come up with a list of possible interview questions the panel might ask. She felt so out of practice. The past few years, she'd been the one doing the interviewing and this felt like starting over. Her phone beeped again.

> **Melissa**
> If the law doesn't work out, consider relationship counseling. THANK YOU! Engagement drinks at the Udder Bar tonight. Hope you can come. Melissa & Scott xx

Happiness for her friend filled her along with the fact she'd played a part in it. She hadn't felt this buzzed since she'd presented a family with an electric wheelchair on behalf of the Kids Plus Foundation. She tried returning to possible interview questions but she couldn't concentrate so she printed off some information to read later.

As the printer hummed, spitting out pages, Amy gazed out the window. Ben was working on Red as he did—a lot. When she'd asked him how often an engine needed to be tinkered with, he'd shot her an incredulous look that said she had no clue what she was talking about.

"Stick to the law, Amy," he'd said.

Well, she hoped she was. God, she wanted this interview to go well. She so needed this job.

Amy watched Ben straddle the bike, his strong legs firmly planted on either side of it, and then he gripped Red's handles.

She held her breath.

He flicked his wrist, kicked down and the throbbing and thunderous sound of the engine broke the stillness of the morning with an explosive roar.

She flinched, telling herself it was concern for his untested shoulder but it was the sound of the bike. There was no turning back. Things were really changing.

Of course they're changing. This time here isn't real life.

He turned and she caught his wide grin. Happiness radiated off him and although he looked as deliciously handsome as ever, there was something else. She realized with a sob that he looked carefree. He was looking forward to his next adventure. Mustering up a smile from somewhere around her ankles, she raised her hand in a stationary wave.

He gave her a thumbs-up with his right hand and then Red was moving forward and Ben was positioning his feet and riding away.

You have two days left.

Her phone beeped again twice in quick succession. She read the first message.

> **Mom**
> Enjoy last day of vacation and tell Ben safe travels. Luv Mom & Dad x

She was sure her parents genuinely wished Ben well. But she also knew this was a check-in text to confirm that she was returning to Chicago.

There wasn't a second message and she realized the other beep must have been an email coming in. She saw it was from the personnel department of Stokes and Bent, most likely containing instructions for accessing the parking garage on Monday.

Dear Ms. Sagar,
Unfortunately, due to a situation beyond our control, we are no longer able to interview you on Monday. The previously advertised position is now under review and at this stage, no interviews will be conducted. We apologize for any inconvenience and wish you every success in the future.
Doris van Loon
Stokes and Bent

A hot flush crawled over Amy's skin and she immediately reread the email thinking she must have scanned it too quickly—that she must have missed the invitation to be interviewed at another time. She forced herself to reread it more slowly but by the time she reached Doris's name, she'd arrived at the same conclusion. The email had a finality to it that couldn't be misconstrued. There was no interview on Monday or at any other time.

Don't panic. She huffed out a breath, trying to slow her breathing that kept hitching in her chest. After four weeks of seeking work, this had been the first interview she'd been able to get and now it was canceled. With her vacation time exhausted, she was officially unemployed.

She ripped the pages of research off the legal pad and violently scrunched them into a ball. Staring at the blank yellow page, she knew she had to rethink her strategy. Widen her search.

Her brain froze, refusing to cough up a single idea.

She pushed back from the desk and walked to the kitchen, her mind spinning with a thousand incomplete thoughts and an overwhelming need to do something. To make something. To have something tangible to show for her actions instead of the nothing she had after hours and hours of futile job seeking. Her gaze fell on the box of vegetables that Keith and Lindsay had sent over for them.

She'd make soup. Ben loved rich, thick vegetable soup. She grabbed an onion and started dicing.

After twenty minutes of frenzied chopping and dicing, she now had all the ingredients for minestrone soup bubbling on the stove. Finally, the calm she'd been seeking descended, stealing through her and reminding her that everything was going to be fine. It would all work out. After lunch with Ben, she'd draw up another list and contact some of the companies she'd ruled out earlier, having considered them too small for the career path she and her dad had always talked about.

You go, girl.

Only her enthusiasm for the task wasn't what it should be. She'd rather be outside watching Ben. Hiking with Ben. Watching a movie with Ben. Making love to Ben.

Loving Ben.

Oh, why had she allowed herself to fall in love? She was seriously hopeless in the relationship stakes. The only solace she could take this time was that at least her taste in men was improving. Ben was caring, kind and honest—the complete opposite to Jonathon in every way. But even thought she'd managed to get that right, it was moot. Her life was in Chicago and Ben's was wherever the road took him.

Her phone sounded again and she picked it up hoping it was another funny photo from one of her sisters—she could do with a laugh. But it wasn't Cindy, Heidi or Sally.

The number on the screen was like a sucker punch to the gut and with trembling fingers, she opened the text.

> Got an interesting call from Stokes and Bent.
> Sadly I couldn't find a way to recommend
> you. Give up trying to work in Chicago. Time
> for a new career? Jonathon

The phone tumbled from numb fingers and a cold sweat broke over her skin. How the hell had Stokes and Bent come to speak with Jonathon? His name wasn't anywhere on her résumé and her list of references didn't include him.

No interviews will be conducted. The words of the Stokes and Bent email peppered her like buckshot.

She gagged knowing exactly what Jonathon had told them. Her career was officially finished.

Ben knew he was grinning like a fool but he'd just ridden Red three miles down the road and back without feeling a single twinge from his shoulder. The relief was exhilarating because the days were shortening fast and he needed to get out of Wisconsin before the weather locked him in. Al had offered him a job over the winter but Ben wasn't eager to stay. The idea of Whitetail without Amy wasn't appealing.

In forty-eight hours she'd be driving to Chicago, which was why he'd done the test ride today. He wanted to take her and Red on a farewell ride tomorrow and then he'd pack his saddlebags, kiss her goodbye and ride out of town. He still had a lot of the country to explore and he planned to winter in the southern states and island hop in the Caribbean. Beyond that, he had no clue.

He made his way into the house to wash up and was surprised to find Amy in the kitchen surrounded by the heady aroma of garlic and onions. He breathed in deeply and then lifted the lid on the simmering pot. Something shifted in his chest.

"You made me minestrone?"

She laughed. "I made us minestrone. Who knew it's as easy as ratatouille?"

He kissed her on the cheek. "Thank you, but I thought I was on cooking duty because you're on a fact-finding mission for your interview."

She dropped her gaze for a moment. "The facts were all running into each other so I took a break." Her fingers started climbing up his chest. "And talking about breaks, the soup isn't going to be ready for half an hour so..."

"So?" he said, being deliberately obtuse because he loved seeing her blush.

The pink started on her décolletage and rose up her neck and along her cheeks. "So I was thinking we could..." She swallowed.

He laughed good-naturedly at her struggle. "See, this is why you should sext. You'd find it much easier typing out this stuff."

"My phone's dead," there was an almost hysterical edge to her voice, "and we're wasting time."

She had a point and he didn't care if she sexted him or not. "We've never done it in the kitchen."

"Tell me what's sexy about cold granite?"

He laughed. "It might be fun to find out."

"I want a bed, Ben."

Something about the quiet way she insisted on a bed rammed it home that this was one of the last times they'd be having sex. "Good idea." He grabbed her hand, took her upstairs and peeled her naked.

As her arms and legs wrapped around him and he buried himself inside her, he used thrust after delicious thrust to block the faint voice in his head saying, *you'll miss her.*

When his orgasm rocked him, thankfully the only sound he could hear was his ragged breathing.

He rolled away quickly so as not to flatten her and he brought her with him, enjoying the way she fitted in against his side and how her hair tickled his nose.

"Thank you." He pressed a kiss into her hair. "And here I was thinking that riding Red was going to be the highlight of my day."

"And there's still soup to come." Her laugh sounded strained and then she pressed a kiss to his chest.

His fingers tangled in her curls. "I want to take you on a ride tomorrow. I thought we could do the trip your folks did with Ella and Al. It sounded pretty."

"I'd love it." She raised her head. "Actually, I've been thinking maybe I could tag along with you and Red for a bit."

His barely settled post-sex heart rate jumped as her words sent adrenaline surging into his system. It was the last thing he'd expected her to say and he struggled to construct a response that didn't sound like, *hell no.*

"What about your job interview? You've been so excited about it?"

She stared at her fingers splayed against his chest. "The more research I've done the less I think this job is really me. Besides," she smiled brightly, "I've never been on a road trip, let alone on a bike so why not?"

So many reasons why not.

Although Amy had always shown an interest in his journey, he'd got the impression she really couldn't fathom how anyone would walk away from a good job and just travel. So why was she asking to tag along? He was used to her uncertainty about a lot of things in her life, but never her work. Then again, being laid off screwed with self-confidence.

"It sounds to me like you've got the interview jitters."

Her large gray eyes swirled with shadows. "I guess you're right."

"Of course I'm right." He kissed her on the nose, unsure which of them he was trying to reassure the most. "Have faith in yourself. Stokes and Bent are going to love you so much they'll hire you on the spot."

She gave a tight laugh, sat up and pulled on her sweats and polo shirt. "I better go check the soup and put the bread rolls in the oven."

His heart rate kicked back slightly at the return to the normal topic of lunch. That and he'd just dodged a bullet. "I'll be down in a bit."

"Sure."

As she left, he simultaneously threw back the covers and heard a beeping and vibrating noise that sounded just like Amy's phone. "Amy!" he called out but she didn't reply or return. The phone kept buzzing and he turned toward the source of the sound to see the phone moving across the nightstand and edging perilously close to the edge.

He threw himself across the bed and caught the phone just before it fell. He couldn't help but notice the text was from one of her sisters.

> **Cindy**
> Another Ben photo for your collection. His butt is super cute in this one

He grinned. There was a photo collection? Justifying that as the photo involved him, he could look at it, he scrolled across the touch screen. Sure enough, there was a photo of him bending over to pick up a rock that had caught his eye on one of the walks with the Sagars.

He laughed at the memory of Cindy telling him soon after he'd shoved the rock in his backpack that the view was worth the walk. Her comment had confused him at the time because they were standing close to a rather sickly-looking pine tree.

As he closed the screen, he wondered what other photos the sisters were sharing about him and that's when he saw the name: Jonathon Wiseman.

Jonathon. The guy her family had expected her to be with. The guy Amy refused to talk about and yet there was a text from him dated today.

A flash of jealousy ripped into him with an intensity he'd never known and he immediately opened the text and read it.

It wasn't at all what he'd expected.

CHAPTER THIRTY-FOUR

IDIOT! Amy jerkily put the hot cookie sheet on a trivet, making the bread rolls bounce. She was furious with herself for giving in to a moment of post-sex weakness and asking Ben if she could join him on his trip. What had possessed her to do that? The question had just blurted out of her unbidden, sparked by the amazing feeling of resting her head on his chest, hearing and feeling the solid beat of his heart, and loving him so much that it hurt.

She'd caught the shock clear and stark on his face. Part of her understood but most of her had wanted him to hold her tightly and say, "Travel with me for the rest of my life."

Yeah, like that's going to happen. Not in a million lifetimes was he going to say that and all she'd done was expose her vulnerability. Tell him she didn't want him to leave without her.

She heard his footsteps on the kitchen floor and turned. He must have jumped in the shower because his hair was damp and tendrils kicked up at his nape as the strands dried. He smelled of soap, liniment and laundry powder and she wanted to bury her face in his chest, breathe him in and bank his scent. Bank it for the long days and nights ahead. Her heart tumbled in her chest at the thought of only one more day with him.

"Soup?" She plunged the ladle into the big pot.

"Sounds good." He grabbed silverware from the drawer, butter from the fridge and placed them on the table before sitting.

She set the soup on the table, placed the bread rolls in a basket, grabbed some napkins and joined him.

He broke open a crusty bread roll, the steam rising in a curl. "So I've been thinking about what you said and sure, why not? If you want to come along as I head south on Red, knock yourself out."

Her spoon clattered into her soup, splashing some drops onto her shirt as the sweet feeling of joy exploded inside her. "You're serious?"

His expression seemed guarded and he leaned forward, his green eyes riveted to her face. "Tell me why you suddenly want to come."

I'm not tied down by a job. "I think all your travel stories have finally convinced me that I need to do some exploring of my own."

"Is that right?" He tugged his hand away from hers and dug into his pocket. The next moment her phone was spinning toward her across the table.

She glanced at it, then at his stony face and rigid body and she didn't understand what was going on. "Yes."

"It's a pretty convenient time for you to suddenly realize you need a road trip," he said harshly.

A cold dread trickled through her. "What do you mean convenient?"

His arms folded hard across his chest and his mouth flattened into a grim, hard line. "You don't have a job interview on Monday, do you?"

Fear tightened her throat, blocking all words from reaching her lips and then a defensive anger burst out of her borne out of incredulousness. "You read my messages?"

"Oh yeah, you go right ahead and make me look like the bad guy here when you're the one who's been lying to me from day one."

The derision in his voice sent her heart thundering into overdrive and she could barely hear let alone think. "I haven't been lying to you."

The pain of betrayal slashed his face and she knew he didn't believe her.

"Oh, I forgot that in your lawyer world you've only been withholding the truth." His words spat at her, viscous and acidic, burning her with his hurt. "Where I come from, Amy, that's lying. Fuck, and I thought you were different."

Her heart tore at the hardness in his eyes and the uncompromising set of his shoulders, and she barely recognized him as the man she loved. He was staring at her as if she was dog shit on a sidewalk and to be avoided at all costs.

She pushed away her bowl, her stomach threatening to immediately eject anything that was put into it, and she forced herself to look at him. To say the words she'd been too afraid to say out loud because it made them real.

"The truth is that I made an error in judgment and now I'm being sort of blackmailed."

"Blackmailed?" He sounded skeptical but then he fisted both hands. "By that dickhead Jonathon you dated?"

She nodded, unable to put her voice to the word *yes*.

Ben's fingers uncurled and he lifted his hand as if he was going to touch her but instead, he dropped it back by his side. "He's taking your money?"

"No." *God, this was so hard.* She swallowed against the lump in her throat. "He took my job and now he's making sure I don't get hired anywhere in Chicago or with companies associated with M.M. Enterprises."

A muscle in his cheek twitched. "How's he managing that?"

She rose and walked over to the window, standing with her back to him. She didn't want to look at him when she told him the tawdry story. Didn't want to see pity on his face or for him to see her shame.

"He has some emails and texts from me that are..." she sucked in a fortifying breath, "...sexual in nature."

"So that's why you won't sext?" He sounded bemused and she felt his breath on her neck. "Stop worrying. Every couple sexts, Amy. They're hardly blackmail worthy."

She wanted to believe him. She wanted to turn and rest her head on his shoulder but she had to tell him the full story. The only way to do that was to stay separate from him. Crossing her arms over her chest to steady herself she said, "Jonathon was my junior at M.M. and I was his mentor. I was in a position of power over him in the office."

For a moment, the only sound in the kitchen was the solid and relentless ticking of the clock. The noise mocked her and she wanted to run. Run fast and run far, far away from the whole sordid mess.

"He's accusing *you* of sexual harassment?" Ben barked out a short, sharp half laugh of incredulity. "That's insane, Amy. You're not capable of sexually harassing anyone. Where does this prick live? I might need to visit him."

The lawyer in her was horrified at the idea of such violence but the woman was overwhelmed by his support. "That's kind of you to say but you don't need an assault charge brought against you. If I've learned anything it's that Jonathon's as cunning as a fox. He's been holding those texts over me like a ticking bomb. I didn't think he'd ever go so far as to use them but he's obviously told Stokes and Bent something because they canceled my interview."

She kept her gaze fixed on the rippling water of the lake, hoping that if she told the story fast and without stopping, it might not hurt as much. "What I hate the most is my stupidity. From the moment I met him I only ever saw him as a colleague. I recognized in him the same drive to succeed that I had. Only I missed the memo that he'd do anything to get promoted, including getting rid of me so it could happen."

She struggled to get the words out. "And he did it so expertly, starting with the accidental one-night stand a year after we'd been working together. We'd worked seventeen hours straight in a hotel room in Denver trying to avert a major contract crisis. I was punch-drunk with exhaustion and high from having saved the day and we ended up in bed. Afterward, he agreed with me that it was probably a mistake and it should never happen again. Looking back, that agreement was all part of his plan to slowly maneuver me into a compromised position. A month later he pushed for more. He said he'd been wrong putting work ahead of us and as long as we were careful, he couldn't see a problem. After all, we were adults and our private life was just that and didn't I agree?"

She finally turned to face him and bit her lip. "I liked him and I was flattered. There haven't been a lot of men in my life who've actively pursued me and it totally screwed with my brain. It made me monumentally stupid."

Ben wound one of her curls around his finger. "There isn't a person out there who doesn't warm to a bit of flattery, Amy. He sounds like a conniving, manipulative bastard. They're clever sons of bitches and I'm guessing he suggested the sexting?"

"He said things were a bit boring and we should spice them up a bit."

"No one wants to be accused of being boring." Ben's eyes filled with genuine empathy. "But I don't get it. If he hasn't publicly accused you of sexual harassment, how did he get your job?"

She shuddered. "I missed a hugely important meeting in Ohio, which didn't go down well, and he went in my place, passing off my work as his own. I thought I'd caught a stomach bug but it turns out he deliberately put something into the surprise supper he cooked me the night before to make me sick."

"Jesus, Amy." Ben slammed a fist into his palm, his anger making her jump. "I've heard of workplace sabotage but this..." his eyes had a dazed look in them, "...this is out of control. You need to go to the police."

She shook her head so fast she saw spots. "There's no point. I can't prove the dinner he cooked me was poisoned and if I go to the police he'll go public on the sexual harassment. That not only means I cannot work as a lawyer, I'll lose any chance of starting another charity."

Tears stung the backs of her eyes. "That idea's worse than not working in the law."

"Shit. What a bloody mess." He wrapped one arm around her and stroked her hair with the other. "No wonder you've been acting crazy every now and then with all this going on."

She breathed in the scent that was Ben and laid her head on his shoulder, feeling for the first time since the phone call with Jonathon that everything was going to work out. As hard as it had been telling Ben, it was like a weight had been lifted off her shoulders. The news was out there and he hadn't judged her. If anything, the vitriol in his voice whenever he mentioned Jonathon made her feel protected. The strength of his arms around her made her feel safe.

Loved.

The thought took hold. "I'm so sorry, Ben. I should have told you earlier but it's not something I'm proud of."

He stroked her hair soothingly and pressed a kiss onto her forehead as if to say, *it's okay. I get it.*

She thought about these past few weeks—how he made her laugh, his generosity of spirit, and his gentle and supportive care. Of how much she loved him. Resting against him, feeling sheltered and secure in his arms, she felt the rickety protective fence she'd built around her heart fall over. She'd never been very brave when it came to men but this time, knowing that she'd found a wonderful man, a man who was her quiet champion, she didn't want to let him go. She loved him and she didn't want to live without him.

Raising her head, she lost herself in the rain-forest-green of his eyes. "I love you, Ben Armytage. I want to be with you wherever you are."

His eyes widened into dark disks and his body jerked violently as if he'd just taken a high-voltage hit. His arms fell away. "No. You don't."

A tremble started in her toes and quickly spread through her. "No, I don't what? Love you or want to come south with you?"

"Both." He rubbed the back of his neck. "Right now, you think running away with me is easier than facing that bastard and fighting for your job."

She shook off his words. "Spending time with the person I love isn't running."

He gave her a withering look. "It is if it prevents you from doing what you're good at. From what you've told me, you've spent years working hard to get to that position and your dad told me how you started that kids' charity. You wouldn't have done any of it if you didn't love the work. If it wasn't important to you."

Did she love it? She loved the sense of purpose it gave her when there'd been no one to share her life with. She'd needed the recognition and pride that her parents took in her achievements because at least she'd made their sacrifices worth something and she'd loved the Kids Plus Foundation. And now she loved Ben. "Yes, but—"

"Then you have to fight for it. Your job is the *one* part of your life where you're confident. Are you going to let that prick steal that from you? Hell, you worked there for five years and the people who respect you will know that you wouldn't have threatened this guy in any way."

His reassuring words weren't enough to stop panic skittering again along her veins. "People are easily swayed. The moment those texts go public, they'll create a tsunami of titillation that will swamp the truth. I'll be left looking either desperate or predatory and no one anywhere will want to hire me. And my parents—"

Her voice broke at the thought of them finding out. "If I fight this, Ben, I lose."

His brows rose as if she was being overly dramatic. "Lose what exactly? You've got nothing now because you've rolled over and played the part of the weak woman he thinks you are. You're allowing that douche bag to control where you can work and you're letting him push you out of your career path."

The icy edges of his words burned her. She didn't need him telling her she had nothing—she'd been living with the fear for weeks. She'd expected him to understand, to appreciate her dilemma, but he stood there like an implacable and disapproving force. Her heart raced.

"I've got nothing?" she said incredulously. "That's pretty good coming from someone who's been running for a year."

"I've been traveling for nine months," he ground out, his voice low, "not running. I'm taking time to sort things out."

"Is that what you call it?" She couldn't stop the puff of irony in her voice. "I don't see a lot of sorting out, Ben, but I do see someone who's putting his life on hold."

"You don't have the right to call me on my life when yours is a bloody shambles."

His eyes blasted her with such fury that she took a step back. "Oh, right, so you can dish out advice but I can't."

His nostrils flared. "Not when you want to use me in the exact same way as Lexie."

His words stung like an open-palm slap. "I'm not using you." She tried holding her voice steady but it sounded like a plea. "I love you."

He shook his head, every part of him rejecting her. "I don't want you to love me."

He may as well have plunged a knife into her heart and turned it ninety degrees. "Love doesn't work that way, Ben."

"How does it work then, Amy?" A sardonic look twisted his handsome face. "Lexie vowed she loved me. Hell, she wanted to marry me so I suppose I should be grateful you haven't suggested that."

His vitriol rained down on her unprotected heart. How could he not see the stark differences? "I'm not Lexie."

"You're hiding from your problems just like she did. Lexie pursued me, convinced herself she loved me because if she did, and if she stood up in front of one hundred and fifty people and married me, then surely she wasn't a desperately unhappy and confused woman struggling with her sexuality. But it was only ever going to end in disaster. Instead of facing up to her reality she tried to hide behind me. I'm finding it really hard to forgive her for putting me into the middle of the chaos of her life."

His resolute gaze bored into her. "I let one woman bring me down with her problems and I'm never letting that happen again."

Amy swallowed. Was she using him to hide? *No.*

May be just a little bit. The idea of going back to M.M. and demanding her job back had fear coalescing in her belly. No one at the office knew how insecure she was about her life outside of work. Fighting Jonathon would bring all that to light.

Your job is the one area in your life where you're confident. Are you going to let that prick steal that from you?

If she had the support of the man she loved, had him by her side, it might not be as bad as she imagined. "If I go back to Chicago and fight this, will you come with me for moral support?"

He shook his head. "I don't think that's a good idea."

His pragmatic rejection of her sucked the air from her lungs, leaving her cramping and empty. Desolate. She'd thought he cared for her. *You're hopeless, Amy. You get it wrong every time.*

Anger burst into flames, leaping in her veins and scorching her. At that moment she hated him.

"So you want me to go back to Chicago and sacrifice myself, my career and my reputation, risk hurting my family and do it all on my own to prove that I really do love you?"

"No." His face filled with a mixture of sympathy and regret. "You have to do it so you can live with yourself. You have to start loving yourself, Amy I'm not looking for love. Yours or anyone else's."

Her heart shuddered, immobilized for the briefest moment by grief. Grief for them both. "Are you not looking for love, Ben, or are you running scared from it?"

His face twisted with regret. "I really like you, Amy, and I know you like me but what we have together isn't love. I'm sorry I've hurt you but you can't take refuge in me."

She shook her head, her curls bouncing wildly. "It is love, but you don't want to acknowledge it because it terrifies you too much. I'm sorry Lexie hurt you, Ben, but I'm sorrier still that you think closing yourself off to love is going to protect you from ever being hurt again."

He ran his hand abruptly through his hair. "That's bullshit."

"You wish it was."

His face blanched but his eyes smoldered with anger. "And you're in such a stable emotional place to make a judgment call like that. This wasn't how I wanted us to end, Amy. We were supposed to have a great day out on Red tomorrow and part as friends but you've totally stuffed that."

She sucked in a breath, hauling it from a place deep down in her soul as her knees threatened to buckle. Her hands gripped the counter. "I'm sorry for ruining your plans. I guess I could have withheld the truth and not told you that I love you but I know how much you hate that."

He flinched. "I'm sorry, Amy. I truly am."

Her mouth dried and she tried swallowing around the lump obstructing her throat. It felt like she was experiencing everything in slow motion—Ben moving forward and closing the gap between them, the brief touch of his lips on her cheek and his agonizingly slow walk toward the door and out of her life.

The man she loved would very soon straddle his bike and, with a thunderous roar, ride away from her taking a piece of her heart with him. Her legs collapsed out from under her and she slid down the kitchen wall as racking sobs consumed her.

CHAPTER THIRTY-FIVE

ELLA HEARD the familiar rumble of a motorcycle but she knew instantly it wasn't Al's chopper. First off, it wasn't loud enough and second, Al had driven his car to Minneapolis and the bike was in the garage covered in a soft cloth until spring. This motorcycle engine lacked the distinct thunder of a Harley and she sighed, sad that it wasn't Ben's bike, Red, either. She and Al had waved goodbye to him a few weeks earlier and she knew Al missed his company.

The throbbing sound ceased. Intrigued, she set down her cake-decorating bag with a clatter and reached for her coat. Pulling it over her apron, she hurried outside and stopped short.

"Al, what is that?"

He was standing in front of an enormous metallic-blue-and-chrome motorbike with a pillion seat that looked like an armchair rather than the tiny box on the chopper. He grinned. "This, Ella, is a luxury touring bike. She's beautiful, eh?"

She was used to Al waxing lyrical about machine, but she ran her hand along the soft leather. "Whose is it?"

"Mine."

"Yours?"

"Yup." He stroked the sleek bodywork reverently.

Ella got a ridiculous zap of jealously and immediately crossed her arms. "What's wrong with the chopper?"

"Nothing at all. But as you so often point out, Ella, I'm not thirty anymore and a man needs his comforts when he's on a road trip."

She was still trying to shift the shock of feeling jealous of a machine when the next wave of surprise hit her. "What road trip?"

Al pulled at his beard. "Got a postcard from Ben last week. He's in New Orleans eating gumbo and something called beignets. Got me thinking that there's something wrong when an Australian's seen more of this wonderful country than I have."

"You do realize the first snow is predicted for Friday? You'll slide into the first drift and break your leg or worse," she said sharply, her anxiety rising fast that he was about to depart. "I'm telling you, I'm not spending my winter looking after you."

He smiled at her. "Relax, Ella. I might be looking for adventure, but I'm not stupid. No, this road trip's gonna take some planning. Where do you think I should go first?"

"I'm sure I don't know." She pulled her coat tightly around her, feeling jumpy, out of sorts and upset that she'd missed him.

"Aw come on, Ella, don't be like that." Disappointment hovered around him. "Where would you go if you had the chance?"

She thought about the places Ron had always talked about them visiting when he got better, even though at the time they'd both known he was dying. "I want to see Old Faithful."

"Yellowstone National Park, eh?" Al tugged at his beard. "If you went there, you'd have to visit the Grand Tetons."

She visualized the maps Ron had pored over as a distraction from his death sentence. "And see the bison in Custer State Park."

"There're a lot of long, straight roads across those prairies for sure." Al's hand caressed the armrest of the pillion seat and he winked at her. "Just as well I got you the world's most comfortable seat. It's even heated for those cold spring mornings."

Shock made her gasp. "You expect me to come along with you on this crazy road trip?"

His gaze, so often teasing, suddenly took on a serious look. "Not expecting, no. Hoping, yes."

His quiet words made her heart jump. "Why?"

"Why do I want you to come along?" He picked up her hand. "I think we'd enjoy it."

His warmth trickled through her just like it had every time they'd ridden together on the chopper. It scared and excited her but she didn't want to love or need a man in her life again. Not now in her sixties when health was a lottery. She pulled away. "We'd argue over directions."

He grinned and pointed to the GPS. "Got that excuse covered."

She huffed out a breath. "We can't just abandon Whitetail. What about the garage and wedding season?"

Al's large shoulders rose and fell. "My nephew in St. Cloud's eager to come run the business and Carol's going to bring the grandkiddies up and vacation. She'll keep an eye on things, eh?"

Thankfully, her brain finally threw up a cast-iron excuse as to why she couldn't go. "That's all well and good for you, but who's going to make the wedding cakes, hmm? I'm needed here for that."

He raised his gray brows. "If you really want to come on this trip, Ella, you'll find someone no problem. It's why I'm giving you six months' notice."

His reasonable answers didn't reassure her. "And if you get sick while we're away, what then?"

He frowned at her. "I haven't had more than a cold in four years. Besides, that's what insurance is for. If *you* get real sick, it would get us and the bike home."

"I'm not going to get sick," she said indignantly. "My mother lived until she was ninety."

"Oh, right, so you've got me in wooden box already but you're gonna be fine."

"No," she whispered. "I'll be the one taking care of you."

"Oh, Ellie." He sighed, understanding filling his face. "You've had a tough few years, especially the last one with Ron."

"He was my husband and I loved him, and I wouldn't have had it any other way, but I don't want to do it again."

He nodded. "I'm not expecting you to give up your freedom, Ella. All I'm wanting is for us to have some well-earned fun and adventure while we're both fit and healthy. It seems a shame to waste our prime, eh?"

"Our prime?" She laughed but then she remembered how alive she'd felt riding the chopper with him.

This was a chance to do something she'd never done before. She was sixty-five years old with a possible thirty years of life left and Al was offering her the chance to have fun. It felt wicked and wild and wonderful. "Where would we sleep?"

"All sorts of places." His eyes sparkled. "Under the stars, in Airbnbs and cabins, but preferably together."

She tilted her head. "Are you suggesting we live in sin, Al Swenson?"

He grinned at her. "We're bikers, Ellie. We're going to grow old disgracefully and spend our children's inheritance."

"The kids are going to be embarrassed that their parents are gallivanting around the country on this beautiful machine."

"Nah, they'll be jealous." He put his arms around her, his pale blue eyes caressing her with their tender gaze. "I couldn't think of anyone I'd rather be spending time with than you."

A zip of need shot through her and she marveled at the fact her body might be sixty-five but inside she was still that bright-eyed eighteen-year-old with an eye for a handsome man. As Al lowered his head to kiss her, she rose on her tiptoes and met his lips with hers.

He kissed her slowly and thoroughly and she reveled in every moment of it. When he lifted his head, his expression was sober. "Of course, I'll happily make an honest woman of you, Ellie, if that's what you want."

"Don't you dare," she said, laughing. "I've been respectable and responsible for years. This time's for us." And she kissed him again.

Amy sneezed as she tied off the thread on the wedding gown she was supposedly altering. It had been so badly made in the first place, she was virtually making it from scratch. She felt sorry for the young bride whose dreams of a feathery gown like the one worn by Sleeping Beauty had arrived from China looking more like a half-plucked chicken.

Melissa stuck her head into the workroom behind the store. "I've brought coffee."

"Thanks. I've got feathers clogging my nose and mouth."

Amy had moved out of the lake house and into Melissa's spare room because she couldn't stand staying at the Rasmussens' on her own. Every room reminded her of Ben so on the night he'd left, she'd slept in the carriage house only to be reminded of her parents. She'd accepted Melissa's offer the next day. She had a tiny window of time to pull herself together before her mom was on the phone, expecting her to be back in Chicago. A tiny window of time to work out what she was going to do with the rest of her life.

Melissa sipped her latte. "Are you sure you want to go back to boring and stuffy law when you can stay in Whitetail and create glorious gowns that make people happy?"

Amy blew a feather out of her hair, not sure about anything. When Melissa had arrived at the lake house to find her sobbing, she'd known Ben had broken her heart, but Amy hadn't told her the Jonathon part of the story. She didn't plan on telling her or anyone else for that matter. She may have been naive once but she was no longer. No man was ever going to use her again.

Ben didn't use you.

Her heart throbbed with the pain of rejection.

You have to love yourself. The painful irony of his words whipped her. Telling him she loved him had been her first step in that journey and look how that turned out.

On and off, she played with the idea of staying in Whitetail. It was true that she got a great deal of satisfaction from sewing, and working with brides wasn't fraught with the nightmares of the corporate world.

"It's tempting, Melissa, but I'd be living on air for a while."

"When you give up your Chicago apartment you'll save a fortune. Rents are pretty low here."

"That's true." There wasn't much point having an apartment in Chicago when she couldn't work there.

"Besides, I need you to make my wedding gown."

Amy's hands stilled on the fabric in her lap. "I thought you had one all picked out?"

Melissa smiled a secretive smile. "That was a gown for a make-believe wedding. Now I need one for a real wedding."

Amy didn't really understand but she smiled anyway. "In that case, I better stay."

"Stay and make my gown or stay and join Weddings That Wow?"

Make people happy. Her life was far from that but if she was able to make brides happy then surely that would rub off onto her. After all, there wasn't anything wrong in exchanging a high-powered career for a quieter one. There were books and magazine articles about people doing that sort of thing all the time.

"I'm going to join Weddings That Wow," she said, hearing the emphatic words and totally surprising herself.

"Yes!" Melissa high-fived her. "That's so neat."

Was it? At least it was a decision and an attempt to start the rest of her life. A mild buzz of excitement rippled through her at Melissa's enthusiasm and she tried to harness it. "I guess it is."

"Of course it is," Melissa said firmly. "I'll go get the wedding diary so you can mark down the dates of our next Meet the Bride sessions and then we have to tell Nicole. Oh, Amy, I'm so excited. This is going to be so great."

As she left the workroom, Amy returned to her feather stitching, happy that she'd made a decision.

You're hiding from your life, Ben's accented voice accused her loudly.

"If I am then so are you, buddy," she said to the empty room.

As Ben's voice faded and she plunged the needle into the material, she heard her father's voice. *It's just a vacation thing, right?*

She was going to have to tell her parents about her change of career. As hard as that would be, at least it didn't involve a scandal that would have their neighbors and work colleagues sniggering behind their backs that the Sagars' talented daughter, whose successes they'd had to hear about for years, had spectacularly failed. She could save her parents that hurt and find a way to live with their disappointment in her.

Her phone rang and her heart jumped. *Ben.*

Irrational hope poured through her and she picked up the phone, only to be plunged into despair when his name didn't appear on the display. She hated how this happened every time her phone rang or a text buzzed in because, in her heart and soul, she knew that he was gone. Gone and never coming back. She just wished her body would catch on.

She didn't recognize the number but she took the call anyway. "Amy Sagar."

"Miz Sagar?" a female voice came down the line. "It's Hannah Bryant, Jasmine's mama."

It took Amy a moment to remember the mother of the little girl with cerebral palsy. "Hannah. How lovely to hear from you. How's Jasmine enjoying the new electric wheelchair?"

"That's the thing, Miz Sagar. She don't got it."

Three days before Amy lost her job, she'd approved the Bryants' application to the Kids Plus Foundation for the wheelchair. It should have been delivered by now. She bit her lip. "I'm so sorry to hear that, Hannah. You may have heard that I'm no longer working at M.M.

Enterprises and Mr.—" she could barely say his name, "—Wiseman has taken over the running of Kids Plus. Have you spoken to him?"

A long sigh shuddered down the phone—one borne of the constant toll of having to fight by inches for her child. "I got a letter saying there's no wheelchair coming and he don't return my calls. Without that wheelchair, Jasmine can't go to school."

Amy had met with the Bryants twice; heck, she'd even gone with Hannah and Jasmine to the wheelchair fitting and supervised the placement of the order. They'd had a celebratory coffee afterward. What the hell was Jonathon up to?

And then it hit her. Fury like she'd never known sizzled in her veins so hot and hard she thought she'd burst into flames. It was one thing to screw her over, but it was another entirely to disadvantage a family just because of their association with her.

Your job is the one area in your life where you're confident.

Oh, God, Ben was right. For weeks she'd been feeling sorry for herself, ashamed, timid and scared, and that's what Jonathon was depending on. He'd attacked her weak spot, expecting her to slink away and she'd done exactly that. But attacking someone she cared about? Someone who needed her to fight for them, well, *that* was a tactical error.

"Hannah, I'll be back in Chicago tomorrow and I'll fix this," Amy said.

Jonathon Wiseman wouldn't know what hit him.

But first she had to tell her parents and warn them of the nastiness that was about to engulf her and, by default, them.

CHAPTER THIRTY-SIX

BEN WAS IN KEY WEST, Florida, and discovering that even though he was only ninety-four miles from Cuba it may as well have been a million. His vague plans of taking Red to the island country had hit a massive brick wall of bureaucracy. It didn't matter that he was Australian—he and Red weren't going to get to Cuba by boat from here.

He'd had glorious sunshine and blue skies on his ride along the Overseas Highway and the impressive seven-mile bridge, and he'd taken a moment to salute the engineers. The Keys, with their turquoise green seas, white, sandy beaches, swaying coconut palms and coral reefs, reminded him of Queensland. After diving off Islamorada, he'd found himself wanting to tell Amy all about the Great Barrier Reef. It wasn't the first time he'd automatically gone to tell her something only to realize that wasn't possible.

You could call her.

But there was no point. She wanted more than he could give and he was done being anyone's crutch.

Just like Queensland, the Keys had the colorful and laid-back lifestyle that comes with a warm climate. There were no early morning frosts or snow down here. Just vacationers out for a good time and, had he wished for it, he wasn't short on bikini-clad women for company. As it was, he'd taken to reading a book on the beach so he wasn't constantly making polite chitchat with women who clearly wanted more than conversation.

He wasn't interested in any of the beautiful women with golden tans and straight up and down bodies who presented themselves to him like models on display. They had a fake perfection compared to Amy's real body of creamy skin and lush, toned curves. Thinking about Amy made him ache and feel restless all at the same time. He missed the sex.

You did without sex for months. You miss Amy.

"I don't," he said out loud, his voice carrying on the sea breeze.

"Dude, chill," a passing Rastafarian said with solemnity.

Shit. He was losing it. Ben left the beach and decided to video-call his parents. Talking to them would bump him out of this odd mood. Dad would tell him about his latest modification to his four-wheel drive and his mum would fill him in on the news of his brothers as well as going off on entertaining tangents, pause, then ask him what she'd been talking about.

Toward the end of the call, his parents made quiet murmurings about the length of time he'd been away.

"Mate, they're advertising for engineers for the M1 widening. It'd make a change from mining," his father said.

"I'll think about it." The words surprised Ben but despite the spectacular scenery, the lure of the road wasn't as appealing as it had been before he'd got stuck in Whitetail.

"Darling, soak up Key West," his mother encouraged. "All that literary history."

They blew him kisses and signed off but the lift in his mood hadn't come. He felt edgy and disconnected and it had been a long time since he'd felt that way. Had the road trip done its job? Was it time to go home? He thought about Australia, picturing Melbourne, but even before he'd come on this trip, he hadn't lived there for a long time and it didn't feel like home.

His mind slid to the lake house and he hauled it away fast. No way was that home.

He took his mother's advice and visited Hemingway's house. He saw the famous typewriter, the six-toed cats, shook his head at the idea of four wives—how much drama had the man wanted in his life?—and then he bought his mother a book of poems. He walked into the gardens, planning to stay awhile but a wedding was taking place and that was his cue to leave.

He rode to Fort Zachary Taylor to glimpse where the Atlantic met the Gulf of Mexico and to catch the sunset. He parked Red and wandered down to the beach. *Bloody hell.* A wedding party was having their photos taken with the setting sun behind them. Key West was worse than Whitetail for weddings and happy couples. He stomped back to Red, his thoughts full of Amy.

Amy.

It stopped him cold. Not Lexie but Amy. He shook his head at the irony. Weddings still made him break out in a cold sweat but for a different reason. He'd ridden two thousand miles from Whitetail but Amy was still making him mad. Why was she letting that asshole railroad her life? Hell, if the sabotage had happened to him, he would have fought the bastard both physically and legally. At least Amy had something to fight for.

When Lexie had come out, he couldn't fight because there was nothing to fight for. All he'd been left with was the shattered illusion of a relationship he'd thought he'd understood, only to discover that all of it was fake. He hated that. He'd have given anything to have had something to fight for. To feel justified. To feel less used.

And then Amy, who he'd thought he understood, had tried to use him too. Did he have a fucking tattoo on his forehead that read, Sucker?

Not wanting to let his mind go there, he rode back to a bar that hugged the Atlantic. Its kitchen not only served up grouper, snapper and swordfish hooked that morning, but the joint had spectacular views and sea breezes. He reminded himself he was in paradise, not a war zone, and he should be a hell of a lot happier.

He took his beer to a table by the window and watched the sky's fingers of orange and red vanish, taking the last of the daylight with them. The game on the big-screen TV came to an end and then the news started.

"Sex, texts and missing charity funds have rocked a Chicago Fortune 500 company," the female newsreader said.

The glass in Ben's hand stalled halfway to his lips as the footage showed a group of suits surrounding a short man with thinning hair before cutting away to a woman walking on her own. A woman with distinctive red curls blowing wildly in the Chicago wind was trying to make her way through a media crush to a taxi.

Amy.

Good for you. His heart pumped harder and he raised his glass to her in salute. He really hadn't expected her to fight back, but it looked like she'd actually listened to him and she was taking control of her life. He truly hoped the process would prove to her that she didn't love him or need him.

"It's lawyers representing lawyers," the newsreader continued, "as two former employees of M.M. Enterprises slug it out with accusations of sexual harassment and theft."

Theft? Amy hadn't mentioned anything about theft.

A reporter stuck her microphone into Amy's face. "Do you regret sending those texts?"

Amy's chin tilted up. "I regret that Jasmine Bryant's suffering and that the Kids Plus Foundation, which I started, has been compromised. That's the important issue here. Disability may not be as exciting to report on but don't let yourself be sidetracked by the smoke screen of sexting and office affairs."

Before the reporter could ask another question, Amy got into the cab and closed the door.

The camera swung back to the group of suits. Ben would stake his life that the short guy was the sleazy bastard Jonathon. Why did he have so many lawyers around him while Amy was on her own? Did the guilty need a show of strength?

Will you come with me for moral support?

The memory of her face after he'd said *no* to her, pierced him. *Shit.* He drained his glass quickly. Where were her former colleagues?

People are easily swayed, Ben.

Why weren't her parents there with her?

Because, you dickhead, she's protecting them from the publicity.

Guilt rammed him hard. Amy really was on her own.

An overwhelming need to protect her slugged him. He should have gone with her. She'd asked him to so why hadn't he?

Because she freaked you out by telling you she loved you.

He'd allowed fear to make him act like a dickhead. He'd let kind, generous yet insecure Amy, who didn't value herself enough to ask people for anything, face this mess on her own. He'd thrown her to the piranhas because he'd thought she wanted to use him. Because he was too damn scared to believe her when she said she loved him.

I love you.

Those three little words were so easy to say. They'd fallen so freely from Lexie's lips. She'd said them to him over and over as if saying them would convince her they were true. And he knew on one level they had been true. He just wished he'd known about the other stuff.

Amy's nothing like Lexie.

Lexie, despite her confusion, hadn't had any problems asking for what she wanted or making demands on him. Amy didn't have any of Lexie's relationship confidence. Sure, she'd gained some in their time together but she still had trouble asking for what she wanted.

I love you.

He choked on his breath.

She'd have known when she said those words that the chances of him rejecting her were high and yet she'd still done it. She'd been brave and he'd virtually called her a coward. Amy had taken a huge emotional risk and he'd been so wrapped up in his own fears that he hadn't believed her.

He'd allowed his own issues to get tangled up in the current chaos of her life.

The chaos of my life. The lonely, miserable, screwed-up mess that was his life and the dispirited restlessness that had become its spine.

You were happy in Whitetail.

And how had that happened? He'd been stuck in a wedding town with an injured shoulder and unable to ride Red.

He thought about how he'd enjoyed tinkering in Al's garage and spending time with Al and Ella, his doppelgänger parents. He'd loved the lake and the hiking.

With Amy.

Cooking in the fabulous kitchen.

With Amy.

The sex with Amy. Happy? He thumbed his nose at the irritating voice in his head.

Making love to Amy. Talking to Amy. Laughing with Amy. Caring for Amy. Arguing with Amy. Being frustrated by Amy.

He wanted to put his hands over his ears.

Loving Amy.

Every cell in his body froze and he tried desperately to argue the thought. He didn't love her. He liked her but that wasn't love.

She's in your thoughts all of the time. You miss her like you'd miss a limb.

He loved her. He truly loved her. "Fuck."

"You okay, man?" asked the aging hippy at the next table.

"I'm an idiot."

He nodded slowly. "Happens to us all, bro. Job, money or women?"

"Women. One in particular."

He held up a shot glass. "I find tequila helps."

And yesterday Ben might have convinced himself that tequila would help too. Hell, an hour ago even, but not now.

His general unhappiness, his restlessness and his discontent had stopped in Whitetail. It had started again the moment he'd left. Amy was the common denominator—beautiful, generous, contrary, confused, complicated Amy.

And dickhead that he was, he hadn't realized he'd fallen in love with her. He'd taken her freely-given, no-strings love then thrown it back in her face with gratuitous advice—so easy to give rather than to take—then abandoned her to cope alone with the biggest personal crisis of her life.

She had every right to hate his guts. He knew he did.

He had no clue how he was going to win her back, or convince her that he truly loved her. Given everything that had been said, he didn't know how he could persuade her he was even worth taking a risk on, but one thing he knew for sure. This time he had something worth fighting for and by God, he was going to fight.

CHAPTER THIRTY-SEVEN

AMY SPREAD out napkins and unpacked the Chinese takeout boxes onto her apartment's coffee table, before shoving serving spoons into them and pouring wine. "Thanks for being here."

Her parents both gave her quiet smiles and accepted the proffered wineglasses. They'd been stoically supportive of her from the moment she'd called them from Whitetail. They'd met her in Chicago and had made sure she didn't watch the news or read the newspapers. While they'd done their best to shield her from difficult people, not once had they asked her why she'd allowed herself to get into such a predicament.

"Thank goodness it's over," Todd said with a pained expression as he served himself some pot stickers. "This has to have been the worst week of your life."

Amy thought about the afternoon three weeks earlier when Ben had left her. She wanted to say, *I've had worse* but instead she said, "It's up there for sure."

They ate in silence because what was left to say? Jonathon had fought dirty just as she'd expected and even though she'd found the evidence that would convict him of theft from Kids Plus, she hadn't avoided the spray of mud. And she hadn't expected to. She'd been foolishly naive and now her colleagues, her parents, their friends, the community she'd grown up in and anyone watching the news knew it.

Just like children never wanted to think about their parents having sex, she was certain parents didn't want to imagine their adult children's sex life, and hers had been "Live at Five." Even if the sex with Jonathon had been amazing—and it had been so far removed from that it wasn't worth thinking about—it would never have been worth it if it meant her family would be faced with the details.

As for Ben, her parents seemed to have assumed that they'd parted as planned or maybe they hadn't, but with everything else going on, Todd and Lisa had never asked. Amy could understand that. Why put your hand up to be told more stuff you didn't want to know?

Her mother put down her empty plate, nudging it onto the crowded coffee table. "Amy, we've been worried about you for weeks. Why didn't you tell us the moment you lost your job?"

Tell your parents. How many times had Ben said that? She swallowed her dumpling. "I couldn't."

"But why?" Hurt and confusion filled her mother's face. "It's not like Daddy and I haven't ever made mistakes."

Tears pricked the backs of her eyes. "Yes, but as I was your big mistake I've pretty much spent my life trying not to make any."

Lisa's eyes widened in shock. "Amy Sagar, you are not one of our mistakes."

She sighed. "Come on, Mom. You and Daddy didn't exactly plan me, and getting pregnant with me changed your lives. And don't try and deny it," she said as her mother opened her mouth. "You never started college and Daddy had to give it up. If you told me once you told me a hundred times between fourteen and twenty not to get pregnant but to get an education."

Lisa looked stricken. "I've loved being a mom but we just wanted you and your sisters to have an easier life. It's easier to study before you have children."

Todd picked up Lisa's hand. "Perhaps we overcompensated. Amy, we love you and we just wanted the best for our smart girl."

And there was the problem. She sucked in her lips to try to hold back her tears. "I know you did...do. Cindy was pretty, Heidi was pretty and athletic, Sally was pretty and devilish, and I was smart."

"And pretty," Todd said firmly. "All of my daughters are pretty."

You're beautiful, Amy.

She shook away Ben's voice. He might think she was beautiful but he couldn't love her. "I loved being the smart one. When I brought home a report card full of As and you put it up on the fridge I wanted it to stay there. Somehow me getting the good grades got tangled up with me not letting you down. When I went to college, that continued and I studied the law and then I got the good job. I did everything you and Daddy weren't able to do and then I lost it."

Bewilderment scudded across Todd's face. "Are you saying you didn't want to be a lawyer?"

She shook her head. "No, I did, I do, but if I'm honest, I did it a little bit more for you than for me."

"Oh, Amy." A tear slid down Lisa's cheek. "Your dad and I have loved you from the moment the doctor laid you in our arms. I'm so sorry that our hopes and dreams for you have been a burden."

"No, Mom, it's not a burden," she said, tears splashing onto her hand. "I loved that you wanted me to succeed, it's just—"

"It's my fault." Todd swallowed hard. "I've loved watching you flourish, getting the career one part of me always wished I had. I loved talking to you about your plans to become V.P., only now I see they weren't just your plans, were they?"

He picked up her hand. "When I was in Whitetail, Ben told me that you didn't like to disappoint people and I agreed with him, thinking about how hard you worked. Now I think he was trying to tell me something."

Ben. Her heart quivered. He understood her but he didn't love her.

"But Amy," Todd continued, his eyes moist, "I love you and you've never disappointed me."

"Not even this week?" she asked weakly, feeling battered and bruised from the fallout.

"Especially not this week." He kissed the back of her hand. "You held your head high, uncovered a crime and won back your job."

"We love you, darling. We just want you to be happy," Lisa said, lines of anxiety bracketing her mouth.

Happy. Amy wasn't sure how that was possible when a piece of her heart was missing. Ben had accused her of hiding and as much as it hurt her to admit it, she now realized that part of her had been hiding all her life. Not from work—she was the smart, educated woman there. But the rest of her life. She'd been the geeky, bookish, timid girl who'd never been prepared to show her real self out of fear of disappointing and being rejected. The one time she'd risked it, she'd been rejected anyway.

These past few weeks she'd learned that she owed it to herself to step out into the light and create her own version of happiness. It started with being true to herself for the very first time.

She sucked in a deep breath. "Mom, Dad, in the spirit of painful honesty, I need to tell you something about my job..."

Ben flew from Florida to Chicago, not wanting to risk the weather closing in on him and Red in the hilly country of Kentucky and stranding him there. Now, as the street lamps came on, he'd arrived in the unfamiliar city and it was like having changed countries. Snow was falling lightly as he stood outside Amy's apartment building at the end of a tree-lined street in Old Town. From the outside, it looked like it had started life as a warehouse. Given the trendy-looking restaurants housed in beautifully restored Victorian buildings that he'd passed in the cab to get here, he got the impression he was in a district of upwardly mobile professionals. He thought of Amy's black business suit, which had been so out of place in Whitetail but would fit in perfectly here. He'd just stepped into her world. He hoped she'd welcome him in.

Back in the bar in Key West, when he realized he loved her, all he'd wanted to do was call her but he'd worried she'd hang up on him. Decision made, he'd booked a ticket to Chicago but he didn't know where she lived and her name didn't show up in the directory. He hadn't wanted to ring M.M. Enterprises and he'd doubted they'd give him that sort of information anyway. Fortunately, he'd managed to find Cindy's number and had called her. Unlike Lisa and Todd, he'd got the impression that Cindy approved of him and at this point he needed all the brownie points he could get. Cindy had given him Amy's address.

So now he stood clutching a bunch of cut flowers he'd bought from a florist down the street who'd charged him half the national debt of a third-world country. Blowing out a breath, he pressed the doorbell under Amy's name. It buzzed loudly.

Be home, be home, be home.

Static sounded followed by, "Hello?"

His heart leaped at the sound of her voice. "Amy, it's Ben." The crackle of the intercom deafened him but she didn't speak. "Can I come up?"

"I want to say no." Her voice sounded unusually firm.

"It's snowing."

"Welcome to Chicago."

Only she didn't sound welcoming at all. "Would you leave an Aussie out in the snow?" he quipped against his rising panic. "There might be snow leopards or the North American cousin of drop bears."

"I hope they're hungry."

"Please, Amy."

There was a long pause, followed by a sigh. "Top floor, apartment six."

The door started clicking and he pushed it open. He took the stairs two at a time, not wanting to waste even a second waiting for the elevator. He arrived at her door panting.

She opened the door at his knock and he stared at her, soaking her in. She was wearing running pants and a hoodie, and a green bandanna was tied over her hair. He immediately noticed that she'd lost weight, which he didn't think suited her because it lengthened her usually round and smiling face. She was pale and her face was filled with strain—dark smudges ringed her luminous gray eyes. She flicked him a derisive look and nothing about her demeanor indicated that she was pleased to see him.

He swallowed. "You look good."

She raised one auburn brow. "I thought you hated lies?"

Touché. If he'd been kidding himself that he hadn't hurt her that much, he was under no illusions now. She walked away from the open door, leaving him standing in the entrance. It hardly counted as an invitation to enter but he took it anyway.

"I brought you some flowers," he said.

"I've packed the vase."

He pulled his gaze away from her and for the first time noticed the apartment. Packing boxes littered every available space. "You're moving?"

She nodded and folded her arms across her chest, every part of her vibrating with loathing. "Why are you here, Ben?"

"I was down in Florida when I saw the news." He smiled at her proudly. "Good for you, showing that bastard what for."

"I'm glad you approve."

Every inch of her said the opposite and a band of sweat broke out on his forehead. "Amy, I'm really sorry."

"What for?"

The words sounded like a slap or a trap or both. He wanted to wrap his arms around her, but nothing about her said she'd welcome his touch. "For letting you go through all of that alone."

She picked at lint on her hoodie. "I wasn't alone. My parents were here."

"Oh." He hadn't expected that. "Well, I'm glad you told them."

The left side of her mouth tweaked up wryly. "Of course you are.

You told me more than once I needed to tell them just like you told me I needed to fight Jonathon. You were right on both counts. I just didn't realize you needed to hear me say it so much that you'd come all the way from Florida. So, Ben, you were right. Now you can take your flowers and go."

This wasn't part of his plan. "That's not why I'm here."

"Oh, really?"

Tell her. "Amy," he blurted, "I love you."

Her nostrils flared as if the words were a toxic stench. "What happened to, 'I'm not looking for love and you need to go sort out your life'?"

She made an odd choking sound in the back of her throat and then marched to the kitchen, putting the counter firmly between the two of them. When she finally looked at him again, her face was ragged with pain and anger tinged bewilderment.

"Oh, my God. Me taking control of my life was some sort of test, wasn't it? Now that I've passed, you've come back to claim me."

"No. Hell no! Amy, there was no test." Shocked the she thought so little of him, he willed her to understand.

Wariness edged with flint flashed in her eyes. "So your realization that you loved me happened before you saw me on the news?"

He couldn't lie. "Actually, it happened at the same time."

"Ben, you need to go."

Her hurt sliced into him. *You've got one chance. Don't fuck this up.*

"Amy, I swear when I left you I was doing everything you accused me of. The idea of you loving me had me running scared. I couldn't even consider that I might have fallen in love with you because I'd sworn I was never going to allow that to happen again.

"And yes, I won't back down from the fact I thought you should fight for your job, but when I saw you on the news, being brave and taking on that slimy bastard, everything inside of me screamed that I'd thrown you to the lions. I should have been there with you, standing next to you. I hated that you were on your own. As much as I wanted you to fight, I wanted to wrap you up in cotton wool and protect you.

I've never felt the need to protect anyone as strongly as I have with you. I want to keep you safe and close, and the thought of losing you is more terrifying than loving you."

Amy stared at Ben, trying to make sense of what he was saying. His arrival was so unexpected and he looked haggard and unkempt, as if he'd slept in his clothes and hadn't shaved in days. A month ago, a declaration of love from him would have sent her into a giddy whirlwind of joy. Only now, she wasn't quite the same person as she'd been then.

She wanted to be loved for herself, not for what she'd done. "And if I hadn't fought Jonathon? Would you have realized you loved me?"

He looked shamefaced. "I only ever want to tell you the truth, Amy."

She braced herself for pain. "Go on."

"It may have taken me a couple more days longer to realize, but it would have happened. I'd ridden two thousand miles to try and outrun you and I'd run out of land. I was in Key West, surrounded by beautiful women and every single one of them paled in comparison to you in your sequined top, shorts and hiking boots. I'd see amazing things and turn to tell you, only to realize you weren't there. I'd go running and expect you to arrive a couple of minutes later, flop down next to me and say, 'I'm never doing this again,' before catching your breath and keeping on going."

She could scarcely breathe as she tried to absorb his heartfelt words.

"I was on beautiful beaches watching glorious sunrises and sunsets and I was miserable." His green eyes begged her to understand. "I thought about going home to Australia but it didn't feel like home anymore and I couldn't work out why I'd been happier amidst the fall colors in Whitetail than I was on any beach. I thought I was missing Whitetail but I wasn't. I was missing you."

He walked around the counter and stood in front of her. "After Lexie, I never wanted to fall in love again but then you happened. You hit me with that torch and you hit me with your love. I'm sorry I wasn't ready to hear you when you told me you loved me, but know this. I love you, Amy Sagar and if you let me, I'll always be here for you."

The plea in his voice, the earnest expression on his face and the worry in his eyes made her sob but she still needed more. "Be with me here in Chicago?"

"Your job's here so I'm here." He gave a hopeful smile. "I'm sure in the home of the skyscraper they need engineers."

Her heart hammered hard at his offer and she wanted so much to accept it but there was one more thing holding her back. "And what if there are times when I'm not brave and I want to hide behind you?"

His green eyes filled with understanding. "I'll stand *next* to you, Amy, and hold your hand."

He loves me. He really loves me.

She reached out her hand toward him and he grabbed it as if it was a life jacket being thrown to him. Then his arms were around her and his face was buried in her hair and she felt the sob in his chest before she heard it.

"I thought I'd lost you." His hands cupped her face and he gazed down at her.

She gave him a wobbly smile. "I know how you feel."

His arms tightened around her. "I'm so sorry for being so idiotically slow to realize that you're the best thing that's ever happened to me."

"I love you, Ben." She smiled up at him, feeling his love wrap around her like a cloak. "But I'd be lying if I didn't tell you there have been days these last few weeks when I didn't want to love you. The thing is, I have no choice. You're part of my heart."

"I promise to take great care of it."

His lips came down on hers in a seal of commitment—his love infusing her with its heady mix of care and unconditional support. She leaned into him, giddy with amazement that she was so fortunate to have this wonderful man in her life.

A few minutes later when they finally came up for air, Amy led

Ben to the couch and snuggled into him. "I need to tell you something."

He frowned. "What?"

She laughed. "Don't look so worried. If anything I should be the worried one because what I'm about to tell you will probably make your head swell. From time to time in Whitetail, you told me I was hiding from things and as much as I didn't want to hear it, I now confess you were right. It had become a habit I didn't even recognize."

He wound one of her curls around his finger. "It's always easier for an outsider to have perspective. You had me pegged about being scared to love so I guess we're good for each other."

She nodded, sucking in a breath. "And you and I, we're about the truth, right? Well, the truth is, I didn't actually fight Jonathon to get my job back. I fought him for the rights of a little girl with cerebral palsy who needs a wheelchair. But along the way I learned something about myself."

"What was that?"

"That I'm in the wrong job."

He stared at her in surprise. "You don't want to be a lawyer?"

"Oh, I do. I just don't want to work in corporate law, so I've quit my job at M.M., the one they *had* to offer me." She laughed. "I'm sure they're secretly relived about it."

"So the packing boxes are because you're moving for a new job?"

"Not exactly." Her fingers fiddled with the zipper on his leather jacket. "My stuff's going into storage and I'm traveling before finding a job in disability advocacy. I realized what I loved most about working at M.M. was my work with the Kids Plus Foundation."

"Good for you." He dropped a kiss on her forehead. "Have you told your parents about the job change?"

She gave him a wry smile. "Yes, Ben, I've told my parents and they're totally on board. Turns out we were all a bit misguided about each other, but we've talked it out and everything's good."

He grinned down at her. "So you want to travel?"

"I do. I've worked continuously for years and I deserve some adventure."

"Where are you planning to go?"

"Australia. I figured if I couldn't have you, I wanted to see where you came from."

His heart, already full, overflowed. "Can I tag along?"

"Yes, please."

"My parents are going to be beside themselves with joy when I bring you home." He paused, struck by a thought. "When you and your folks were having your heart-to-heart did you mention the travel?"

"No."

"Ah."

"Ah, what?"

"Your dad's already told me not to take you away. He'll have my balls."

She laughed. "I doubt it. Visiting Australia has always been on Mom and Dad's wish list."

"Would they come for a wedding?"

Amy sat up fast, her heart thundering so hard she was sure Ben could hear it. "Is...is that a marriage proposal?"

He blinked at her in surprise as if he couldn't quite believe he'd said the words. Then his eyes darkened, overflowing with love. "Yes," he said firmly.

The next moment he was on the floor, on his knees and holding both her hands. "Amy Sagar, will you have me for better because you already know the worse, for richer although possibly financially poorer if we keep traveling, and in sickness and in health for the rest of our lives?"

She leaned forward, loving him so much. "Given you're a health freak, I'm guessing it will be more health than sickness."

"I'm hoping so. I plan to live to a hundred and you better keep up with me. Marry me, Amy."

Tears overflowed. "I will."

"Thank you." He grinned at her, his handsome face radiating love. "I never thought it was possible to be this happy."

"Neither did I."

She thought her heart would burst from joy. This amazing and wonderful man had literally ridden into her life and changed it in ways she could never have imagined. She wasn't naive enough to know there wouldn't be bumps along the road but she knew down to the tips of her toes she was loved and adored, and she loved and adored him back. This was their insurance. This was what would cushion the road ahead for them both.

She dropped her head and kissed him, excited to start the rest of her life.

CHAPTER THIRTY-EIGHT

MELISSA RUSHED into the Monday town meeting, waving photos. "Ben and Amy got married!"

Al grinned and slung an arm around Ella's shoulders. "Don't be too disappointed, Ellie. Fortunately, you've still got me."

Ella rolled her eyes. "Don't you worry. I'm planning on enjoying the view of all the young bikers in their leathers who we meet on our trip," she said, leaning into him with a smile.

"Why didn't they get married in Whitetail?" Nicole said disappointedly. "After all, they met here and we would have thrown them an amazing wedding."

"Ben wanted something really quiet," Melissa said softly.

A collective *ah* of understanding went around the room. No one knew the full story, but they all knew Ben had been jilted once before. The photos got passed around while Melissa read out a letter from Amy.

"'Ben and I got married on a beautiful tropical island off the Australian Queensland coast. It was a glorious day, the sky was blue, the sea the most amazing turquoise green and so clear that we could see fish. Apart from Ben and me and the marriage celebrant, the only other people present were my parents and Ben's. As you can see from the photos, Ben was beyond handsome in a white linen, open-neck shirt and rolled-up chinos. I chose a simple, full-length chiffon sheath.'"

Melissa laughed. "Ben has crossed out *simple* and added *sexy*."

Everyone smiled.

"'I didn't have a bouquet but wore frangipani in my hair until my curls tossed them out. We held hands and stood with our bare feet buried in the warm, white sand and pledged our love to each other. Ben gave me a Russian wedding ring because he says the three intertwined rings of white gold, gold and rose gold, without an obvious beginning or end, mean never-ending love. I cried. So did he. So did our parents.

"'Our favorite photo is the one of us standing inside a huge love heart, which my dad drew in the sand for us. After the ceremony we drank champagne, ate crayfish—which is like lobster—and then we all went snorkeling. It was an amazing and special day and I hope you and Scott have one just as special next year.'"

"Hear, hear," John Ackerman said as everyone joined him in agreement.

"There's a bit more," Melissa said, continuing to read.

"'G'day, everyone, Ben here. Now I've got a ring firmly on Amy's finger, I've decided that weddings aren't that bad after all. We had such a great day we want to do it again, only this time with Amy's sisters, my brothers and all our Whitetail friends. As Amy's promised Melissa she'd make her dress, we'll get married again when we return and we want to use Whitetail Weddings That Wow as our preferred wedding company. Al, start putting together a group of vintage Harleys for our wedding transport.'"

"I know a guy with a 1969 pearl-white classic," Al said. "Now that would be perfect for a wedding."

"I'll come with you to make sure a bride in a wedding dress can fit on the pillion seat," Ella said.

"Shh," Nicole said, "I want to hear the rest of the letter."

"'Could you also contact the Rasmussens and ask them if they'd rent the house to us because when we add up all the Sagars and the Armytages, it comes to a lot of people. I'd love to write more but my wife's just put on her running gear and I can see her bending over and lacing up her shoes. I best go catch her up. Take care and we'll see you all soon. Ben.'"

As Melissa put down the letter, everyone sighed and then clapped. Whitetail Weddings That Wow had another wedding to plan and the town couldn't be happier.

Missing Whitetail? Why not read *Boomerang Bride*, the book that launched the *Wedding Fever trilogy*. Available in print, eBook & audio.

ALSO BY FIONA LOWE

The Wedding Fever Series

(Romance Fiction)

Saved by the Bride

Picture Perfect Wedding

Runaway Groom

Women's Fiction Novels

Daughter of Mine

Birthright

Home Fires

A Home Like Ours

A Family of Strangers

Coming in 2023

The Money Club

Did you know BookBub has a new release alert? www.bookbub.com/
authors/fiona-lowe

Romance Novels 2006-2018

Fiona has an extensive backlist of Australian-set romances. For a full list head
to http://www.fionalowe.com

ACKNOWLEDGMENTS

Enormous thanks to Annette who gave me her valuable time and explained the intricacies of dress making and the step-by-step process of making a wedding gown from the concept sketches through to the glorious finished product. This book couldn't have been written without her help and expertise!

Thanks also go to Sharon and Glenn who cheerfully answered my frantic emails about Harley-Davidson engines and vintage bikes. I'm so lucky to know such generous people and I love it that they're "growing old disgracefully."

A big shout-out to Cindy and Mike, Wisconsin friends with matching Harleys, who were with me in spirit when I wrote this book along with the memories of long conversations with Gold Wing riders on convention in Wisconsin. Happy days!

Thanks to my wonderful editor, Charlotte, to Barton for the fab cover and to Vicki for reading this up-dated 2022 edition and finding the typos. And a big squishy hug to all my wonderful readers. Thank you for spending time with my books.

Last, but by no means least, thanks go to my wonderful readers. Your emails and social media comments are valued and appreciated, and they keep me going. I wish you days of being able to lose yourself in a good book.

ABOUT THE AUTHOR

FIONA LOWE has been a midwife, a sexual health counsellor and a family support worker; an ideal career for an author who writes novels about family, community and relationships. She spent her early years in Papua New Guinea where, without television, reading was the entertainment and it set up a lifelong love of books. Although she often re-wrote the endings of books in her head, it was the birth of her first child that prompted her to write her first novel. A recipient of the prestigious USA RITA® award and two Australian RuBY awards, Fiona writes books that are set in small country towns. They feature real people facing difficult choices and explore how family ties and relationships impact on their decisions.

When she's not writing stories, she's a distracted wife, mother of two 'ginger' sons, a volunteer in her community, guardian of eighty rose bushes, a slave to a cat, and is often found collapsed on the couch with wine. You can find her at her website, fionalowe.com, and on Facebook, TikTok, Instagram and Goodreads.

www.ingramcontent.com/pod-product-compliance
Lightning Source LLC
Chambersburg PA
CBHW020328120726
47904CB00002B/317